Black
Water
Rising

ATTICA LOCKE

Black Water Rising

HARPER

An Imprint of HarperCollins*Publishers*
www.harpercollins.com

BLACK WATER RISING. Copyright © 2009 by Attica Locke. All rights reserved. Printed in the United States of America. No part of this book may be used or reproduced in any manner whatsoever without written permission except in the case of brief quotations embodied in critical articles and reviews. For information address Harper-Collins Publishers, 10 East 53rd Street, New York, NY 10022.

HarperCollins books may be purchased for educational, business, or sales promotional use. For information please write: Special Markets Department, HarperCollins Publishers, 10 East 53rd Street, New York, NY 10022.

FIRST EDITION

Designed by Betty Lew

LIBRARY OF CONGRESS CATALOGING-IN-PUBLICATION DATA

Locke, Attica
    Black water rising / by Attica Locke. — 1st ed.
        p. cm.
    ISBN 978-0-06-173586-8
1. Lawyers—Fiction. 2. Petroleum industry and trade—Fiction.
3. Corporations—Corrupt practices—Fiction. I. Title.

    PS3612.L247b57 2009
    813'.6—dc22   2008041950

09 10 11 12 13 OV/RRD 10 9 8 7 6 5 4 3 2 1

FOR MY GRANDFATHER

If we are blinded by darkness,
we are also blinded by light.

—ANNIE DILLARD

Black
Water
Rising

Part I

Chapter 1

Texas, 1981

The boat is smaller than he imagined. And dingier.

Even at night Jay can tell it needs a paint job.

This is not at all what they discussed. The guy on the phone said "moonlight cruise." City lights and all that. Jay had pictured something quaint, something with a little romance, like the riverboats on the Pontchartrain in New Orleans, only smaller. But this thing looks like a doctored-up fishing boat, at best. It is flat and wide and ugly—a barge, badly overdressed, like a big girl invited to her first and probably last school dance. There are Christmas lights draped over every corner of the thing and strung in a line framing the cabin door. They're blinking erratically, somewhat desperately, winking at Jay, promising a good time, wanting him to come on in. Jay stays right where he is, staring at the boat's cabin: four leaning walls covered with a cheap carport material. The whole thing looks like it was slapped together as an afterthought, a sloppy attempt at decorum, like a hat resting precariously on a drunk's head.

Jay turns and looks at his wife, who hasn't exactly gotten out of the car yet. The door is open and her feet are on the ground, but Bernie is still sitting in the passenger seat, peeking at her husband through the crack between the door and the Skylark's rusting frame. She peers at her shoes, a pair of navy blue Dr. Scholl's, a small luxury she allowed herself somewhere near the end of her sixth month. She looks up from her sandals to the boat teeter-tottering on the water. She is making quick assessments, he knows, weighing her physical condition against the boat's. She glances at her husband again, waiting for an explanation.

Jay looks out across the bayou before him. It is little more than a narrow, muddy strip of water flowing some thirty feet below street level; it snakes through the underbelly of the city, starting to the west and going through downtown, all the way out to the Ship Channel and the Port of Houston, where it eventually spills out into the Gulf of Mexico. There's been talk for years about the "Bayou City" needing a river walk of its own, like the one in San Antonio, but bigger, of course, and therefore better. Countless developers have pitched all kinds of plans for restaurants and shops to line Buffalo Bayou. The city's planning and development department even went so far as to pave a walkway along the part of the bayou that runs through Memorial Park. The paved walkway is as far as the river-walk plan ever went, and the walkway ends abruptly here at Allen's Landing, at the northwest corner of downtown, where Jay is standing now. At night, the area is nearly deserted. There's civilization to the south. Concerts at the Johnson and Lindy Cole Arts Center, restaurants and bars open near Jones Hall and the Alley Theatre. But the view from Allen's

Landing is grim. There are thick, unkempt weeds choked up on the banks of the water, crawling up the cement pilings that hold Main Street overhead, and save for a dim yellow bulb at the foot of a small wooden pier, Allen's Landing is complete blackness.

Jay stands beneath his city, staring at the raggedy boat, feeling a knot tighten in his throat, a familiar cinch at the neck, a feeling of always coming up short where his wife is concerned. He feels a sharp stab of anger. The guy on the phone lied to him. The guy on the phone is a liar. It feels good to outsource it, to put it on somebody else. When the truth is, there are thirty-five open case files on his desk, at least ten or twelve with court time pending; there wasn't time to plan anything else for Bernie's birthday, and more important, there hasn't been any money, not for months. He's waiting on a couple of slip-and-falls to pay big, but until then there's nothing coming in. When one of his clients, a guy who owes him money for some small-time probate work, said he had a brother or an uncle or somebody who runs boat tours up and down the bayou, Jay jumped at the chance. He got the whole thing comped. Just like the dinette set he and Bernie eat off of every night. Just like his wife's car, which has been on cement blocks in Petey's Garage since April. Jay shakes his head in disgust. Here he is, a workingman with a degree, two, in fact, and, still he's taking handouts, living secondhand. He feels the anger again, and beneath it, its ugly cousin, shame.

He tucks the feelings away.

Anger, he knows, is a young man's game, something he long ago outgrew.

There's a man standing on the boat, near the head. He's thin and nearing seventy and wearing an ill-fitting pair of Wranglers. There are tight gray curls poking out of his nylon baseball cap, the words BROTHERHOOD OF LONGSHOREMEN, LOCAL 116, smudged with dirt and grease. He's sucking on the end of a brown cigarette. The old man nods in Jay's direction, tipping the bill of his cap.

Jay reaches for his wife's hand.

"I am not getting on that thing." She tries to fold her arms across her chest to make the point, but her growing belly is not where it used to be or even where it was last week. Her arms barely reach across the front of her body.

"Come on," he says. "You got the man waiting now."

"I ain't thinking about that man."

Jay tugs on her hand, feels her give just the tiniest bit. "Come on."

Bernie makes a whistling sound through her teeth, barely audible, which Jay hears and recognizes at once. It's meant to signal her thinning patience. Still, she takes his hand, scooting to the edge of her seat, letting Jay help her out of the car. Once she's up and on her feet, he reaches into the backseat, pulling out a shoe box full of cassette tapes and eight tracks and tucking it under his arm. Bernie is watching everything, studying his every move. Jay takes her arm, leading her to the edge of the small pier. It sags and creaks beneath their weight, Bernie carrying an extra thirty pounds on her tiny frame these days. The old man in the baseball cap puts one cowboy boot on a rotted plank of wood that bridges the barge to the pier and flicks his cigarette over the side of the boat. Jay watches it fall into the water, which is black, like oil. It's impossible to tell how deep the bayou is, how far to the bottom. Jay squeezes his wife's hand, reluctant to turn her over to the old man, who is reaching a hand over the side of the boat, waiting for Bernie to take her first step. "You Jimmy?" Jay asks him.

"Naw, Jimmy ain't coming."

"Who are you?"

"Jimmy's cousin."

Jay nods, as if he were expecting this all along, as if being Jimmy's cousin is an acceptable credential for a boat's captain, all the identification a person would ever need. He doesn't want Bernie to see his concern. He doesn't want her to march back to the car. The old man takes Bernie's hand and gently guides her onto the boat's deck, leading her and Jay to the cabin door. He keeps close by Bernie's side, making sure she doesn't trip or miss a step, and Jay feels a sudden, unexpected softness for Jimmy's cousin. He nods at the old man's cap, making small talk. "You union?" he asks. The old man shoots a quick glance in Jay's direction, taking in his clean shave, the pressed clothes and dress shoes, and the smooth hands, nary a scratch on them. "What you know about it?"

There's a lot Jay knows, more than his clothes explain. But the question, here and now, is not worth his time. He concentrates on the floor in front of him, sidestepping a dirty puddle of water pooling under an AC unit stuck in the cabin's window, thinking how easy it would be for someone to slip and fall. He follows a step or two behind his wife, watching as she pauses at the entrance to the cabin. It's black on the other side, and she waits for Jay to go in first.

He takes the lead, stepping over the threshold.

He can smell Evelyn's perfume, still lingering in the room—a smoky, woodsy scent, like sandalwood, like the soap Bernie used to bathe with before she got pregnant and grew intolerant of it and a host of other smells, like gasoline and scrambled eggs. The scent lets him know that Evelyn was here, that she followed his careful instructions. He feels a warm rush of relief and reaches for his wife's hand, pulling Bernie along. She doesn't like the dark, he knows; she doesn't like not being in on something. "What is this?" she whispers.

Jay takes another step, feeling along the wall for the switch.

When the light finally comes, Bernie lets out a gasp, clutching her chest.

Inside the cabin there are balloons instead of flowers, hot links and brisket instead of filet, and a cooler of beer and grape Shasta instead of wine. It's not much, Jay knows, nothing fancy, but, still, it has a certain charm. He feels a wave of gratitude—for his wife, for this night out, even for his sister-in-law. He had been loath to ask for Evelyn's help. Other than his wife, no one seems more acutely aware of Jay's limits than Evelyn Annemarie Boykins. She's been on him for two weeks now, wanting to know was Jay gon' get her baby sister something better for her birthday than the robe he bought Bernie last year, what cost him almost $30 at Foley's Department Store. He couldn't have done tonight on his own, not without his wife suspecting something. So he was more than grateful when Evelyn offered to pick up some barbecue on Scott Street and blow up a few balloons. Everything will be ready, she said. In the center of the room is a table set for two, a chocolate cake on top, with white and yellow roses, just like Evelyn promised. Bernie stares at the cake, the balloons, all of it, a slow smile spreading across her face. She turns to her husband, reaching on her tiptoes for Jay's neck, pressing her cheek to his. She bites his ear, a small, sweet reprimand, a reminder that she doesn't like secrets. Still, she whispers her approval. "It's nice, Jay."

The boat's engine starts up. Jay feels the pull of it in his knees.

They start a slow coast to the east and out of downtown, beads of water rocking and rolling across the top of the air-conditioning unit. The moist, weak stream of air it offers isn't enough to cool an outhouse. The room is only a few degrees below miserably hot. Jay is already sweating through his dress shirt. Bernie leans against the table, fanning herself, asking for a pop from the cooler.

There's a Styrofoam ice chest resting in one corner. Jay bends over and pulls out a soda can for his wife and a cold beer for himself. He flicks ice chips off the aluminum lids and wipes at them with the corner of his suit jacket, which he then peels off and drapes on the back of his chair. Next to the cooler is a stereo set up on a card table, black wires and extension cords dripping down the back and onto the floor. Jay kicks the wires out of view, thinking of someone tripping, a slip or a fall. Bernie soon takes charge of the music, fishing through Jay's shoe box, passing over her husband's music—Sam Cooke and Otis, Wilson Pickett and Bobby Womack—looking for some of her own. She's into Kool & the Gang these days. Cameo and the Gap Band. Rick James and Teena Marie. She slides in a tape by the Commodores, which at least Jay can stand. *Just to be close to you* . . . the words float across the room. Jay watches his wife, swaying to the music, dancing, big as she is, the tails of her two French braids swinging in time. He smiles to himself, thinking he's got everything he needs right here. His family. Bernie and the baby. All he has.

There's a sister somewhere.

A mother he isn't talking to.

Old friends he's been avoiding for more than ten years. He hasn't spoken to his buddies—his comrades, cats from way, way back—since his trial. The one that nearly killed him. The one that drove him to law school in the first place. He started missing meetings after that, skipping funerals, ignoring phone calls, until, eventually, his friends just stopped calling. Until they got the hint.

He counts himself lucky, really.

A lot of his old friends are dead or locked up or in hiding, out of the country somewhere; they are men who cannot come home. But Jay's life was spared. By an inch, a single juror: a woman and the only black on the panel. He remembers how she smiled his way every morning of the trial, always with a small nod. It's okay, the smile said. *I got you, son. I'm not gon' let you fall.*

After the trial, after he'd checked himself in and out of St. Joseph's Hospital, he learned the juror, his angel, was a widow who stayed out on Noble Street, down from Bernie's church, the same church where her father, Reverend Boykins, had loaded a bus with half his congregation every morning of Jay's trial. They were women mostly, dressed in their best stockings and felt hats and cat eye glasses with white rhinestones. They rode to the courthouse every day for two weeks simply because they'd heard a young man was in trouble. No questions asked, they'd claimed him as one of their own. They sat through days of FBI testimony, including a secret government tape that was played in the hushed courtroom—a tape of a hasty phone call Jay had made in the spring of 1970.

The prosecutors had him on a charge of inciting a riot and conspiracy to commit murder of an agent of the federal government—a kid like him and a paid informant. They had Jay on tape talking to Stokely, a phone call that ran less than three and a half minutes and sealed his fate. Jay, nineteen at the time, sat at the defense table in a borrowed suit, scared out of his mind. His lawyer, appointed by the judge, was a white kid not that much older than Jay. He wouldn't listen and rarely looked at Jay. Instead, he slid a yellow legal pad and a number 2 pencil across the table. Anything Jay had to say, he should write it down.

He remembers staring at the pencil, thinking of his exams, of all things.

He was a senior in college then and failing Spanish. He sat at the defense table and wondered how old he would be when he got out, if they gave him two years or twenty. He tried to imagine the whole of his life—every Christmas, every kiss, every breath—spent in prison. He tried to do the math, dividing his life in half, then fourths, then split again, over and over until it was something small enough to fit inside a six-by-eight cell at the Walls in Huntsville. Any way he looked at it, a conviction was a death sentence.

He remembers looking around the courtroom every morning and not recognizing a soul. His friends all stayed away, treating his arrest and pending incarceration as something contagious. He was humbled, almost sickened with shame to see the women from the church, women he did not even know, show up every day, taking up the first two and three rows in the gallery. Never speaking, or making a scene. Just there, every time he turned around.

We got you, son. We're not gon' let you fall.

His own mother hadn't come to the courthouse once, hadn't even come to see him in lockup.

He didn't know Bernie then or her father, didn't know the church or God. He was a young man full of ideas that were simple, black and white. He liked to talk big about the coming revolution, about the church negro who was all show and no action, who was doing nothing for the *cause* . . . a word spoken one too many times, worked into one too many speeches, until it had lost all meaning for Jay, until it was just a word, a shortcut, a litmus test for picking sides.

Well, he's not on anyone's side anymore. Except his own.

There are other American dreams, he reasons.

One is money, of course. A different kind of freedom and seemingly within his reach. If he works hard, wears a suit, plays by the new rules.

His dreams are simple now. Home, his wife, his baby.

He watches Bernadine, moving to the music, wiping sweat from her brow, pasting stray black hairs against her bronze skin. Jay stands perfectly still, lost in the sway of his wife's hips. Right, then left, then right again. He smiles and leans over the cooler for a second beer, feeling the boat moving beneath his feet.

An hour or so later, the cake cut and the food nearly gone, Jay and Bernie are alone on the deck, trading the hot, humid air inside the cabin for the hot, humid air outside. At least on the deck, there's the hope of a breeze as the boat travels west on the water. Bernie leans her forearms against the hand railing, sticking her face into the moist night air. Jay pops the top of his Coors. His fourth, or maybe his fifth. He lost count somewhere near Turning Basin, the only spot between downtown and the Port of Houston where a boat can turn around on the narrow bayou. They are heading back to Allen's Landing now, but are still a few miles from downtown. From the rear of the boat, Jay can see the lights of the high-rise buildings up ahead, the head-quarters of Cole Oil Industries standing tall above the rest. To the rear of the boat is a view of the port and the Ship Channel, lined with oil refineries on either side. From here, the refineries are mere clusters of blinking lights and puffs of smoke, white against the swollen charcoal sky, rising on the dewy horizon like cities on a distant planet.

Between the refineries and downtown Houston, there's not much to look at but water and trees as the boat floats through a stretch of nearly pitch-black darkness. Jay stands next to his wife on the deck, following shadows with his eyes, tracing the silhouette of moss hanging from the aged water oaks that line the banks of the water. He finishes his beer, dropping the can onto the deck.

They are about to head back inside when they hear the first scream, what sounds at first like a cat's cry, shrill and desperate. It's coming from the north side of the bayou, high above them, from somewhere in the thick of trees and weeds lining the bank. At first Jay thinks of an animal caught in the brush. But then . . . he hears it again. He looks at his wife. She too is staring through the trees. The old man in the baseball cap suddenly emerges from the captain's cabin, a narrow slip of a room at the head of the boat, housing the gears and controls. "What the hell was that?" he asks, looking at Jay and Bernie.

Jay shakes his head even though he already knows. Somewhere deep down, he knows. It wasn't an animal he heard. It was a woman.

The old man ducks into the main cabin. A few seconds later, Jay hears the music stop . . . then silence, nothing except the soft whisper of water lapping against the sides of the boat as they creep slowly along the surface of the bayou.

The old man emerges from the main cabin. "Y'all heard something?"

"Over there," Bernie says, pointing to the brush along the embankment.

Jay strains to make out any buildings behind the trees, trying to place where they are. He makes quick calculations, judging their distance from downtown with his eyes, trying to gauge how long they've been drifting westward. But in the darkness and with his drunken sense of time, he can only guess. They are somewhere near Lockwood Drive, near Fifth Ward, that much he can tell. He can see part of the Freedman's National Bank clock from here, rising high behind the trees. It's late, he realizes, just shy of midnight.

He's had a couple of cases come out of Fifth Ward. Property disputes and petty theft. But also fistfights and holdups and one kid who knifed another one just for playing his music too loud. Jay knows they are floating through the back side of the one of the roughest neighborhoods in the city.

Bernie turns to her husband. "Something's wrong out there, Jay."

Behind them, there's another scream, a howl really, a plea.

A woman's voice, shaped into two very distinct words: *Help me.*

Jay feels a slight flutter across his chest, a tiny hiccup of dread.

Bernie's voice drops to a whisper. "What in the devil is going on out there?"

The old man disappears into the captain's cabin.

A few seconds later, he emerges carrying a flashlight. Bernie and Jay clear the narrow deck, giving him room to pass as he starts for the rear of the boat. He shines the weak light into the brush on the north side of the bayou, calling out into the darkness, to a face none of them can see. "You okay out there?"

There's no response. The old man waves his light through the trees. They're traveling at an even clip, creeping slowly, but surely, farther away from her. The old man calls out again. "Hey . . . you okay out there?"

A gunshot cracks through the air.

Jay's heart stops, everything going still. He has a fleeting, panicked thought that . . . *this is it.* He actually looks down to see if he's been hit, an old habit set off by firecrackers and bad mufflers, a holdover from his other life.

There's a second shot then. It echoes and rolls across the air like thunder.

The old man lets out a low, raspy moan. "God in heaven."

Bernie mutters a prayer under her breath.

Jay grabs for his wife's hand, pulling her toward the door to the main cabin, away from the open deck. Bernie yanks her hand free of his, the movement strong and decisive, the force of it causing her feet to slide a little on the slick surface of the deck. She steadies herself on the railing, turning to face the old man in the baseball cap. "Sir, I think you'd better turn this thing around."

The old man in the baseball cap stares at Bernie, sure she's not serious. "I can't," he says to her and Jay. "The bayou's too narrow. 'Sides the basin, ain't no place to turn her around 'til we get back to Allen's Landing."

"Then stop the boat," Bernie says.

The old man shoots a quick glance in Jay's direction, making it clear that he intends to take no instruction from the pregnant woman, not without her husband's say-so, which only infuriates Bernie. "Stop this boat," she says again.

In the end, the old man relents, starting on his own for the captain's cabin.

Jay grabs his arm. "Don't."

"Somebody's in trouble out there, Jay!"

"There are *two* people out there, B," he says. "The girl and who or whatever it is she's running from." He's picturing a street fight or a knock-down, drag-out between lovers or something worse . . . much, much worse.

"Leave it alone," he hears himself say.

Bernie stares at Jay, her voice hushed. "What is the matter with you?"

Her disappointment in him, no matter how it cuts, is not the point.

"Somebody's shooting out there, B," he says. "You got me and him on this boat . . ." he says, pointing to the only other able body on board, a man almost seventy. "And my wife," Jay adds, lowering his voice to match hers, trying to get her to see it his way. "I, for one, am not willing to put you or myself at risk to step into some trouble we don't know the first thing about. We don't know that girl, don't know what kind of trouble she brings," he says, hearing the cynicism in his voice, hating it, but feeling pressed to speak it anyway. The oldest con in the book, he thinks to himself, is the damsel in distress, the girl with the flat tire by the side of the road, the one with a boyfriend waiting in the weeds to jump you as soon as you stop to help. "Just leave it alone," he says.

Bernie stares at him for a long, painful moment, squinting around the edges of her eyes, as if she's trying to place him, someone she used to know. "Oh, Jay," she say with a sigh.

"We'll call the police," he says, deciding it just then.

It's a good plan: clean, simple, logical.

The old man is sheepish, slow to move, shuffling the ball of his right foot on the deck's floor. "We ain't got a city license to run this thing after hours."

"What?" Jay says.

"Oh, God," Bernie mumbles.

"Call the police, man," Jay says firmly.

The old man sighs and walks to a dirty white phone that's smudged with oil and grime and resting outside the door to the captain's cabin. He lifts the phone, what looks more like a walkie-talkie or a CB receiver. He dials, then pauses, listening, straining, it seems. Jay and Bernie wait, watching as the old man punches the buttons on the phone a few times. Hearing nothing, he finally slams the receiver in its cradle. The phone, apparently, is not working.

"Fucking Jimmy," the old man says.

There's another scream, closer this time.

Bernie grabs the flashlight from the old man's hand, swinging the cloudy white light toward the embankment in time to see a flash of motion in the trees, a rustling in the brush. They watch as a body drops, rolling zigzag down the steep bank, bumping up against weeds and uneven soil. It rolls all the way down the embankment, then . . . it disappears. Jay hears a quiet splash, a sucking sound, the bayou swallowing something whole.

Then . . . nothing. For what seems like an eternity.

Bernie looks at Jay. He can hear his own heartbeat, low in his throat.

A moment later, a ripple breaks the still water, its waves spread like arms offering an embrace. "Somebody's moving out there," the captain mumbles.

There's a burp and gurgle of air. Something surfaces on the water.

Jay hears splashing, then a cry, hoarse and starved for air.

Bernie waits for no one's permission. She marches into the captain's cabin. The old man makes a move to stop her, then thinks better of it. Bernie can barely fit her body inside the small captain's cabin. She has to reach past her belly to touch the key sticking out of the control board, turning it to the left.

The engine sputters, then falls quiet.

No one on the deck moves, no one says a word.

Bernie and the old man are both looking at Jay.

He moves quickly, without a word being said, removing his watch, but not his wedding band, thinking to himself that this is one of those times when being a man, or rather trying to play the part to any convincing degree, trumps his better judgment. He's not exactly a big guy to begin with, and the years have softened his once wiry frame. He kicks off his shoes, then lifts his shirt from his pants, past the slight paunch around his middle. He starts to take it off, but changes his mind. He makes an awkward climb onto the deck's railing, takes a deep breath, holding it tight and precious in his chest, and jumps.

The water is warm and bitter. It comes in everywhere, in his mouth and throat, through his clothes. Beneath the black surface, the bayou is alive, pulling at him, tugging at his arms and legs. He feels twigs and leaves and what he hopes are only fish brushing against his arms and legs. He has some vague sense of the light from the boat, but his eyes are burning. It's impossible to see clearly. He moves blindly through the darkness, reeled in by the sound of her voice.

When he feels something stringy in his hands, tangling around his fingers, he knows he's found her; her hair is in his hands. She's gurgling, spitting and coughing. He wraps an arm around her sternum and pulls. He turns toward the boat, momentarily disoriented by the white light shining in his eyes. He pulls and swims, swims and pulls, until his legs burn, until his arms ache, until he is sure they will both drown. Within a few feet of the boat, he pushes harder, past what he thinks is his limit. When he reaches a thin ladder at the back of the vessel, he strains to lift her body overhead. The captain reaches over the side of the railing to help lift the woman, weak and limp, onto the boat's deck.

Jay is bent over, his hands on his knees, trying to line up one breath after another, trying not to pass out. Out of the corner of his eye, he gets the first good look at the woman he carried across the bayou, the life he's just saved.

She's white and filthy.

There's black dirt coating her skin, dead leaves clinging to her arms. She's terrified, shaking, staring at a room full of black faces, each of whom is staring back at her. The boat's cabin is still and quiet except for the AC unit buzzing in the window and the drops of water raining off their bodies, hers and Jay's.

"He follow you?"

It's his first question, before her name, before he asks if she's okay.

She can't, or won't, speak. She sits on the edge of one of the folding chairs at the table, her teeth chattering, blue and yellow balloons swaying incongruously over her head. Bernie, in the other seat, reaches across the table for a stack of wrinkled paper napkins. She offers them to the stranger, who is soaking wet. But the woman won't let go of her purse long enough to take one.

"Are you okay?" Bernie asks gently.

Jay's eyes skim the woman's body, her arms, her legs, her face.

She has not been shot, he sees right away. The skin beneath her neck is red and swollen, but Jay can't be sure if that was his doing—when he grabbed her in the water—or someone else's. Other than that, there isn't a scratch on her. She looks up, aware that Jay is watching her, and tightens the grip on her purse, as if she half-expects him to make a clean snatch and run away with it. He senses this white woman is afraid of him. He ignores the insult, stuffing his rising anger, an emotion that will in no way serve him.

"Where is he?" he asks.

Still she doesn't speak.

"Where *is* he?" Jay asks again, harder this time.

"I don't know," she says, opening her mouth for the first time, her voice sweet but raw, like a rusty church bell swinging on its hinge. "I ran, I just ran."

Jay, still thinking there's a gun somewhere close by, turns to the old man in the baseball cap. "Start the boat," he orders the captain. "Now."

The old man slips through the cabin door, and a few moments later, Jay hears the engine start. He turns back to the woman. "What happened to you?"

She lowers her eyes, her face taking on a hot, crimson color.

She is too shamed, it seems, to look him in the eye.

"He attack you?"

"Jay," Bernie says softly. She shakes her head at her husband, a silent suggestion that whatever went on behind those trees, maybe this woman, terrified and shaking, is not ready to say it out loud, in mixed company no less. Jay nods, backing off, but he doesn't take his eyes off the stranger. She lost her shoes somewhere in the water, but Jay can tell by the cut and fabric of her dress that it isn't cheap. She's also missing an earring. Its twin is round and gold with a diamond in the center. There's a diamond on her ring finger too—right hand, not left—a rock three times bigger than the one Bernie is wearing. Her purse, the one she won't let go of, has little *G*'s printed all over it. It's Italian, Jay knows, like the ones those rich insurance company lawyers carry into the courtroom.

Eyeing the clothes and the rock, Jay asks, "Where were you?"

"Excuse me?" the woman says, a surprising edge in her voice.

"Where were you coming from?"

She stares at him blankly, as if she doesn't understand the question, but Jay catches an unmistakable flash of recognition in her copper-colored eyes. He thinks she knows exactly what he's asking: what was a woman like you doing in a neighborhood like this, 'round about midnight, alone?

She cuts her eyes away from Jay, turning to Bernie instead. "Is there a washroom I can use?"

Bernie points to a swinging door across the room. It stops short of the floor, offering little privacy except for a small painted sign that says OCCUPIED, a smiley face drawn inside the *O*. Bernie offers the paper napkins again. The woman is slow to move, her body stiff, like a broken doll, held together at this late hour by sheer will, as if she's afraid that any tiny motion might break her in two. And she won't let go of her purse. Bernie reaches for the handbag, as if to set it on the table for the woman. But the move startles her. She lets out a small cry in protest, her eyes alight with a kind of panic. Bernie lets go of the purse instantly, and the bag tumbles from both their hands. They all watch as it falls onto the floor, landing with surprising softness. Its mouth open to the room, the purse, Jay sees, is empty. It contains nothing, not a lipstick case or a book of matches, not even house keys or a few coins. Like her missing shoes and earring, it seems the contents of the woman's purse were lost somewhere in the bayou. Lost, or *dumped*, he thinks, the word occurring to him unexpectedly, lodging itself stubbornly in the back of his mind, like a sharp pebble in his shoe.

Bernie and the woman reach for the purse at the same time.

"Don't touch it," Jay blurts. "Don't touch a thing."

Just leave it alone, he thinks.

The woman picks up her bag. She stands, turning her back to them, and slips behind the bathroom door. Jay can hear the metal latch catch on the other side. The old man is now leaning against the cabin door, smoking another cigarette, pinched between his thumb and forefinger. He nods toward the white woman, her legs showing beneath the bathroom door, then looks at Jay and shrugs. "Ain't nothing to do now," he says. "Just ride her on in, I guess."

Jay watches her in the rearview mirror.

She's in the backseat, eyes closed, turning her diamond ring over and over, fingering the icy stone as if it were a talisman or a rosary, something to bring luck or a promise of redemption. They're only a few blocks from the central station. They ride in silence, the stranger in the back and Bernie in the front passenger seat. Jay keeps the Buick Skylark at an even thirty-five miles an hour, careful not to draw any undue attention. He's keenly aware of the irony, his fear of being stopped by cops on his way to a police station. But driving a strange white woman, whose name he never got, at this time of night, in *this* city, makes him edgy, cautious. He wouldn't have offered to drive her at all if Bernie hadn't insisted. His clothes are still wet with the stink of the bayou.

There's no one in front of the police station when he pulls up to the curb.

Jay parks the car, but leaves the engine running.

Downtown's central police station is an older building, a rarity in a city that has a curious habit of razing its own history. The station was built in early midcentury, before the city was a boomtown, before the postwar explosion of American highways made gas the most coveted commodity in the country, before 1973 and the embargo, before the crisis, before oil made Houston.

"Should we go in?" Bernie asks, her face turned to her husband.

The woman in the backseat opens her eyes. They meet Jay's in the rearview mirror. "I'm fine from here." Her voice is mannered, calm. "Thank you."

She steps out of the car and walks up the first steps to the police station, then stops. She's gathering her strength maybe, or, Jay thinks, she's stalling.

"You think she's okay?" Bernie asks.

Jay puts the car in drive, fresh sweat breaking across his brow.

Just the idea of being anywhere near a police station at this time of night, looking like a ragged dog, tangled up in some white woman's mess makes him more than a little dizzy. He knows firsthand the long, creative arm of Southern law enforcement, knows when he ought to keep his mouth shut.

He locks the doors and pulls away from the curb, stealing a final glance in his rearview mirror. He watches the woman standing alone in front of the police station and wonders if she's going inside.

Chapter 2

Monday morning, the hooker shows up wearing a neck brace. Jay takes one look at it and tells her to get rid of it. She starts to take it off right there in the hallway. "Not here," he says, surprised, again, by how much instruction she needs. He looks up and down the hallway, making sure opposing counsel hasn't witnessed this whole routine, his client's backstage preparations. He nods toward the ladies' washroom across the way. "And don't let anybody see you."

The hearing is due to start in three minutes, and it won't look good for them to be late before this judge. Jay is going to need as much goodwill and mercy as the court will see fit to offer. His case is as thin as ice milk, and they all know it. He runs his finger along the crease of his suit pants, a poly-fiber blend made exclusively for JCPenney, and the nicest pair he owns. He smooths his shirt beneath his jacket, lifting his arms slightly to check the moisture level in his pits. He feels hot and slightly off his game. He's had the same headache since he crawled out of the bayou Saturday night, a dull ache behind his ears, a near constant pain that nags at him, a vague feeling that something is wrong.

It's just a hearing, he reminds himself. *Just get Hicks to agree to a trial.*

He stares at the closed door to the ladies' washroom and wonders if he ought to send someone in after his client.

But the fourth-floor hallway is nearly deserted.

Monday mornings at the civil courthouse are usually slow going. The place lacks the focus or feeling of purpose of the criminal courthouse, a building that practically crackles with the electric energy of righteous indignation, a feeling running under everything, even the most mundane office tasks, that something huge is at stake. There are murderers and rapists in the hallways, crooks and thieves roaming the building; there are handcuffs and officers with guns. The spectacle alone is enough to fill everyone with a sense of heroic purpose, or at least a heated feeling of excitement. In a civil courtroom, there is only one thing at stake: money. Questions of right or wrong, who did what to whom, are stripped of their morality here and reduced to a numerical equation. What is your pain worth? What's the going rate for sorrow? If it's not your money or pain that's at stake, it's kind of hard to get too fired up about the proceedings, nor do they draw much of a crowd. Judge Hicks's courtroom is nearly empty when Jay walks in, save for the bailiff and the court reporter and Charlie Luckman, who is sitting at the defense table in a cream-colored suit and tan 'gators, the only one in the room wearing a smile.

"Where's your client?" he asks Jay.

"Where's yours?" Jay nods toward the empty seat next to Luckman.

"I advised my client not to attend, lest we give these proceedings more weight than they deserve," Charlie says, twisting a gold pinky ring on his right hand, just above his thick knuckle. "And anyway, I got the cop," he adds, picking up an affidavit lying on the defense table, next to his shiny leather briefcase. "I told Mr. Cummings not to dignify the charges with his presence. He is, after all, out doing important work for this community."

Jay's papers are held together in a sagging accordion file folder. He lays them on the table in front of him. "Maybe your client should have thought about his position in the community, his wife even, before he put a hooker in his car."

"What hooker, Mr. Porter?" Charlie says with a wink.

The door to the judge's chambers opens. The clerk comes out first, then the judge. They all stand. Jay turns and looks over his shoulder. His client is just now entering the gallery, the neck brace on open display in her right hand. As she approaches Jay, she whispers, rather loudly, that she had the damnedest time getting the thing off. Jay closes his eyes and takes a deep breath. He's up first.

On the stand, the hooker has a name: Dana Moreland. And a new profession: "escort." She speaks softly, with a practiced vulnerability that Jay knows she's been working on over the weekends, like trying to learn a new dance step in time for the prom. This is her moment in the spotlight after all, her chance to tell it the way she wants it heard. Her story: a friend set her up with a Mr. J. T. Cummings ("No, sir, he is not present in the courtroom"; Jay wants that on record). She agreed to meet him in the parking lot of a Long John Silver on the north side of town. They negotiated a price and drove off in his car. She then asked her "date" to take her to Gilley's, out 225, in Pasadena. She'd seen *Urban Cowboy* at least ten times and wanted to dance at the place where John Travolta and Debra Winger got married. For a couple of line dances and a b.j., J.T. was happy to oblige. ("A 'b.j.'?" Jay asks, 'cause he has to. She leans forward on the stand, into the microphone, as if she's going to demonstrate right then and there. "A blow job," she explains.) Her "date" drove her some twenty, thirty miles outside the city limits ("no small thing, gas being as high as a dollar thirty-five a gallon in some parts"). They were having such a good time at the club that Mr. Cummings lost himself and drank one or two ("maybe it was three") Long Islands past his limit, and on the way home, he was weaving and driving erratically. She asked him several times to please pull over. But he refused, and she was, after all, in his employ. Somewhere along the way home, Jay's client reports, Mr. Cummings got into a one-car accident: he hit a telephone pole.

"And where were you at the time of the accident?"

"In his lap."

The court reporter looks up. The bailiff cracks a smile.

"Well, really . . . just my head."

The judge lets out a little cough.

They're all laughing at him, Jay thinks, with his JCPenney suit and his shitty case. He's heard this story a dozen times, and it has never sounded more ridiculous than it does right now, with her on the stand. He frankly never expected the case to get this far. He was sure just the mention of Ms. Moreland's name and profession to the defendant's lawyer, the fact that she claimed any association with Mr. Cummings, would be enough for an instant settlement. He actually imagined the whole thing would be handled in a single phone call. But he grossly underestimated Charlie Luckman's propensity for bluff calling.

Jay looks down at his notes. "An Officer Erikson arrived on the scene?"

"A state trooper, yes."

"And when he discovered Mr. Cummings behind the wheel, drunk, with your head wedged between his legs . . . what did Officer Erikson do?"

"Nothing."

"Nothing?"

"He was practically apologizing to the guy."

"And what did you make of that?"

"That he recognized J.T., and he didn't want to get him in any trouble."

Jay is waiting on the objection: "calls for speculation," "lack of foundation," "irrelevance" . . . something. But when he catches Luckman out of the corner of his eye, Charlie is leaned way back in his chair watching the whole thing like a sporting event he is only mildly interested in.

"He offered you no medical attention?"

"No, sir."

"So, the extent of your injuries that night may never be fully known, since you did not get immediate medical attention?"

Again, he waits for it: "witness is not a medical expert."

But Charlie says nothing.

He just watches as Jay guides this train wreck, walking his client through the rest of her testimony—a description of her injuries, aches and pains, and seemingly a million reasons why she never made it to a doctor. His final question: It was Mr. Cummings who put your head in his lap, was it not?

"I definitely wasn't down there for my health."

By now, she's lost the rhythm of the whole routine. The vulnerability is gone and a huskiness has crept back into her voice. Jay can suddenly imagine all the laps she's ever had her head in, can see her whole career in full color.

"Nothing further, Your Honor."

Charlie passes on a cross-exam. For his direct, he walks a stapled stack of papers to the judge's bench: the cop's affidavit and the original police report. The judge reads the pages in silence while they all wait. The court reporter checks a chipped nail. The bailiff looks at his watch. Out in the hallway, they can hear rubber soles squeaking on the linoleum and one side of an argument about who has the best catfish plate, Delfina's on Main or Guido's.

Finally, Judge Hicks looks up, looks right at Jay.

"The cop pulled him over for a busted taillight."

"Yes, Your Honor, but—"

"There's nothing in here about an accident, no mention that Ms. Moreland was even *in* the defendant's car."

"Your Honor," Charlie says. "Defense respectfully requests the court to grant a motion for summary judgment and to dismiss all claims at this time."

"Slow down, Counselor," the judge says.

He turns to Jay as if he's not sure what Jay expects him to do in this situation. Jay clears his throat. "It is our contention, Your Honor, that Officer Erikson, catching Mr. Cummings, a port commissioner and a former city councilman, in a 'compromising' position, wrote Mr. Cummings a ticket for a minor infraction, carefully leaving out the fact that Mr. Cummings was drunk and had a lady friend in the car, a woman other than his wife."

"So she's claiming the *cop* broke the law too?" Charlie says.

The judge holds up a hand to keep Charlie out of it. He asks Jay, "And you can prove this how?"

"The testimony of Ms. Moreland clearly states—"

"My client has never even met the plaintiff, Your Honor," Charlie interrupts.

Judge Hicks looks at Jay. "You do have something other than the girl, right? Some other evidence? A witness, something?"

"I'm working on it."

Judge Hicks lets out a sigh, a tight little puff of air, like he's passed gas after a bad meal, like they've all wasted his entire morning. He looks back and forth between Charlie and Jay, then waves defense counsel to the bench, calling him by his first name. Jay wonders how well the two men know each other. Charlie, in his mid-forties now, is a former prosecutor with some renown in the city. He was almost elected district attorney of Harris County, Texas, twice in his heyday, the same years he won Texas Prosecutor of the Year and had a near perfect conviction record. And now, as a defense attorney, he's in the peculiar (and rather lucrative) position of being on friendly terms with nearly every prosecutor and judge in the county. Jay watches the two men, their heads pressed together at the judge's bench, both doughy about the jowls and pink with summer heat, as if they each spent the weekend playing golf—together, for all Jay knows. The two men are whispering, sharing words he can't hear.

. The hooker tugs on his jacket sleeve. "What's that all about?"

Jay ignores her.

A few seconds later, Charlie walks back to the defense table, smiling.

The judge intertwines his fingers, pressing his palms together. "Mr. Porter, I don't suppose I need to remind you that Mr. Cummings is an important member of our community. If this is some sort of extortion attempt—"

"No, Your Honor."

"And if I let this go to trial, put a man like Mr. Cummings on the stand, you better come to the table with more than you walked in here with today."

"Yes, sir."

"I'm not interested in wasting the court's time or Mr. Cummings's."

The judge looks down at the cop's affidavit again and the police report. He looks up at the hooker sitting next to Jay. "It's her word against his."

"The basis of every trial I've ever come across, Your Honor. Somebody's word against somebody else's."

The judge stares at Jay for what seems like an hour.

Then he nods, deciding it. "I'm gon' let it stand."

At the defense table, Charlie Luckman clears his throat rather loudly.

The judge, rising from his seat, pretends not to hear him.

The court reporter stretches her arms. The bailiff makes a quick phone call. The hooker asks for a ride home. Jay glances at his watch. He hasn't been to the office all day, but he agrees to the ride anyway. He doesn't need her walking and possibly picking up another notch on her rap sheet before they even get to trial.

On his way out of the courtroom, he feels a hand on his back.

"I admire your fortitude, Porter," Charlie says, throwing charm on top of any hard feelings. "Maybe we can work something out on this deal after all."

"Talk to your client," Jay says. "Let me know."

He arrives at his office already behind for the day. His head is throbbing, and there's nothing in his desk but an old bottle of Pepto and a tin of Sucrets lozenges. For lunch, he has a couple of bags of Fritos out of the vending machine in the strip mall where he works. He eats them alone at his desk.

Eddie Mae, his secretary, is MIA, today leaving a note about her grandbaby's dentist appointment. He's on his own with the phones.

He interviews two potential clients.

The first is a woman in her seventies who slipped on a black grape in the produce section of a Safeway mart. He's pretty excited about this one, until he asks the woman about her legal history. It turns out that in the last sixteen months, the woman slipped on a cantaloupe at Kroger, depilatory cream at Walgreens, and soapy water at a car wash on Griggs. When he tells her he won't be taking her case, she calls him a fool. "I won them cases, sugar, every last one."

He wishes he could say the rejection was some great act of legal integrity. The truth is, the case would cost him more than he would make, Safeway being a national corporation with deep pockets and a bevy of in-house attorneys, one for every day of the week if they want. They would assuredly do their best to tie up the case with court hearings and brief filings and depositions for everybody from the store's manager to his client's high school boyfriend. Jay, a one-man operation, doesn't have that kind of time for anything but a sure thing.

The second prospect he interviews is more promising.

The man actually comes into the office, says please and thank you when Jay offers him coffee. He's got a good story about a motel out near Katy. His little girl is holed up in a local hospital down that way. She got cut up pretty bad by some broken beer bottles left by the side of the motel's pool. The manager offered to cover their room, but balked at the notion of paying their medical bills, and now the man's got a hospital tab that's growing by the minute and no money to pay it. He left his daughter at the hospital with his wife because he didn't know what else to do. "I got a good case, I know I do," he says. "But right now, I'm just trying to get my little girl home."

Jay sets his pen across his desk. By now, he's onto the hustle.

"If I could just get a little money," the guy starts. "I'll pay you back, I swear. Or you can just take it off my bill, soon as we win this."

Jay stands and shows him to the door.

The hooker is the only bright spot on the horizon.

He tries a couple of phone numbers Ms. Moreland scratched on the back of a gas station receipt, looking for the girlfriend who set up the date between his client and J. T. Cummings, the only person Dana can think of who can corroborate her story. The first number is disconnected. The other is the home of a Mexican woman who sounds to be about eighty. She's never heard of Dana Moreland. Jay leaves a note on Eddie Mae's desk: they've got to find the witness.

He gets home late, after eight o'clock. Bernie is already in bed, snoring.

She left a plate for him on the stove. Jay takes off his tie and eats in silence at the kitchen table. Afterward, he washes his plate and fork and leaves them in the rack to dry. He tries to clean up some, make himself feel useful around the house, but Bernie has already cleared and washed the pots and pans and wiped down the counter. He cleans out the refrigerator instead, pulling out leftovers from Bernie's birthday two days ago: barbecued meat, dried and rubbery by now, old potato salad, and beer, a can of which he drinks standing up, holding open the door to the fridge. He burps and reaches for another to kill his lingering headache. He finishes the second beer standing over his stereo, flipping through his LPs, trying to find just the right one. He picks out an Otis record, his favorite, and sets the needle down on track number five.

I want security, yeah, and I want it at any cost.

Finally, he sits down with the mail, the bills he's been avoiding, the kitchen calculator, and his checkbook. He runs the numbers two and three times and comes up short every time. He rearranges the bills, deciding which ones he has to pay now and which ones can wait. What's left in the register seems hardly enough to eat on, let alone raise a family. He looks around their tiny one-bedroom apartment, cramped as it is with mismatched furniture, law books, and borrowed clothes for the baby, and worries that they'll never get out of here. Back against the sofa, his financial life spread across the worn carpet, he thinks through his case-load, the open files on his desk, like running lottery numbers in his head, trying to guess which cases to play, where to put his money and time.

It's become a game for him, a gamble.

It didn't start out this way. One of his first cases out of law school was a police brutality lawsuit against the city. A rookie cop had allegedly roughed up a sixteen-year-old black kid who was nervous and fumbling for his license. The way the boy told it, the cop dragged him from the car, yelled a few epithets, and knocked him to the ground, hard enough that it left bruises and a scar that was still showing by the time they made it to trial. Jay took the case pro bono, going head to head with the city attorney, a white man who had at least a decade of litigation experience over Jay. But Jay had, in so many ways, been preparing for that trial his whole life. His own legal troubles were not so far from his mind. He remembered what it was to sit at a defense table, remembered what it felt like to have his basic civil liberties up for debate. The anger was still with him then. And he let it guide him the whole way. He went after the cop with a vengeance, making the poor man stand in for everything that was wrong with a country and a government that applied the law willy-nilly. By closing arguments, half the jury was nodding along to his every other word, and Jay won the case.

But it was a moral victory, not an economic one. What he made off the city's meager settlement wasn't enough to cover his expenses or to make up for money he lost by ignoring his other cases during the trial. His performance in the courtroom got his name in the papers, for the second time in his life, and before he knew it, he had folks lined up in his office, all asking for his help. They'd heard he took that boy's case for free and wanted to know what he could do for them. Their problems were low rent, the stuff you find in any black neighborhood in the country: a son in jail or a cousin who'd been let go on his job or an ex-husband who wasn't making his child-support payments on time. They never had any money, and Jay could hardly make his own rent. Practicing law, he would soon find out, is like running any other small business. Most days he's just trying to make his overhead: insurance and filing fees, Eddie Mae's meager salary, plus $500 a month to lease the furnished office space on West Gray.

He, quite frankly, can't afford his principles.

He needs a win, a jackpot.

And if it comes in the form of a prostitute with a neck ache, then so be it.

He shoves the bills together into a messy pile, stuffing them inside his checkbook, and decides on another beer. He drinks it slowly, leaned up against his couch, staring at the boxes of baby gifts that have been piling up for weeks now. The long, flat box is from his wife's parents, the Reverend and Mrs. Al Boykins. Bernie has asked him on more than one occasion to get a move on it.

Jay stands and crosses the room, using his car keys to tear into the cardboard. The crib spills out in pieces. Jay sets it on the floor and walks to the hall closet, hunting for his toolbox. Inside, beneath his screwdrivers and drill bits, he finds a crumpled pack of Newports. He supposedly quit when Bernie got pregnant, but he keeps a stash here and there, in his car and at the office. He pockets the pack of cigarettes and carries the toolbox into the living room.

The whole thing takes him over an hour, but he manages to get piece A to fit with B, and B to fit with C, and so on. Before long, he has a crib. He lays the tiny, vinyl-covered mattress inside and runs his fingers along the handrailing. It's white-painted plywood, cheap but sturdy. They'll have to get some little sheets to go with it, maybe put up a mobile sometime, one that plays a melody. He tries to picture the little one who will sleep here soon, and wonders if she'll have Bernadine's dimples or her toothy smile . . . or if he'll have Jay's eyes, brown and wide and set in his face like two river stones, weathered and deep.

He crumples the instructions, shoving them in the empty box. On his way to the back door, he pulls the trash from the step can by the kitchen stove and grabs a stack of old newspapers. He drags the whole mess down the back stairs.

The waste bin out behind his building is overflowing with paper grocery bags full of chicken bones and black, moldy heads of lettuce, dead leaves and beer bottles and boxes of old clothes. The trash has a putrid smell, rotten and sickly sweet. There are flies buzzing over everything. It's been sitting like this, untouched, for almost two weeks, what with trash pickup in Houston getting more and more sporadic. It's one of the city's dirty little secrets, that for all its recent economic prosperity—the fastest-growing city in the country two years running, the oil crises of the late '70s a boon for an oil town like Houston—the city can barely keep up with its own growth. It is literally busting at the seams, its trashy insides spilling over everything. Sanitation workers put in overtime but can't keep up with the new businesses and housing developments going up every week. Residents in tony neighborhoods like River Oaks and Memorial hire private companies to haul their shit away, but on streets like Jay's in Third Ward, lined with cheap rental units and shotgun houses, working people are at the mercy of the city. Jay dumps the empty crib box and his kitchen trash on top of the rotting heap in the bin. He tosses the newspapers next, watching as they dribble down the huge mound of garbage, landing back at his feet.

Jay reaches for the cigarettes in his pocket and makes a seat for himself on top of a broken TV. He strikes a match on the concrete at his feet and lights the end of a bent Newport. He takes a drag and picks up one of the old newspapers, killing time between this cigarette and the one he knows is coming next.

Cole Oil Industries, the largest oil and gas company in the city, made the business page, along with some other big names in petrol, Exxon and Shell. Cole Oil is reporting a slowdown at their main refinery near the Port of Houston; a shortage in barrels coming in from overseas is listed as the cause. There's something lurking behind the words in print, a hint, a threat really, of another oil crisis on the horizon. Jay doesn't think he can afford much more than he's paying at the pumps now, up to $1.37 at the PetroCole station by his house.

Below the fold is more on an ongoing story about labor problems at the port, dockworkers threatening to strike over wage issues. Jay reads the article carefully, thinking of Mr. J. T. Cummings and his position on the port commission. Mr. Cummings, Jay knows, is up for reappointment to the commission, and a strike at the port could possibly hurt J.T.'s chances and help Jay in his civil matter. His job on the line, Mr. Cummings and his slick lawyer are likely to want to settle as quickly as possible, before word gets out about the hooker. Jay stores this information about the strike in the back of his mind. He takes a couple of short puffs on his cigarette and turns the page.

And that's when he sees it.

The City Beat, page 2.

Sunday morning, somebody found a body.

A white male, shot twice, found in an open field in the 400 block of Clinton, near Lockwood Drive in Fifth Ward, not fifty yards from Buffalo Bayou.

Police were called to the scene to investigate.

They talked to a female companion of the deceased, at her home near Memorial. The dead man's name is not mentioned, nor is hers, only the name of the groundskeeper who found the body, a part-time worker for Quartz Industrial, Inc., a broken concrete wholesaler whose warehouse is on Clinton.

The whole bit is just five lines, something right out of a police blotter.

Jay, transfixed, reads it two more times.

Buffalo Bayou. Fifth Ward.

White male, shot twice.

His first thought is of *her*, the woman from the boat. He remembers the rock and roll of water beneath their feet, the screams and the gunshots, two, one on top of the other. He remembers the taste of the bayou water, bitter and foul.

They've mentioned her only once.

Sunday morning Bernie lay in bed and told him the dream she'd had the night before. They were on an island somewhere, riding around on a bus. The woman from the bayou asked the driver to stop. And when the driver said he couldn't, she opened the nearest window and jumped out. They all watched her float out across the water, wave at them, and then dive headfirst into the ocean.

Later, two cops came on the bus.

"One of them was Mr. Hempnill, the one who runs the funeral home down by Daddy's place. I kept saying, 'Hi, Mr. Hempnill,' and he said he didn't know anybody by that name." Bernie turned to Jay, as if they were on the bus right then. "I said, 'Jay,'" she whispered. "'That's Melvin Hempnill if I've ever seen him.' And you shushed me. Well, then the cops turn to you. They looking at you now." She smiled, enjoying her own story, the clever turns it was taking.

It was early. Jay was on his side, facing the wall. He had not slept two consecutive hours all night. He slid a hand under his pillow and felt the .22 nestled there. This is his morning ritual, the way he greets the world.

"So now the police want to know what you got to do with the whole thing," Bernie said. "This woman jumping out a window like it's nothing."

Jay sat up and swung his legs off the side of the bed.

"'We got some questions need answering,' something like that."

Jay stood and started from the room barefoot.

"Jay."

"I'm listening."

There's only one bathroom in their three-room apartment, in the hallway between the bedroom and the kitchen. Jay left the door open. "So like I said, old Hempnill is looking at you, and everybody else on the bus is staring at you too. So you get up . . . and this is the crazy part . . . you get up and go out the same window she did. Only you don't float at all. You drop like a bag of bricks."

He put the toilet seat down and walked back to their bedroom.

"Ain't that something," she said. She was sitting up in bed, a paperback resting on her belly. Jay realized she'd been up for a while, that she'd waited before waking him. "You left me on that bus, didn't wave back or nothing."

Jay found that amusing, the idea of him leaving her any-where.

Bernie slid the paperback off her belly. "I told Evelyn about it."

Jay hiked his pants on over his shorts, keeping his mouth shut about his sister-in-law. "Maybe we shouldn't have left her out there," Bernie said softly.

She fiddled with her paperback, sliding a bookmark back and forth between the same two pages. He saw she was upset, but in some way he didn't recognize or understand. "We didn't do anything wrong," he said.

Outside, by the thin light of a nearby streetlamp, Jay reads the newspaper article again. The date at the top of the page makes his stomach turn. The article, he sees, is from today's paper, which means the body was discovered yesterday, the day after their boat ride. He wonders if his wife read these same words, and if she did, why she didn't say anything to him about it. Maybe she read the article and thought nothing of it. Hell, there must be a couple of shootings a week in Fifth Ward, Saturday night being the favored day for mischief making. The gunshots they heard on the water and the report of a shooting death in the area are surely no more than an uncomfortable coincidence. Still, the whole bit bothers him enough that he takes the time to tear the page from the newspaper, folding the article two, then three times, and sliding it into his pants pocket.

Bernie's awake when he comes into the apartment.

She's standing in her house shoes and a faded brown robe that won't close over her belly. She stares at Jay standing in her kitchen, smelling of smoke, newsprint stained on his fingers. She looks him up and down, lingering about his face, trying to read his expression, why he's breathing funny.

"I heard you go out," she says.

"I was taking out the trash," he says.

Bernie nods. This makes sense to her, makes her feel better.

"You gon' put another bag in?" she asks.

"I always do."

"No, you don't, Jay."

He reaches under the sink and pulls out a black trash bag, snapping it open to make his point. "You gon' fight with me about trash bags?"

"I'm just saying. Sometimes you don't."

She's mad with him about something. He doesn't know what, and he doesn't think she knows either. They've been kind of short with each other since Saturday night, their nerves slightly on edge, their collective, unspoken anxiety masked as ill temperament. Jay closes the lid on the trash can, deciding then and there he won't tell her about the newspaper article. It'll only upset her, and for no good reason he can think of. Besides, he's still hoping it's nothing.

Chapter 3

Eddie Mae pokes her head into Jay's office, where he's been working since seven o'clock this morning. She leans against the door frame, kicking at a piece of carpet that's coming up on the floor, holding a stack of pink message slips. Her wig is red today. Which means she's in a bad mood. Or a drinking mood. Or she's got a date to play dominoes after work. Jay can't remember which, can't keep up with Eddie Mae's changeable temperament. He wants her to leave the messages on the left corner of his desk like he's taught her to and leave him to his work. He does not want to give her the idea that he's gon' stop everything every time she walks into the room. Eddie Mae is cheap labor—no paralegal training and not a day spent in secretarial school—but she's costly in other ways. She won't let him alone half the time, always checking up on him and henpecking about what he eats for lunch. She's a black woman and a grandmother, no matter the tight polyester tops that tug against her chest, and she treats him like a son or a nephew. She seems to sense something in Jay that needs caring for.

"Your father's on the phone," she says.

"Excuse me?"

"Mr. Boykins. He's waiting on line two."

His father, right.

Jay sets his pencil down. "You find the witness in the Cummings thing?"

"I'm working on it," she says, scratching at the wig's scalp, getting to hers underneath. "I know where she work, but the dude at the club won't give me her phone number, and she ain't returned none of the messages I left."

"What club?"

"The Big Dipper, out 45."

Jay nods, motioning for her to leave the message slips on his desk.

Then he picks up the line. "Rev."

"You know I wouldn't bother you at work unless it was something," his father-in-law says straightaway. His voice is hoarse this morning, overworked and strained. "Son, we got us a big problem."

Jay reaches for his pencil, thinking a kid at the church must have gotten himself in some kind of trouble. A bar fight or joyriding or maybe petty theft. One time, a girl, barely sixteen, knocked the front teeth out of her boyfriend's mouth. Jay gets these calls from his father-in-law several times a month, usually with somebody's mama crying in the background. He searches for a clean slip of paper to write down the facts, the kid's name and where they're holding him, already weighing what a trip to the station will do to his afternoon schedule.

"You got some time tonight, son? Time we can talk?"

Something in the Rev's tone makes Jay pause. "What's going on?"

"I'd rather we talk in person. Can you come by the church tonight, sometime around seven thirty?"

"Yes, sir."

"Good. We'll see you then."

Reverend Boykins hangs up, leaving Jay to wonder who *we* is.

He tries to go back to his work, but finds he can't focus.

It's more than the cryptic call from his father-in-law. He's also had trouble putting the newspaper article out of his mind, the one from yesterday's paper. Before he left the house this morning, he actually tucked the newspaper clipping into his pants pocket because he simply couldn't bring himself to throw the thing away. He's had a few halfhearted thoughts of phoning the police. But to say what exactly? He doesn't know that the gunshots they heard Saturday night have anything to do with the shooting death in the newspaper. And no matter how hard he tries, he simply can't picture himself walking into a police station and offering information that ties him to some other shooting . . . certainly not with his felony arrest record. Free advice he gives to any prospective client who walks through the door: don't volunteer anything to a cop that he didn't ask for in the first place. Keep your fucking mouth shut.

He already checked the *Post* this morning, standing over his kitchen table in his shorts and bare feet. There was no more mention of a white male, shot twice in Fifth Ward. It's as if the whole thing was simply forgotten, and Jay tries to convince himself that he can do the same. He puts his mind and body to work, diving into the mound of paperwork on his desk.

The rest of the day passes in a blur.

Eddie Mae gets a stomachache around four o'clock, the symptoms of which are very vague. She comes out of the bathroom wearing lipstick and fresh powder, asking if she can go home early. She practically skips out the door when he says yes. At a quarter to seven, Jay grabs his suit jacket and heads for his car.

First Love Antioch Baptist Church is located on the northeast side of Fifth Ward, out by the railroad tracks, where the Ewell Line runs east-west three times a day like clockwork, shaking the church's fake stained glass. The church is small and poor and set in the middle of a residential street lined with one-room shacks. Jay parks right in front. He lights a cigarette and stares at a gray house down the street. She would be nearing eighty, he thinks. The juror at his trial. He used to bring her things, a bag of groceries every now and then or flowers, any little thing just to say thank you. She's been dead three years, and her people, the ones who stay in the house now, won't hardly ever open the door. They don't know Jay or what their grandmother did for him, the life she saved.

He tosses his cigarette and steps out of his Buick, into the reckless path of a late-model Cadillac thumping by on the street, blasting music on the stereo, so loud the whole car shakes, rattling gold chains hanging from the rearview mirror. Jay feels the crush of bass in his chest. He stares at the group of young men in the car. They're no more than nineteen years old, brothers with do-rags mashed against their foreheads. They regard Jay with open suspicion, his pressed clothes and polished shoes. They seem to know he doesn't belong here, in their neighborhood, in their time. As the car continues up the street, Jay can't help but think of where he was at nineteen. Marching, strategizing, planning. Fighting for a hell of a lot more than gold chains hanging from a Coupe de Ville.

He turns for the church steps, hearing the last ringing chords of "Jesus, Come Walk with Me" on the church's aging pipe organ. Choir practice is ending, Jay thinks, or just getting started. Inside the sanctuary, he walks down the blue-carpeted center aisle between the pews, where he walked on his wedding day. The man at the organ bench is small and thin, with a cheap, greasy Jheri curl slicked against the sides of his head. He's scooping up sheet music. The woman standing next to him is packing up her hymnal.

It's only then that Jay notices the men down front, filling up the first three rows. There's got to be more than a dozen of them, men dressed in scuffed work boots, grimy jeans, and stained T-shirts, a few of which read BROTHERHOOD OF LONGSHOREMEN, LOCAL 116 in letters that are cracked and fading.

In an instant Jay knows what this is about, what he's walked into. He can read it on the men's stern faces, their rough, calloused hands, the nylon caps clenched in their fists. He can smell it on them. The salt of the Gulf.

He knows this is some trouble about the strike.

Reverend Boykins stands in the center aisle, down in front of the pulpit. He waves a hand for Jay to come forward. "We've been waiting on you, son."

They have all turned around now. They're all looking at him.

In the crowd, Jay spots a familiar pair of dark brown eyes.

Kwame Mackalvy, who dropped "Lloyd," his given name, sometime during their junior year at the University of Houston—"Lloyd" was a banker's name, he'd said, an "establishment" name—is sitting in the second pew, wearing a union T-shirt over his loud and colorful dashiki. He runs a hand along the fresh, clean T-shirt as if admiring a new costume, getting into character. This is Kwame's scene, Jay thinks, always some fight to be had, a cause to get behind. Kwame runs a community center a few blocks from Jay's apartment, but the two men haven't spoken in years. They run in different circles now, Jay with his middle-class aspirations and Kwame still holding notions of a coming revolution.

"Jay Porter," Kwame says, drawing out the name, eyeing Jay's suit and his close-cropped hair. He lets out a slow, catlike grin, his teeth white and unnaturally large. "White man still got you, huh, bro, one way or another."

"It's good to see you too, Lloyd," Jay says flatly.

He's relieved when Reverend Boykins opens the meeting, if only to move out of Kwame's political crosshairs. His father-in-law speaks to Jay first. "Son, you heard about the trouble we've been having down at the Ship Channel?"

"Yes, sir."

"Well, we got a bigger mess on our hands here."

The Rev nods toward an older gentleman in the first pew. He's wearing a Houston Independent School District janitor's uniform, a pack of cigarettes rolled up in his sleeve. Awkward and shy in front of the group, the man starts to put his hands in his pockets, forgetting he's in his uniform, which doesn't have any pockets. He rests his hands at his sides instead; then, with an elbow, he nudges a young man beside him. The boy, eighteen or nineteen, stands and turns, facing the rest of the men too. He's wearing a sling on his left arm. His face is beaten something awful, bruised and discolored, his lip busted and swollen. One of his front teeth is chipped. "Mr. Porter," the janitor says. "This here's my son." He puts a hand on the boy's shoulder. "You can see they beat him good. They drug him from his car, coming from one of the meetings, broke his arm in two places."

"Who?" Jay asks, though by now he's already guessed.

"Some of the ILA boys."

The ILA is the International Longshoremen's Association, the white union down at the docks. The Brotherhood of Longshoremen belongs to the blacks. The two labor groups were ordered to integrate a few years back and are still operating under a government consent decree to do just that. But the process has taken longer than anyone expected, except for maybe the longshoremen themselves. "Some of them ain't too happy about us talking about a walkout," one of the men says, his ashy elbows propped on the back of the first pew, his hands in two tight fists. "We supposed to all be brothers now, part of the same union. Government say so. If some of us strike, we all got to."

"ILA ain't having none of that," one of the dockworkers says.

From what Jay has read in the papers, talk of a strike originated in the Brotherhood's camp. The two unions technically operate under the same voting body, pay into the same pool of funds, but the black workers are routinely paid less than their white brothers, and the Brotherhood is using a new round of negotiations with the shipping companies to get more pay. They've got enough white ILA men promising to join their ranks, enough for a bona fide strike.

"They got some good white ones down there," one man says.

"But the rest of them crackers is up to no good," another man says, pulling a gnawed toothpick from his mouth. "They trying to scare us out of a strike. And the police ain't doing a damned thing about it."

"He drove himself to the station," the janitor says. "My boy looking worse than he do now. They wouldn't do nothing, wouldn't let him fill out a report, nothing. Even though Darren says he saw the men who did it."

"Police making a bigger mess out of this than it is," somebody chimes in.

"They're doing everything they can to make trouble for the mayor," Reverend Boykins adds. "The police department has made no secret of the fact that they don't like her."

"We gon' strike either way," the man with the toothpick says. "We talking about walking out as early as this week. Soon as we get the votes."

"Place wouldn't be nothing without us." An older man speaks, his chest puffed out, gray hairs peeking out of his union T-shirt. "All the money they making off our backs, and we ain't seeing none of it. Folks can't put food on the table, businesses can't sell 'less we load and unload them ships. It's time they start paying us what we're worth, least what the other boys is getting."

"I mean, what was all that 'we shall overcome' stuff," Ashy Elbows says, glancing vaguely in Jay's direction, "if I can't pay my rent?"

The men are all staring at Jay, waiting. He doesn't understand what they want from him, what exactly they think he can do about any of this. Reverend Boykins seems to read his mind. "We understand you know the mayor, Jay."

Kwame turns to Jay and winks.

Jay feels a stream of sweat running down the center of his back.

Yeah, he knows the mayor.

Of course, she's been trying to forget him ever since she ran for office, paying a whole slew of consultants to bury her past. A couple of reporters tracked him down during the mayoral race, asking all kinds of questions about their days together at U of H. But Jay didn't say a thing, not one word about the fact that she joined SNCC when she was twenty-one, then the more radical SDS a year later. He didn't say anything about the guns she kept in her dorm room or about the marches she organized single-handedly. Cynthia Maddox was just a girl he went to college with. Maybe they'd had a class together, maybe they hadn't. Maybe they'd had a cup of coffee together one time . . . it wasn't for him to say.

"We figure," the Rev says, "maybe you can talk to her."

"And say what exactly?"

"We need to send a message, son. Let the city know these young men are serious about a strike. And if some of the ILA keep acting ugly, our men are going to need police protection. The mayor is going to have to get off the stick, talk to the chief and get some uniforms down there watching these boys."

"You been involved in this type of thing before, Mr. Porter," the janitor says. "I followed your other case, the one against the police department a few years back. If the city sees you representing my boy in this thing—"

"Wait a minute. You're not talking about a lawsuit, are you?" Jay asks.

"A lawsuit is just the thing we need," Kwame says. "Blow this issue wide open in the courts, drain the city's resources, make 'em know we mean business." He stands suddenly, getting pumped by his own rhetoric. "We got to take charge of this opportunity, shut the motherfuckers down if we have to."

Kwame has badly miscalculated his audience and forgotten he's in a house of the Lord. Reverend Boykins shoots him a look of disapproval. Even the sweat-stained dockworkers seem turned off by the sudden outburst. They don't want a revolution. They want a bigger paycheck. "Well, now, let's hold on there, Mr. Mackalvy," the Rev says. "Let Jay talk to the mayor first."

"You'll do that for us, Mr. Porter?" the janitor asks, a hand on his son's one good shoulder. Jay looks at the boy's father, then at the Rev, the closest thing to a father he's ever had. He nods without thinking. "Yeah . . . I'll do it."

The meeting moves on after that to talk about strategies for the strike, getting the word out to black day laborers that they are not to cross the picket line, should it come to that, and deciding whose wife or mother will make sandwiches or some chicken while they're on the line. Jay tunes out most of it. He can tell they've finished with him, but there isn't any way to leave without him seeming rude. A few minutes later, they end the meeting with an awkward prayer, the men fidgeting, uncomfortable holding hands. Jay ducks out as soon as he can, nodding once as the Rev asks, "You'll call on her, won't you, son?"

Outside, Kwame stops him on the church steps, his face flushed with the heat and excitement of the meeting. "It's just like old times, huh, partner?"

Jay looks at Kwame's hand on his shoulder. "Don't touch me, Lloyd."

He practically jogs to his car, hot to get out of there.

There's no way out of this thing, he knows. His father-in-law made him promise. And Jay, for the most part, is a man of his word. He has no idea how he's going to get to the mayor. What's he supposed to do, call her up after more than a decade? Just show up at city hall? He reaches into his pocket for his cigarettes, and the newspaper clipping slides out, fluttering briefly before sinking softly in the humid air, landing at Jay's feet. He stares at the scrap of paper, the facts of a murder laid out before him in black and white.

A moment later, he climbs into his car. Clutching the newspaper clipping in the palm of his hand, he kicks the engine in gear. Highway 59 to I-45 is the quickest route home, but Jay drives past the nearest on-ramp. He tells himself he's taking the long way home. But deep down, he knows. He's heading for the water.

Chapter 4

Jay left home when he was fifteen. He took his summer earnings from working in his mother's shop in Nigton, up in Trinity County, and left. He was headed to Nacogdoches. That was his plan. But at the bus station he met a pretty girl who was headed south, toward the Gulf, and he changed his mind on the spot. He bought a ticket to Houston instead. If he was gon' do this, he was gon' do it big. He arrived in the city at dawn. He didn't know a thing about where he was, didn't know a soul. He spent half a day talking to a janitor at the bus station, asking about a place to stay. He ended up in Fifth Ward because it was black and therefore safe. He found a room on the first floor of Miss Mitchell's boardinghouse, where it was clean and there was always fresh coffee. His upstairs neighbor was a transves-

tite burlesque dancer whose stage name was Effie Dropbottom.
They sat up most nights, when Effie wasn't performing, smoking
cigarettes and playing records. Wilson Pickett and Ray Charles
and any Motown. Or they listened to the *True Confessions* show
on 1430 AM.

He found a job at a bakery, cleaning ovens and sweeping up
after hours. He scratched out a living and called home when he
was ready. It was his sister he wanted to see about. He felt awful
for leaving her behind. It was a cowardly thing to do, he knew.
But he couldn't protect her from his mother's third husband—
the nasty, sidelong glances and midnight gropes—and that fact
alone had been more painful to a young boy trying to be a man
than any guilt about leaving. They talked a couple of times, he
and his sister. He sent her a postcard once. It was a picture of the
Astrodome, the words "8th Wonder of the World!" scrawled in
silver glitter across the top. Sometime after that, he heard she
went to stay with her father, his mother's second husband, up
around Dallas.

Jay never finished high school. But when the University of
Houston was making noise about integrating, trying to head off
at the pass any radical violence or government injunction, he
went down to the admissions office without an appointment. He
scored near 100 percent on the entrance exam, and they let him
in without a diploma. He moved into a segregated dorm a couple
of miles off campus and said good-bye to Fifth Ward for a long,
long time.

Driving through the neighborhood now, Jay stares out of
his car window, thinking how much Fifth Ward has changed.
Down Lockwood Drive, fine-dining restaurants and clothing
shops have been replaced by liquor stores and Laundromats with
single women inside, folding clothes alone. There are boarded-
up buildings on nearly every corner and empty fields thick with

weeds and flattened soda cans, shards of broken glass, trash and used furniture. Even the sidewalk in front of the Freedman's National Bank, the first black-owned bank in the state, has dead grass coming up through cracks in the cement. Jay remembers the neighborhood differently, remembers when it was a point of pride for black folks to say they lived near Lockwood Drive or had a little place on Lyons Avenue or went to Phillis Wheatley High School. He knows plenty of doctors and lawyers who came out of Wheatley. Fifth Ward was a place where black people thrived. People made a little bit of money, made a nice life for themselves. The neighborhood wasn't much, wasn't fancy or rich, but it was theirs.

And then, of course, came integration.

Black people suddenly had a choice, in theory at least, and the ones with any money almost always chose to leave Fifth Ward behind. Just because they could. Because wasn't that, after all, the very thing they had been fighting for?

Jay lights another cigarette and makes a right turn onto Clinton.

The newspaper said it was the 400 block.

He wants to see it for himself.

If only to put this whole thing out of his mind.

He drives parallel to the bayou, along Clinton, a narrow two-lane road, heading west. There are warehouses on the south side of the street, tall trees and brush behind them, and then the bayou, which Jay knows is there, but can't see in the darkness. There are no streetlights or even city signs on this stretch of road. Jay flips on his brights, taking a curve in the road, his head-lights swooping past the warehouses, dark and deserted at this hour, past grain silos and steel machinery and yards of chain-link fence. A few feet ahead, there's a sudden turnoff in the road, a path of dirt and gravel to the left that winds around to the back of a warehouse . . . and toward the water. Jay takes the left turn, slow and easy. He drives cautiously, maybe ten, fifteen miles an hour, tossing his cigarette through the crack in his car window. Dirt and gravel kick up a fine dust that swirls in the hazy white light of his high beams.

Around back of the warehouse, there's a locked gate.

Behind it, Jay sees the silhouette of small hills, mounds of broken concrete and quartz, finely crushed, like tiny sand dunes. A sign on the fence reads QUARTZ INDUSTRIAL, INC. Jay remembers the name from the newspaper.

In front of him, the dirt road ends abruptly.

Jay slams on his brakes, almost running into a thin film of yellow police tape. It's blocking off a large, burnt-up patch of grass, probably twenty-five yards wide. Jay shuts off the engine to his car, but leaves his headlights on, shining them past the field of dirt and grass to the hawthorn trees and bunches of scrub oak and Spanish moss on the other side. He still can't see the bayou from here. If he didn't know better, he would laugh if somebody told him there's water on the other side of those trees, running right through the middle of the city.

Part of the crime scene tape has come loose and is trailing in the dirt. It seems the cops have already come and gone, their business done, which makes Jay feel better about getting out of his car. He notices the white spray paint right away. Four *X*'s in a rectangle mark a ghostly shape of something once there and now gone. Jay takes a careful step over the yellow tape to get a better look. Up close, he sees tire tracks. Somebody was parked here, he thinks. There's another mark in the grass, a misshapen oval of white police paint, indicating something that once lay beside the tire tracks. *White male*, Jay thinks, *shot twice*. At Jay's feet there's a dark patch of motor oil . . . or blood. He is too afraid to touch it, to have any of this on his hands. He backs up suddenly, overcome with the feeling that this was a superbly stupid idea. He should never have come out here.

It's when he turns to leave, toward his car and the street, looking back the way he came, that he sees something in the distance, high above the trees.

The lights of the Freedman's National Bank clock:
9:37   78°

It's the same thing he saw from the boat Saturday night, the same image, the same angle. He turns and looks behind him, past the trees to the downtown skyline. It's all the same. He's standing on higher ground, some twenty or thirty yards above the surface of the water, but there is now no doubt in his mind:

This is where she must have been standing when they heard the shots.

The thought makes him ill, the fact that he carried that woman with his bare hands, spirited her away from what he now realizes was a crime scene.

There's a sudden flash of white light on the main road, a pair of headlights coming down Clinton. The car hits the same curve in the road, its lights momentarily streaking down the dirt path, hitting Jay in the chest. In an instant, he sees himself in the driver's eyes: a black man, after dark, standing inside police tape. For all he knows, it's a cop on the road. For all he knows, this is still an active crime scene. He watches the car's brake lights come on as it slows on the main road. If his eyes are right, the car is backing up toward him.

His first thought is to hide.

It's a few long strides to his car, the path to which is awash with the light of his high beams. It's much easier, safer, he reasons, to step backward, out of the light and into the thick brush. He moves quickly, crouching low, pushing his body through the trees. The branches pull at his clothes, grazing his face, digging into his skin. He feels a hot sting on his cheek. Knee-deep in weeds and a fog of mosquitoes and moving by a thin stream of moonlight through the clouds, Jay tries to feel his way. His ankle turns on a piece of uneven earth and gravity seems to grab him whole. He slips feet-first down the embankment. He quickly reaches for the nearest tree branch, but it breaks off in his hand, causing him to slip again on the soft earth. He manages to turn onto his stomach as he hits the ground, clawing the dirt to keep from sliding all the way to the black bottom. He can hear the bayou whispering softly, kissing the sides of the bank below him. He remembers the sound of her falling, rolling into the water.

If you didn't know it was here, Jay thinks.

How easy it would be to make a mistake, a wrong turn.

He thinks of her. The screams, the gunshots. The confusion. A man dead, and her out here alone. Someone passes by, and afraid, she hides.

Just like he's doing now.

Jay reaches for another branch, clinging tightly. He looks through the tangle of trees, checking for the car on the street. Its taillights are already fading in the distance. The car is back on its course, up Clinton Road and far away from Jay. He doesn't know if the driver saw him, doesn't know who it was or if they're coming back, but he's not waiting around to find out. He wants to get back to his car, to the main road, to the freeway and home. Fingernails digging in the dirt, Jay drags himself through the choke of weeds, moving an inch at a time.

He hears something above him, some movement in the brush. For a tense moment, he fears a run-in with a bayou rat or a raccoon. Then he hears footsteps crunching dead leaves and twigs and knows he's not out here alone.

"I help you with something?"

It's a man's voice, no doubt about that.

Jay has no idea where he came from . . . or how long he's been watching.

Caught, Jay crawls through the brush, slowly, pulling himself out of the grass like a snake. He's lost one of his shoes, and his sock, soiled up to the ankle, is coming off at the heel. He scrambles to his feet, brushing dirt off his pants and what was once a clean shirt. The man, Jay sees, is older than he is, in his sixties maybe, and smaller, more compact. He's black, in coveralls smudged with motor oil and grass stains and cut at the sleeves. He's got a cigarette tucked behind his ear. He stares at Jay, his filthy clothes and missing shoe.

Jay opens his mouth to speak, faster than he can think of some reasonable explanation to come out of it. He stands in the dirt, mute and slick with sweat.

"You ain't supposed to be back here, you know," the man says.

Jay thinks of making a run for his car, but doesn't want to make himself look any more suspicious than he already does. The man in the coveralls rocks back on his bowlegs, digging his heels in the dirt. He slides the cigarette from behind his ear and uses the head of the filter to pick something from between his two front teeth. He stares at Jay, eyeing his clothes, studying his every little move, trying to settle something in his mind.

"You a reporter or something?" he asks bluntly.

Jay is on the verge of correcting him, but stops when he catches the fleeting glint in the man's eyes, the flash of perverse excitement. For the first time, Jay notices a wheelbarrow parked by the chain-link fence, a shovel sticking out of it. He takes another look at the man's coveralls, coated in grass stains.

The groundskeeper, Jay remembers, the one from the paper.

And according to the news article, the one who found the body.

"Can I get one of those?" Jay asks, motioning to the pack of

Carltons peeking from the man's front pocket. He's stalling, of course, trying to buy himself some time, a moment to get his head around this. He wonders what the old man knows.

The groundskeeper purses his lips, upset that he's being held to answer to some unspoken code, between black men or smokers or both. He reaches into his coveralls and taps out a crumpled cigarette for Jay, tossing him a book of matches. In the man's side pocket, Jay spots the top of a liquor bottle.

The man catches Jay staring at his stained coveralls and fifth of Seagram's. "This ain't my regular gig, you know," he says, as if he feels he needs to explain himself. "I'm just picking up a little extra cash right now, that's all. I come by a couple of times a week to clear out the trash, beer bottles and such. I'm keeping an eye on the place nights now . . . you know, since the shooting."

"It was you, huh?" Jay asks carefully. "The one who found him?"

The man shakes his head to himself, whistling low.

"Man, I ain't ever seen no shit like that in my life, and I seen some shit, let me tell you." He snatches his book of matches from Jay's hand, striking one to light his own cigarette. "You can quote me on that if you want to."

He actually pauses, waiting for Jay to produce a pad and a pencil, to make sure he's getting all this down. So this is his big moment, Jay thinks, his little piece of fame. The man's name in the paper and everything. More than his mama ever dreamed for him, probably. Jay, playing the part, pats his pockets. "I must have left my notes in the car," he says, trying to sound casual, jaded even, a beat reporter who's seen everything. "What happened out here?"

"Hell if I know," the groundskeeper says. He takes a single, lusty pull on his cigarette, sucking it nearly to the filter. He stares out across the field at the police markings, the ghostly shapes in the dirt. "It was early when I got out here Sunday morning, around eight, like I always do. I come up the walk here," he says, pointing to the dirt road. "And I set my buggy over by the fence." He points to the wheelbarrow resting against the fence now. "I stopped to get a little sip, you know, just to warm me up." He reaches for the bottle now, reenacting the scene, pulling the Seagram's from his pocket. He takes a hearty swallow, nodding his head toward the field. "And that's when I seen the car. I mean, it was just sitting right there." He nods toward the white markings in the grass.

"What kind of car was it?" Jay asks, remembering the woman from the boat, her nice clothes and diamond ring.

"It was a Chrysler, kinda gold-like," the man says. "It was a rental, that much I remember, 'cause the sticker on the back said LONE STAR RIDES. I got a good look at it too. I come up on it real close," he says, tiptoeing on his bowlegs, walking through the open field like it's a graveyard, careful where he lays his feet. "The driver-side door was wide open. The light was still on inside." He gets within a few feet of the white police paint, the lumpy circle in the dirt, and then stops short, his voice almost solemn. "He was laying right here."

"Who was he?" Jay asks.

The man shrugs. "Cops pulled an ID off the man, but who knows?"

"It was a white guy, though, right?"

The man nods. "Laying right there, hanging out of the car, on his back."

Jay looks out across the empty field. There are black mosquitoes dancing in the white light of his high beams, crickets humming to themselves in the brush behind them. Jay turns from the view of the field to look at the empty warehouse and the dark, nearly deserted street. At this hour, the place looks like an industrial wasteland. What in the world was she doing out *here?* "If he was on the driver's side," Jay mumbles to himself, repeating the groundskeeper's description, arcing around the four *X*'s that mark the car, to what would have been the Chrysler's passenger side, "then she must have been riding here," he says softly, thinking out loud, still trying to piece together some kind of a story. He wonders if the dead man picked her up somewhere, if the two knew each other.

When he finally looks up again, the groundskeeper is staring at him.

"How do you know it was a woman?" the man asks.

"Excuse me?"

"I said . . . how do you know it was a woman he was with?"

It takes Jay a moment to understand what the man is asking, to realize the mistake he's made, the single clue he let slip from his mouth. The panic, when it hits him, is swift and forceful, and he actually feels himself sway just the tiniest bit. Then, remembering the article from the paper, he repeats a few of the details. "The cops talked to a lady friend," he explains. "It was in the police report."

"Is that right?" the groundskeeper asks, a knowing smile creeping across his stubbly face. He pinches off the head of his cigarette, letting the cherry fall to the dirt and pocketing the dirty butt. "Well, I know why they talked to her."

"You do?" Jay feels the panic again, and he has a sudden thought of Jimmy's cousin, the boat's captain. It's the first time Jay has considered him since the night of the boat ride. And it now occurs to him that the old man might have seen the same blurb in the paper and gone straight to the police. He's so caught up in what that might mean for him, wondering if the cops already have his name, that he almost misses the next words out of the groundskeeper's mouth.

"Dude's pants were coming down," the man says.

"What?" Jay asks, not immediately comprehending.

"The dead man," the groundskeeper says. "The belt, the fly . . . his pants was wide open. The cops was all over it. And they was taking pictures of the ground over there." He points to the dirt and grass where Jay is standing. "There were footprints, real small-like, you know, like a lady's shoe." Jay remembers the woman's bare feet on the boat, her missing earring too. "But we don't really know it was a woman," the groundskeeper says. *We*, like he's in on the investigation, like he and the cops are working this one together. "We don't know what that man was into. Hell, when I seen him, he was wearing leather in August, had on gloves up to here," he says, demonstrating high on his forearms. "Ain't no telling what kind of freaky shit was going on. That mighta been why he was hiding out here in the first place." He lowers his voice, speaking the seemingly impossible. "I mean, it coulda been a dude he was with."

The groundskeeper helps himself to another Carlton. "Now ain't that some shit," he says. His expression has cooled somewhat, and he seems to have turned his investigative gaze on Jay, taking a second look at Jay's soiled clothes and his missing shoe, seemingly calling his whole presence at the crime scene into question. Jay doesn't like the way the man is looking at him, or what he thinks the man may be insinuating. It would be ridiculous, the idea of Jay being in any way involved in a murder, if it weren't so . . . plausible. Even a rookie cop knows that more times than not, the perpetrator returns to the scene of his crime.

"You with the *Chronicle* or the *Post*?" the groundskeeper asks.

"I freelance," Jay answers, a little too quickly.

"Maybe I could get your name, in case I remember something else."

The smirk is faint, but impossible to ignore.

The groundskeeper stares at Jay, waiting for an answer.

"Ernest Pennebaker" is the first ridiculous name out of Jay's mouth. He delivers it as convincingly as a practiced closing argument, thanking the man for his time and reaching for his car keys. He nods good night as he slides into his front seat. Through the dusty windshield, the groundskeeper watches him, the Skylark's headlights carving deep shadows beneath the man's suspicious eyes. Jay throws his car into reverse, driving faster than he should, churning up reddish brown dirt across his rear window, creating a blinding haze of smoke.

He rolls up his window and turns on the radio, trying to shut out the noise in his head. The box is set to 1430 AM, black radio. They're in the middle of another hour of *Confessions*. Wash Allen is talking to a woman, a caller who's sleeping with a married man, has been for years. She's wondering if he'll ever leave his wife, and if he doesn't, where in the world will that leave her? The show is call-and-response, a rhythm borrowed from blues or the church, where black people come to lay down their problems. The callers have on-air names like CB handles. "This is Stormin' Norman calling . . ." "Yeah, Wash, this is your girl Sunshine . . ." "Dark 'n' Lovely here, Wash, and I got something to say . . ." They're all calling in, hot to give their opinions, to tell the woman on hold that she's a stone cold fool.

Chapter 5

The next morning, he stands over the sink checking his cut in the bathroom mirror. It's at least an inch long where the tree branch got him. There's a thin slash just below his cheekbone, a little too high to be explained away as a shaving mishap. He would put a Band-Aid on it, but he doesn't want to draw any more attention to it. It's bad enough it looks like the scratch of a woman's fingernail, an act of aggression or passion, neither of which would be easy to explain to his wife. He doesn't want her to know where he was last night. Not yet at least. Not until he gets ahold of Jimmy's cousin. For it has become fairly clear to Jay that he will have to make some kind of statement to police detectives. He thinks it's better if he contacts them first, before they come looking for him. Bernie, were she to hear about the shooting in the paper and the woman's apparent involvement, would demand that she and Jay march down to the station this morning, which Jay is not the least bit inclined to do, not without another witness, preferably one he's not married to. He wants someone other than his wife to testify to his fundamental innocence in this situation. Otherwise, how to explain his odd behavior? The fact that he's waited four days since the shooting to say a word about it or, more important, why he was at the crime scene last night. He feels sick when he thinks about the traces of himself he carelessly left behind—the Newport he tossed out the window as he was coming up the dirt drive, his footprints and tire tracks, and the shoe he lost in the brush—all of it just sitting out there, waiting to be discovered. He could hardly sleep last night for imagining the groundskeeper talking to homicide detectives, telling them about the stranger out after dark, sneaking around their crime scene. Jay thinks all of it can be easily explained away, but he wants to talk to Jimmy's cousin first. If the old man hasn't done so already, maybe he and Jay can make a statement together.

He opens the cabinet over the sink and pulls out a tub of Vaseline. He rubs jelly into the cut on his cheek, then uses one of Bernie's compacts to cover the mark with bronze powder. He tries to make it blend in, to make himself look at least presentable and, at best, credible. When he's done, he wraps a towel around his waist and picks up the .22 that's resting on top of the toilet's tank.

Jay has three guns: a .38 in his glove compartment, a hunting rifle in the hall closet, and the nickel-plated .22 he keeps under his pillow, always within arm's reach. He's tried to break the habit of carrying it into the bathroom with him. But most days it's right by his side. Some people, when they're in the shower, imagine they hear the phone ringing. Jay imagines people breaking into his apartment with guns drawn.

He lost a buddy that way. Lyndon "Bumpy" Williams had been Jay's roommate his first year at U of H, when the dorms were still segregated. It was Bumpy who joined SNCC first, who took Jay to his first meeting. He was one of Jay's oldest and closest friends. By the summer of 1970, the feds had some heavy intel on Mr. Williams, courtesy of COINTELPRO. They broke into his duplex on Scott Street while Bumpy was in the shower. He never heard them coming, never heard their orders to come out with his hands up. The first flash of movement behind the shower curtain, they shot him thirteen times. He was only twenty years old. Now, eleven years later, Jay still sleeps with his .22 and carries it into the bathroom with him. He also can't take sudden noises and won't sit with his back to the door, and several times a year, he catches himself, by rote, unscrewing the mouthpiece of his telephone, looking for bugs.

Back in his bedroom, he returns the gun to its hiding place beneath his pillow and makes the bed by himself, a routine he and Bernie came up with in their first months of marriage. "I don't like guns," she'd said. "I don't want to see a gun." There's an AM radio propped on the paint-chipped windowsill. It's picking up bits and pieces of a local news show on 740. Jay dresses quickly, listening to a report about talks between the dockworkers and the shipping companies. As he slips on his shoes, he remembers his pledge to call the mayor.

His clothes from last night are piled on a nearby chair, where he tossed them in the dark last night. On his way out, he scoops up the dirty, grass-stained clothes and rolls them into a tight ball, hiding the whole mess under his arm. When Bernie comes in from the kitchen, her robe open at her belly, she eyes the pile of laundry he's got wadded under his arm. "What are you doing?"

"Going to work," he says simply, holding the soiled clothes as if they were an attaché case, a part of his usual uniform. He tries to pass her in the narrow doorway, but she does not move, blocking him with her belly, waiting for him to say a proper good-bye. When he bends down to kiss her on the cheek, Bernie screws up her nose, pulling away from him and wiping at the side of her face. She looks down at her fingertips, staring at a glob of brown jelly.

"Are you wearing makeup?"

"No," he says, turning away from her. "Of course not."

Outside, beneath the carport, he tosses the dirty clothes into the back of his Buick, which, he notices, is still covered with the reddish dirt from the open field by the bayou, the location of a murder. He stops at a car wash on the way to his office. With two dollars' worth of quarters, he washes the Buick twice, rinsing any trace of the crime scene from his car. He uses the soiled clothes from last night to dry the soapy water. Then he pitches them into the trash.

He arrives at his office late, his suit damp and wrinkled from the car wash. Eddie Mae has a message from Charlie Luckman, saying he wants to meet for lunch. This is settlement talk for sure, Jay thinks. But the relief he feels about the possibility of a quick financial resolution to the case is tempered by the morning he's had. He knows he's being paranoid—chucking his clothes, washing his car—but he can't seem to stop himself or calm his racing nerves. He goes into his office and shuts the door, lights a cigarette at his desk and picks up the phone.

He starts with a guy named Tim.

Tim was Jay's client a few months back, the one with the outstanding bill. Jimmy, Tim reminds Jay, was dating Tim's sister. Fine, Jay says. He doesn't care. He's trying to get in touch with Jimmy's cousin. It's another half hour before he's able to track down Jimmy, at a bar on Calumet. There's loud music playing in the background, and it takes a while to make Jimmy understand who Jay is or why he's calling. Jimmy, who frankly sounds drunk at nine o'clock in the morning, tells Jay he hasn't seen his cousin in days.

"You got a number for him, some way I can reach him?"

"You might try his girl's place," Jimmy slurs. "He's kind of in between digs right now."

"You have her phone number?" Jay asks.

"Well, let me see if I can find it," Jimmy says, as if he keeps a Rolodex right there on the bar top. "Here," he says a moment later. "Try this one: 789-3123. Gal's name is Stella."

"Thank you," Jay says, jotting down the information.

"You get ahold of him, you tell him I don't appreciate how he left my boat. He left dirty dishes on the floor. Didn't even bother to straighten up or nothing. It ain't right," he says. "You tell him I don't appreciate it one bit."

"Yeah, sure."

Then Jay adds, "You know if he talked to any cops recently?"

"About what?"

"Nothing," Jay says, thinking better of it. He hangs up the line.

Stella's number is busy the first five times Jay tries it. When he finally gets through, the line rings some twenty times before Jay simply gives up.

He thinks of calling the cops on his own, but can't bring himself to do it.

He remembers his own advice: *Keep your fucking mouth shut.*

It's a warning that lives under his skin, in his DNA. *Keep your head down, speak only when spoken to.* A warning drilled into him every day of his life growing up in Nigton, Texas, née Nig Town, née Nigger Town (its true birth name when it sprang up a hundred years ago in the piney woods of East Texas). A warning always delivered with a sharp squeeze from his mother's hand before crossing the street or going to school, and especially before going out after dark.

He's not proud of his fears, but there they are, pinching at him from all sides like too tight shoes, restricting his movements, limiting his freedom. A shame, considering the real reason he marched so many years ago was to prove fear was dead, that it belonged to another time, to men like his father.

Jay sits at his desk, thinking about Jerome Porter.

The same image always comes to him, like a well-worn photograph in his mind, a snapshot of another time. It's an image of his mother, eighteen, sitting in the front seat of her daddy's pickup truck, Jay's father, twenty-one and strong, behind the wheel. They were newlyweds, the way Jay always heard the story. His mother, Alma, was just starting to show. They were riding on a farm road that ran behind Jay's grandmother's place, a barbecue joint and greengrocer, where his parents were both working the summer after they married. Jay's father was driving his young wife home 'cause she wasn't feeling too good on her feet.

There was another truck on the road that day, riding their bumper and honking the horn, two white men in the cab and a loaded rifle rack in the back window. This was Trinity County, 1949, a lawless place for men like Jerome Porter. The police were white. The sheriff and the mayor. And they made it known that the countryside belonged to them. There had been a rash of poultry theft that fall and winter, somebody (or bodies) sneaking onto people's farms after dark, spiriting away valuable hens, sometimes going so far as to slit a guard dog's throat in the process. Wasn't no way to tell who it was, but white folks got it in their minds that it was niggers' doing. They set up vigilante groups, guarding property with rifles and axes, questioning folks coming in and out of the grocery store, even harassing little boys coming out of the colored elementary school. They stopped people on local roads, demanding to search their cars and making citizens' arrests if anything was out of order. And local law enforcement didn't do a damn thing to stop them.

Jerome, Jay Bird, as Alma called him, was careful not to go above thirty miles an hour. He didn't want to give the men in the truck any excuse to stop the car, which it turns out they did anyway by pulling their pickup ahead and blocking the road. Jay's parents were in Alma's daddy's truck, and she knew he kept a pistol in the glove box. She reached for it, but Jerome told her not to make it worse. He got out of the car, let the men have a look around, and asked them politely to let them go on their way. "My wife's not feeling well," he explained.

Something about the self-satisfied way he said it seemed to set them off. Maybe they didn't have wives or didn't like the ones they had, but they got kind of rough then, poking around on the passenger side, near Alma, making Jay's father understand that nothing in this world really belonged to him. It was all within their reach. His father was a tall man, taller than Jay. He stood up straight, looked the men in the eye, and said, "Y'all need to get away from there now. Leave her be." The men turned to each other then, agreeing on something, an approach, something choreographed from their repertoire. They were small and squat, and they charged at him like yard dogs, coming at him from two sides. Within the first couple of blows, it was clear they would not be satisfied by some regular beating, a few kicks in the dust. They were going for something else, scratching past his skin and bones, punching at his spirit. They had him near 'bout to the ground when Alma got the gun out of the glove box, a little .25-caliber pistol her brothers had taught her to shoot. "Your daddy took one look at me with that gun and said, 'Alma, don't you dare.'"

As a kid, Jay listened to this story in disbelief.

It was nothing like the cowboy movies he watched on television. There was no explosion, no gut shot, no hero. Not his father anyway. Jerome Porter wouldn't let his wife save him, afraid of what would happen to her if she pulled the trigger. There was no coming back from shooting a white man in Trinity County, 1949. If a mob didn't get you, the courts would.

It turned out the gun scared them anyway, it was shaking so in Alma's hand. The men couldn't be sure Jay's mother would heed her husband's instruction not to shoot. They ran back to their truck and took off. A red Ford was all anybody ever remembered. No license plate, no names.

Jay's daddy was beat pretty good about the head.

He managed to get himself into the truck. He turned the engine over, but never got the car into gear. He turned to his wife and said, "Alma, I think you better drive." He passed out a few moments after that. She pushed him over to the passenger side by herself, even in her condition. The nearest colored hospital was all the way to Lufkin. She didn't think Jay Bird could make it that far, so she drove him to St. Luke's Faith Memorial in Groveton. In the waiting area, the nurses went so far as to let Jay's mother fill out all the paperwork, let her think her husband would be the next one in line. Alma sat with him, holding his hand, his head resting on her lap, wondering why they were letting other people go ahead of Jerome. It wasn't until late in the evening, the waiting room empty and the two of them the only ones still waiting, that she understood what was going on, that this white hospital had no intention of treating her husband.

She laid his head softly on the bench, then got up and called over to her parents' place. Somebody needed to run up to Jerome's mama's house, she said, and let Mrs. Porter know her boy was in trouble, that it looked bad. She asked her brothers to drive down, to help her get her husband all the way to Lufkin.

They got him out of St. Luke's and into Alma's brother's Dodge so Jay's father could lie out in the backseat. He came to at least once, but he never said a word. Just looked at Alma and kind of smiled. He died somewhere between Groveton and Lufkin. That was December. Jay was born five months later.

He would never be like his father; he'd decided that a long time ago. He was going to live to see his son. Or a little girl. Two maybe. The world would be different for him. As a kid, he watched King, Bayard Rustin, and the others, watched the boys in clean sweaters and pressed pants at the lunch counters in North Carolina, getting spit on and pushed around. And even then he thought they were missing the point. Even then he thought he'd shoot a motherfucker before he'd let them spit on him. He wanted something more than the early movement's fight for legal equality and freedom in the streets. Jay's dream was for freedom in his own mind, liberation from the kind of soul-crushing fear that took his father's life. So he marched and wrote speeches and armed himself for a coming revolution . . . until they arrested him and locked him in a jail cell, threatened to take his life away, holding him to answer on shaky evidence and flat-out lies. It was a courtroom instead of a country road. Still, they killed his spirit.

He's older than his father now. His daddy is somewhere, still twenty-one.

Jay thinks about that fact every day, thinks of what he has to live for now, the family he wants to protect, and how, in his own way, all these years later, he's become just as conservative as his father's generation. He is just as afraid.

Chapter 6

Charlie Luckman keeps an eye on the black girl, the one on the right side of the stage. Her ass is hanging out of a little burgundy number, her long, pointy nails painted to match. She ducks coyly behind the pole, wrapping one leg around it, then the other, as she makes a graceful dive backward, until she is practically hanging upside down, dark nipples spilling out of her costume.

Jay looks down at his watch.

He's been fidgety and unfocused through most of lunch, bumbling through the appetizers and small talk, feigning interest in the girls onstage, all the time thinking about police detectives combing the crime scene by the bayou.

The black girl arches her back, sliding down the pole like a cat.

Charlie, fascinated, can't take his eyes off her.

J. T. Cummings, the port commissioner, is on the other side of the table, halfway between Jay and Charlie. He's sweating, hunched over the remains of a filet he's too nervous to finish. He's been sucking on a roll of Tums for the past twenty minutes.

"We get down to business already?" he says, rolling an antacid around his tongue. "My whole goddamned political career is on the line here, and I'd just as soon get this over and done with before I'm back at the office."

Charlie glares at his client. Whatever script they worked out before Jay got to the table, J.T. is decidedly going his own way, making no secret of the fact that he's worried about a trial. Charlie, on the other hand, is trying to act casual—the reason for meeting in this place, Jay realizes. Or maybe it was meant to throw Jay off his game. It's a certain kind of man can look at pussy while he eats, never mind talking business at the same time. "Did you know," Charlie says, "that there are more gentlemen's clubs, or titty joints, depending on your preference or income level, per capita in Houston, Texas, than there are in any other city in the state? The whole nation, in fact." He plucks a pearl onion out of his glass with his thick pink fingers and pops it into his mouth, practically swallowing the thing whole. "And lord knows I've been to my fair share. I consider myself somewhat of an expert on the local industry. And let me tell you what I know for sure . . . I have never seen a girl like *that* in a place like this."

He's pointing to the black girl.

"Maybe at the Boom Boom Room or the Wet Bar or Pussy-cats, you know, joints off the freeway. But not an upscale place like Wynston's."

"I wasn't aware this is a whites-only establishment," Jay says, his voice rising, Charlie's casual insult getting the better of him.

He's had a couple of drinks with lunch. Not his usual habit, but then again neither is steak at lunch.

"Well, there's no sign on the door, nothing crass like that. But the price list here alone . . . I wouldn't think most blacks and Mexicans could afford this kind of establishment, right?" Charlie says, directing his question to Jay, the expert.

Jay looks around the posh club, peppered with businessmen and city officials. He is, in fact, the only black man in the room. Money, it turns out, is the new Jim Crow. Jay looks at Charlie, feeling a heat spread beneath his collar, imagining yet another motive for bringing Jay to this place, with its creamy leather chairs and sterling silverware, the twenty-dollar steaks and Kenny Rogers pumped through hidden speakers. Around the dining room, Jay counts at least three sitting judges, several of whom have nodded Charlie's way or come by the table to offer regards and well wishes. This is all to let Jay know how well connected Charlie is and just who has the upper hand.

"Don't get me wrong," Charlie says. "I'm for equal rights and all that." He smiles, raising his martini glass in a toast to the black girl onstage. "As far as I'm concerned, this is an affirmative action plan we can all get behind."

"Jesus, Charlie. Can we get on with it?" J.T. says, popping another Tums in his mouth. "Tell the man what we came to, what we're prepared to offer."

"You want to let me handle it?" Charlie says to J.T.

Then he turns to Jay. "You'll never win a jury trial."

"I'm not going to trial, Charlie! Goddamnit, I can't!" Cummings is practically shrieking. "That goddamned dyke down at city hall is already making me do a dog and pony show just to keep my goddamned job. I can't have something like this getting too much attention." There are salty, cloudy streaks running down his face. Jay can't tell if Cummings is sweating or crying.

"J.T.," Charlie says, his voice steady and self-assured. "You are still missing the point, the beauty of the thing. There is no police record that says that woman was ever *in* your car." He leans back in his white leather chair, feeling good about the whole thing. "Your girl don't stand a chance with a jury," he says to Jay. "Her story don't hold up, Mr. Porter. And you and I both know it."

"If you're so sure about that, then why are we here?" Jay says.

J.T. starts to say something. Charlie holds up a hand.

"Look, I'm as fair as the next man," he says to Jay, as if he's doing him a big favor. "I want to come up with something *reasonable* for all parties involved."

"Is that an admission of guilt?"

J.T. starts to answer. Again, Charlie holds up his hand.

"Not at all," he says. "Let me put it to you this way . . . Mr. Cummings is not a *bad* man. I mean, he really *cares* about people, is what I'm trying to get at." Charlie leans forward, lowering his voice, soft and smooth as a lothario charming a virgin into his bed. "If some little gal even thinks that she might have been hurt in some way, in some fashion that Mr. Cummings never intended—"

"Well, I'd like to make it right," Cummings says, catching on to the script now, the general direction in which Charlie is headed.

Charlie, whose afternoon buzz seems to be wearing off, ignores Cummings completely. "I'm sure we could come up with something that might make her feel better about what she imagines may have taken place."

"How much?" Jay asks.

J.T. pops another Tums in his mouth, and Charlie runs his fingers along the rim of his martini glass. "One thousand dollars," Charlie says.

Jay laughs out loud, the first time in a week.

Charlie cuts an eye toward his client. Cummings nods.

"Five thousand dollars," Charlie says, tossing the words across the table like a winning roll in a dice game. "Can't beat that."

If he'd said ten, Jay would have taken it on the spot. He'd had that decided before he walked in the door. His cut would run about three thousand, minus expenses. Nothing that would turn his life around. But still something, without having to worry about the expense of a trial, which, by the way, there is a good chance he will lose. He's still looking for a witness, somebody to put his client in Cummings's car. Without that, he's screwed. He would have taken ten in a heartbeat. Five, he can't do. "I was thinking more like twenty," he says.

"Now, wait a minute." J.T. slams his fist on the table. "I'm going to do right by this girl. But twenty thousand dollars is horseshit."

Jay shrugs, as if his hands are tied.

"I can't advise my client to entertain this any further, to even consider such an outlandish suggestion, Mr. Porter."

"See you in court then," Jay says, pushing back from the table, hoping somebody will try to stop him.

"Seventy-five hundred," Charlie says.

"That gal woulda lived like a queen on five," J.T. says.

Jay and Charlie both ignore him.

"Least you can do is put it to your client, see how she takes it."

"I'll talk to her," Jay says. "But I can't promise anything."

J.T. looks at the two of them, not sure if he should be pissed off or celebrating. He turns to his very expensive lawyer. "That's it?"

"He said he's gon' talk to the girl."

"Damnit, Charlie, I said I wanted this wrapped up today." He sounds more confounded than angry, as if he can't understand why a man of his stature should be subjected to the machinations of a low-rent call girl. "This is a fucking nightmare."

"Your faith in me is remarkable, J.T.," Charlie says.

He turns away from his ungrateful client, catching sight of a familiar face across the dining room floor, a man in his early fifties wearing a gray summer suit the exact color of his eyes.

"Thomas Cole," Charlie calls out eagerly.

As the man turns toward their table, Jay recognizes his face from pictures in the papers. He's the CEO or some such bigwig at Cole Oil Industries, the homegrown oil and petrochemical giant started by Johnson Cole in the late 1940s and now run by his sons Patrick, John, and Thomas. The Cole name is sprinkled throughout the city and its surrounding environs. They have buildings at both Rice University and U of H, and they sponsored construction on a research wing at NASA. Lindy Cole, their mother, and only living parent, has an elementary school named after her in Baytown, where she was born. The Coles are the closest thing to royalty this city has (the Coles and maybe Jerry Hall, or George Bush, depending on your political sway). As Thomas Cole starts across the room to their table, Jay can see Charlie's face kind of light up at the fact. Charlie eyeballs the room, wanting to know who all is watching Thomas Cole walk over to *his* table. He stands as Thomas approaches, pumping the man's hand up and down.

"Mr. Luckman," Thomas says, patting Charlie roughly on the back, his eyes never straying too far from the girls onstage. "How's Rita?" he asks.

"You see her, you let me know," Charlie says with a frat boy's smile.

"Well, they do come and go," Thomas says.

He tells Charlie to expect a call from him, and then he's off, stopping at another table.

Cummings watches Thomas work the room. "If the union moves forward with this strike," he says, his voice almost a whisper, as if he's speaking the unspeakable, like a cancer or a death in the family, "the whole port will shut down. Nothing coming in, nothing going out. The whole goddamned economy will come to a screeching halt in a matter of days, and we'll all be in a huge heap of shit. The mayor's getting pressure from both sides, but she can't decide if she's business or labor. She can't hardly decide anything 'cept what color lipstick to wear or how she's fixing her hair this week." He shakes his head, as if he can't believe they let women vote these days, let alone serve in public office.

"They're not going to strike," Charlie assures him.

"You better hope you're right, Charlie. Rest of the country ain't doing so hot. You get north of Oklahoma and it's a whole different story, boy. The rest of the country is on the verge of a goddamned recession. Oil's the only thing keeping this goddamned city afloat. And we're down to thirty dollars a barrel as it is. That's another five from last week. Now you throw a port strike in the mix—"

"Oil don't run through the port, J.T. That's not your jurisdiction. Those oil tankers up and down the Ship Channel dock on *private* land. The Coles, Exxon, Shell . . . they all got their own refinery workers. The longshoremen, the ones unloading little plastic dolls from China or some shit, they don't have a goddamn thing to do with oil. They can picket all they want to."

"You haven't heard the latest then," J.T. says, smiling darkly, happy to impart bad news if it means he knows something that Charlie doesn't. "OCAW's talking about walking out too . . . in solidarity." OCAW, the Oil, Chemical, and Atomic Workers Union, is one of the largest labor groups in this energy-obsessed city. "They strike too . . . and this has everything to do with oil."

Charlie's eyes narrow momentarily, then he breaks into a lopsided grin, shaking his head at J.T. as if J.T. had tried to pull a fast one, telling Charlie a tall tale about the Loch Ness monster or Big Foot, something only a fool or a child would believe. "Oh, hell, J.T., look around you. This economy is foolproof," Charlie says, motioning to the room of wealthy white men in case anyone needs reminding that everything is as it should be. "Do these men look nervous to you?" he asks, pointing in particular to Thomas Cole, a few tables over. "He don't look nervous to me." Charlie motions for the cocktail waitress. "Have a drink, J.T. Matter fact, have two drinks. You worry too goddamned much."

After lunch, Jay tries Stella again, from a pay phone on Richmond. She picks up on the second ring. She hasn't seen Jimmy's cousin either, not for a week. He owes her $20, so she doesn't imagine she'll be hearing from him anytime soon. She tells Jay to try a lady named Mary Patterson who stays off 288.

Jay finds a street address for M. Patterson in the phone book.

He hops in his car and drives back to his side of town, to a neighborhood just south of Sunnyside.

The house, when he finds it, is green and white with an aged pecan tree shading most of the yard and littering the driveway with broken shells. There's a woman in her late forties leaning up against the back side of a '67 Lincoln. She's wearing a red halter top and house slippers, a pair of shears in her hand. There's a teenage boy in front of her. He's perched on top of a blue suitcase that's sitting upright, a bath towel draped around his shoulders. The woman looks up once as Jay walks up the drive, then goes back to cutting hair, holding the boy's head still whenever he moves. "I'm not taking no new customers today," she says matter-of-factly to Jay. "This here's just a favor I'm doing for his mama."

"I'm looking for Marshall," Jay says, meaning Jimmy's cousin.

She glances at Jay again, his suit and dress shoes.

"Me and Marshall are through."

"You know how I can get ahold of him?"

"I ain't the one to ask," Mary says, her expression as stoic as if she were reporting on the weather. She picks up a pink can of Afro sheen from the top of the Lincoln's trunk and sprays the boy's head, instructing him to cover his eyes. "Marshall was supposed to be home Saturday night, said he'd done a run up the bayou and that he'd be over just as soon as he cleaned the boat. But that son of a bitch never showed." The news of which Jay finds odd, remembering Jimmy's complaint that his cousin had left the boat a mess, dirty plates and trash on the floor.

"You got any idea where he went?" he asks.

"I'm guessing he went back to *her*."

"Stella?"

Mary purses her lips, refusing to speak the other woman's name.

She gives the boy's 'fro a final pat, then whisks off the bath towel, shaking curly black hairs onto the pavement. She folds the towel, hugging it to her chest. Her voice betrays the first pinch of emotion. "I was about tired of his shit anyway," she says to Jay. "You see him, you tell him that for me, will you?"

Chapter 7

That afternoon, Eddie Mae finally manages to get the witness for Dana Moreland on the phone at her place of employment, interrupting Jay's search for Jimmy's cousin Marshall. The woman agrees to talk to Jay, and as a favor, Bernie rides with him to the Big Dipper, out I-45, past Gulfgate Mall, almost halfway to Galveston. Bernie brings a paperback book and finds a table in the back. She orders a Dr Pepper and a plate of french fries. Starla, the girl he's interviewing, keeps looking in Bernie's direction. The book, the belly, all of it.

"That really your wife?"

"Yes, ma'am."

"What'd you bring her in *here* for?"

Jay looks around the small, dark bar, a far cry from Wynston's, the glitzy gentlemen's club where Charlie Luckman had him to lunch. This place, with its velvet wallpaper and mirrored ceiling and tables covered in white plastic, is low class all the way. Conway Twitty is squawking through the speakers overhead. The bartender, arms folded across his barrel chest, is mouthing the words to the song. *You want a lover with a slow hand . . .* He's watching the redhead onstage. The girl, wide through the hips, is on the floor, pumping her pelvis up and down. She's staring at the ceiling, caught up in her own reflection, or maybe she's going over her grocery list in her head. She looks hopelessly bored.

Jay nods toward the naked girl onstage, then his wife, making his point.

"She likes to keep an eye on me."

Starla smiles. "I'll bet."

The truth is, he had to beg Bernie to go with him. And it certainly wasn't to put his wife at ease. After years of practicing law, he's learned that women put men in one of two categories: the ones they know are trying to fuck them and the ones they're not so sure about yet. Bringing his wife on interviews helps female witnesses relax. It roots him in some way that matters to women.

Starla asks him two more times if he wants a drink. She seems to get a kick out of him, his suit, and his pregnant wife. "So what you wanna know?"

She props her scrawny knees against the lip of the table. They're scratched and bruised, the skin broken in tiny lines like streets on a map. Jay thinks he can almost trace the course of her life across her skin, the events that brought her to this place. She takes a putty-colored ball of gum out of her mouth and rests it on her left knee, then lights a cigarette, leaning back, absently playing with her lighter. It's got a cartoon picture on it, Elmer Fudd holding a rifle in each hand; it says SIX FLAGS across the bottom.

She can't be more than nineteen. Her fingernails are bitten to the quick, and she smells musty, like a kid coming in from playing outside in the dirt. He can think of a dozen reasons why a jury won't believe her. But right now, she's all he's got.

He pulls a pen out of his pocket.

"You know a woman named Dana Moreland, that right?"

"Look," Starla says, sitting up suddenly, blowing smoke in a girlish curl out of the side of her mouth. "I'm pretty much gonna say whatever you want me to, okay? I owe Dana some money and after this we're gonna be square. So you might as well just tell me what it is you're looking to hear."

Jay sighs and looks at his watch, feeling this was a waste of his time. "You have any personal knowledge that Miss Moreland was on a date with Mr. J. T. Cummings on the night of June twenty-ninth of this year? Other than what she told you?"

"No."

"You have any personal knowledge that she was in Mr. Cummings's vehicle?"

"No." She puts out her cigarette, then picks up the gum on her knee. She's about to pop it back into her mouth when she stops, smiling all of a sudden. "But she did give me a handkerchief she got out of the old man's car."

"Yeah?" He's skeptical, but also a little desperate.

"It was real silk, red with gold paisleys on it. She lifted it out of his jacket pocket. I used it in my stage show a couple of nights ago." Her smile widens. "That personal enough for you?"

He makes her write down her address, tells her he needs to see the handkerchief. When she asks him if she should wash it, he tells her no, that won't be necessary. He thanks her for her time, and is about to grab his wife and get the hell out of there when Starla says softly, almost reluctantly, "Wait."

She sits up in her chair again, popping the wad of gum back

into her mouth, shaking her head, kind of. "Dana'll kill me if she knows I told you."

"What?"

"Well, I'm not the only one knows she was with Cummings that night."

"I need a name," Jay says, inching back into his seat.

"There's a bouncer out at Gilley's who sometimes sets up dates for girls like me and Dana. When those roughnecks come in off the oil fields or the rigs out in the Gulf, first place they go when they get a dollar is to Gilley's. And the ones that ain't married or got girlfriends or whatnot need a little company, you know? Girls like me and Dana can make a lot of money out that way."

"The bouncer is a *pimp*?" Jay asks.

"Well, I wouldn't put it that way."

"What's his name?"

"Clyde."

Jay pulls out his pen. "Clyde who?"

"I don't know." Starla shrugs. "Clyde."

Jay writes down the name and underlines it.

"He gets kind of funny about us bringing in our *own* dates, you know," Starla says. "He don't much like us working on our own. Dana told me Clyde threw her and Cummings out of Gilley's the night they had the car accident. If he wasn't getting paid, he didn't want her on his turf."

"So the bouncer saw them together?"

"Oh, yeah." Starla nods. "And Dana said he was some kind of pissed."

"I don't understand . . . if this Clyde guy corroborates her story, why wouldn't she want me to know about it?"

"Oh, Dana don't want him having his hand nowhere near a lawsuit. This is her deal, through and through. She's probably afraid Clyde'll try and take a cut. I mean, she's already paying you, what, twenty, thirty percent, right?"

"Right," Jay says, rolling his eyes at being compared to a pimp.

Outside in the parking lot, Bernie asks, "How'd I do?"

The Big Dipper sign is flashing over her head, next to an animated neon painted lady who's opening and closing her legs, on beat, every three seconds.

"You were perfect," he says.

She eases her way into the Buick, balancing one hand on the car's frame.

"You washed the car," she says, noticing for the first time.

"This morning." He shrugs coolly. No big thing.

He closes the car door and walks around to the other side.

There's a late-model Ford LTD on Jay's side, black and long. Jay is careful not to scratch it with his door. Inside the Buick, Bernie asks him to turn up the air-conditioning. He makes some halfhearted complaint about gas prices—$1.37 at the Exxon on OST—but turns up the AC full blast anyway. "What was that one about anyway?" Bernie asks. She's picking at a tear in the beige seat cover.

Jay looks through the windshield, watching as I-45 slows to a crawl. The rusted pickup truck in front of him has a NATIVE HOUSTONIAN bumper sticker pasted across the back window of its cab. The driver is propped up on twenty-inch wheels, smoking a cigarette out the window, looking at the tangle of taillights spread out before him. The traffic problem in the city has only gotten worse in the last year or two, as the city's population reaches nearly three million. And still the people keep coming, hundreds by the week, from all over the country, spreading out into new housing developments that pop up like mushrooms in this humid city. They come with dollar signs in their eyes and too many episodes of *Dallas* ringing in their heads. They come chasing oil.

The guy in the truck honks his horn twice. But the traffic doesn't move.

"That girl back there? What was that all about?" Bernie asks.

"She's a witness."

"To what?"

"It's just a case, B." The details of which he'd just as soon keep to himself.

Traffic picks up after the I-45/610 split.

Jay puts on his right-turn signal, wanting to ease over in time for the 59 exit that'll take him to Fifth Ward and Bernie back to her father's church, where she was typing the programs for Sunday's service when he picked her up before the interview. He looks in his rearview mirror, searching for an opening in the next lane. The Native Houstonian is behind him now, one lane over. Jay waits for the truck to pass, then moves over to the right lane, pulling right in front of a black late-model Ford. He studies the car in his rearview mirror.

At first he can't make sense of it, why the sight makes him so ill at ease.

Then he remembers the strip club's parking lot.

There was a Ford LTD, black like this one, parked next to him. And now here's one again, some fifteen miles down the freeway, riding right behind him.

Jay rolls down the driver-side window, sending a hot gust of exhaust into the car. He adjusts the side-view mirror, pivoting the glass just so, until he can, through smoke and freeway dust, make out a rough image of the Ford's driver: a white man wearing sunglasses and a tie, with close-cropped hair. The driver is smoking a cigarette, which he, just then, throws out of his win-

dow. Without signaling, the man abruptly changes lanes, jumping out from behind Jay and into the next lane over, cutting off
a blue station wagon in the process. As the Ford passes Jay on
the left, the driver turns in his direction, looking right into the
car, looking right at Jay. It's no more than a few seconds, but it's
just long enough to anchor the feeling in Jay's gut: someone is
tailing him.

As the freeway splits, concrete parting ways, the black Ford
continues on 45 North as Jay veers right onto the exit ramp for
Highway 59. He tries to make out the Ford's license plate number, not watching where he's going. He almost rear-ends the car
in front of him. Bernie puts her hand on the dash, bracing herself. She turns and looks at her husband, the sweat coming down
his face. "Roll up the window, would you, Jay? It's got to be at
least ninety degrees outside."

Jay does as he's told, and it's suddenly quiet in the car again.

"What is the matter with you anyway?"

"What do you mean?"

Bernie snaps off the radio. "You been acting funny, Jay, for
days."

This would be his shot, he realizes. His chance for a confession, to tell it all: the article in the paper, his trip to the crime
scene, and his fears about being connected to a murder. But he
doesn't mention a word of it. "It's just work, B."

He reaches over and pats her knee. Bernie looks down at his
hand as if someone had laid a cold fish in her lap. She lifts the
hand, returning it to its owner, then turns and stares out the
window on her side, watching the cars in the next lane. There's
something she wants to say to him, and he can tell she's searching for the right tone. "You don't talk a lot, Jay," she starts. "I
knew that when I married you. You don't talk about your mother,
your father, and you sure won't talk about your sister." She sighs,

the sound a kind of sad whistle through her front teeth. "But it's six years now, Jay, you and me. I guess I thought you'd have let me in by now, that's all."

She turns the radio back on, lets the music fill the space between them.

"I have a doctor's appointment on Friday," she says finally. "Can you take me or should I ask Evelyn?"

"I'll take you," he says.

"Fine."

The rest of the ride back is stiff.

He drops Bernie off in front of her father's church, but doesn't go inside. He takes surface streets back to his office, checking his rearview mirror every few seconds. He thinks of the black Ford and the guy behind the wheel. White, early forties maybe. A suit and tie, sunglasses, and close-cropped hair. In a late-model American sedan. A good description of a cop if he's ever heard one.

Back on West Gray, near his office, Jay drives around the block two times before going inside. He checks every car in the alley out behind his building. There's no sign of a black Ford, and he starts to seriously consider that he made the whole thing up, that he's seeing things, his old paranoia flaring up again. He doesn't trust his mind the way he used to, not the way he did when he was young, so sure of everything. The car in the club's parking lot. It was black, yeah. *But was it a Ford?* He only looked at it for maybe a couple of seconds. It could have been an Oldsmobile or even a Cadillac. And the guy driving the Ford, Jay would have remembered him inside the Big Dipper. White men like that, the ones who look like cops or feds, he never forgets. He can't afford to. There's no way that guy was in the club with him. That much he's sure of.

He makes his way into his office, reminding himself that he's done nothing wrong. He heads straight for his desk, ignoring the pink message slips in Eddie Mae's rhinestone-covered hand, and makes a cursory effort to tackle the papers on his desk. But the words blur on the page. His eyes are no good today. He feels another headache coming on, and, because there is no other remedy at hand, he takes two swigs from the open bottle of Pepto-Bismol in his desk. Wanting something stronger, he opens a pack of Newports hiding in the back of the drawer. He lights the last cigarette in the pack, right there at his desk, kicking the door to his office closed when Eddie Mae starts coughing in the hall.

He buys another pack on the way home, stopping at a filling station on Almeda. He's got half a tank as it is, but the prices at this Shell station are a good ten cents a gallon cheaper than the PetroCole by his house. Jay leaves the nozzle hanging out of the Buick and goes inside to pay: $7 on number 2, a pack of Newports, and a carton of milk because Bernie called him at the office asking if he wanted macaroni and cheese for dinner. He's walking back to his car when he sees a black Ford LTD parked across the street. Jay stops cold in the middle of the gas station's parking lot, feeling the milk cool against his side, the paper bag wet and soft with condensation. There's no one behind the wheel of the Ford. Jay looks to his left and right, scanning the faces in the parking lot, looking for a white man, early forties, suit and tie, close-cropped hair. He sets the milk on the roof of his car and crosses Almeda on foot, wanting a look at the Ford's license plate:

TEXAS. KLR 592.

There's no city seal on the vehicle, nothing to mark it as official.

Jay walks along the side of the car, peering through the windows. There are paper cups and fast-food bags on the floorboards and a tape recorder on the front seat, next to a legal pad. Pressing the sides of his palms to the glass to shield the late-afternoon sun, Jay tries to make out the tightly coiled handwriting.

"What the hell do you think you're doing?"

Jay turns and finds himself face-to-face with a large black man who's carrying a greasy take-out bag that smells of fried chicken and mustard greens.

"I know you?" the man asks.

Jay holds up both hands to show he means no harm.

"Naw, man, I don't know you," he says.

"Then I guess you best get the fuck away from my car."

"Sorry, man," Jay mumbles, backing away and into the street, almost walking into the front end of a Honda hatchback going thirty-five miles an hour on Almeda. The driver punches his horn. Jay staggers back to his Buick. He pulls the grocery bag with him into the car, resting the carton of milk in his lap. Through the windshield, he watches the black guy across the street sliding into the front seat of the Ford LTD, which, on second glance, Jay realizes, is dark blue.

Chapter 8

Sometime late, after midnight, Jay opens his eyes, sure he's heard something, a noise inside the apartment. He turns over in darkness, but can't make out the lines on the clock by his bed. He reaches for his gun. He's up and into the hallway in a matter of seconds, into the kitchen before he realizes the phone is ringing. The noise he heard. It rings a second time. Jay flips the light switch and looks at the clock above the stove: 2:37. The phone rings again. This hour, the news can't be good. He fears this is the moment he's been dreading.

"Jay."

His wife is standing behind him in the doorway, her faded brown robe around her shoulders. She's staring at him: bloodshot eyes, hair mashed to one side, a .22 in his hand. Her look is something past concern. She actually seems afraid of him. The phone rings again. Bernie goes to answer it. Jay picks it up first. He turns his back to her and clears his throat, speaking into the phone with a clear, calm voice, one he uses for juries . . . and cops. "This is Jay Porter."

"Son, you got to come out here."

It's his father-in-law, wide awake.

Jay feels relief at first, thinking this is another legal service call, another kid in trouble. He sets the gun on the kitchen table, reaches for pen and paper.

"You hear me, Jay?" his father-in-law asks. "They shooting out here."

"What's that?"

"They shot up a house on Market Street, man's wife and kids sleeping in the next room. By a miracle, a sheer miracle, they wasn't hit."

"Who? Who's shooting?"

"ILA."

"Jesus," Jay mumbles, forgetting for a moment who he's talking to.

Then he asks, "How do you know for sure it was—"

"They've been harassing these boys all week, son, after every meeting. The union's gon' vote on this thing soon, and some of the ILA are bent to see it come out their way. This boy here, man's house I'm in, he's been getting calls all week, saying what they gon' do to him and his family if he votes for the strike. There are shells everywhere, broken glass right in the man's living room."

"You call the police?" Jay asks. He glances at his wife, not wanting to alarm her, knowing she's listening to every word.

"We're waiting on 'em now. But we're not gon' see this go down like the last time. They got to take us seriously this time. We need a lawyer down here."

"Now?"

"They almost killed the man, Jay, his wife and kids, you hear me?"

"Yes, sir."

"The police have got to know there's gon' be some repercussions if they don't do their part to protect these men. You understand?"

"Yes, sir."

Jay looks at his wife, wondering how he's going to explain this to her, him leaving at three o'clock in the morning. "It's your father," he whispers.

Bernie seems to understand at once. He doesn't belong to only her.

She turns and pads softly out of the room.

She's sitting up in bed when he gets off the phone. He returns the gun to its hiding place beneath his pillow, then puts on the same clothes he was wearing only a few hours ago. "Union boys are running into some trouble," he says, his voice thin with fatigue. "I'm driving out to the north side." He slips on his dress shoes, putting on the costume, knowing he ought to at least look the part.

"You got to stop this, Jay."

No shit.

Only she's not talking about the phone call, him leaving in the middle of the night. "You can't grab a gun every time the phone rings," she says. "I can't have this around my kid, Jay." Then, a whisper, "I won't."

"Don't start that now."

"You're not right, Jay."

He stands in the middle of the room, eyes on his shoes.

Bernie looks up at her husband, her voice halting. "You're not . . . right."

Jay slides his wallet into the back pocket of his slacks.

"I don't know when I'll be back," he says.

"I figured that part out already," his wife says.

He turns and leaves without kissing her good-bye.

He checks the .38 in his glove compartment. It's in a small leather case underneath his registration papers, the only gun for which he has a permit. It would be illegal to have the .22 in the car or else he might have brought that along too. Reverend Boykins said he thought the gunmen had gone, but there is no way of knowing if they're coming back, and Jay has no intention of walking into an ambush. The late-night drive is unsettling, the air kind of heavy with the knowledge that this is trouble's hour. Jay pushes in the car lighter and rolls down his window. He lights a cigarette and thinks about his wife.

She was just a kid when they met, thirteen years old when her father brought her by the courthouse, the day the verdict came down. Jay remembers getting dressed that morning, leaving his cell for the last time, either to go home or to the Walls in Hunstville. And he remembers the judge's warning. There were to be no outbursts in the courtroom, no matter the verdict. Then, adding his own two cents, the judge said, "I don't have an ounce of respect for you, boy. The nigra issue is an important one in this country. But you boys goin' 'bout it the wrong way. And that's all I'm 'on say on it."

Jay remembers looking at the jury box, at the black lady in particular, the one who stayed down the street from First Love Antioch Baptist Church. She wouldn't look at him. She was in black from head to toe, and she had her head down, hands clasped around a wrinkled handkerchief, her lips moving slowly.

She was praying.

Jay threw up right there in the courtroom.

He managed to get his head between his legs, so most of it spilled out across the floor. Black coffee and some chunks of white bread they'd served him in lockup. Some of the church ladies in the back stood up. So did members of the press. Reverend Boykins was sitting behind Jay, with his wife and two daughters. He put a hand on Jay's shoulder. Jay remembers turning around. He was shaking his head, trying to say something, ready to make his bargain with God, the Rev as his messenger. But he couldn't get any words out. He couldn't speak, for days, it would turn out. He was finally out of speeches.

The Rev whispered in Jay's ear. He spoke of God and faith.

He's got you, son. He's not gon' let you fall.

The judge made them all wait until a maintenance crew could be located in the building. They lugged buckets and mops into the courtroom, cleaning up Jay's insides in front of everybody. He was long gone by then, lost in the swamp and stink of his fears, steeling himself against what he thought was inevitable.

But the verdict, when it came back, was *not guilty*.

The judge read it twice, as if he didn't believe it either. The lady in black, his angel, was weeping. She held her thin, prayerful fingers up to the ceiling, up to the sky and the Lord on the other side, to thank him, as it was clear she didn't trust her vote on a piece of paper, didn't trust white folks' doing. She dabbed at her eyes with an eyelet handkerchief; then, finally, she looked at Jay. Despite the noise in the courtroom, he thought he could hear her heartbeat, soft as a whisper in his ear. She gave him a small nod, just as simple and courteous as if they had passed each other on the street. Then, one by one, the jurors were led out.

He doesn't remember the faces in the courtroom, doesn't remember meeting the reverend's family or his future wife. He doesn't remember the parting words from the judge. He looked in the gallery for one face, and when he didn't see it, he was ready to go. He walked out of the courtroom with maybe thirty dollars in his pocket and no place to stay. He walked around the city for hours, and then days. He spent six dollars seeing *Beneath the Planet of the Apes* twice, eating popcorn for lunch and dinner; he slept in MacGregor Park one night. His third day out of jail he had breakfast at a Wyatt's cafeteria, eggs and coffee. Then he took the bus to St. Joseph's Hospital downtown. When the admitting nurse asked what was bothering him, he wrote down on a piece of paper: *I'm tired.*

The next time he met Bernadine Boykins he was in his last year of law school. She was a senior at the University of Houston, a school he hardly recognized anymore. By 1977, the student population was over 10 percent black, and the dorms were fully integrated. There were an Afro-American studies program and classes in Chicano history. The only activists left on campus were the feminists, white girls who felt entitled to everything.

He'd seen Bernie around the church, times he went by to pay his respects to her father. He thought she was cute, but just a kid. In truth, Evelyn, Bernie's sister, was probably, at the time, more to his liking. There was something kind of solid about her looks. Jay hadn't been with a woman in a long time and thought it best to start with one who might not mind taking the lead. To this day, he's pretty sure that's what the Rev and Mrs. Boykins had in mind when they invited him for dinner one Sunday; they were trying to set him up with their eldest girl.

But five minutes into the meal, he knew he could never make it with Evelyn, who was pouting about the heat, pouting about her lips, and couldn't someone pass her a better piece of chicken.

After dinner, he took a cigarette on the porch, and Bernie brought him a glass of tea, floating a slice of lemon on top. She sat on the porch steps, pushing her skirt between her knees, and asked him if he'd seen *Cooley High*, what kind of music he liked, and if he'd ever been roller skating. Then she asked if he'd like to go out with her sometime.

"I've had a crush on you since I was thirteen years old," she said.

He couldn't explain, even then, why this moment grabbed him so, why it hit him at the knees. It was about the sweetest thing he'd ever heard, offered up with such sincerity, such simplicity. Bernie was so at ease with her feelings, and Jay admired that, was drawn to it even. He took a good long look at her that day. She was nearly twenty by then and shapely, with soft brown eyes and a heart-shaped face that looked up at him, waiting for some answer. He told her he'd have to ask her father. She laughed out loud, showing her long, white teeth.

They dated off and on that summer. She was answering phones at a dental office on the north side of town. He had a car by then and would pick her up sometimes when she got off work. They went to the movies mostly, held hands in the dark. She helped him study for the bar exam, made up flash cards even though she didn't understand half the terms she was writing on them. And a couple of months into his first job—handling traffic tickets and DWIs at a low-rent shop across the street from a municipal courthouse—Bernie told him to go out on his own if he hated the job so much. "Do your thing," she said.

He got to thinking that he loved her.

She held him up in ways he had never expected from a woman. So he married her. She moved into his small one-bedroom apartment and never once complained. She loved him in an uncomplicated way, not at all weighed down by false expectations. She seemed to understand the limits of his emotional fluency, the things he simply could not, or would not, talk about.

It was a good fit for him. So much had changed in the world in so few years, they were almost of two generations, though he was only seven years older than she was. And he liked it that way. There were things about his past he didn't want to be reminded of. With Bernie, he could start new. He went along with her friends, made do without any of his own. And over the years, they made a pact, unspoken but as real and present in their marriage as the furniture in their apartment, the bed they slept on every night: she didn't ask questions. About his trial, where he got those guns, why they never saw his mother at Christmas or Thanksgiving. But lately, the baby coming and all, she seems to want something more from him. He can't bear to disappoint her, but he won't be pushed into places he's not willing to go. That was never a part of the deal.

He doesn't notice the headlights in his rearview mirror right away, at least they don't mean anything to him at first. It's not until he's exiting the I-10 freeway, going south on Lockwood, that he gets the feeling again, the sour ripple at the base of his chest, the tickle in his gut. He looks in the rearview mirror and realizes the square white lights have been behind him for some time, on the freeway and now here on Lockwood Drive. He tries to keep his nerves on an even keel as he glides into the right lane, waiting for the car to pass. The driver stays behind him, in the left lane, keeping a steady pace. Jay slows, then speeds up, then slows again. But no matter what move he makes, the driver stays on his tail, eventually sliding into the right lane, directly behind Jay. Its headlights blast through the Buick's back window, bouncing off his rearview mirror and momentarily blinding Jay. He can't tell the make or model of the other car, can't see the driver's face from here. In his mind's eye, he pictures a black Ford, a white male at the wheel, and wonders again if the guy is a cop, if he ought to pull over.

When Market Street comes up on the right, Jay makes a sharp turn without signaling, his car fishtailing widely as he speeds onto Market. He cranks the wheel heavily to the left to keep from slipping into a steep ditch lining the side of the narrow road. When he finally manages to straighten the car, he looks into his rearview mirror. The square white headlights are behind him still.

Up ahead, past Phillis Wheatley High School, Jay sees half a dozen cars parked in front of a graying wood-frame house. There are lights on in the neighbors' front windows, folks peeking from behind curtains to watch the commotion, the police activity on their block. There are two squad cars parked in front of the gray house and uniformed officers standing on the patchy lawn.

The car behind Jay stops suddenly in the middle of the road.

Its headlights snap off.

Jay can finally make out the shape of the car, its long, boxy silhouette. It's a Ford LTD for sure, black as the night on all sides. The driver starts to back away from the house, away from the cops and the scene on the street, pivoting on the narrow road, almost dipping into the ditch on the left side to make the turn. The driver heads east, back toward Lockwood Drive, picking up speed. Whatever his business with Jay, he does not want to handle it here, in the company of others. This only deepens Jay's apprehension, the nasty feeling in the pit of his stomach that the man in the black Ford means nothing but trouble.

He parks in front of the gray house, leaving his .38 in the glove box, and steps into the red-and-blue swirling haze of the cop cars. He recognizes some of the union men standing in the front yard. They're smoking cigarettes and drinking out of mismatched cups. Somebody took the time to make coffee, to pass it around. This is union business now. Kwame Mackalvy is standing on the cracked driveway, arms folded across his chest. He's talking to a young Hispanic woman who's scribbling Kwame's every word onto a notepad.

He called the fucking press, Jay thinks.

As he steps onto the grass, walking toward the front door of the house, a cop puts out a hand to stop him, landing a firm shove in the center of Jay's chest.

"Who the hell are you?" the cop asks.

He's a kid, black. Jay's got ten years on him, at least.

The black cop cuts a look at his white partner, showing off. "I asked you a question," he says, digging his finger into Jay's sternum.

Jay is slow to answer the cop, resenting the need to justify himself to a kid who wouldn't even have a job on the police force if it weren't for the civil rights Jay's generation marched and died for. "You want to take your hand off me?"

"What did you just say?" the cop barks.

Reverend Boykins crosses the patchy lawn. He's in a suit and tie, impeccable, even at this hour. "This is Jay Porter, Officer. He's a lawyer."

These are the magic words. The cop releases Jay without another word.

Kwame Mackalvy waves Jay over to his spot on the driveway. "I got Sylvia Martinez from the *Post* here. You want to make a statement, bro?"

"No," Jay says bluntly and without breaking his stride.

He walks up the cinder-block steps and into the house. Inside, the air is a good ten degrees hotter than it is outside, more humid too. There must be thirty people piled into the tiny house. Union men, neighbors, kids up past their bedtime. There's a woman in a cotton nightgown crying on the couch, a man kneeled in front of her, holding her hand. He's wearing nothing but blue jeans and house shoes. Jay walks to the family, speaking to the woman first. "You okay?" he asks.

She doesn't look up or acknowledge where the voice is coming from. She simply nods, her eyes glazed over as she stares blankly through the hole in her front window, watching police officers pick up shotgun shells from her yard.

"Mr. Porter." The man, young for a husband and father, stands, still gripping his wife's hand. Jay recognizes him from the church meeting a few nights ago. "Donnie Simpson," the man says. "'Preciate you coming out here."

Jay nods, shaking the man's hand. "What happened?"

"Three shots, right through that window."

"Nobody was hit?" Jay asks.

"No, sir. The kids was sleep in the bedroom with us."

Across the room there are two little girls and an older boy in T-shirts and pajamas, sitting at a card table with a bowl of plastic fruit resting on top. They're eating Frosted Flakes out of the box, the older boy doling out equal portions to his sisters. The girls are watching the cops, the excitement in the house. None of the kids is more than ten years old, all of them tall and lanky like their father.

"They stay out here on the let-out couch usually. But late summer like this, we keep them in the back room with us, where the window unit is."

Jay nods, looking at the kids, thinking the same thing as Mr. Simpson.

"If they had been out here . . ." Donnie says, his voice low.

"You see who did it?"

"No, sir. We was sleep."

"How do you know it was ILA?"

"Like I told them," he says, nodding toward the cops. "The ILA been calling my house all week, man, talking about I better not vote to strike. And I'm not the only one neither. Other brothers been getting the same phone calls, all time of the day and night. They trying to shut us down, Mr. Porter."

Reverend Boykins and the two police officers step inside the house. The bare bulbs on the ceiling catch them in a harsh light, throwing deep shadows beneath their eyes, lighting up the greasy sweat running down their necks. The reverend wipes at his face with a handkerchief. "Come on, now," he says, waving a hand out across the room, trying to get the men's attention. "Let's let the gentlemen talk now." He steps to the side, giving the cops the floor.

"All right, all right," the white cop says.

Kwame Mackalvy and the brothers outside crowd onto the front porch, trying to listen in through the open front door. June bugs and mosquitoes wiggle past them, into the funk and sweat and feast of human flesh in the house.

"We got a lot of information tonight," the cop says. "I want you to know we take seriously what's happened here."

"Then what you gon' do about it?" one of the men on the porch asks.

"Let the man finish now," the Rev says.

"We'll take the information we have here and file a report at the station."

"A report?" the man on the porch says.

"That's it?" Donnie asks.

"You gon' have to do better than that, brother," Kwame says, looking at the black cop, holding him, especially, accountable.

"There's no eyewitness to the shooting," the white cop says.

"We *told* you who did this," Donnie says.

"ILA motherfuckers, that's who," somebody in the room says. "They beat up a kid last week."

"The ILA is a big union with a lot of members, some of whom support you boys," the white cop says. "Now, you want to tell me specifically who shot a gun through this house, who's been calling you . . . I'll go talk to 'em myself."

"What if we got you a list of names?" Donnie says, turning to the other men. "Come on, y'all, we all at the same meetings. We know the ones that get up in front of everybody, trashing the strike, saying what they gon' do to stop it."

"Now I want to be clear here," the white cop says. "I'm not gon' go around accusing folks without some kind of real evidence."

"Isn't that your job, to *find* the evidence?" Kwame says.

"You get us a list, we'll be sure to put it in the file," the cop says.

"That's it?" one of the men asks.

"Man, get the hell out of my house with that shit."

"Donnie, that's enough," Reverend Boykins says.

"Hey, we're just trying to do a job here," the black cop says.

Kwame clucks his teeth, shaking his head at the kid.

The white cop passes his business card to Reverend Boykins, who passes it to Jay, who doesn't know why he's the one suddenly in charge of the thing.

"Call us if something changes," the white cop says to Jay.

By four o'clock in the morning, the men are still working on their list, calling out names to each other across the room, going over any beef they've ever had with any member of the ILA. Donnie's wife is in the back room now, trying to get the kids down for what's left of the night.

Jay turns down the third cup of coffee he's been offered. He stands alone by the door. He doesn't know what more they need from him, why he even got out of bed for this. He pulls the cop's card from his pants pocket and turns it over to Donnie. "You tell your wife I'm real sorry," he says on his way out.

"Wait a minute now." Donnie looks at the Rev and the other men in the room. "We're ready to move on to the next step with this thing . . . right?"

Jay turns to his father-in-law. "What's he talking about?"

The Rev takes a deep breath and a step toward Jay. "We think Kwame was right, son. We think a lawsuit may be our best chance to be heard."

Kwame, on the other side of the room, stands with his hands clasped behind his back, firing up a speech. "The police department is not doing enough to protect these men. As we move forward with a strike, we need to know that the city and the mayor back their right to peaceably assemble."

Jay sighs to himself. He's been here before. The late-night strategy session, the caffeinated rhetoric. He is suddenly very tired and wants to go home to his wife. "Lloyd," he says to the man Kwame used to be, "the cops came, they did their job. You know who did this, it's a different story, but—"

"Not *this*. Forget this," Kwame says. "We're going with the kid."

Jay looks around the room, not immediately understanding.

"Darren Hayworth, son," Reverend Boykins says. "The young man with the busted arm. You met him and his father at the church."

"They beat the shit out of that kid," one of the men says.

"He was coming home from a meeting, you remember," the Rev explains. "He was headed to a second job when they cornered him out Canal Street, near the tracks. After they left him out there, bleeding all over, the boy drove himself to the north side station, not even half a mile from the ILA headquarters on Harrisburg. The cops there wouldn't even take his statement."

"And he said he seen the ones who did it," Donnie says.

"He's got names?" Jay asks.

"Naw, but he say they was at the meeting that night."

"As far as we're concerned, the Houston Police Department failed in its duties to protect one of its citizens, to see the law carried out," Kwame says. Then, writing the press release in his head, he adds, "He's a good-looking kid, hardworking . . . just the kind of message we want to send."

"You talk to the mayor yet?" his father-in-law asks.

"I'm working on it." A lie to a man of God, and family to boot.

"Well, tell her a lawsuit is coming. That'll get her attention," Kwame says.

"Look," Jay says, trying to think of a way to slow them down, a way he can get out of this. "I don't even know what kind of case you'd have, and second, I'm not sure I'm the right guy. I can't really take on something of this magnitude right now. I do have other cases, other . . . obligations."

The Rev nods to some of the men across the room, one of whom pulls a brown paper sack out of a metal lunch pail sitting on the kitchen counter. The man, in faded Levi's and mud-crusted work boots, walks toward Jay in the center of the room, handing him the paper sack. Inside there are bills: $20s and $10s mostly, some singles and loose change. "The Brotherhood ain't a real group no more, not legally," the man says. "We don't have our own funds. But we got this together since just last week. We'll try to get you some more soon."

Jay looks at the men in the room, men who work just as hard as he does for what little they have. He hands back the paper bag. "I can't take this."

The men in the room look at each other, not sure what this means.

"I'll get in to see the mayor this week," Jay says. "She'll take my call."

He knows it's true as soon as he says it. He's always known she would see him if he pushed. And maybe that's why he's never tried. "I'll talk to her."

Chapter 9

The morning of, Bernie lingers a bit longer than usual in the bathroom, watching him shave, the way he combs his hair, the extra time he's taking to groom himself. She's taking note of everything, filing it away. In the bedroom, Jay makes a show of *not* choosing his best shirt and tie. Bernie sits on the bed, rubbing at the underside of her belly. "You coming by the church after?"

"I got some stuff I have to get to at the office." He slides on his shoes.

"I promised Daddy I'd finish up the programs for Sunday this morning. I thought you could meet me at the church later."

Jay looks up at his wife, not immediately following.

"The doctor's appointment, Jay?" she says. Then, seeing the blank look on his face, she sighs. "If you can't take me, I'll get someone at the church to drive me." She's pouting a little, cupping her belly like a schoolyard ball, turning away from Jay, as if to let him know, this is mine, not yours. She's aiming to hurt him, it seems, and he resents her for it. He didn't ask to go talk to the mayor. This was her father's idea. "Just tell me what time, B," he says.

The phone rings in the kitchen. Bernie shuffles out of the room first.

When Jay comes into the kitchen, his suit jacket folded over his arm, Bernie is holding the phone receiver, pointing it in his direction. "It's for you."

He takes the phone from her hand. "This is Jay Porter."

The voice on the line is gruff and slow. "Marshall's dead."

"Who?"

"My cousin." It's Jimmy calling.

Jay lays his jacket across the kitchen countertop. He glances at his wife, who is buttering a slice of bread at the table. Apparently, Jimmy didn't share this news with her. His wife probably had no idea who she was just talking to.

Jay lowers his voice anyway, turning away from her. "What happened?"

"They found him in a ditch on Elysian," Jimmy says, his tongue thick and uncoordinated this early in the morning. Jay can't tell if it's grief in his voice or Jack Daniel's. "He must have run off the road is what they're saying, fell asleep or had a heart attack, a stroke or something, just run right off the road. They saying he mighta been out there two or three days." Then a sigh. "My God."

"I'm sorry to hear it," Jay says, because he can't think of anything else.

"You saw him Saturday night," Jimmy says. "He look all right to you?"

Jay glances at his wife again. "Uh, yeah."

"Well." Jimmy sighs again. "That's what it is, what I wanted to tell you."

He asks Jay for the name of a good funeral home, one that might work out some kind of payment plan. Jay claims ignorance, mainly because he wants to get off the phone as quickly as possible. He feels mildly sick to his stomach. He's nervous about going to the mayor's office, for sure. But the phone call, the news from Jimmy, has also left him feeling unsettled. It's not exactly sadness he feels for Jimmy's cousin, but a vague sense of dread. When he hangs up the phone, Bernadine is looking at him, the buttered toast half-gone in her hand.

"The doctor's appointment is at three, Jay."

He nods. "I'll be there after lunch."

The mayor's office is on the third floor of city hall, a squat limestone building dwarfed by steel and glass on all sides, high-rises that have come to dominate downtown Houston. In 1939, when city hall was built, the city's dream for its future didn't reach past eight stories. The state flag sits on top of the government building; it is several feet wider and longer than the Stars and Stripes flying alongside it. There's a reflecting pool in front of the building, on Bagby. And across the street is a gilded archway leading to Cole Towers, twin office buildings that house the headquarters for Cole Oil Industries. The Cole name, in huge block letters, crowns the two towers, casting a heavy shadow across city hall, falling, at this hour, right into Jay's lap. He sits beside a large window just outside the mayor's private suite, where's he's been waiting for over an hour.

He folds and refolds his hands across his lap, trying to keep them still, passing the time staring at the framed photographs lined end to end on the beige walls of the anteroom: pictures of the mayor with Vice President and Mrs. Bush; Governor Clements, the state's first Republican governor since Reconstruction; even a snapshot of her with Congressman Mickey Leland, a Democrat and former political activist. Jay can discern no political rhyme or reason to the images on the walls. In picture after picture, in one pastel-colored suit after another, Mayor Cynthia Maddox is shaking hands with Democrats *and* Republicans, Teamsters *and* members of the Business League. Everyone has a hand on her in the photos, laying their claim to a woman who ran as a Texas Democrat, but garnered nearly 30 percent of the Republican vote, a woman who spoke vaguely on the campaign trail about her commitment to civil rights but still managed to reassure moneyed conservatives that she could keep their neighborhoods lily-white. In Mayor Maddox, people see what they want to see.

Jay looks at his watch for the third time. The mayor's secretary gives him a tiny shrug. "I'll let 'em know you're still waiting," she says, pressing a button on the intercom. Then, hearing something, she twists her torso around to look at the mahogany-stained double doors leading to the mayor's suite. She lifts her finger off the intercom button. "Oh, here . . . I think they're coming now."

It's not until the doors open that the weight of the moment finally hits him. His face is suddenly flushed with heat . . . and also the bitter sting of shame. He's embarrassed to be undone by her still, all these years later. He bites the inside of his cheek until he tastes his own blood, until he remembers what senseless pain feels like, until he remembers what this woman is capable of.

It's not the mayor at the door anyway, just another secretary or aide of some sort, a boy in his twenties with a clipboard tucked under his arm and a tie that comes up too short of his waist. He waves at Jay impatiently, as if they've been waiting for *him* all this time. Jay stands and straightens the front pleats of his pants. Slowly, he makes his way through the double doors, dragging his feet as if he's walking through sand. The boy with the clipboard leads Jay down a short hallway. "Her conference call ran over," he says. "She's got about fifteen minutes before she has to be at a luncheon across town. I'd make it quick."

The boy opens another set of doors at the end of the hallway.

A rush of cool air, crisply air-conditioned and sweetened with rose water perfume, hits Jay in the face, along with a lingering hint of cigar smoke, a reminder that this room, the inner sanctum, was once the domain of men.

The current mayor is leaned up against the front side of her desk, dressed in a plum-colored suit, a bloom of frilly white fabric knotted at her throat as if she couldn't decide between a lace scarf or a man's necktie. At the base of her legs, covered with thick, nude-colored panty hose, she's wearing Keds.

"The car's waiting downstairs," the boy says.

The mayor waves in his general direction, her head tilted back.

There's a makeup artist, a woman in her sixties wearing a green lamé top and matching eye shadow—whom Jay would probably not trust to put on the face he shows the world—sweeping a pencil across the mayor's left eye.

It's quiet a minute, and Jay wonders who will speak first.

"I want to thank you for coming," Cynthia says.

Jay looks down at the thick carpet, fingering the change in his pockets.

"Your support means the world to me," she goes on.

The presumption irritates him. He's about to correct her, to explain that she's misunderstood his reason for coming. He is not here to let her off the hook.

Cynthia keeps her eyes closed while the makeup artist pats

powder the color of corn silk onto her nose and cheeks. "What's the next part, Kip?"

There's a typewriter going behind Jay.

The boy, Kip, types another line then rolls the paper to the top of the page. " 'As this city enters the golden age of its greatest opportunity,' " he reads flatly.

" 'As this city enters the golden age of its greatest opportunity,' " the mayor repeats, with some romantic flourish. " 'It's organizations like yours—' "

"You're jumping ahead. That line goes after you say the part about Houston being the fastest-growing city in the nation, the hope of a new decade."

"I want to open with that. 'Houston is the fastest-growing city in the country . . .' blah blah blah . . . 'and it's organizations like yours, the Daughters of the Texas Revolution, who maintain our heritage and tradition, our precious link to the past.' That's enough, Marla," she says to the makeup artist.

Cynthia stands upright then, finally opening her eyes. Jay's is the first face she sees. The smile starts somewhere behind her too-made-up eyes, slowly, like a neon sign kicking on at dusk . . . a few sparks, then light. "How do I look?"

To tell the truth, if it weren't for her name on the door, he would hardly recognize her. The suit is square and covers nearly every inch of the body he once knew so well, as if she is well aware of its liability in public office.

He cocks an eyebrow. "Daughters of the Texas Revolution?"

Her smile broadens, a spot of mischief behind her docile, coral-colored mouth. It's *this* face he recognizes. She angles her head to one side. "Oh, Jay," she says. Remorse maybe, or else pity, for him, the things he still hasn't learned.

"Touch it up once before you get to the podium," Marla says, lugging an alligator makeup bag on her way out the door.

Cynthia nods, waving her off. Then she says to Jay, "I'll have you know, those ladies gave me five thousand dollars during the campaign." She crosses behind her desk and plops into an over-size leather chair. Jay can't help thinking she looks like a kid playing dress up in her daddy's office. "'Course, they gave the other guy ten . . . but I can't afford to hold a grudge."

The other guy was Buddy McPherson, the mayor's challenger in the general election. A former sheriff and county commis-sioner, the Big Mac ran a particularly nasty campaign, one that ultimately backfired. Sure, Cynthia Maddox *was* probably too young to be mayor, with too little political experience—a few years as Senator Lloyd Bentsen's aide in D.C., then home to serve a year on the local school board and on to the comptrol-ler's office—but the Mac's very public attacks on her intelligence and maturity (repeatedly referring to her as "that gal") and his frequent remarks on her mannish affect ("Something my grand-daddy always said: 'Son, don't ever trust an unattractive woman; they got way too much to prove'") didn't go over well with the public. And the fact that on the campaign trail, Mac repeatedly brought up the news that Cynthia Maddox had never married was universally regarded as being in poor taste.

Cynthia picks up the can of Tab on her desk, drinking it through a straw so as not to mess up her lipstick. She looks at Jay and shrugs. "The DOTR are having their annual in Houston this year, and they asked me to speak at the luncheon," she says, picking up a plastic fork and stabbing at a boxed salad on her desk. "They're not all Republicans, you know. They didn't all vote for Reagan."

"Did you?"

She looks up at Jay, mouth full of lettuce, and shakes her head. Not an answer to the question so much as a reprimand for asking in the first place.

"Nice picture," he says, nodding over her head at the two oil portraits hulking on the wall behind her, between the Texas and American flags. One is the governor, William P. Clements; the other is Ronald Reagan.

Cynthia doesn't even bother to turn around. "They came with the office."

"We have to get these remarks down before lunch," Kip says.

"You finish up," she says.

"You want me to leave?"

"No," she says quickly. "We're not going to be long, are we, Jay?"

Kip goes back to typing, reworking her speech. Jay goes back to fiddling with the change in his pocket, turning nickels over in his hand. He turns and looks out the wall of windows on the northwest side of the office. The mayor's suite is on the third floor of city hall, not a grand view, but high enough that Jay can see a swatch of the 45 freeway from here. It's under construction, as usual, as is almost every pocket of the city; this is a restless, adolescent city, forever picking at its pimples, never satisfied to leave well enough alone. Below the I-45 overpass are Allen Parkway and Buffalo Bayou. Jay can just make out a piece of the water from here. In the afternoon light, it looks chocolate brown, as inviting as a cup of coffee, completely harmless. He thinks of the woman on the boat. Her face comes to him, as uninvited as the night his path crossed hers. That, and the mystery of the black Ford, the man behind the wheel.

Cynthia lets out a soft belch. "Pardon me for all this," she says, dumping the rest of the salad into a trash can at her feet. "But I stopped eating in public after *Texas Monthly* described me as 'stout' in their winter profile. You read that shit? I swear, I can't win. I put on weight just to stop people harping that I got in on my looks. Now, I got half the city talking about my thighs. Everybody's got some fucking thing to say." She shakes her head in disgust, leaning down to open a bottom desk drawer. She pulls out a pair of black pumps, kicks off her Keds, and slides on the high-heeled shoes. "Kip, make sure that door's closed."

"It's closed," he says without looking up from the type-writer.

Cynthia reaches for a purse resting on a sideboard behind her desk. She pulls out a pack of Vantage 100s. She slides one out and lights it, then exhales, waving the smoke away from her hair, which is teased to hell in a round dishwater-blond helmet. She used to wear it long, Jay remembers. He used to have a goatee. And back then neither of them would have been caught dead in a suit. And yet here they are. Cynthia looks at him through the smoke, maybe thinking the exact same thing. *So here we are.*

"What are you doing here, Jay?"

There's no simple answer to the question of why he came all this way instead of talking to her on the phone. It was a test, maybe, just to see if he could. "There was a shooting a couple of nights ago, out on Market Street," he says, sticking to the script he was given. "That's on the north side of Fifth Ward."

"I *know* where it is," she says. "Anyway, I heard about it."

"You read it in the paper?"

Cynthia shakes her head, blowing a thin stream of smoke through her lips, then stubbing out her cigarette after just a few quick puffs. She points to a stack of papers on the corner of her desk. "I get briefed by the police chief every morning. Every armed robbery, every rape, every shooting, I hear about it."

Jay looks at the typed briefs on her desk. There must be fifty or so, going back a couple of months. Somewhere in that stack of papers is a report about the body by the bayou, maybe even word about the investigation. He wonders how much the mayor knows about the case or if Jay's name is on one of those pages. The news this morning about Jimmy's cousin means Jay has no way of knowing what, if anything, the old man might have told police detectives about Saturday night.

"Crime's a big topic in this city," Cynthia says, zipping up her purse. "The worst thing is to be at some function, a ribbon cutting for a grocery story or something, and have a reporter ask me about a couple of dead bodies somebody found the night before, and I don't know a thing about it. Let me tell you, it don't look good. I almost didn't make it into office on the crime issue alone. People think a girl can't keep things under control." She walks from around the back side of her desk, motioning to Kip that it's about time to go. "Fifth Ward is one of our hot spots, so, yeah, I heard about it. Why?"

"The dockworkers, the ones talking about a strike . . . they think the ILA had something to do with it."

Cynthia's blue-gray eyes widen slightly. She seems to instantly comprehend what this means, the trouble it brings. "Jesus."

"To the Brotherhood, it's an act of war."

"The cops told me they don't know who did it," the mayor says, hopeful.

"The Brotherhood has reason to believe this was stress over the strike. It wasn't that long ago when some of the ILA beat up a nineteen-year-old kid coming home from an organizing meeting."

"What?"

"It was three men. The kid says he'd seen them at the ILA meeting the night he was attacked."

"Well, give me their names. I'll take them to the chief of police myself."

She reaches for a notepad on her desk. Jay shakes his head. "The kid already tried talking to the cops. He drove himself to a station with a busted arm, somewhere on the north side. Cops there wouldn't even take a report."

Cynthia rolls her eyes.

"Those unions bowl together, you know," she says. "The Policemen's League and the ILA. The boys in blue are pretty protective of their buddies at the port." She goes to run her fingers through her hair, a nervous habit, he remembers. But she's forgotten the amount of hair spray her groomer encased her in. Her fingers get stuck a few inches above her ear. "This is a goddamned mess. If the city council would go my way in terms of who we seat on the port commission, then maybe I can push this strike situation in the right direction."

"What about Cummings?" Jay can't help asking.

"He's part of the problem, you ask me. It's the port commission that started this trouble in the first place." She goes on to tell Jay that the labor crisis actually started several months back when the port commission cut deals with some of the major shipping companies, allowing them to berth, or dock, their ships several hours earlier than has been customary for twenty years. Starting earlier means more ships docked in a day, more goods unloaded and loaded, more business. It also means extra hours of work for the dockworkers, most of whom don't get overtime, a point on which the stevedoring companies refuse to budge. They're already paying plenty of overtime to their foremen, who get compensated for the extra responsibility they take on. To management, this pay scale is based on a time-honored hierarchy. The problem, Jay knows, is that the hierarchy falls along racial lines. The foremen, the men supervising, holding clipboards, dipping into air-conditioned trailers for doughnuts and coffee anytime they want to, are disproportionately white. The ones doing all the manual labor, the lifting and loading, are almost all brown. And the stevedoring companies are slow to promote blacks, and especially Latinos, to the more lucrative positions.

"I'm all for equal rights and equal pay," the mayor says. "But now is just not the time for this kind of fight. There's a time and place for everything, Jay."

"Ten years ago you and I would have laughed if somebody told us we ought to wait patiently for our civil rights. *Wait* is just another word for *no*, and you know it."

"Look, Jay," she says firmly, almost like a schoolteacher scolding a mouthy pupil. "There's not a goddamned one of us can afford a strike right now. This is the second-biggest international port in the country. You know that? You got any idea how much money floats on that water? Not to mention the oil. The *oil*, Jay. Those petrochemical workers go on strike too, and this whole country's going to feel the effects of it. I got people calling me left and right. Business leaders, oil and gas folks, the unions. People are starting to panic, Jay," she says, shaking her head gravely. "This just isn't the time."

"They're talking about suing the city, Cynthia. The kid's family."

"For what?"

"Their position: the Houston Police Department and the city that funds and manages said department both failed in their duties to protect a law-abiding citizen and to carry out the law to the fullest extent of their abilities."

Cynthia stands perfectly still, her high heels dug in the blue carpet, staring at him with those pale blue-gray eyes, hot pink flushing across her cheeks. For the first time, she actually looks angry. "You're not taking the case, are you?"

"They asked me to talk to you, that's all I'm doing."

"Because you *can't*." Then, catching herself, she says, "Not that I'm in a position to tell you what to do—"

"So long as we're clear about that," he says.

"I'm just saying, you don't have to do this, Jay, just to punish me."

She waits for him to say that's not what this is, not the reason he came all this way. "Why would I want to punish you, Cynthia?" he asks pointedly.

"Don't do this to me, Jay."

"I'm not doing anything to you, Cynthia."

"That's not true," she says warmly. "You're here, aren't you?"

She gives him a wistful smile. It betrays a weakness he didn't know was there, an acknowledgment that his presence holds some power for her as well. "You telling me you came all this way to talk to me about a union? Really, Jay?"

He looks into her eyes and tells the truth. "I don't know why I'm here."

The answer seems to irritate her in some way, and she makes a quick, rather graceless switch from sly courting to an outright plea for mercy. "Look, I'm in a struggle with this police department as it is, and everybody in this goddamned city knows it. I'm only eight months in. I cannot have a *lawsuit* against the police department. It'll be an indictment against me, proof that I can't control those men. They'll hang me, Jay."

"The Brotherhood just wants protection," he says. "In the very likely event there's a strike, they want to know that they'll be safe on the picket line."

"You sure sound like you're representing them."

"Just doing a favor, that's all. The only outsider they're taking any real cues from is Reverend Al Boykins, the minister over at First Love Antioch."

"Your father-in-law?"

This stops him, completely unnerves him. He had no idea

she knew he was married, that she knew anything about his life anymore. "Just talk to the chief, okay," he says. "They're going to strike. It'll be a hell of a lot better if no one gets hurt, and it ends quickly. For them and for you."

He turns and starts for the door.

He hears her voice behind him, his name landing softly at his back. "Jay."

He turns to look at her, wondering if she'll finally say it, here and now.

"If you get me the names of the men who hurt that boy," she says, her voice cool and businesslike. "I swear I'll do everything I can."

"'Preciate that."

He nods to Kip on his way to the door, stealing a final glance at the first woman mayor of Houston: the fruity suit, the stiff black shoes, the helmet hair; the American flag and Reagan watching over her shoulder. He looks at Cynthia and thinks of the girl he once knew . . . and tries to guess which one is the lie.

Chapter 10

He doesn't remember when he stopped loving her. It would be neat and tidy to say his arrest. Those frantic and confused days after he turned himself in, long hours spent in lockup, trying to explain to his court-appointed lawyer what exactly had happened, trying to understand it himself . . . all the while waiting for her to call, to prove his worst fears wrong. He doesn't remember when he stopped loving her, or when exactly he started. They never called it anything or gave it a name. In the beginning she was just a scruffy kid who started coming around to meetings. He was the one who had been appointed to tell her, as forcefully as need be, to stop. They didn't want her help. Her political awakening was on her own time, not theirs. Besides, in those days, the sisters were still frying chicken and going on beer runs for the meetings, walking ten feet behind the men at campus marches. If the brothers hadn't run her off, the sisters surely would have. No way a white girl was gon' get in line first.

He went to tell her in person, even though he didn't have to. He could have waited until she showed up at the next meeting at the duplex on Scott Street, where they spent most of their days—organizing marches, skipping classes, eating whatever somebody's little paycheck could scrounge up, drinking beer and fooling around with women, whoever was in the building at the time. He could have waited and made a show of the whole thing, putting down the white girl in front of everybody. But he had no desire to be cruel. This movement wasn't about keeping score or getting even, at least not for him. He really believed they could change things. And he didn't see any reason why whites shouldn't be a part of that too. Hell, they had made this mess of racial inequality in the first place; why shouldn't they have a hand in cleaning it up?

His comrades though, his brothers-in-arms, were, for the most part, leery of white folks. They didn't fool with hippies— white kids who didn't wear shoes and were always telling people to relax—and they were even more suspicious of the whites who showed up in pressed khakis and Top-Siders, who joined SNCC and Students for a Democratic Society, who talked the talk. Their anger was some days focused as much on pissing off their parents as it was on the president or voting rights or racist cops across the South. But, hey, Jay thought, at least they showed up. They went to campus marches and organized their own. Cynthia Maddox was all right in Jay's book; she got credit for just showing up.

So Jay went out of his way to tell her to please *stop*.

She took the news well.

After calling him a racist and a chauvinist, a word he had to look up when he got home, she told him she thought he was the only one in his group who had any sense. She asked him if he wanted to join her for dinner, her treat.

Jay, who had holes in his coat and was working on a few in the soles of his shoes, was quite grateful for the offer.

They went to a barbecue stand on Telephone Road, her choice. She ordered chicken and mustard greens and pushed him toward the hot links and potato salad since she had never tried those before. Halfway through the meal, she was reaching across the table every few minutes to pick at his plate.

All through dinner, she ran through a laundry list of things she'd been saving up, stuff she would have said at the meetings if they'd ever let her talk. How they should work the system from the inside, plant one of their own on the school's admin board, or even better, the city council. "Infiltration," she said, chomping on an ice cube soaked in Big Red soda. "The FBI ain't all crazy."

She thought they could pull it off too.

But they would need somebody unassuming, somebody the establishment would never suspect. She licked the corners of her mouth and smiled, an indication that she knew such a person, maybe someone sitting across the table from him right now. "You may need me more than you think you do."

And she had more to say too.

She claimed their meetings were disorganized, too much eating and smoking and not enough focus. She also thought the Panthers were on to something with their uniform look. "Have y'all ever thought about getting matching outfits? Something jazzy, like with rainbows on the back."

By then, Jay had heard enough. He mumbled something about a paper he had to write. He thanked her for the meal and hitched a ride back on his own.

He, frankly, didn't think he'd ever see her again.

But Cynthia Maddox was insatiable and full of ideas. She was on a full scholarship and making straight As; she had a lot of time on her hands. She stopped coming by the house on Scott Street and starting calling him up at his dorm, on the hallway phone, all time of the night, wanting to run her ideas by him. She was a member of SNCC by then, a group she'd finally talked her way into, and was starting up one of the few SDS chapters in the state. She wanted to know what he thought about this or that. Would he look at a draft of a press release she was writing, urging a boycott of the student union cafeteria (because they bought canned peas and tomatoes from a plant that didn't hire blacks or Mexicans)? Could she get him to agree to give her a heads-up about any marches he had planned so she could coordinate something with her groups and present a unified front to the school, the city, and the local press? And what did he really think of nonviolence? "I mean, really, don't you think we're past all that?"

Finally one day, just to shut her up, he asked her where she was from, where she'd gone to high school. She grew up in Katy, she said, out west, off the I-10 freeway. She'd come to college late, already in her twenties, and before that, she'd spent her entire life within a fifteen-mile radius. To Jay, it explained a lot. She was like a spring chicken that'd been running around in a too tight cage and had finally been let loose. It was an energy he recognized in himself. They were both kids who'd grown up in the dirt in rural East Texas, itching to get past the social confines of all that open, lawless space. They kind of got to be friends that way, talking about home. Turns out Cynthia (Cindy to everybody but him; he didn't like the name, didn't think it suited her much) didn't know her daddy either. She had a bastard stepfather too, a guy not even ten years older than she was, who used to look at her funny when she was coming out of the bathroom.

It was weeks before Jay would tell her his story.

The soft footsteps he used to hear in the dark, his stepfather padding past, on the way to Jay's sister's room. He'd always hear his mother next, shuffling on the same worn carpet in the hallway, walking into her daughter's room to stop whatever had happened or was about to. Jay, who was just a boy then and scared to death of his stepfather—the beatings that sprang up like hurricanes on the Gulf, with no advance warning and no time for retreat—never did a thing to stop him. The next morning they'd all sit around the breakfast table like nothing had happened, like there wasn't a snake sitting right there at the table, sipping Sanka and sopping up his eggs with a biscuit. His mother was still married to the guy, wondering why Jay never came home for Christmas.

He'd tried to tell his buddies once. He and Bumpy Williams and Lloyd Mackalvy were sharing a bottle of Jack on the front porch of Bumpy's mother's house in Third Ward one night, long after a card game had broken up. Jay tried to talk to them about his family, what tore it up. He tried to talk about what it is to be a man, to feel such a need, a call really, to protect the ones you love, and the hollow, gnawing pain of being unable to do so. But his friends weren't interested in personal tragedy; they were out to save a race of people. There was a war going on; this was no time for baby sisters and family squabbles. Plus, they were slow to condemn Jay's stepfather. In their eyes, a brother could be forgiven anything. Hadn't they all been through enough as it was?

But Cynthia listened.

She said it wasn't his fault.

"You should call her," she said, meaning his sister.

Their phone calls started to stretch so long that some of the boys on his floor complained, and he and Cynthia took to meeting off campus. Beer joints and taco stands, sometimes sneaking off to the movies, something he never did with Bumpy or Lloyd. And they hit every blues hall in Third Ward. Once they saw Lightnin' Hopkins play at the Pin-up Club. Cynthia nearly fainted from the heat, the stench of sweat and perfume, and the shots of hooch she kept accepting from a group of sisters who were having a little fun with her, playing like they were her friends, laying out sly compliments about her stringy hair and laughing at her behind her back. Jay ended up having to drive her home. It was too late to try to sneak her into the girls' dorm, so he drove in circles around town, Cynthia laid out across his lap in the front seat of her green Ford Econoline truck, waiting for her to sober up. Near dawn, he settled into the parking lot of an elementary school out in the Heights. It was Sunday morning by then, and no one was around. Cynthia came to around dawn. She sat up and looked out the window and asked where they were. Jay had taken his coat off at some point. He'd rolled up his sleeves and was smoking a cigarette out the window.

Cynthia turned and looked at him.

He can still see her now.

Her hair was messed up and tangled . . . and it *was* stringy.

She had mascara smudged under both of her eyes.

Still, she was beautiful, a fact he finally allowed himself to admit.

And she was, at that moment, probably the best friend he had.

"I like you, Jay," she whispered.

He felt something flutter in his stomach then, and he was suddenly, terribly aware of how hungry he was, how empty he'd been for years.

"I like you," she said again.

There was no way he would make the first move. She seemed to know this without anything needing to be said. When she finally kissed him, the taste was big, meaty and warm and kind of bitter, like blood. He couldn't restrain himself any longer. He put his hands everywhere, cupping her doughy flesh, wanting to fill what he could with her. Before long they moved to the bed of the truck, lying on top of Jay's ratty coat, his backbone pressed against the metal bed, as she (of course) insisted on being on top. There, on his back, eyes stretched past the ponderosa pines to the starlit sky above, Jay held his breath.

There were many other times. In the truck, in the basement of her dorm, and once on top of a picnic table after midnight in MacGregor Park, one of the stupidest thing he's ever done. He never told his friends, and she never told hers. It was just between the two of them. They met in silence most nights, reaching for each other like a salve, slick, wet kisses to wash away everything past the reach of their young arms. By the time the feds killed those boys in Chicago in the winter of '69, everyone was on the lookout for rats. The administration was cracking down. There were cops on campus, cops everywhere, it seemed. The FBI and local law enforcement had moved on to new strategies. They'd grown tired, it seemed, of billy clubs and water hoses. They were just flat out shooting people now. What had started some fifteen years earlier with peaceful sit-ins and boycotts had disintegrated into guerrilla warfare. Something ugly was happening around them. Dark clouds were moving in, marching in martial formation, threatening to break everything wide open.

King was dead by then, Malcolm and two Kennedys.

Death was everywhere.

Cynthia asked him once about getting a gun.

He feigned ignorance and told her to watch herself. He didn't want her getting hurt. SNCC was falling apart, Cynthia was spending more and more time trying to get attention for her fledgling SDS chapter, getting deeper and deeper into her own rhetoric, her ideas that they should meet fire with fire. She started speaking around campus more and more, standing on classroom chairs outside the administration building, screaming until her throat was raw, always quoting Malcolm, as if the rest of them had never heard of him. She got her name in the school paper, but the *Post* and the *Chronicle* mostly ignored her, treating her as little more than a groupie, a white girl caught up in nigger fever, as sure as if the Temptations had come to town.

Chapter 11

The report to his father-in-law goes something like this: the mayor has expressed tremendous concern for labor instability at the docks, as well as compassion and understanding for the longshoremen's wage struggles; she will speak to the chief of police about getting adequate protection for the dockworkers in the event of a strike; she passes on words of sympathy to the kid and his family; if he can ID the ones who jumped him, she'll do all she can to see that charges are brought. In all, the mayor is a friend to labor.

It's only marginally true. But Jay can see no reason to escalate the situation by repeating verbatim any of the things she said. He played his part as the messenger boy. The end of it, as far as he's concerned.

"Now wait a minute, son. We still need you on this thing."

"Rev, with all due respect, I'm not sure you have much of a lawsuit here. You got the mayor herself saying she'll make sure the men are caught. The problem is, you're saying the boy doesn't really know who did it."

"Not by name, but he *saw* them, Jay. Well, one of 'em, at least."

Jay sighs. The story seems to keep shifting.

"Meet with the boy again, hear him tell it, what those men did to him."

"I can't afford to take any more time away from my business."

"I understand, son, but they're going to vote on the strike, this week maybe. They're going to call it. Come out to the union meeting and let the boy point the man out. We'll get his name, then take it to the mayor's office—"

"You don't need me for that."

"You're the one who has her ear. Now look, the lawsuit was just a tactic. The main thing is, we need her on our side, get the whole city behind us."

Jay sighs, feeling again that the rules keep changing.

This is not my fight, he wants to say. *This ain't my deal.*

"I got a baby coming, sir," he says. "I have to work."

"How did it go with the doctor?" the Rev asks.

"He says Bernie's looking real good, doesn't expect any complications."

"Well, we'll pray on that, son, that's for sure."

"Yes, sir," Jay says.

He's about to hang up the phone when his father-in-law pipes up again.

"Think about coming to the meeting, son. This is history, you know."

=

He's been stalling on the hooker case. Between the union drama and his anxieties about the shooting death in the newspaper, he's let his work slip. And time is not on his side. It was two days ago that he promised Mr. Luckman he would present the settlement offer to his client, but in truth, Jay's been avoiding her altogether—not returning her calls and telling Eddie Mae to inform her he's out of the office if she should drop by unexpectedly. He doesn't want his client to know about the offer. Dana Moreland would probably think $7,500 was enough to retire on. Jay is still holding out for more. If he can come up with a witness who saw J.T. and the girl, he thinks he can scare five digits out of Cummings and Charlie Luckman. That in mind, he heads out to Gilley's after sundown, this time dropping Bernie off at her sister's, going it alone. It's safer this way, he reasons, remembering the black Ford on his tail just two nights ago.

And anyway, Pasadena, Texas, is not exactly a pleasure destination.

There's a sign on Red Bluff Road as it crosses Highway 225, the major artery in and out of Pasadena, Texas. It's a homemade billboard, white with hand-painted black letters. It's been there for more than a decade. A relic, some could argue. A holdover from another time. The sign has faded some, taking a beating from hundreds of South Texas storms. But cruising along at a cautious speed on Highway 225, Jay can see the words quite clearly from his car window:

PASADENA, TEXAS

"PROUD HOME OF THE KU KLUX KLAN"

Nearly every citizen in town, every cop and city official, including Pasadena's mayor and the police chief, drives by the sign maybe two, three times a day, Jay thinks. On the way to the grocery store or work or taking their kid to the doctor. You can hardly get to city hall without driving past it. Folks on their way to church Sunday mornings see this sign every week, rising some fifty feet in the air, high above the buildings and trees. There has never been a campaign launched to tear the sign down, no arguments made in the local newspaper that perhaps this is no longer the time for such unapologetically racist fare, at least not broadcast so loudly. Hell, the city could just come in and break the sign down in the middle of the night if they were moved to. And yet here it is, lit eerily from below by city streetlights, the white of the billboard stark against the black sky. It still stands on high as the unofficial town welcome.

Make sure you know where you are, boy.

In an odd way, Jay finds the sign comforting. He has come to appreciate these kinds of visual clues. To see a Confederate flag flying outside someone's home or in the back window of a pickup truck is about as accurate a warning system as a man could hope for, like the engine light coming on in your car a few miles before something may or may not blow up; it's a caution before trouble starts, offering a clean window of time in which to make a run for it.

He would not be out here now if weren't for business. There's nothing appealing about Pasadena, Texas. It's flat land, cow pastures and overworked strawberry fields turned over for cheap housing, strip malls and liquor stores, gun shops and honky-tonks. And somewhere in the middle of all of it, a small-time country singer opened the world's largest nightclub, capable of holding more rednecks in one location than Jay ever wanted to encounter in a lifetime. Mickey Gilley's place made the city of Pasadena, Texas, famous.

The dance hall sits on several acres, including the parking lot, which, at a quarter to ten, is filled with dozens of Chevy and

Ford pickup trucks, most of which have a red-and-white Gilley's bumper sticker above their tailpipes or pasted in the back windows of their cabs. There must be dozens of people huddled in groups outside the club. They're getting an early buzz on, drinking beer out of coolers propped up in the beds of their trucks, listening to Waylon Jennings or the Charlie Daniels Band on their car stereos. At the front doors, there's a group of girls waiting in line, their hair feathered up to the brims of their pink-and-white cowboy hats. They're popping gum and sharing a can of hairspray. They glance in Jay's direction, nudging each other as he drives through the parking lot, where all eyes are on him: a black man in a crisp white button-down, no pearl buttons or tassels, no beard on his face or even a mustache, driving a Buick Skylark no less. He is clearly not one of them.

Jay parks at the far end of the lot, the front end of his Buick tipping dangerously over the edge of a steep ditch that separates the gravel lot from the cars passing by on Spencer Highway. He has a sudden, bothersome thought of Jimmy's cousin, an image of the old man driving off the side of the road, his body discovered in a ditch, just like this one. And he wonders, not for the first time, why Marshall told his girl he'd be home after cleaning the boat, but when Jay spoke with Jimmy, he complained that his cousin had left it a mess.

He is about to open his car door when something hits the glass on the driver-side window, right by Jay's ear. He jumps, thinking it's a rock, that somebody is throwing stones at his car. He turns and sees a couple of roughnecks standing outside the driver-side door, one with his arms folded across his substantial chest, the other motioning for Jay to roll down the window. The man taps the window again with his pinky ring, a turquoise stone the size of a small biscuit. When Jay doesn't respond fast enough, the one with the chest pushes his friend out of the way and taps on the glass harder. Slowly, Jay rolls down the window halfway. He can immediately smell the liquor on them, the sweat from a good day's work. The one with the chest says, "You lost, boy?"

Jay rolls down the car window a little more, far enough so the men can see the .38 sitting in his lap, where he laid it about a half mile outside Pasadena's city limits. He puts a hand on the butt of the weapon. "I believe I'm all right . . . *boy.*"

The one with the chest backs away first, pulling his friend with him.

Jay keeps one hand on his gun, watching their retreat in his side-view mirror. He takes his time getting out of the car, lighting a cigarette. Then he makes the long walk across the parking lot, keeping his eyes straight ahead.

At the front doors, there's no one on duty who goes by the name of Clyde, and no one who'll tell him if Clyde is anywhere on the premises. Inside, the club is as warm as a midday barbecue, even with air-conditioning going and ceiling fans whirling overhead. The dance floor, seemingly half a mile of parquet wood flooring, is a sea of cowboy hats, ducking and swaying. Jay can hear the thump and shuffle of boots across the wood floor. He counts three bars under the pitched roof, each with a line of cowboys gathered, dollar bills folded lengthwise in their hands, waving at the girl bartenders for 75-cent longnecks of Lone Star.

Jay stands in the entryway, wishing he'd at least put on some jeans or a pair of boots and pretended to be some long-lost descendant of Charley Pride.

People are starting to stare.

He decides to start with the bar on his left, working his way to the front of the line. The gal behind the bar gives him a can of Gilley's beer even though he ordered a Michelob. He imagines she didn't hear him over the music, that or she's fucking with him, or maybe Mickey makes all the girls push his brew.

She pops the top for him, twirling the cap on her pinky finger, motioning to the next man in line. Jay sips at the beer; it's thin and not to his taste. He pulls out a $5 bill and orders a Michelob, louder this time. He tells her to keep the change. She looks at Jay anew, raising an eyebrow. From the cooler behind the bar, she pulls out two sweating bottles of Michelob. She opens one and slides it to Jay, pops the cap on the other and takes a sip herself. She leans across the bar. "I don't drink the shit either." She winks at him, pocketing the rest of his change.

He watches her work for a while, thinking he's got an in.

She moves with grace, able to fill one order while she's taking the next, making sure the women in line get served first. Her hair is stick straight and dirty blond, and she wears it straight down her back like Crystal Gayle. She's older than the other barmaids at her station. There's a weariness in her hips; too many years on her feet, he gathers. This is career work for her. He bets she's in here at least five nights a week. The next time she's down at his end of the bar, he asks her about Clyde. "He's off tonight," she hollers above the music, moving back and forth between the bar top and the cooler of beer. Jay orders another Michelob. "You got a phone number for him or something?"

"Depends on why you're asking? You're not a cop, are you?"

From his back pocket, Jay pulls out a Polaroid picture of his client, one he took the first day she came into his office. He lays the picture of Dana Moreland on the bar top, along with another $5 bill. "You seen her in here before?"

"She a friend of yours?"

"Something like that," Jay says.

The bartender nods at Jay's wedding ring. "Your wife know you're friends with a girl like that?"

"So you know her then."

"I know what she and Clyde are up to, if that's what you mean."

The line behind Jay is getting rowdy, pushing up against him.

The bartender finishes the rest of her Michelob in two clean swallows. She goes back to taking one-dollar bills, pulling beers, popping tops. Jay tries to talk to her over the noise. "You seen her in here with him?" he asks, pulling out a smudged newspaper photo of Mr. Cummings, a shot of him with the other port commissioners standing on one of the public wharves. The bartender snatches the picture from Jay on her way to the cash register.

"Maybe," she says.

"He wasn't one of Clyde's customers, if that rings any bells."

"I said 'maybe.'" She pulls the tab off two cans of Gilley's beer, slides them down the bar to a couple wearing matching black-and-silver cowboy shirts. She crosses back to the cash register, studying the smudged newspaper photo, holding it next to the Polaroid of Dana Moreland. "Yeah, all right," she says.

"Are you sure?" Jay asks.

"This one looks real familiar," she says, pointing at Cummings's picture. "I remember him not wanting to leave so early, getting huffy with Clyde."

"On the night of June twenty-ninth?"

"That sounds about right."

"You saw these two people together?"

"I guess so," she says, not sounding as sure as she did a moment ago.

"And what about Clyde? You got a number for him or something?"

"Why? What's this all about?" She leans over the bar top, smiling, her breasts mashed together under a pink-and-red Gilley's T-shirt. "What'd she do?"

Jay puts another $5 bill on the countertop. He hopes she won't ask any more questions. She pockets the extra money and reaches for a matchbook on the bar top. From somewhere in her waterfall of hair, she pulls a stub of a pencil and jots something on the inside flap of the matchbook. "Clyde's number," she says. Then, smiling, she adds, "And mine." Jay actually feels himself blush.

It's after midnight by the time he picks up Bernie at Evelyn's house. He's whistling, in a good mood, and Bernie catches his spirit. She's on the baby now, day and night. Since the last doctor's appointment, she's started packing her suitcase and scribbling baby names on the back of any piece of paper she can get her hands on—takeout menus and circulars from the paper, even paper napkins.

"What about Donna?"

He shakes his head, making a face.

"Gayle?"

"No."

"Angela?"

"No."

"Ellen?"

"Maybe."

They're playing a string of Sam Cooke songs on 1430 AM. *At first I thought it was in-fatuation, but ooh it's lasted so long.* Jay turns up the volume. "Don't you have any boy names?"

"Well," she says. "I was thinking Jerome . . . for your father."

He's always thought of his father as gone. It never occurred to Jay that his daddy might come back again, in some small, wholly new way. "Yeah . . . okay."

In the dark, across the torn front seats, he reaches for her hand. When they arrive at their apartment building, Jay lets his

wife up the back stairs first, following behind, providing a buffer between her and the hard concrete, in case she should lose
her balance. She goes into the apartment first, heading toward
the bedroom. Jay stops in the kitchen and grabs the trash out of
the step can. Alone, he walks it to the Dumpster in the alley out
back.

Over his shoulder, he hears his wife scream.

Jay turns, dropping the bag at his feet. It splits open like a
cracked egg, spilling coffee grounds and chicken bones. A light
comes on in a neighboring apartment as Jay races up the stairs
to his building. At the back door, Jay pushes his way into the
kitchen, tearing the hinge loose from the wall. He runs to his
wife, in their bedroom, in a panic over what he might find.

Bernie is standing in the middle of the tiny room, staring at
the bed.

Jay immediately goes for his gun.

He slides his hand under his pillow, feels the cool fabric
beneath it but does not find his .22. He looks under the mattress
and under the bed. But it's gone. The look he gives his wife is ice
cold. He's furious with Bernie, thinking she moved it, taking it
from him when they need it most, when *this* is what it's for.

He grabs a broken-off broom handle he keeps under the bed,
gripping it like a baseball bat. He checks the bathroom, the hall
closet, and the living room.

His worse fear—an intruder, someone lying in wait—passes.

There's no one in the apartment but the two of them.

Bernie calls out his name, calmly this time, as if she were calling him in to dinner. Jay walks back to the bedroom and sees
his wife standing stock-still, where she was. He stares at her, not
comprehending. "What is it, Bernie?"

She points to the bed, her hands shaking. He is looking so
hard for a spider or a rat, what he's by now suspected is the root

of the problem, that he misses the bigger picture. It takes a moment for him to see the room clearly, like eyes adjusting to bright white sunlight after stepping out of a cool, dark shade. A few seconds, then finally everything comes into focus. On the bed, Bernie's suitcase, the one she's been packing carefully in bits and pieces for the last few days, is turned over, upside down, the clothes strewn across the bedspread and spilling onto the floor. Someone has gone through every piece of it, her panties and nightgowns and every magazine; they even opened an envelope with the doctor's instructions in it, the name and address of the hospital.

The dresser drawers are open. So is the drawer on his nightstand; a bottle of aspirin and a tin of hair grease have been fished out and thrown across the bed, along with his AM radio. The nightstand drawer on Bernie's side has been pulled clean out of its socket. It's sitting on the floor, along with paperback books and a spiral notebook that Jay didn't even know his wife kept by the bed. Bernie looks at her husband. He's sure she's about to cry. He glances over at his side of the bed and sees his overturned pillow and the empty spot beneath it. It's clear now that his wife didn't move his gun. Someone came in here and took it.

Bernie walks out of the room first, carrying her notebook.

He finds her in the kitchen, checking the refrigerator of all things. His checkbook is still sitting on top of the stereo speaker in the living room. The television is there. And their books. Even a basket of folded laundry Bernie'd left on the couch. All of it untouched. The only thing he finds out of place is his wedding picture, one he had framed for their first anniversary. Someone has turned it facedown on the coffee table, pressing their noses to the glass.

In the kitchen, Bernie is counting a roll of bills stashed inside a cleaned-out tub of Parkay margarine. She folds the money back into its hiding place, seemingly satisfied that it's all there. She closes the refrigerator door and walks to the wall phone between the kitchen countertop and their three-piece dinette set. When she picks up the receiver, Jay panics. "What are you doing?"

"Calling the police."

"Bernie, wait." He takes the phone from her hand.

"Jay, we are calling the police. Just because we live on this side of town does not mean we don't deserve to live in peace. I'm not having this in my house, Jay. I'm not putting up with it." She shoves his hand out of the way, like she's swatting at a persistent fly. She grips the phone receiver and starts to dial.

"Bernie. *I* did this."

It's the first thing that comes out of his mouth. He doesn't tell her what he's really thinking, his worst fear—that it was police officers, homicide detectives, who broke in here in the first place, possibly looking for information on him. The television, Bernie's cash, even his checkbook, weren't touched. This was not a burglary, that's clear. The only thing missing is the .22. And he would be a fool to mention a missing gun to any beat cops who would show up at this hour, reporting a gun for which he has no permit. He presses his finger on the hook, hanging up the line. "The mess in the bedroom, B, I did that."

"What are you talking about?"

There's a rap on the front door. Two times, then again, louder.

Jay makes sure to get to the door first. All the noise they've been making, someone might have already put in a call. If these are cops at the door now, he wants to do the talking. He turns to his wife before opening the door. "I did this, Bernie. Okay?" He waits for her to agree with him. Her face is completely blank. She stares at him as if he's a stranger, the true intruder in her home.

Jay opens the door, pulling it just a crack.

The eyeball on the other side is red-veined and rheumy about the insides.It's Mr. Johnson from downstairs. "Mr. Porter, y'all doin' all right?" he asks, scratching at his gray beard, trying to peer past Jay and into the apartment. "I heard your wife screaming. Somethin' not wrong, is it?"

"Bernie saw a rat is what it was."

"You get him?"

"No, sir. He made it out the back door."

"Lord, don't tell me that. My wife hear about another rat running around, and she's gon' keep me up all night about it." He chuckles, wanting to share a husbandly laugh with Jay. But Jay just stands there, saying no more than he already has. "And you're sure that's all it was?" Mr. Johnson asks.

"Yes, sir," Jay says.

He mumbles a curt good night to his neighbor and quickly shuts the door.

"What in the world, Jay?" his wife says.

"I don't want that man in our business, B."

"I'm talking about that mess in the bedroom."

"I'm sorry, B," he says, talking too fast. "After I dropped you off at Evelyn's, I realized I forgot something back here, something I needed for the interview. It was a good thing I remembered too, before I got all the way out to Pasadena. I tore the place up, in a hurry, you know. And I'm sorry."

He walks past her calmly, into the bedroom, as if he does this sort of thing all the time, tearing up her things, scaring her half to death. He starts picking through the mess in the room. Bernie stands in the open doorway, leaned against the wood frame, watching him. "What was it?" she asks.

He looks up. "Pardon?"

"What was it you were looking for?"

"A sheet of questions, names my client told me to look into."

"I don't remember seeing it," she says. Then, "Where'd you find it?"

"Hm?" he says, stalling.

"Where did you find it, Jay?"

"That's the funny part. It was in my car the whole time."

He smiles. She does not smile back.

"Come on, Bernie. If anybody really broke in here, they would have taken the TV, the radio or something. Your 'frigerator money's still there, ain't it?"

Softly, he adds, "You got no reason to be scared, Bernie."

"I'm not scared. I'm thinking." She runs her finger inside the doorjamb, fingering the cheap, pulpy wood. There's a lot he's not telling her, and she seems to know it by the look on his face. "I'm sorry about the mess," he says, putting the dresser drawers back. Bernie watches him for a while, then slowly joins him in the cleanup, repacking her flowered suitcase piece by piece.

About an hour before dawn, he's still up, sitting on the living room sofa, a tool chest at his feet and a can of beer in his hand, trying to think of how they got inside. He checks the front door and the one in back, where the hinge is still hanging loose from when he pushed his way into the apartment. He wonders if that was the point of entry, if they kicked the door in and then sloppily tried to repair the damage, replacing the hinge. But as he hunches on his knees, refastening the screws on the brass-plated hinge, he considers what little sense that makes. Why would anyone bother? Why tear the place apart, make a show that you'd been there, then take the trouble to cover your tracks?

No, somebody wanted him to know they were here.

Which is why he can't sleep now.

'Cause the more he thinks about it, the more a nagging feeling starts to sink somewhere in the back of his mind, like dirt and debris settling after a hurricane. At this late hour, the air finally still, he can, at last, see things clearly.

It was not a cop who broke in. He's almost sure of it now.

Jay used to have break-ins all the time. His dorm room, the duplex on Scott Street where he stayed sometimes, even his first apartment after his trial, a one bedroom rattrap in the Bottoms in Third Ward. The feds and local law enforcement often came and went as they pleased, going through his things, bugging the phones. But they never left more than a faint trace: a lamp out of place, a phone book moved a few inches to the left of where it had been, or his papers rearranged in a slightly different order than before. Everything else was exactly the way he'd left it, down to the cigarette butts in the ashtrays and the dirty dishes in the sink. The only firm clues that someone had been in his place were the tiny recording devices he used to pull out of his phone receivers.

He's already checked the kitchen phone tonight.

In a fit, he took the whole thing off the wall and tore it apart, laying the pieces across the dinette table, studying them under the light. When he didn't find anything, he tried to put the thing back together and couldn't, and he got so frustrated that he started to laugh out loud, a dark, bitter sound that led to tears.

You're not right, his wife had said. *You're not right.*

It's been almost a week since Bernie's birthday dinner, since he helped a stranger out of the bayou, a woman he doesn't even know for a fact to be a murderer. No cops have come beating down his door; no one's even called to ask him any questions. He's done nothing wrong. And yet here he is, three o'clock in the morning, sitting over his dead phone, what he broke apart with his bare hands.

This is what his life has done to him.

He looks at his wedding picture on the coffee table, the one that was turned facedown. He thinks of the mess they made of his wife's things and knows this was meant to intimidate him. Someone wanted him to know how easy it would be to get to him. Into his apartment, into his bedroom, the deepest part of his marriage. He doesn't know why someone would have taken the gun. Except that taking it would rattle his nerves, which, in fact, it has.

Jay runs through a list of clients in his head, ones who might be disgruntled enough to pull a stunt like this. But his mind keeps coming back to the longshoremen, the strike, and the violence that's erupted over the last few weeks . . . and the fact that he let himself get pulled into a very public fight.

He thinks of the black Ford and the white driver and begins to wonder if he hasn't been reading this whole thing wrong from the get-go. He remembers the car tailing him on Market Street a couple of nights ago, how quickly it turned and sped off when they came upon the lights of police squad cars. What if it was never a cop following him, he thinks, but someone aligned with the ILA, the faction that's against the strike? What if their new tactic is to come after *him*?

He opens his eyes at about a quarter to six. Bernie is standing over him, pushing at his left shoulder to wake him. He's laid out on the couch, where he must have nodded off sometime during the night. He does not remember how much of it was a dream. The darkness is gone, and he feels washed clean.

He follows the smell of coffee into the kitchen. Bernie sets a steaming cup for him on the table. The phone is still there, broken into a dozen pieces. She does not ask him about it, probably knows she wouldn't get the truth if she did.

Chapter 12

Two days later, not even a full forty-eight hours after he told his father-in-law he didn't want to get involved, Jay is standing on the docks at the Port of Houston, an hour before the dockworkers union is set to vote on a strike. He waits on wharf 12, next to a roach coach that smells of coffee and fried bologna and pork tamales. He lights a Newport and keeps his eyes peeled, on the lookout for a white man in his forties with a buzz cut and sunglasses, the one driving the black Ford, and the one he now suspects broke into his apartment.

Wharf 12 is a public dock run by the port authority. It's sandwiched between two other docks that are considerably larger and move a lot more inventory in a day. Over the years, wharf 12 has become a kind of de facto break room for longshoremen working up and down the Ship Channel. Here the ones who didn't get a work assignment for the day wait around to see if their luck might change; they gather to get a bite or call home or play cards. The doors of the pier's warehouse are open, and a group of men sit inside, taking advantage of the shade. It's a half hour to dusk, and still, it's nearly ninety degrees outside.

For Jay, the sun and the salt water at the port, the smell of fish tails caked up on the shore and the fuel from the barges all mix into a heady cocktail. He feels dizzy and hot. He tosses his cigarette and buys a grape Nehi from the food truck. Standing in the shade of the warehouse, he watches ships in the distance.

There are men in motion everywhere, up and down the Channel, dressed in coveralls or Wranglers, lifting bags of pure cane sugar, bales of cotton, and boxes of computer chips. They load and unload fan belts and air-conditioning units and sacks of grain, baby dolls and skis and grain mustard, doing the work by hand, in teams of two, lifting and loading, their backs bent at a harsh angle. They labor in near silence save for the grunts of their breath.

A few of the wharves operate by forklift. Two or three men work the machines, which load goods mechanically into long rectangular metal containers that look like boxcars on a train. The containers are then transported onto the ships by even bigger machines. Even at a distance, Jay can see it's an infinitely more efficient way of going about things, easier and faster too. In an instant, he gets a clear picture of how labor problems might be solved in the future: machines.

At a quarter to seven, the kid shows up. He's alone, his arm still in a sling.

His name is Darren. He's nineteen, as Jay guessed. He grew up on the north side, went to high school out in Kashmere Gardens, a rough neighborhood north of the Loop, full of Section 8 housing and street toughs. He likes football and Michael Jackson (the new stuff) and is thinking about taking a few classes at a community college in the fall. "I need a job I can work if *both* my arms are broken." Smart boy, Jay said to him over the phone.

Jay offers to buy the kid a soda. Darren says no, that he doesn't want to bother Jay with anything. But Jay insists. Ten minutes later, he leaves the food truck with two sodas, plus a hot dog loaded with mustard and onions and a bag of Fritos, all for the kid. They sit on a couple of empty crates inside the warehouse while Jay watches the boy eat. His lip's healed, and the bruises have faded along his jawline. The thought actually crosses Jay's mind: did someone get pictures, some physical record of the injury, something besides the arm sling?

He shakes the thought and reminds himself that this is not a real case.

He's going to help the kid, sure. If Darren can identify the guys who jumped him, if he can provide a name or two, Jay will pass it along to the mayor. Beyond that, it's out of his hands, and he'll carefully advise his "client" that pursuing this any further than that is foolish. In the meantime, the kid gains him entry into ILA headquarters, and maybe Jay gets to make an ID of his own. Since the break-in last night, he's wondered more than once if the man in the black Ford and the guy who jumped Darren are one and the same, and he's ready to tell the man, in no uncertain terms, to think twice before he crosses Jay again.

"You look good," Jay says, nodding at the healed cuts on the kid's face.

Darren nods, stuffing Fritos into his mouth. "I'll be all right." He wipes grease and salt on his pants leg. "I get one of those?" he asks, pointing to Jay's cigarettes. Jay passes the kid his Newports, watching him fire one up, which the kid does with ease and grace, blowing smoke out of the side of his mouth. "So, I guess you want to know how it happened, huh?"

"You told your father and the rest of them that you were coming home from a meeting at the ILA headquarters," Jay says.

"It was a week ago, about," the kid says. "The union was just getting into this thing serious. Some of the Brotherhood camp was making their case about the wage discrepancy." He trips over the word, as clumsily as if he were wearing too tight shoes. Jay finds himself nodding along, encouraging him. "How many people were at that meeting?" he asks.

"A couple hundred, maybe more," Darren says. "It was the first time some of the white ones came out and said they gon' stand with us if we walk."

"What time did you leave that night, Darren?" Jay asks.

"I cut out early, before nine o'clock. That's when my shift at the bakery starts."

Jay scratches his chin. "So you think they actually followed you out? Watched you leave, then cut out after you?"

"Looks that way, don't it?"

"You speak up at the meeting, say anything, for or against the strike?"

"No, sir. I only been in the union a year now. I can't even remember when there was a Brotherhood. It's only ever been one union, far as I've known. This ain't a black or white thing for me. I just want to get a little extra money in my pocket, you know, hold on to a girlfriend for more than a couple of weeks."

Jay nods, as if he completely understands, as if these were his only concerns when he was Darren's age. The kid starts in on his second Dr Pepper.

"And you saw them at the meeting, the men who jumped you?" Jay asks.

"One of 'em at least. He was standing right outside the hall, in the doorway, catching a smoke. I remember 'cause he looked at me kind of funny when I was walking out to my car."

He runs down the rest of the story for Jay:

He left the meeting, must have been about a quarter to nine because he remembers thinking he was going to be late clocking in at the bakery—it's almost thirty minutes to get out to his second job at the Meyer Bread factory. He was heading west on Harrisburg. He was gon' pick up 59 and carry that to I-45.

But of course, he never made it that far.

There was a pair of headlights in his rearview mirror, not even a couple of blocks from ILA headquarters. He says he knew right away that he was being followed. How, Jay asks. Just a hunch, a feeling, the kid says. He tried to duck the car, speeding up, then slowing down, but the lights were right on his tail the whole way. Jay nods; all of this sounds eerily familiar. The kid admits he made a pretty big mistake. He took a sharp turn down a side street, thinking he could lose them that way. But he ended up at a dead end. The car behind him, a truck, it turned out—A truck, Jay asks twice. You sure it wasn't a car? A sedan, like a Ford?—the truck pulled sideways and parked across the road, so that when the kid turned around trying to get onto Canal Street, they blocked him in. Two of 'em jumped out with baseball bats. The one driving stayed behind the wheel. Darren locked both his doors, but the men broke his driver-side window, yanking him out. Looking at Darren's lean frame, Jay acknowledges that this was possible, but still the kid must have been cut up something awful.

Yes, sir, he says.

He never got up after the first blow, a mean lick across the back of his neck. It was two against one, plus the dude in the cab of the truck. One of the men yanked Darren's arm behind his back, pinning it there with his boot, which is how the bone broke. The other one made a few kicks at Darren's face, spitting at him the whole time about how a vote to strike would mean trouble for him and his family. From the ground, Darren couldn't see much but tar and concrete. There were lights on inside some of the houses on the street, but no one dared to come outside. He doesn't know if there were any witnesses.

Except for the dude sitting in the truck.

He was behind the wheel, smoking a cigarette out the window, watching the whole thing, sometimes offering direction to the other two. "Telling them to twist my arm a little harder. He seemed like the ringleader," Darren says.

"What'd he look like?"

"A white guy, 'bout your age, I guess, maybe older."

"Blond or brown hair? Was he wearing it short or long?"

Darren shrugs. "He was wearing a baseball cap . . . and glasses."

"What kind of glasses? Like sunglasses?"

"No, like regular glasses."

"And you're sure it was the same guy you saw at the meeting? Even though it was dark out, and he would have been at least a couple of yards away from where you were laid out on the ground?"

"The one who was looking at me funny when I left the union hall, that guy was wearing a baseball cap too, just like the dude in the cab of the truck. It was red on white . . . just like the dude in the truck."

"If you see him tonight at the meeting, you point him out to me, all right?" Jay says. "Let me handle the rest."

"Yes, sir," Darren says, smiling through his chipped front tooth.

They leave the port in different cars, agreeing to meet in front of the union hall a few minutes before eight o'clock. The ILA parking lot is overflowing, and Jay sees at least two press vans parked by the curb out front. At a pay phone by the doors, he calls over to Evelyn's and asks to speak to his wife. Without making a big thing of it, he had asked Bernie to stay out to her sister's for the night. After what happened the other day, he doesn't want her home by herself. Of course, the story he cooked up for her had something to do with a concern that she could go into early labor and he wouldn't be anywhere around. Bernie agreed. But now, on the phone, she sounds tired and ready to go home. In the background, Jay can hear Evelyn cackling at George Jefferson on television. He asks Bernie to hold out for a few more hours. He'll come get her before ten.

Darren shows his union card at the door, introducing Jay as his lawyer; they let Jay in without a fuss. The hall is already at full capacity. Some of the men are starting to spill out through the double doors. Jay squeezes through a wall of bodies to get inside. The room is hot and packed, the air thick with cigarette smoke and the stench of grown men's fears, men who have families to feed, rents and mortgages to pay. They are at least four hundred deep in the hall, black and white and a few brown, their skin tight and leathery, cured by the sun and the salt of the Gulf. They're chain-smoking cigarettes and sipping free coffee and nibbling at iced cookies wrapped in paper napkins, their work caps tucked under their arms. They stand idle, staring at the stage, where a lone microphone waits.

Jay follows Darren to the black side of the room, over to the left. He recognizes some of the faces. Men from the church meeting, men he met on the night of the shooting on Market Street. They pat him on the back, offer extended hands in his direction. Donnie Simpson is standing against the back wall, drinking black coffee out of a Styrofoam cup. Jay asks about his family, how the kids are holding up. Donnie says the kids are fine, but his wife hasn't slept good since the shooting. It's a couple more paydays before he can fix the broken window, and in the meantime they're sleeping with a thin sheet of plywood between them and the outside world. He offers to get Jay a cup of coffee. Jay waves him off, says he'll get it himself. Can he get Donnie a refill?

He takes Donnie's empty cup and cuts across the room, scanning every face, looking for one that's familiar to him. Through the smoky air, he studies every beard and mustache, every haircut, the cut of everyone's collar. He cannot picture any of these men behind the wheel of a black Ford LTD. And didn't Darren say his guy was driving a truck? And wore glasses?

The coffee station is a handful of thermoses lined up on a card table. There's a photographer hovering nearby. He's wearing khakis and Top-Siders and a *Washington Post* press badge around his neck. Apparently, this isn't the only economy sweating over the outcome of one hot, smoky meeting in South Texas. The rest of the country waits too.

Just then, the double doors to the union hall slam shut.

Jay hears footsteps on the plank wood of the stage. They belong to a white man in his fifties, who's graying about the temples in two patches that shoot out like tusks. He's wearing a checkered button-down shirt with sleeves rolled up to his elbows and carrying a clipboard, a name tag pinned to his chest. He taps on the microphone twice then points to the crowd of men. "Somebody oughta push those doors back open. Otherwise we like to suffocate in here."

He waits for two obedient young men at the back of the hall to prop open the double doors using a folding table and a couple of chairs; then the man onstage continues, leaning into the micro-

phone. "Brothers of the International Longshoremen Association," he says. "I just got off the phone with—"

"Name please!" a reporter yells.

"Pat Bodine, B-O-D-I-N-E. President ILA, Local Fifty-six,
Houston, Texas." He waits, making sure the press gets it right.
Then he smiles and says, "I just got off the phone with Wayne
Kaylin, president of OCAW, Local One-eighty, not fifteen min-
utes ago. If we walk, gentlemen, the oil and chemical workers
walk with us."

The whole black side of the room erupts in applause, plus a
good number of whites in attendance. If Jay had to guess, he
would put the glee at a little over 50 percent, a thin but real
majority. The other men in the room, the ones not clapping,
hooting, or hollering, are shaking their heads to themselves or
cutting eyes at each other. One of the men down front shouts,
"What about the Teamsters!"

"Hold on now, hold on," Mr. Bodine says, waving his hands
out across the crowd, signaling everybody to hush. "Hold on
now. The Teamsters ain't come down with a final word yet. But
they're our brothers in labor as much as OCAW. I think in the
end they'll come around."

"I heard some local companies are talking about locking the
Teamsters out, to put pressure on us," the man standing down in
front says, hands tucked in the back pockets of his Lee jeans.

"That is a possibility, yes, sir. Something we all got to think
about."

The head-shakers start mumbling among themselves, slowly
drowning out the pro-strikers. Their voices blend into an ugly
murmur, full of piss and dissent; it spreads like a contagious dis-
ease across the humid room. Suddenly Jay is not so sure of his
original count, just where the majority lies. He takes particular note of the white head-shakers in the room, looking for the

driver of the black Ford. Darren, who is also scanning the faces in the hall, his eyes sweeping from the foot of the stage all the way to the back of the hall. When Jay makes it back to the Brotherhood side of the room, the kid whispers, "I don't think he's here, Mr. Porter."

"All right, all right," Mr. Bodine says onstage, trying to hush the crowd. "We all know what we're here to do tonight. And I want to give everyone a chance to talk, them that want to. But let me start by putting my two cents in, speaking on behalf of the board, and also just my personal opinion on the thing." He shifts his clipboard from one arm to the other. "Now, look here. I love this union. I'm proud of my brothers. I've seen us come too far to let this kind of thing tear us apart. Overtime is an issue for all of us. Black, white, whatever. We cannot let the stevedores think that we're still operating as two unions. 'Cause if we do, it's not going to stop here. Every issue that comes up in the future, every negotiation, they're gonna frame the argument in terms of race. Divide and conquer. We've got to send a message right now, once and for all." He holds up his index finger to make his point. "We are one union."

There is halfhearted clapping across the room, as if no one is exactly sure what being one union means. A black man with a Brotherhood cap on his head holds up his hand. "And the rules got to be the same for everybody now!"

The pro-strikers clap for one of their own.

"That's fucking bullshit," one of the head-shakers calls out. "I don't get paid what my boss gets, and he don't get what his boss gets. That's just the way of the world. People got to work their way up. Everything ain't gonna be handed to you," he says, looking directly at the black side of the room.

"This ain't about no handout," one of the black workers says.

"I been with Gulf Port Shipping nearly fifteen years now," a man in steel gray coveralls says. "I've seen white men younger than me get promoted to foremen or some other management gig. And I'm still out on the docks."

"And now we all gotta get out there two, maybe three hours early just to make sure we get a slot for the day," another black worker says. "Y'all getting paid for that and we not. That's bullshit."

"Hey, man, *I'm* not management either," one white man says. "I'm out there pulling and loading just like you. But you don't hear me complaining, asking for special treatment."

"You a fool, then," somebody hollers.

"Let's do this one at a time, please," Mr. Bodine says, pointing to a white man with a drinker's complexion and thin, greasy hair. "I got a kid, seventeen," the man says, "coming out of Galena Park High School next year." There are a few catcalls in the room from former graduates. "My boy wants to follow his daddy's footsteps. And I want him to have it better than me. If he's got to put in the extra time, he ought to get paid for it. Period."

There is a lot of applause for the sentiment, a man looking out for his son.

Mr. Bodine points to another man in the room, an older white man, a few years shy of retirement. "We go back a ways, Pat. I voted for you twice. But I think it's goddamned irresponsible to be talking about a strike right now."

This gets the head-shakers stomping on their feet and clapping. One man stands on a table. "You put us on the picket line tomorrow, and there'll be a couple hundred Mexicans working our jobs before noon. You mark my words. The ones that's coming over the border, they'll scab. They don't fucking care."

More applause from the head-shakers.

"Fuck scabs," the man in the back says. "That ain't even hardly our biggest problem. I know you're busy up here at the union offices, Pat, but when was the last time you actually set foot on the docks? You see what's going on here?" He looks out across the room. "Come on, y'all, somebody's gotta say it."

There are nervous faces around the room, men looking down at their shoes, biting their fingernails.

"Containers," the man says. "You know what I'm talking about."

"Now wait a minute, Tom," Bodine says.

"Another five, ten years, and it's all machines loading containers onto the ships. We got merchants hiring their own people now, loading the containers right at their home base, getting rigs to drive 'em to the docks, already set to load. The machines do the rest. The Teamsters aren't stupid. Everybody needs a driver. But the rest of us . . . every one of us in here might be out of a job."

This silences everyone, the pro-strikers and the head-shakers.

"That is a trend we're seeing," Bodine says, keeping his voice even and calm, even as the dark, wet spots under his arms are spreading fast. "But we believe that full-scale containerization, at seventy-five percent or more, is a good ways off."

"The stevedores are hiring less and less every year," Tom says. "Tell the men the truth, Pat. If you're gonna ask them to dig their own graves, they might as well know what it's all about."

The reporters in the room are scribbling furiously. The photographer from the *Washington Post* takes a picture of Bodine on the stage, his jaw slack and sweat on his upper lip. "Tom, you're scaring these men unnecessarily," Bodine says. "This is about equal wages, not the merchants' shipping practices. And this thing with the containers . . . it's out of our control."

The room goes silent a moment, the men made painfully

aware of their precarious situation, the fact that their leader can't protect them, not really.

Jay looks at his watch. He's hot and ready to go home. He hasn't seen the man from the black Ford, nor has Darren Hayworth seen the man who orchestrated his beating; there is no way of knowing if they're the same person. He could stay here all night, listening to the rhetoric being lobbed back and forth, but again, this is not his fight. By about a quarter after nine, they start passing the ballots around, even while people are still talking and arguing. A team of union officers passes around shoe boxes full of mismatched ink pens. There are two voting booths on the right side of the room, in front of the stage. A line quickly forms. Bodine, onstage, says he'll hear from just one more speaker. He calls on a young black man who says he can't worry about containers and machines and what's gon' happen in five years. He needs a good wage . . . right now.

Jay tells Darren he'll be in touch. The kid nods, grabbing a ballot and a Bic pen from a passing shoe box. Jay turns and leaves the hall alone. Out front, most of the reporters are at the pay phones. Jay hears the words "economic crisis," "a blow to Houston's golden age," even one man asserting that "there's no way they'll vote to strike." Jay lights a cigarette and waits for a guy from the *Post* to finish up a call. When the phone is finally free, he dials over to Evelyn's place.

"She's not here," Evelyn says, right off the bat.

"What?"

"Johnny drove her home, 'bout an hour ago."

Johnny Noland is Evelyn's on-and-off-again boyfriend.

"I told B I was picking her up," Jay says.

"Well, I guess she didn't feel like waiting around. And Johnny was looking for any excuse to get out of here."

Jay can hear the television going in the background.

"She got home okay?"

"I'm sure," she says.

"She call you?"

"I'm sure she's fine."

Jay sighs. He can feel himself starting to sweat again.

"Look, Johnny ain't right about a lot of things, but he wouldn't just leave her out on the curb," Evelyn says. "I'm sure he saw her to the door."

"Right."

"What you so testy about anyway?" He can hear her sipping at something on the other end, ice cubes clinking against glass. "Bernadine told me you broke into your own house. You not running some kind of insurance scam, are you? Don't you get my baby girl in trouble now." She takes another sip of whatever it is she's drinking, sucking an ice cube into her lonely mouth and rolling it around. It occurs to Jay that she is quite possibly drunk.

"Good night, Evelyn."

He hangs up the phone, fishes another dime out of his pocket, and dials home. When his wife picks up, she's short of breath and in a sour mood. "Where's that white fan, the little plastic one you brought home from the office?"

"It's in the hall closet," he says, relieved to hear her voice. "Don't fool with it. I'll get it down when I come home." He bites at the meat of his thumb. "You all right, then?"

"I'm eight months' pregnant, Jay," she says. "I had the air conditioner on an hour before I saw you'd left it set to eighty degrees. I tell you every time, it costs more money to cool the place down than if you just left it at seventy-six the whole time. It's like an oven in here."

"I won't touch it again, I promise." He smiles.

The men are starting to trickle out of the meeting, in twos and threes, their heads down, caps pulled low over their brows. Jay can't read their faces, only their sluggish gaits, the heavy sense that something solemn passed through this hall tonight. Bernie practically reads his mind. "They gon' strike, Jay?"

"I don't know, baby," Jay says into the phone. "I don't know."

He checks the rearview mirror a few times on the way home, but there's no one on his tail tonight, and he feels a familiar sense of relief at the end of a long summer day, the bright white sun safely tucked in for the night and the black air around him cool enough to breathe. He cuts the AC to save on gas and rolls down both his windows, leaning across the front seat to reach the one on the passenger side. The air is soupy, fogging up the windshield. Jay wipes at the inside of the glass with the palm of his hand. Then he turns up the radio.

On 1430 AM, there's a gal on the line making a breathy late-night confession. Wash Allen is holding all other calls, trying to talk her through it. "I know you got something to say now. Old Wash is right here. I'm listening."

"I don't know if I can tell it," the girl says. She's young, maybe eighteen. There's a jump and shake in her voice, like she can't sit still, like a kid who's had to pee for an hour. Finally, she spills it, a sordid story about messing around with her mother's boyfriend, a man twice her age. They planned to tell her mother a dozen times, but never got around to it. "It just never seemed the right time." And now, without saying a word to her about it, "That man gone and asked my mama to marry him." She starts crying. "I just don't know what to do." Should she confess to her mother or take it to the grave, facing every Christmas and Fourth of July and Juneteenth picnic in the foreseeable future knowing where that man has put his hands?

At first, Wash is kind of on her side, making a point that the man ought to have known better, that he had no business foolin' with a kid, a girl as young and impressionable as this one quivering on the line. "He's a snake, Wash, he is," she says. "I told him we got to tell Mama, we *got* to. And he saying if I do, he gon' tell my husband what I been up to, clubs I be hitting when he's out of town."

"Wait a minute. You're married?" Wash asks.

Jay turns up the volume.

"You ain't tell the people that part. How old are you, girl?"

"I'll be thirty come October."

"Oh, Looo-rrd!" Wash whistles into his microphone.

The phone lines are lit up for this one. The first caller to get through is a cat calling himself Mellow Yellow. "That girl gon' have to clean this mess up herself," he says. "She married and grown. She oughta known better."

"Yeah, Wash, this is Smokey here. And it's not all that girl's fault. Her mama need to look at what *she* ain't been doing to hold on to her man."

"You see, Wash, you see how they do us?" the next caller asks, a woman, a frequent caller named Sunshine. "The men always putting it on us."

And on and on they go, one call after another, turning this gal's very personal, very particular problem into a forum for all manner of grievances men and women have against each other. Before long, the conversation descends into talk about how cheap black men are. To which one caller replies, "Y'all ladies got better jobs than us half the time, shoot. Y'all oughta pay sometime too."

Wash goes to commercial break, playing a Betty Wright song as the out.

Jay is a couple of blocks from home when the DJ comes back

on the air, claiming to have the girl's lover and future stepfather on the line.

Jay parks in the alley behind his apartment building.

On the radio, Dark 'n' Lovely tells the old man to keep his thing in his pants, to leave the girl and her mother alone.

Solid Gold takes the men's side, turning on her fellow sister, saying gals like that "give the rest of us a bad name."

Colt 45 wants to know who was better in the sack. The future stepfather says Mom's got some skills, "but twenty-nine-year-old hips are hard to beat."

Jay snaps off the radio. He sucks his Newport down to the head, then tosses it out the window, catching a glimpse of something moving in his side-view mirror; it's just a flash, gone before it even registers. He looks out the window, down the length of the south side of the alley, but doesn't see anything unusual. He checks in the other direction. Beyond the lone bulb on the back side of his building, the alley is dark. From his vantage point, nothing seems out of the ordinary. Not the trash Dumpsters or the broken TV that's been there for weeks or Mr. Johnson's Pontiac. Jay rolls up the driver-side window. Then he leans across the front seat, reaching for the window handle on the passenger side.

A hand, pale and hairy, reaches into the car, pressing down on the glass.

Jay stops cold. He looks up and sees a man standing on the other side of the passenger door, a man in his late forties probably, hair cropped close on the sides. He's wearing a white button-down and a sports coat, the start of tomorrow's beard growing at this late hour. He lifts his pinky finger up and down, tapping the glass with a rather large gold ring. "I want to talk to you."

He's not dressed like the longshoremen Jay came across tonight, or any he's ever seen, frankly, and the thought flashes across his mind: this guy *is* a cop.

Jay clears his throat. "You want to tell me what this is regarding?"

The man looks up and down the alley, then leans his impressive torso inside the car. Jay can smell liquor on his breath, scotch probably, and the faint hint of tobacco and mint. "I'd rather we get someplace private," he says.

"You got some identification on you . . . sir?" Jay asks.

The man from the black Ford smiles. "Sure."

He stands tall then, pulling back the side of his sports coat, revealing a holstered pistol, a .45 as far as Jay can tell. He makes sure Jay gets a good look at it, that he's made himself perfectly clear: this is all the identification he needs.

Jay feels his stomach sink. This is dirty.

Nothing about this feels right. The fancy threads, the gold ring, the scotch. "You're not a cop . . . are you?"

The man shakes his head.

Jay makes a dash for the .38 in his glove compartment. He barely gets a hand on the weapon before the man from the black Ford cocks his .45. It's a horrible sound, sharp and threatening. The power of the gesture pushes Jay back in his seat. "Don't be stupid," the man says. "I just want to talk to you."

He keeps the gun on Jay and nods for him to get out of the car.

"Not here," Jay says, almost a whisper. "Not in front of my wife."

The man from the black Ford runs his hand along the inside of the door. He unlocks it, then opens the car door and slides in next to Jay. He props a foot against the glove compartment. Boots, Jay notices. Alligator, with gold stitching.

"Drive," he says.

Jay holds his hand over the key in the ignition. He thinks of his wife in the apartment upstairs, above them. He thinks of his baby. And he has a sudden, overwhelming desire to do whatever this man asks, whatever keeps Jay alive and unharmed from this moment to the next. He pulls out of his parking space.

"You know, I could drive this car straight to a police station," he says.

The man from the black Ford settles into the torn fabric of the passenger seat. "I got a nickel-plated twenty-two in my possession says you probably won't."

Jay remembers his stolen gun, the one missing from his bedroom.

An unlicensed weapon with his fingerprints all over it.

It's the final clink in the trap.

"Where are we going?" Jay asks.

"Just drive."

Part II

Chapter 13

He has Jay pull into an abandoned rail yard, instructing him to park on the tracks, across from a busted-out trailer with broken windows and a missing door. Jay does as he's told, then places his hands, clearly visible, on top of the steering wheel, awaiting further instruction. The man in the passenger seat reaches for Jay's car keys. He kills the engine. In the silence that follows, Jay hears the man's heavy, even breath and the almost musical jingle of metal on metal as he slides Jay's keys into the pocket of his sports coat.

Jay is careful not to move. The mouth of the gun is still pointed in his direction. His captor shifts several times in his seat. Out of the corner of his eye, Jay sees him reaching underneath his sports coat for something in his waistband.

It's a large manila envelope folded in half.

The man lays it on top of the dashboard, motioning for Jay to pick it up, which Jay is not the least bit eager to do. The man in the passenger seat fishes a cigarette out of his coat pocket, his hand still on the .45. He pops in Jay's car lighter and once more motions for Jay to pick up the envelope, which Jay, finally and reluctantly, does. He's surprised by the weight of it, like a brick in his hands.

"Open it," the man says.

The car lighter pops out. Jay jumps in his seat.

The man smiles, enjoying this. He lights the cigarette. "Open it."

Jay unfolds the envelope in the darkened car, fumbling with the fastener. Inside, he sees stacks and stacks of one-hundred-dollar bills, each bound neatly by a rubber band. "It's yours," the man says. "Twenty-five."

Jay stares at the pile of money in his lap.

"Thousand," the man adds, as if he needed to clarify.

It's more money than Jay made last year, more than he's ever held in his hands at one time. He feels light-headed at the thought.

"What is this?"

"Consider it a business proposition, an exchange of sorts," the man says. "The money is for your . . . discretion."

Somewhere in the distance, Jay imagines he hears the rumble of a freight train. He glances over the man's shoulder, out the window and down the long length of railroad tracks. He wonders if this is still a working line.

To the stranger, he says, "I'm not sure I follow you."

The man shifts in his seat, refreshing his grip on the gun. He sighs, as if he's searching for the right words, the right way to put this. "August first," he starts, looking at Jay. He pauses then, waiting for Jay to catch up.

August first, Jay thinks, the night of Bernie's birthday.

"You didn't see anything, understand?" the man says, lifting the gun slightly. "You follow me now?"

"I think I do."

"Good," the man says. "The money is just a show of my appreciation."

"I can't take this," Jay says. He folds the envelope in half and lays it back on the dashboard. "I don't want it."

The man from the black Ford laughs.

Again, Jay is sure he hears the rumble of a train on the tracks.

"Twenty-five thousand dollars is a lot of money, Mr. Porter," the man says. "But I suppose if I have some show of good faith from you, if I find I can trust you, I suppose there might be more down the line."

"I'm not *negotiating*," Jay says. "I don't want the money."

His voice cracks on the last word, a sour note hit so strongly that it echoes inside the car. It betrays a feeling he didn't know was there. How good the money felt, the weight of it in his lap, nestled so securely there.

"Who are you?" he asks.

"Not important."

"Why should I go along with this, I don't even know who I'm talking to?"

"I think the *why* is fairly obvious," the man says, gun still in hand.

Over the man's shoulder, Jay can see a pinpoint of light down the tracks, maybe a half a mile in the distance. It could mean only one thing: a train coming.

Jay holds out his hand. "Give me the keys."

"I need some assurance that I've been heard here," the man says. "Do we have an agreement, Mr. Porter?"

"Give me the keys now!"

"Relax, Jay. I'm not trying to hurt you. I believe this is a solution that benefits you greatly. You could have gone to the police already. But I know for a fact that you haven't. I'm offering to pay you to stay out of something you don't want to be involved in anyway. I'm not sure I see what the problem is."

The train is coming from the northeast, headed right in their direction. Still only a light in the distance. There's still time. Jay puts his hand on the door handle. He pulls the lever, ready to jump. The man in the passenger seat grabs his arm, twisting the skin, making it burn. "Do we understand each other?"

The light of the train is growing brighter by the second, coming closer.

Jay tries to reason with the man. "If the cops were to ask me anything—"

"They won't," the man says. He doesn't even flinch at the roar over his shoulder, the vibration on the tracks.

"How can you be so sure?" Jay asks.

"I wouldn't propose a deal to you, Mr. Porter, if I didn't have my end of it squared away. Your part is simply to keep your mouth shut."

She must have told him about the boat, Jay realizes.

She must have told him everything: the late-night rescue, Jay and his wife out on the water. He wonders if the guy posed as a cop . . . and thinks how easy it would have been to get Jay's name and address from the boat's captain.

My God, he thinks, suddenly remembering the car accident. He gets a sickening image of Jimmy's cousin lying in a ditch, his body twisted in the wreckage. Jay's legs go stiff and heavy. He's almost paralyzed by the realization of the true danger he's in, at the mercy of the armed man sitting next to him. He manages to speak, his voice low and etched with fear, the words a near whisper.

"The captain from the boat?"

"I offered him the same deal," the man from the black Ford says with unnatural repose. "But I didn't feel I could trust him . . . not to my satisfaction, at least." He takes a puff on his smoke. "So we worked out another arrangement."

"He's dead."

The man gives Jay an affable smile, as if he's only trying to be helpful, considerate even. "Take the money, Mr. Porter, buy your wife something nice."

Jay goes hot at the mention of his wife. "Leave her out of this."

"I don't want to see anyone hurt, I really don't, Mr. Porter. You and Mrs. Porter are the only two people who know what happened that night . . . and I'd like to keep it that way. You keep your mouth shut and everybody wins."

"Where's my gun?" Jay asks, remembering his missing .22.

"I'm going to hold on to that," the man says. "For a little insurance."

"Where is it?"

"Don't worry. I plan to keep it safe. I'd hate to see it get in the wrong hands. I wouldn't want the police to get the idea that you've got something to hide about the shooting or that, God forbid, you were in any way involved."

The threat lands across Jay's chest with an unbearable heaviness. The air in the car is thick with smoke and musk. The light of the locomotive is a perfect circle now, just over the man's right ear. A few hundred more yards and it's a bullet or the train. Jay has to decide.

"And if I don't take the money?"

The man shrugs. "Shame to see it go to waste."

He looks over his shoulder, as if he's just noticed the train for the first time. "Either way," the man says, "if anything goes wrong with our agreement, you can bet I'll be in touch." He reaches into his right pocket for Jay's car keys, dropping them on the dashboard, right on top of the manila envelope.

He opens the car door and is gone in a flash, jumping across the tracks, leaving Jay alone with the train and the money.

The white light of the train's front car has encircled the Buick, burning across Jay's face. His arms are leaden with terror, his fingers numb and thick. He fumbles with his car keys, nearly dropping them before he manages to get them in the ignition. The train sounds a horn, a shrill warning. Jay makes a quick decision to dump his car and save only his life. He pushes open the driver-side door, moments from the greatest leap of his life.

But he can't bring himself to leave the money behind.

He glances back at the envelope on the dashboard and makes a quick grab for the money, pulling the envelope by a corner. It unfolds in the middle, sending the money, stacks of $100 bills, spilling across the floor of his car and rolling underneath his seat. Jay feels along the carpeted floor for the money. He looks up at the coming train and makes an impulsive decision to start the car. The engine coughs and starts on the first try, an unimaginable blessing. Jay throws the Buick in reverse, backing it over the tracks at fifty miles an hour, getting only a few feet to safety before the train rumbles past, shaking Jay's car like a leaf in a late-summer storm.

He's halfway home before he stops the car, pulling into the parking lot of an all-night food mart. There are two brothers sitting on milk crates out front, one of 'em shaking something in his hand that Jay takes for dice. His heart still racing, Jay locks the doors, then bends over to scoop up the money. He stuffs it back into the envelope, fastening the clasp, folding it over again in half.

He knows he can't keep it. But he can't bring himself to get rid of it either. In this envelope is Jay's first house. A down payment, maybe, with money left over to pay off his car and the loan he took out to start his practice. In this envelope is a front yard for his baby and money so Bernie won't have to go back to work in a couple of months. It's a way out of the tight spot he's in. All just for keeping his mouth shut . . . which, hell, he was planning to do anyway.

But it's a fool's dream, he knows.

There's no way he can spend this money.

Or turn it over to the cops.

Like it or not, he's stuck with $25,000.

He's too skittish to stash the money in the apartment.

So he buries it in the trunk of his car, beneath a box of legal pads. Then he covers the whole thing with a rusted tire iron and dirty oil rags and walks up the back stairs into the apartment, where his wife is so caught up in a late-night showing of *Cooley High* on channel 11 that she does not seem the least bit concerned about where he's been for the last hour and a half. On the couch, she lifts her lips to meet his when he says hello, but never takes her eyes off the television screen, never gets a good look at the fear on her husband's face. Jay walks alone down their narrow hallway to the bathroom. Inside, he locks the door. He lifts the porcelain lid to the toilet's tank, laying its heavy weight up against the bathroom door. Inside the tepid water, he keeps a pint of Ezra Brooks whiskey. He stands over the sink, the cap to the liquor bottle rolling around the mouth of the drain, and finishes the bottle in two clean swallows.

He catches a startling glimpse of himself in the mirror. His tawny skin has gone a flat, ashy gray. His eyes are red-rimmed and veiny, and the cut on his cheek has left an unsightly mark.

He fingers the ugly scab, thinking of the new wounds that have opened up tonight, the new questions . . . about the money in his trunk, the man from the black Ford, and the woman on the boat.

Her face comes to him at once. Almond-shaped and pale, eyes dark like her hair. He remembers the way she looked at him on the boat—her fear, which Jay now realizes he misread at first. His own racialized disposition, his sensitive, almost exquisite sense of the world as black and white, mistook her fear as a fear of *him*—a fear that he might snatch her purse or pull her hair or harm her in some way. But he had missed the whole picture, the subtle shade of gray. She was not afraid of him because he was black or even a man . . . but because something in his countenance that night must have told her that he was not convinced, even then, that she was a damsel in distress. What he saw that night was a woman on the wrong side of town at the wrong hour and for all the wrong reasons. And whatever this woman's secrets, she's apparently willing to kill for them.

But he still doesn't know who she is.

Since that first bit in the paper, there has been nothing else mentioned in either of the city's two major newspapers about a white male, shot twice, in Fifth Ward. There has been no mention of an arrest made in the case or even a suspect the cops might be talking to. Jay doesn't know what this woman may have already told the police about *him*. For all he knows, they could have been watching him tonight . . . watching him take an envelope full of cash, what could easily look like payment for something else; the man from the black Ford said he could make it look as if Jay had something to do with the shooting.

He can't help feeling that this whole thing is a setup, the money nothing but bait. But why, he thinks, would anyone want to trap *him?* His whole life he's made no enemies he can think of . . . save for the U.S. government, of course.

The thought is like a hand grenade tossed under his bathroom door.

He watches it roll across the floor, taking up position at his feet.

The blow, when it comes, takes his breath away.

He has a sudden, sharp memory of Charlie Wade Robinson, a Panther out of Detroit, Michigan. Back in '69, the feds tried to nail him on a charge of conspiracy to commit mayhem and engage in unlawful assembly, which one progressive judge promptly threw out of his court. When the feds couldn't get Charlie Wade on that, they tried to put him away on an illegal weapons charge. But he dodged that bullet too. Two years ago, the way Jay heard it, Charlie Wade Robinson was coming out of a McDonald's restaurant in Atlanta, Georgia, his six-year-old daughter in tow, when federal officers arrested him on felony tax evasion, right there in the parking lot. Long out of the politics game by then, Charlie Wade had started an arcade business with an investor he'd met at a party, and the IRS claimed they'd played fast and loose with the accounting. The feds had finally found a charge that would stick. He's been locked up ever since.

Same thing happened to a Natalia Greenwood, out of Clarksville, Mississippi. She cut her teeth during Freedom Summer in '64, and went on to Washington with Fannie Lou Hamer and the Mississippi Freedom Democratic Party later that year. When they wouldn't let the folks from the MFDP vote at the Democratic convention, Natalia Greenwood turned radical. She started talking about taking up arms 'round about the time the Deacons for Defense were getting going in Bogalusa, Louisiana, long before the Panthers. She was rumored to have an FBI file two inches thick. She was arrested several times, for crimes as serious as conspiracy to overthrow the United States government and as petty as not paying her phone bill. But she was never actually charged with anything in court. Except in 1978. She followed a girlfriend into the bathroom of a Manhattan disco and was arrested along with half a dozen other women who were doing lines on the countertop. For a cocaine-possession charge, Natalia Greenwood spent two years in lockup and the state took away her kids.

The names and faces come back to him:

Lionel Jessup, Camille Bodelle, Ronnie Powell, M. J. Frank, Carl Petersen.

Men and women who fought on the front lines for what they believed in and were labeled radicals, had their lives threatened on a daily basis, and somehow managed to escape the reach of the federal government in their prime . . . but who now, in their thirties and forties, suddenly find themselves in trouble with the law again, arrested and locked away in jail.

They were fools back then, Jay thinks. Young and naive to believe they could raise voices and guns against a superpower and get away with it. Weren't they always meant to pay . . . someday, some way? Hasn't he, deep down, been waiting for this very moment? The day when they would come for him again?

He wakes up hours later, mouth dry, his head a throbbing mess.

In the light of a new day, he tries to rein in his paranoia.

After all, Hoover dropped dead in '72; COINTELPRO had been officially discontinued the year before. Jay had his day in court, and they let him go home. That was the end of it. This is a different time, he tells himself; it's only your mind that can't move out of the prison of its past.

It's all in your head, man.

Nobody was watching him tonight.

The man from the black Ford made sure of it. He had Jay drive out to an abandoned rail yard, didn't he? A place surrounded by empty fields?

But, of course, this does nothing to put Jay at ease.

The facts of this story, the last twenty-four hours of his life, are laid out before him like the disparate pieces of his broken phone, pieces that don't line up neatly or make any sense together: a man hands him a stash of cash to keep his mouth shut about a murder he didn't actually witness. This is dirty, any way you look at it.

The strike made the front page, headline news.

Above the fold is a report on the vote last night and speculation about the outcome. An inside spread in the *Post* has a collection of quotes from local business leaders and oil company honchos, all espousing various doomsday scenarios, describing what a devastating blow a strike would be to the local and national economies. AM talk radio is hot on the news too, people calling in panicked. Things have been so good in Houston for so long—oil companies getting rich, setting the tone and pace for the rest of the economy; people coming from all over the country to get in on the action; hell, *New York* magazine did a piece in '80 calling Houston the city to beat—that a lot of people in the city can't remember when things were any different. On 740, there's a woman caller who works in human resources at C & C Petrochemicals, a Cole Oil Industries subsidiary that makes plastics and other synthetic goods from oil waste. She was still in high school during the crisis in '73, she says, but the other girls in her office remember they laid off several hundred people back then.

Jay snaps off the radio when Bernie pads out of the bathroom. She's moving more and more slowly these days. He can't tell if it's the pregnancy or the heat, or both. He tells her not to fool with his breakfast this morning. He wants to get into the office early. The idea is to get there well ahead of Eddie Mae, but he does not tell his wife that. Instead, he offers to fix her something quick on his way out, scrambled eggs or toast. But she's already in bed, halfway back to sleep by the time he gets his shoes on.

Outside, he checks the trunk of his car, checks to make sure the money is still there. Satisfied, he slams the trunk closed, looking both ways up and down the alley behind his building, checking over his shoulder for nosy neighbors. He doesn't want a soul to know what he has in his possession. Finally, he slides into his car and heads for work, watching for a black Ford in his rear window.

Traffic is heavier than normal at this hour. Every gas station he passes has at least three cars waiting at each pump, some lines spilling into the street. One man at a Gulf station on Almeda is filling up gas cans, loading them into the back of his truck. It's a sight Jay hasn't seen in years, people hoarding oil, scared there won't be enough. He cannot believe all the hubbub over a small number of men asking for a better wage, the way this thing is reverberating across the city, like an echo across a valley, where a small whistle can make a very big noise.

Jay keeps a lockbox for petty cash underneath his desk. Only $23,400 fits inside. Until he can think of something better, he pockets the rest of it. Eight hundred rolled up in each of his pants pockets, held tight by two rubber bands from his desk drawer. He secures the lockbox with a key, then hides the money in the bottom of a filing cabinet. Then he picks up the telephone on his desk, purposely not thinking this through, not even completely sure he can go through with it. He cradles the receiver against his shoulder and dials the mayor's office. And just as calm as if he does it every day, he asks to speak to Cindy.

Chapter 14

The name gets him past the mayor's secretary. She puts him on hold for what seems like an hour but by his desk clock is really only four and a half minutes. When the mayor comes on the line, her voice is so abrupt, so coarse and loud, that it actually startles him. "I can't do this right now, Jay. I have a meeting at eight o'clock. The port commissioners, Pat Bodine from the ILA, some of the OCAW boys, the stevedores . . . they're all coming *here*," she says, sounding very much like a harried housewife who's still got curlers in her hair and dirty dishes in the sink less than an hour before her guests are set to arrive.

"Thomas and Patrick Cole just walked over here from across the street," she says. "They've been waiting outside my door for the last twenty minutes. And now OPA's saying they want in on this meeting." The Oil Producers Alliance, a group of local refinery owners, is one more lobbying group pulling at the mayor's attention. "They sent the Cole brothers as their representation. The *Cole* brothers, Jay," she says, drawing out what is universally considered the most powerful name in the city of Houston. The Cole brothers—Patrick, John, and Thomas—run the largest industrial complex in the city and one of the largest corporations in the entire country. "This whole thing has blown way out of control," Cynthia says. "This is between the stevedores and dockworkers, nobody else. I don't know what the hell everybody expects me to do about it."

All of this is beside the point. Jay doesn't give a shit about the strike.

"Cynthia," he breaks in.

"Look," she says quickly. "I know I said I'd help you with this thing, that boy getting beat up and all, but this just isn't the time to be pointing fingers. Let's stop this walkout before it starts, and then we'll get on the other matter."

"I need a favor," he says, stopping her. "No questions asked."

There is a long, flat silence on the other end.

"I'm cashing in my chip," Jay says. "After this, we're even."

Cynthia is silent, her breath completely still. She's bracing herself, it seems, as if she's been expecting this moment for a long, long time. Finally, she speaks, softly, almost timidly. "Jay," she says. "There's something I need to say to you."

"Not now." He's not prepared to hear a confession now. "Just do this for me," he says.

"What is it?"

"On the right-hand corner of your desk, there's a stack of papers." He waits for her to find it. On the other end of the line, he hears a rustling of papers, then stillness. He imagines her with the pages in her hand, trying to follow him, to guess what this is all about. "Okay," she says. "I think I've got it."

"The police briefings. Yes?"

"Jay, what is this about?"

"August third," he says. "It was a Monday. Whatever you got from the chief's office that morning would have made mention of activity over the weekend. I'm looking for a homicide. White male, gunshots. They found a body in an open field by the bayou, on the south edge of Fifth Ward."

"I remember that one."

"Okay, then," Jay says. "I want you to tell me everything they told you."

There is no reply, no shuffling of papers, no searching for the right page, nothing to suggest an easy and immediate granting of his request.

"Cynthia?" he says.

"Kip, could you step out for just a second?" Her voice is muted, as if she's got her hand over the receiver. Jay had no idea she wasn't alone. "Tell them we'll get started in a minute," she says to her assistant. Then, waiting until Kip is well out of earshot, she says to Jay, "What the hell is going on?"

"Just tell me what they told you."

"Why?"

"No questions, remember?"

"Are *you* representing the girl?"

He assumes she means the woman from the boat.

"I need her name," he says. He wants to know who he's dealing with.

"Why?" She sounds worried now, or just plain confused.

"I can't answer that question."

"Well, I can't *give* you this report, Jay. It's sensitive information."

"Not asking you to give it to me. Just tell me what's in it."

She lets out a sigh. "I can't do that."

"No one will hear a word from me about it. I won't tell a soul we talked."

"It's an ongoing investigation. The police let me in on it just as a courtesy. This is not my information to share. Not even the press have this—"

"I'm asking you for a favor, Cynthia. This is between me and you." He plays the one card he's got. "I think you know you can trust me."

For a moment, he hears nothing on the other end.

When Cynthia's voice returns, it's cold and flat.

"Her name is Elise Linsey."

Jay reaches for a slip of paper on his desk. "Who is she?"

"I don't know anything but her name."

"You have an address?" he asks.

"No."

"Date of birth?"

"No."

"They arrest her?"

"I don't know," she says. "But I doubt it."

"Why?"

"Evidence was light."

"What'd they have?"

"A body," she says. "And fingerprints in his car. That's it."

"*Her* fingerprints?" Jay asks.

"That's what it says."

"What about the body, the dead guy? You got a name for him?"

"They're not releasing it, not even to me."

"So that's all you have?"

"White male, shot twice," she says bluntly. "They found two

bullets, one outside the car, the other in his skull, both twenty-two caliber."

"Let me guess," he says. "They haven't found a gun."

"No."

The murder weapon is a .22, just like his missing gun.

"Oh, God."

"Jay," Cynthia says. "Do I want to know what this is about?"

He has a moment's thought of telling her about Jimmy's cousin and the car accident that killed him, what Jay now knows was probably murder. She could take the information to the police, start an investigation for the man's family. But he's afraid of what leaking the information would do to him or his wife, so he keeps it to himself. He underlines the name *elise linsey* on the paper in front of him, pressing so hard that the pencil lead snaps. "I appreciate this, Cynthia."

"Jay?"

He hangs up the phone.

There's an E. Liddie in the phone book.

An E. Linney.

An E. Linnwood.

And at the bottom of the page, his finger practically pressed on top of it, there's an E. Linsey: 14475 Oakwood Glen, phone number not listed. Jay writes the address on the back of a cease-and-desist order he's been drafting. There's a street map on top of the phone books Eddie Mae keeps under her desk. Using the index, he tries to find Oakwood Glen. By the name, it's no surprise that it's located on the west side of town, home to dozens of new housing developments and subdivisions, each one full of Oaks and Glens and Hills and Estates.

The front door opens, and Eddie Mae blows into the office,

bringing a warm gust of August air behind her, thick and moist and laced with the burnt smell of engine exhaust from the parking lot. Her wig is a caramel-colored number full of ringlets that don't suit her face or age. And it's crooked on one side. She's wearing sunglasses and no makeup and blowing hot air about her current boyfriend and his long list of shortcomings, starting with a fight they had at six o'clock this morning, carried over from the night before. From what Jay can gather, it had something to do with a dominoes game and a missing six-pack of beer. Jay butts into her rant long enough to tell her he's stepping out for a while and doesn't know when he'll be back. She waves him off, still running down her boyfriend, muttering on about his crusty feet and tuna fish breath.

Jay takes his time heading west, circling the streets around his office building until he feels certain he's not being followed. Then he makes his way to Memorial Drive, watching the landscape change before his eyes with every westward mile. He drives past furriers and diamond retailers in the Galleria shopping district and four-star restaurants off Post Oak Boulevard, into a plush residential community of newly constructed homes. One hundred years ago, this would have been logging territory. Developers have since tamed the area into a forest of subdivisions and planned communities. Memorial Drive is dotted with large, elaborately decorated signs, each enshrined in lush landscaping, announcing the entrance to one private housing community after another: Plantation Oaks and Pecan Grove Estates and Briar Meadows and Maplewood Glens.

According to the street map, he's to turn right on Wilcrest, a few miles past Town & Country mall, then make another right on a street called Autumn Oaks Lane. Here he finds the entrance to Oakwood Estates. Oakwood Glen runs down the center of the subdivision, lined on both sides with town houses made up to look like stately French Tudors. The street is wide and freshly paved, and there are newly planted pin oak trees in each yard; they are tiny and childlike, like something borrowed from a toy train depot. There's not a stitch of shade to be found in the whole subdivision. Jay squints against the sun, checking house numbers through his windshield.

The fourth town house on the right-hand side is 14475.

From the car, Jay studies the front windows of Elise Linsey's home, looking for some sign of activity. He has no idea if anyone is home or what exactly he'll say when the door opens, when he sees her face again. He checks his side mirrors before getting out of the car. There are few vehicles on the street at this hour. Oakwood Estates is quiet and still. Jay climbs out of the Skylark.

At the front door, he rings the bell twice. But there's no answer.

He waits a good five minutes before trying again.

There are four or five newspapers, Jay notices, still wrapped in plastic, stacked neatly inside the door frame, along with grocery store circulars and an advertisement for something called "cable television," all neat and tidy, as if someone left them there on purpose—either the occupant of the town house or a neighbor who knows she's been away for a while. Jay pokes through the contents of the mailbox, which is overflowing with dozens of envelopes that haven't been touched. It seems that Elise Linsey hasn't been here for days.

Jay tries the doorknob. It's locked.

He tries the bell a third time.

He crosses the front lawn next and kneels in front of one of the windows, behind a low-lying bush of jasmine, making himself less visible from the street. With the glare of the sun behind him, Jay can't make out much inside the town house beyond a vague sense of disarray. It appears that some of the furniture has been turned upside down. The sight gives him a start. He backs away from the window suddenly, almost losing his balance in the tangle of jasmine at his feet. He walks back to Elise's front door, not sure of his next move. It's only when he turns, deciding finally to head back to his car, that his left foot skids across a piece of paper he didn't notice before, sticking out of the welcome mat.

The paper is folded in half with Elise's name scripted across one side, just above Jay's shoeprint. The note isn't sealed, nor does it bear a federal postmark, which makes him feel better about what he's about to do. Looking both ways up and down Oakwood Glen, he scoops up the piece of paper and unfolds it.

The note inside is handwritten, the penmanship flat and simple:

> I tried you by phone several times.
> I'm hoping we can sit down and talk.
>
> —LON PHILIPS

The paper was peeled off a preprinted notepad.

The words *Houston Chronicle* are engraved across the bottom of the page.

Jay folds the note in half, returning it to its spot beneath the welcome mat. He turns and stumbles back toward his car. The sun has hiked a few more miles into the sky. The day is moving into its worst hours, the midday boil. Jay slides behind the wheel of his car, thinking about the note from Lon Philips. If a reporter is getting this close, Jay thinks, then surely the cops are too. He thinks of the disarray inside the woman's town house—a possible break-in, yes, but just as likely a sign that police detectives have been through with a warrant; picking through every inch of the woman's home. The cops are looking for a .22, he remembers. And somewhere, out of Jay's control, there's a .22 with his fingerprints on it. He thinks of how incredibly easy it would be to plant *his* gun inside 14475 Oakwood Glen. He has a criminal arrest record, for God's sake.

He's sweating now, shirt clinging to his back, his legs on fire under the cheap poly blend of his suit. That he's an innocent man, as he was back then, all those years ago, is no real comfort. He knows cops and prosecutors have a natural talent for bending evidence, twisting the truth this way and that, all in the name of putting *somebody* behind bars.

Jay starts his car, keeping the AC as high as he can stand it, then he turns the car around, heading back the way he came, out of Oakwood Estates. He takes Memorial Drive into downtown, running through his phone call with Cynthia Maddox the whole way.

They found her fingerprints in the car. That's what she told him.

Fingerprints mean Elise Linsey has a criminal history. An arrest certainly, maybe even a trial. The county keeps a record of every criminal case before a judge, going back a hundred years, on file in a basement warehouse in the Criminal Courts Building. The clerks make you fill out an information request form with a case number if you have it, or at least the person's name, then they feed it into a computer terminal in the back office. A printout tells them the location of every trial transcript, sentencing order, or brief ever filed in relation to the case. It's all public information for those who know it's there.

The clerk's office is on the first floor of the building. Unlike the rest of the judicial facility, done up in stately marble and official-looking mahogany and brass, the clerk's office is a narrow, poorly ventilated room that always smells of paint and copier fluid. It strongly resembles the waiting room of a public clinic, with rows of plastic straight-back chairs and a take-a-number system of operations. There are three Plexiglas windows cut into the wall, behind which sit three women, one of whom—a busty black woman sipping soda out of a Del Taco cup at ten forty-five in the morning—Jay knows to be the office manager. There are only women in this office. They work with the radio on, greeting cards and family pictures tacked up on the walls. They chat breezily while they type and do paperwork, seemingly enjoying themselves, in no real hurry to get through the day. Jay has already been waiting for half an hour, his knee pumping up and down, keeping a nervous beat, one eye always on the door.

When his number is finally called, he walks straight to the middle window. The clerk behind the glass is in her forties, with a tiny face and big black hair fanned out like crow's wings. Her nameplate says M. RODRIGUEZ. She has a small fan on her desk, blowing right into her face, whipping up her wings, as if she's in the middle of a photo shoot instead of sitting behind Plexiglas in a government office. Jay hands her his information request form, most of which he left blank. She pulls a pen from an Astros mug on her desk.

"I'm not understanding this, baby," she says, popping gum.

"I'm looking for any and all cases in which this person was a defendant."

"Everything?"

"Everything."

"Okay," she says, nodding. "Name?"

"Elise Linsey. It's there."

She writes the name again, in her own, more legible handwriting.

"Date of birth?" she asks.

"I don't have it."

"Social Security number?"

"Don't have it."

"Race?" she asks.

"White."

She writes the word in big, block letters across the bottom of the page.

"Okay," she says. "But it's gonna take a while."

Jay glances in the manager's direction, making sure she can't hear what he's about to ask next. "You have access to arrest records, don't you?" He nods toward the mainframe behind M. Rodriguez, lowering his voice. "Sheriff's department and HPD . . . you guys have copies of their arrest files, right?"

"Yes."

"You think I could get a look at those? Arrest records for Elise Linsey?"

"Sure, long as you show me a piece of paper from a judge or a cop or somebody at the DA's office saying you got permission to 'get a look.' Otherwise, you gotta file a discovery motion." She gives him an admonishing look because she senses he knows better. Arrest records are absolutely *not* public information. "Look," she says, growing impatient. "Unless you have another request form for me, I'm going to have to get to the next one in line."

"Come to think of it," Jay says quickly. "I do have something else."

Before he got out of his car, he took a single $100 bill off the roll of $800 in his right-hand pocket. He folded the bill over several times, then, once in the waiting room, he wrapped it inside a blank Harris County criminal courts information request form. He now slides the form beneath the Plexiglas, watching as she unfolds the paper. The money springs open like a blooming flower. M. Rodriguez looks up at him, then back at the money, staring at it as if she doesn't immediately understand its meaning, its sudden appearance on her desk. She turns slowly, glancing in the direction of her boss, two windows down. Jay imagines she's about to call the manager over, that he has made a grave miscalculation. Then M. Rodriguez covers the money with her small hands, cupping her blossom. "I'll see what I can do," she says.

He's there another hour, eating lunch out of a vending machine in the hall. Funyuns and a can of orange pop. From a pay phone in the hall, he calls home twice to check on Bernie, making a point of asking both times if there've been any visitors, if anyone has stopped by the apartment unexpectedly, thinking specifically about the man from the black Ford and his promise to stay in touch. He checks in at the office next. Eddie Mae is on the other line with her boyfriend when he calls and she puts him on hold for almost ten minutes. She comes back on the line with a la-di-da, ain't-life-funny tone in her voice, announcing that she and Rutherford have made up. Jay asks about his messages.

The building manager called, wanting to know about the rent check.

The hooker called twice. "And she sounds pissed."

"What about Luckman? He call?"

"No."

So he's stalling, Jay thinks.

He wonders if the first offer is now completely off the table, if he should have grabbed it while he had the chance. He puts another dime in the machine and calls over to Charlie Luckman's office himself, only to be told that Mr. Luckman is with a new client on urgent business and can't be disturbed.

When Jay returns to the clerk's office, M. Rodriguez calls

him to her station. She taps on the glass, pointing him in the direction of an adjacent room. There's a carpeted hallway leading from the waiting area into a smaller reading room, painted the same shade of hospital green, fluorescent bulbs flickering overhead. M. Rodriguez emerges in the doorway a few minutes after Jay sits down. She's holding a stack of thin legal-size folders. They are the only two people in the room. "Return these to the office when you're done," she says, sliding the folders across the round table in the center of the room. Then, from inside her cropped blazer, M. Rodriguez pulls out a thick clump of papers, stapled together and folded in half down the center. "These you can keep."

Jay reaches for the arrest records. M. Rodriguez slaps her hand on top. "You didn't get it from me," she says. She bends over at the waist, making sure to catch his eye. "I've never done nothing like this before," she says. "It's for my kid, you know. I'm gonna get him something nice for once."

Jay shrugs. He doesn't give a shit. It's not his money.

When he lays it all out, page by page, the picture that develops does not in any way match the image he's been holding in his head. Beneath the story he told himself about the woman from the boat—what he gathered from her creamy complexion, the cut of her fancy clothes and jewelry—is a life laced with problems. With a criminal history going back almost ten years.

There are five trials for Elise Linsey, defendant, in 1976 alone. Two in '77.

According to the trial papers and sentencing orders, Elise Linsey, last known address West Eighth Street, Galena Park, Texas, did two six-month stints in County for writing hot checks; thirty days for marijuana possession; four months for cocaine possession and intent to sell; and ninety days for stealing headsets from a Radio Shack. The court gave her time served (two weeks) for a misdemeanor assault charge: she punched some guy she claimed was her boyfriend, and he never showed up to testify. Ms. Linsey was also on probation twice during this time period, both to settle charges of solicitation. In other words, prostitution.

The arrest record goes back even further, to 1972.

There are more charges of solicitation, theft, hot checks, plus trespassing and public intoxication. These are poor people's crimes, Jay knows, the stuff you find in the worst neighborhoods, places where people live on the edge of society, their lives frayed and their economic situations completely unstable.

What Jay finds most puzzling about this woman's life and her run-ins with the law is that it all stops—the trials, the arrests—sometime in the fall of 1980. Elise Linsey simply drops out of the system. Only to show up a year later in a town house on the west side, flush with jewelry and expensive clothes and, apparently, money to throw around. Jay hovers over the pages, trying to make sense of what he's reading. There's one question that keeps playing over and over in his mind, hammering away at him, making his head ache: how in the hell did she get from West Eighth Street in Galena Park—a marshy stretch of land a few hundred yards from the Ship Channel that smells of chemical waste and the salt of the Gulf—to Oakwood Estates? According to her birth date, printed on nearly every piece of paper in front of him, Elise Linsey is only twenty-four years old.

Chapter 15

That was their M.O. back in the day.

Find a kid with a boatload of problems, most especially problems of a criminal nature. Find a kid who's got nothing to lose. And cut him a deal.

Jay remembers how it was done.

In the late '60s and early '70s, there was a war going on, right here at home. It was initially a war of ideas, going back to the '30s. Civil rights as a commonsense argument: people are people, eat and shit the same, ought to be able to eat and shit in the same places. Then black folks got on voting, wanting something real, and law enforcement ratcheted up the violence, finding more and more creative ways to beat the shit out of people, publicly humiliate them and test their souls. The next generation coming up—Jay was only a kid when King organized the bus boycott in Montgomery, Alabama—wanted more than a lunch counter at which to eat, more than the right to vote for one knucklehead over another. They wanted true political power, not crumbs off a moldy piece of bread. They wanted the whole establishment turned on its head.

The federal government's response:

They used tax dollars to build a stealth army to take down these activists and agitators, who were mostly students, mostly kids. The FBI had plenty of young agents working COINTEL-PRO, their well-financed counterintelligence program, but the feds quickly discovered that academy-trained officers didn't always make the best moles, not for groups like SNCC or SDS, certainly not for infiltrating the Weather Underground or the Black Panthers (whom Hoover called "the greatest threat to the internal security of the country"). These groups were suspicious by nature, not likely to trust *any* outsiders. Given the chance, they probably would have burned the Trojan horse to the ground before they ever got around to seeing what was inside the thing. The FBI couldn't pull off their plan in-house, not convincingly at least. So they outsourced it, pulled in hired help for their elaborate hoax, the sting of all stings.

From Chicago's South Side to Detroit to East Oakland and Watts, to places as desolate as Fifth Ward, Houston, Texas, they pulled kids out of lineups and pool halls, pulled them off the streets and offered them a hand up, a way out of whatever legal or economic predicament they might have found themselves in. They paid these kids with promises—to make a felony assault charge go away or to knock a few years off a stay at Angola or San Quentin—paid them to learn the Panthers' ten-point program, to be able to recite Chairman Mao's *On Contradiction* backward and forward, to know their Marx from their Lenin. They paid them to blend in. And in return these spies provided the feds with precious information: the location of a secret meeting house, the date and time of a rally, phone rosters and floor plans, or where one might find an arsenal of illegal handguns. Sometimes the information provided was as simple as the physical location of a group's leader, the key ingredient to any successful raid.

Everybody knows that's how they got Fred Hampton.

December 4, 1969, 4:00 A.M. They shot him in his sleep.

The federal government called the raid on the headquarters of the Chicago chapter of the Black Panther Party a success, publicly praising the Chicago Police Department, their partners in crime, citing the officers' bravery in an extremely volatile situation—a house full of sleeping black folks, one of whom was eight months' pregnant. But they failed to mention their secret weapon, their secretest of secret agents—the young felon they had spying on Fred for weeks, the man who made Fred's last meal, lacing a glass of Kool-Aid with secobarbital, and quietly slipping out of the house long before the bullets started flying.

It was all a setup. And policy back then.

The federal government was essentially paying kids to kill kids.

Cynthia was the first one to point out Roger. "Something's wrong with that guy," she said one night, lying on her back in the sand. They had driven Cynthia's truck out to West Beach, in Galveston, where the seawall ended and the colored beach began, a place where heads would turn, surely, but no one was likely to call the police. They could be lovers in public and in peace.

The Dells were playing on a transistor radio resting on top of Jay's jacket, which was laid out like a blanket on the sand. The air was salty and soft, and warm for this time of year. It was March

1970, his senior year at U of H. Jay was propped up on his elbows next to Cynthia, broken conch shells digging into his flesh. The discomfort was nothing, though, compared to the quiet thrill of catching her in this moon-swept light, still and yielding. He held her hand.

The music played. *Stay in my corner . . . honey, I love you.*

The words he couldn't say on his own.

Cynthia sat up, stuffing the bulk of her prairie skirt between her legs, dusting sand off her ankles. She wanted to talk about Roger Holloway.

"He's all right," Jay offered.

There was another couple on the beach that night, their feet hanging out of the front seat of a baby blue Ford Fairlane that was parked across the sand. Jay could hear the woman laughing, high-pitched squeals that melted into the soft, wet air, sounding like wind chimes. He thought he could stay out here all night. He rested his chin on Cynthia's shoulder. She smelled like cloves.

"He come around Scott Street?" Cynthia asked, still on Roger.

"He wants to get more involved with the Africa thing."

"You know he was hanging around SDS last semester," Cynthia said.

She picked up his right hand and held it open like a seashell. She ran her fingers across the inside of his palm. "He asks a lot of questions. You ever notice that?" She looked up, staring at the shoreline, the salty caps doing a languid two-step, back, then forward, then back again. "That's all I'm saying."

Roger Holloway had indeed been coming around the duplex on Scott Street for months. He was a skinny kid they were always bumming smokes from, who always had extra change in his pocket if somebody was hungry. He said he'd dropped out of Prairie View A&M the year before, but Jay suspected he'd never spent a day inside a college classroom. Not that Prairie View was Harvard, but still, Roger seemed to lack some basic grasp of American history, the Constitution and the Bill of Rights. But he knew who Karl Marx was and claimed to read the *Workers World* newspaper. And he was hot on Africa. Which was Jay's baby, where he was finally finding his true political voice.

Years earlier, Jay had stumbled on his first sit-in on the way to class and decided then and there he'd rather be a part of history than study it. After that, there was no turning back for him. Once one dorm was integrated, they all had to be. Once one black professor was hired, there had to be a dozen more. He would settle for nothing less than total equality. Jay rode this initial wave of activism as a rank-and-file member of SNCC, the Student Nonviolent Coordinating Committee, which had a strong presence on campus and across the South. SNCC came out of the SCLC tradition, the Southern Christian Leadership Conference, Dr. King's group through the '50s and '60s. It was a tradition steeped in the assumption that moralism is a real and potent weapon, or the presumption, rather, that you could shame white people into acting right.

Well . . . that was one way of doing it.

But it required a kept tongue and an unyielding faith in a higher power, something Jay did not have. Much as he would go on to preach on the limits of a spiritual approach to civil rights, much as he would chide the churchified for taking it lying down, he always, deep down, admired men like King, for whom the ability to love was a gift, like an ear for music. Jay, on the other hand, lived a life of constant struggle against his own cynicism, his well-earned knowledge of the limits of human grace. To tell the truth of it, he was as angry with his stepfather as he was at any white man, and angrier at his own father for leaving him behind.

But it wasn't just Jay. A lot of the young people were getting tired of the we-shall-overcome way of attacking an increasingly complex problem. So in '67, Jay and Bumpy Williams, Lloyd Mackalvy and Marcus Dupri started meeting at Bumpy's mother's place on Scott Street. She was a night nurse at Ben Taub Hospital and rarely home. They named their organization Coalition for Better Race Relations and nicknamed it COBRA. They were still doing stuff with SNCC, but beyond the campus agenda, they worked within the local black community to help find decent housing for folks, get somebody's son a lawyer if he needed one, and they funded (Jay pointedly never asking Bumpy where the money came from) an after-school program at Yates High School.

Sometime in the late winter of that year, Bumpy got arrested for passing out flyers on Texas Southern University's campus. He was promoting a rally in support of two older gentlemen who'd been picked up for loitering while waiting at a bus stop on Dowling. Bumpy was booked on charges of trespassing and being an all-around public nuisance. It was Jay who came up with the idea for a march to the courthouse downtown. He walked the campus, going dorm to dorm, walked the neighborhood around the college until the soles of his feet bled, until he got nearly five hundred people to agree to march with him. They would meet on campus, cut up Wheeler to Main and walk in unity, storming the courthouse, not leaving until they got justice for Brother Williams and the two other men in lockup. He wrote the press release himself, stayed up typing all night, drinking black coffee and smoking cigarettes, listening to Otis Redding on his turntable.

They were at the courthouse almost seventy-two hours, a round-the-clock vigil. Jay didn't have a law degree then, but he knew enough to know the cops couldn't hold people indefinitely, not without a formal indictment. He got the *Post* and the *Chronicle* there, got his name and face in the paper. He made the mistake of sending the clipping to his mother in Nigton. She mailed it back about a week later with a note saying she'd raised him better and wasn't he due for a haircut. Still, Jay became something of a hero. Bumpy was released, and a few days later, they let the other two men go as well. COBRA was now a force to be reckoned with, getting more attention than the local SNCC chapter.

It was Jay Porter whom Stokely Carmichael, chairman of the national chapter of SNCC, called when he was coming through Texas for the first time. An antiwar rally was happening in Austin that April, and Stokely wanted to speak in Houston while he was visiting the state. All through that winter and spring, he'd been traveling the country, speaking on campuses or wherever he could get a hall, reworking and refining a position paper he was calling "Toward Black Liberation." The remarks, which Jay and his group had not yet heard (as no Houston paper would print them), were apparently so inflammatory that Carmichael was being blamed for riots all across the country. According to local police, wherever Stokely spoke, there was gon' be trouble.

Texas Southern, just a few minutes from the U of H campus, flat-out wouldn't have him. The University of Houston also said no. Jay simply ignored them. The night Stokely came through town, Cullen Auditorium was free. So that's where they held the rally . . . just went in and took it over. Word got around campus, and some three hundred people showed up, more than the hall could hold. They were spilling out into the hallway, onto the grass lawn outside. Some of them curious, wanting to be a part of *the* thing that everyone was talking about. But there was also a contingent of rebels—conservative white students who didn't want this loudmouth nigger on their campus—and they raised painted signs and fists to make it known. And just beyond the doors, in martial formation on the lawn outside the auditorium, were a hundred officers from the police and sheriff's departments, dressed from head to toe in riot gear.

It was after 9:00 P.M. by the time Stokely took the podium, after Bumpy and Marcus Dupri gave two fiery introductions. Some of the rebels had pushed their way to the front row. The air in the hall was muggy, thick with the breathy heat of anticipation, everyone waiting and wondering . . . just what was this brother gon' say? Stokely came onstage dressed clean as a whistle, in a pressed suit and thin black tie, not a wrinkle on him, and he was wearing shades, black and wide, like Ray Charles. Dude looked like the bass player for Booker T. and the MG's, like a blues philosopher. He leaned over the podium, into the mike, pushing his shades up on the bridge of his nose as if they were prescription glasses, as if their darkness helped him see things clearly.

Jay can still remember his first words.

Stokely looked directly at the white rebels and said, "One of the most pointed illustrations of the need for 'black power' in a society that has degenerated into a form of totalitarianism is to be found in the very debate itself." Then to everyone else, "Welcome, brothers and sisters."

The crowd went hog wild, black students whooping and cheering.

The white students in the audience, rebels and liberals alike, were struck dumb, silenced by the sheer force of words they didn't understand, their own language turned against them. Backstage, Jay felt his whole world was busting wide open. Here was this brother onstage, achingly hip and capable of intellectually skating over all of their heads. No one had heard a speech like this, a framing of the fight for justice in such fundamentally political and theoretical terms. The term "black power" was relatively new; it had started at a rally in Greenwood, Mississippi, the year before, one night after Stokely was arrested for the twenty-seventh time. "The only way we're gonna stop these white men from whuppin' us is to take over," he'd said. "We been saying 'freedom' for six years and we ain't got nothing. What we gon' start saying now is . . . black power."

The term caught on and contributed to Stokely's militant reputation, but as he began to lay it down that night in Cullen Auditiorium, to lay out his case, it sounded less radical to Jay and more like good old common sense. It was, frankly, gospel. The black students waved their hands in the air, clapping and calling out to Brother Carmichael as if they were in church.

"The concept of integration is based on the assumption that there is not value in the Negro community . . ."

Mm, hmm. That's right.

"So they siphon off *acceptable* Negroes into the middle class . . ."

Preach on it, brother.

"And each year a few more Negroes, armed with their pass-ports—their university degrees—escape into middle-class America . . ."

Come on now. Tell it.

"And one day the Harlems and the Wattses and the *Fifth Wards* will stand empty, a tribute to the success of integration."

Right on, man.

"You know, Marx said that the working class is the first class in history that ever wished to abolish itself. And if one listens to some of our 'moderate' Negro leaders, it appears that the American Negro is the first race that ever wished to abolish itself. And, my black brothers and sisters, it stops tonight."

The crowd was clapping and stomping, so loud that Jay could feel it backstage, as if the walls were shaking. He could not believe the heat this man was generating, like a lightning rod in a prairie storm. It wasn't just the man, but, really, the ideas, the words . . . *two* words: *black* and *power*.

"So what you're preaching, man," one of the white students down front asked, a cat dressed in cords and a denim patch jacket, "isn't it just racism of a different color? Isn't 'black power' inherently anti-white?"

"See, you're still putting yourself at the center of it, jack. That's what you ain't yet getting. Black folks ain't talking about you, or *to* you, no more."

He had to be escorted out the back entrance that night, not because of rioting, but because so many people wanted to shake his hand, wanted a word with the brother. Jay had to shuttle him out of the rear of the auditorium to avoid a mob. He shoved Stokely into Lloyd Mackalvy's VW bug, and the three of them rode on to Austin that night, to accompany Stokely at the antiwar rally at the University of Texas.

That was the first night somebody put a gun in Jay's hand.

The Klan had threatened publicly to meet Mr. Carmichael on Highway 71 that night, stopping the car before it got past Bastrop. They promised a good show for anyone man enough to come out and watch. Lloyd kept a little .22 pistol under the front seat. He handed the gun to Jay and appointed him lookout.

Stokely talked the whole way on the road that night, his head leaned against the passenger-side window, coat turned around and tucked under his chin like a blanket. He was mumbling softly over the radio about how they were gon' change the world, how it was gon' be better for their kids. Jay remembers Aretha had a new cut out that spring, a haunting cover of Sam Cooke's "A Change Is Gonna Come." The music was so slow and pretty that Lloyd turned up the radio, and the three of them rode in silence in the car, smoking cigarettes and listening to Aretha sing of hope, Jay with Lloyd's pistol still in his hand.

Stokely would shortly leave SNCC for the Panthers, joining Eldridge Cleaver and Huey Newton and Elaine Brown. The civil rights movement as any of them knew it would never be the same. Black nationalism became the order of the day, less a focus on integration than on self-reliance and full-scale support of black pride and culture, entrepreneurship and political uplift, to the exclusion of everything and everybody else. Bumpy got on this big-time. He pushed for the complete disbanding of COBRA. The old Scott Street group reinvented itself as AABL, Afro-Americans for Black Liberation, or "able." Bumpy and Lloyd Mackalvy had fallen head over heels in love with black nationalism.

But something else was happening to Jay.

His political focus was beginning to shift to a higher plane. The more he read, the more he was starting to see injustice as a global problem. Oppression was pandemic, like a cancer; wherever it existed, it would spread. And maybe justice could work the same way; maybe it could spread too. Which meant that the problems in Africa, say—poverty and the imperialism that created it—were as important as the problems here at home; they were actually one and the same.

While Bumpy and Lloyd got more and more heated about "black power"—refusing to coordinate rallies with SNCC or any white groups on campus—Jay kept an eye on the war and communism, and global economics in particular, working the topic into speeches and editorials for local papers and traveling on his own dime across the lower states to speak to other colleges and political leaders.

He knew he was being followed.

They found bugs in the phones on Scott Street. They spotted undercover cops at every rally. And Jay knew somebody was staging break-ins, stealing drafts of speeches and fund-raising rosters. But it wasn't until the feds shot those boys in Chicago that Jay began to believe his life might be in danger—not just a random act of violence, but a planned execution. By 1970, you could feel the tension running under everything. There were suddenly guns on the table at every meeting. No one knew who they could trust. Even brothers and sisters who went way, way back, had been friends for years, were suddenly tight lipped around each other. They started spending almost as much time testing each other's loyalty as they did talking about their fledgling political programs.

It was a brilliant strategy.

If no one knew who the rats were, then no one could be trusted. It was just the kind of thing that would tear a political organization apart.

In all this, Roger Holloway had completely escaped Jay's attention. His lack of political passion and his high-level interest in bedding most of the sisters affiliated with Jay and Bumpy's group made Jay think of him more as a lazy lothario than a revolutionary, a fox who'd found his way into a well-stocked henhouse. He did, however, take a strong interest in something Jay was trying to pull together: an African liberation rally to be held on campus. It was already shaping up to be the biggest political move of Jay's life. Jay wasn't sure Roger could find Africa on a map, but he was willing to do grunt work—making cold calls and mimeographing flyers—so Jay kind of took him in, teaching him how to organize a rally, who to call for money, and what lies to tell the administration to keep them off your back. Alfreda Watkins was on fund-raising then, a one-woman committee. She was a beautiful, long-limbed sister with a big soft Afro, and Jay had a sneaking suspicion she was Roger's true African inspiration.

Cynthia turned away from the water, turning her whole body around to face him. She wrapped her hands behind his neck, locking them. He could feel the heels of her bony feet digging into the small of his back. She rested her forehead on his. "I love you," she whispered. "You know that, right?"

He dug his fingers into her flesh, the folds of her skirt.

Please stay, the song went. *Stay in my corner.*

Cynthia pressed her cheek against his.

She whispered in his ear, "I'm just saying . . . be careful, Jay."

He would think about this night many times over the years. He would remember her face in the moonlight and the salty kisses. And he would wonder why he hadn't noticed Roger sooner, why he needed Cynthia Maddox to point out Roger's suspicious behavior . . . and why she had been so eager to do so.

Chapter 16

When Jay first started practicing law, when he first went out on his own, he was interested only in criminal law; he initially built his whole practice around it. He was six months in before he realized there was no money in it. Maybe for men like Charlie Luckman, with his political connections and well-financed clients who are capable of spending large sums of money to take care of their legal indiscretions. Most of Jay's clients are walk-ins or people who get his name out of the phone book or friends of Bernie's extended church family. People who, for the most part, cannot afford to pay him. Over the years, he's engineered all manner of creative financing plans. Monthly installments and deferred payments. In lieu of cash, he's taken everything from used furniture to free haircuts. One client actually tried to pay him with fresh buttermilk he said he'd drive up once a month from a cousin's farm in Victoria.

But Rolly Snow was a different story altogether.

Sometime in the spring of 1978, Rolly walked into Jay's office and took a seat across from his desk. Half Creole and half Oklahoma Chickasaw, he was long and lean, with caramel-colored skin and jet black hair that he wore in a short ponytail. He never shaved, and he had his name tattooed across the knuckles of his right hand. He'd shared a cell once with Marcus Dupri, who had apparently gotten heavy into drugs about a year or so after Jay's trial, after AABL disbanded for good. Rolly announced that Marcus Dupri had said Jay was an all right dude, that Rolly wouldn't have nothing to worry about.

His problem was domestic in nature. About a month prior, HPD had responded to a neighbor's late-night phone call reporting loud noises and shouting and a woman screaming. The cops showed up at Rolly's apartment and found his girlfriend with a three-inch gash across the side of her face. She was bleeding heavily and cursing Rolly's name, and he was arrested inside of three hours. He swore up and down he wasn't home when the beat-down occurred, that he'd never hit a woman in his life—though after a few hours in lockup, he told Jay, he was starting to rethink his position. He'd only let the girl in his apartment that day so she could do her laundry and maybe get a little something to eat. And with an alarming lack of gratitude, she'd gone behind his back and fucked some other dude in his bed. Rolly knew it was the other guy who had popped her. All he needed was a lawyer to help him prove it in court.

It turned out to be one of the easiest cases Jay ever had.

His client had done all the work.

Rolly ran a bar on the north side, out in the Heights, a working-class, largely Hispanic area of town, but he picked up a second income working as an amateur sleuth, a poor man's private eye. For a few hundred dollars, he could find a distant cousin or a husband who'd taken off in the middle of the night. He could tell you who your wife was seeing on the side, where the dude lived, and what he liked to eat for dinner every night. If the price was right, Rolly Snow would go through anybody's trash, follow anybody you asked him to.

He worked his own case as well as he would for a paying customer. He found a fingerprint on his headboard that the police hadn't even bothered to lift. He went to the biker bar his girl liked to frequent and got the name of the dude she was two-timing him with, and he found a witness who could put the two of them together on the night in question. The whole thing was settled in a preliminary hearing. The judge threw out the prosecution's case and offered Mr. Snow an apology. Jay was so impressed with Rolly's investigative work that when it came time to settle his bill, he offered Rolly an alternative to paying cash: would he like to do some work for Jay on the side? When Jay assured him, several times, that he would not have to wear a suit, Rolly agreed. They met on a case-by-case basis. Rolly helped Jay find witnesses or dig up dirt on defendants or find out which of Jay's civil clients were lying about their injuries. Rolly seemed to like the work at first. He even asked Jay for engraved business cards, and when Jay refused, Rolly made up some of his own, going around for months telling people that he worked in a law firm until Jay had to order him to stop. The arrangement didn't last long. Much as Rolly liked the idea of doing "serious" legal work, he also liked to drink a lot and smoke weed on a daily basis. Jay couldn't always find him when he wanted to, and Rolly didn't like being tied down. He kept meticulous records, creating a homemade balance sheet on the back of an envelope he stashed behind his bar, keeping track of all the work he'd done for Mr. Porter. He knew, down to the hour, when he'd finally paid Jay everything he owed him. After that, the two men parted ways.

Jay can't recall the name of Rolly's bar, or the street it sits on.

He will have to do this by memory.

He leaves the Criminal Courts Building and drives east, out of downtown.

The air is cooler out here in the Heights. Less concrete and more trees, tall oaks reaching out to touch their neighbors across the street and weeping willows so full of the blues their leaves almost dust the ground. There are Victorians dating back to the turn of the century and sturdy bungalows built by the early craftsmen who moved to the Heights in the late 1800s to get away from the swampy, mosquito-infected city of Houston.

Time has not been good to the area.

Once-grand homes have fallen into disrepair, carved up into cheap rental units with sagging porches and chipped paint. There are cracks and potholes along Heights Boulevard. And too many Laundromats and liquor stores to count. Despite its perch some twenty feet or so above Houston's city center, the Heights have, over the years, taken on a distinctly inner-city look. Jay drives past aging, boarded-up storefronts and *taquerías*, discount super-markets and tire yards.

The name of the bar comes back to him suddenly: Lula's, at Airline and Dunbar. Named after Rolly's mother or sister or some girl he picked up along the way. Jay crosses over to Airline and drives in the direction of Dunbar, keeping his eyes open for a squat black box of a building with steel bars over the windows and, out front, a painted mural of an Indian chief at a disco.

There's a baby-blue El Camino parked in front of Lula's,

beneath a flamingo-pink neon sign that's off at this hour. Jay remembers that Rolly used to drive a truck just like it. He shuts the engine on his Buick and crosses the street. Inside, Lula's is hot and moist and smells like peanuts and spilt beer, not to mention the faint, skunky aroma of marijuana. There's crushed-velvet wallpaper on the walls and Billy Dee Williams on posters advertising malt liquor. The air-conditioning unit in the front window is blowing out useless puffs of air.

Rolly is behind the bar, wearing a vest and no undershirt, flipping through a beat-up copy of *McCall's* magazine and playing a hand in a card game at the same time. He hasn't gained an ounce in three years, doesn't look like he's aged one bit. His only customer is a tubby white guy in short sleeves and a tie. He lays a spread across the bar and calls out, "Gin!" Rolly barely looks up from the magazine. The only other person in the bar is a woman with her feet up, fishing at the bottom of a bag of Lay's potato chips. She's wearing white jeans, a gold leotard, and no shoes. "I help you with something?" she asks Jay.

Jay steps over the threshold, letting the door swing behind him. It lands with a soft thud, and the room falls into a kind of bluish haze, courtesy of the bedsheets someone's tacked over the windows and the film of cigarette smoke in the air. Rolly finally glances his way. A corner of his mouth turns up. "Well, look what the devil drug up," he says, smiling. "Ain't this some shit. Jay fucking Porter."

"It's your hand," the tubby at the bar says.

"Let Carla sit in for me."

"I hate gin rummy," Carla says, licking potato chip grease off her fingers.

Rolly walks to the end of the bar. "Jay motherfucking Porter," he says, smile widening. "What the hell you doing here, man? Can I get you a drink?"

Jay runs through the last twenty-four hours in his head: he was face-to-face with a .45; he talked to Cynthia Maddox for the second time in ten years; he buried nearly $25,000 in his office; he rifled through someone's mail; and he bribed a county clerk. By his count, he's committed at least two felonies, and nearly lost his life, and the sun hasn't even set yet. "Yeah, I'll take a drink."

He watches Rolly pour two shots of whiskey. Jay sucks his down in a single gulp, then asks for a beer chaser. When he pulls out his wallet, Rolly waves away his money, making a point to add that the *first* one is on the house. The beer is cool and crisp and feels good going down Jay's throat. He taps a cigarette from his pack to go with it. Rolly pours Jay a second shot without being asked. "What are you doing out this way, man? You still doing the law thing?"

"There somewhere we can talk . . . in private?" Jay asks.

Rolly nods down the bar. "They're cool, man."

Jay lowers his voice anyway. "I need your help, Rolly. It's serious."

From his pants pocket, he pulls the folded pages of Elise Linsey's arrest records. He slides them across the bar. "I need information on her."

"How much do you want to know?" Rolly asks, getting right down to business. "And how badly do you want to know it?"

Jay rehearsed this part in the car, the negotiation, and made a brash decision that when the time came, he would go for broke. He pulls the two rolls of money from his pants pockets, $1,500 total. "I want to know everything."

He sets the money on top of the arrest records. Rolly pockets it without counting it. The weight tells him everything he needs to know. "Who is she?"

"You tell me," Jay says.

Rolly picks up the arrest report. He flips through the pages, stoically, as calmly as he'd been reading the women's magazine just a few moments before.

"Where you want me to start?"

"The last few years," Jays says, watching as Rolly pulls a ball-point pen from the back pocket of his Levi's, making notes in the margins of the arrest report. "She stays out on the west side," he adds, "14475 Oakwood Glen. I want to know how she's been spending her time and with whom. And most important, I want to know where she works . . . and how she gets her money."

"She got money?" Rolly asks, his interest piqued.

"I don't know," Jay says flatly, keeping quiet about the $25,000. "But, hell, look at it, Rolly," he says, pointing to the arrest report. "She was in and out of shit for years, and then *poof,* it just stops. Suddenly she's sitting in a town house on the west side. No more arrests, no more problems. What the hell happened?"

"Maybe she cleaned up her act," Rolly offers.

"Well, I'm willing to bet she got some help."

Rolly nods, following the logic.

Jay is afraid to tell him more: the money and the murder, his fears about a setup, people coming after him. He doesn't want to scare Rolly off the job . . . or get him killed. He remembers Jimmy's cousin and the high price he paid.

"I want to know who she's working for," he says vaguely.

"What's your piece in it?" Rolly asks. "Why you so interested?"

"Just find out what you can," Jay says.

"I got you." Rolly nods, respecting his client's need for discretion.

"Be careful, though. You might not be the only one sniffing around."

"Cops?"

"Maybe." But, of course, it's more than that. "Just be careful." Jay says. "There might be trouble, for both of us, if anybody knew you were looking into this."

"Won't nobody know the difference then." Rolly holds out his hand to seal the deal, giving Jay a lopsided smile. "It's good seeing you again, man."

Jay buys a six-pack with his gas card on the way back to the office.

He drinks two of the beers sitting at his desk, hiding the paper bag underneath, down around his feet. About four thirty, Eddie Mae asks to cut out early, claiming she's got to pick up one of her grandkids from band practice. By Jay's count, she's got something like twelve grandchildren, all boys, half of whom he's long suspected she made up (he once asked her to name them all, watching as she got confused around number seven, repeating Damien and Darnell twice). She's always got some dentist appointment or after-school program or T-Ball game she has to leave work early for. "Got to be there for my grandbabies."

Once she's gone, Jay pulls down the shades and locks the door. Then, on his hands and knees, he counts and recounts the remaining cash in the lockbox and has a fleeting, drunken thought of spending it all. He eventually returns the money to its hiding place at the bottom of his filing cabinet, but not before peeling off a couple of hundred-dollar bills, telling himself it's only for the ride home, only 'cause banks are closed and it's hot and he doesn't want his wife to cook. Maybe he can pick up a chicken dinner on the way. Another $200 . . . what difference does it make?

He's drunk by the time he gets to his car.

On the way home, he stops at Mimi's, on Almeda, and forces

himself to drink three cups of black coffee. He orders two number fives—baked chicken and peas, mashed potatoes with spiced gravy—before leaving. By the time he's back in his car, his hands are shaking and the muscles in his arms and legs feel like warm butter, soft and useless, the caffeine and alcohol meeting at a crossroads in his nervous system. He pulls over unexpectedly, into the back lot of a Rice supermarket, parking by the Dumpsters. He opens the car door and vomits.

Kwame Mackalvy is in his living room when he gets home.

He stands when Jay, takeout platters in his hand, walks in. Bernie is sitting on the couch. She's wearing a pink-and-yellow maternity dress and brown slippers. She looks at her husband and shrugs. "He just stopped by."

"I get a minute with you, brother?" Kwame asks Jay. He's hopping on the balls of his feet, like a runner preparing for a sprint, itching for the gun to go off.

Jay's stomach is still raw, and his head aches.

He doesn't want this now, in his living room.

"We're getting ready to eat, Lloyd."

"It's official," Kwame announces. "As of three forty-five, the union is on strike."

"Who called you?"

"Donnie Simpson. He heard it from Rickey Salles, who heard it from someone down to the church."

"You want me to call Daddy?" Bernie asks.

Jay shakes his head. "What about OCAW?" he asks Kwame.

"They're in," Kwame says, smiling.

"Teamsters?"

"Fuck 'em. We don't need 'em."

We. Right.

"ILA's preparing a statement for the ten o'clock news," Kwame says, still talking. "I've already been in contact with Sylvia Martinez over at the *Post*. This is a chance to put our two cents in, put the story out there the way we want it."

WE.

"Bernie and I are about to eat dinner, Lloyd," Jay says.

"I'll be at the docks tomorrow morning, keep an eye on things," Kwame continues, not at all getting it. The only "we" in this house is Jay and his family.

"Kwame," Bernie says from the kitchen. "Come on, let me fix you a plate." Jay looks over the counter at his wife. She winks at him and passes him a handful of silverware. Jay sets the table for three. Kwame mumbles thank you, shyly taking a seat. Bernie scoops out the food from the Styrofoam containers, carefully dividing the portions, making sure that Kwame gets as much chicken as she and Jay, making sure he feels welcome. Grace is a simple two-sentence affair, Bernie mindful of at least one rumbling tummy at the table. Jay hasn't eaten anything since the vending-machine junk at the courthouse, and he's finished with his entire plate, including a little broke-off piece of corn bread, in less than four minutes and is left with no further distractions, nothing to provide a sensory buffer between himself and Kwame's ongoing rant. "I'm thinking of organizing a march," Kwame says between mouthfuls of gravy and potatoes.

Bernie pushes back from the table, fanning herself with a paper napkin.

"You all right, B?" Jay asks.

"I'm hot, Jay," she says, sticking out her bottom lip and blowing air up toward her nose, trying to cool herself with her own breath.

"I'll look at the box in a minute."

Kwame stares across the table at Jay. "I want you in it with me, man."

It is offered as tenderly as a proposal of marriage. "Just like the old days," Kwame says. "You and me, bro? We show 'em how it's done?" His leg is pumping up and down under the table, making a faint rat-a-tat-tat and gently knocking the plates on the table. Bernie presses her hand firmly on the tabletop to stop it from shaking. Kwame stills his leg. The room is suddenly quiet.

"People need to remember we was about something once," Kwame says.

"We were kids, Lloyd. We were just kids."

"Aw, come on, man," Kwame says. "Are you so far gone?"

"Let me ask you something," Jay says. "This march you're planning . . . how much of this is about the longshoremen and how much is about you?"

"It's about all of us, man. 'Injustice anywhere is a threat to justice everywhere.' You remember that, don't you?"

"Answer my question, Lloyd. Really, man. Answer the question. Far as I know, you never worked a dock in your life. So what is this? What are you trying to do here? Is this just you needing some platform to stand on?"

Kwame stares at Jay, his old buddy, his comrade.

"You telling me you don't miss it, man?"

"Miss what?"

"Come on," Kwame says, his tone wistful and unexpectedly soft and dry with longing. "We were really doing something back then, man."

"I'm doing something now, Lloyd. I'm trying to raise a family."

Bernie has kept her eyes on her plate, pushing her peas around.

"Ain't nobody trying to take this away from you, Jay," Kwame says. "I'm talking about a march, a single afternoon."

"I'm not interested," Jay says. "It's not my deal."

"Man," Kwame says, shaking his head. "They really got to you, huh? They got you good. I guess you doing your twenty years on the house."

Jay slaps his hand across the table, shaking the silverware.

"That's enough, Lloyd."

Kwame picks up his napkin, balls it up and tosses it onto his plate. "I know you got your practice and everything, but I guess I always thought that when push came to shove, if the right issue came along, you'd be right there."

"I'm not interested."

Kwame nods. He's heard the message loud and clear.

"Man," he says. "She really did a number on you, didn't she?"

Bernie wobbles to her feet then, loudly stacking the dinner plates without asking if anyone's finished and slapping away Jay's hand when he tries to help. Jay shoots Kwame a harsh look, and Kwame finally stands. "I didn't mean you no offense, Bernie," he says contritely. "I wasn't talking about you."

"I know," she says, carrying the plates to the kitchen sink.

Kwame starts for the front door. He stops once and turns to Jay. "People look up to you, man. Always have. Hell if I know why. But people listen to you. They trust you, Jay," he says. "I'm not sure you always see that." He shoves his hands into the pockets of his gray carpenter's pants. "I just thought you might want to help." He nods good night to Bernie, then sees himself out.

They're in bed by seven thirty, both exhausted by a litany of things the other doesn't understand. Jay finally got the thermostat down to an insanely expensive seventy degrees, and Bernie takes in the cool air like a sedative. She can sleep only on her right side these days, so they've switched their usual sleeping positions. Jay presses into Bernie's backside, still in his trousers, too tired to fully undress. He lays a hand on her belly and feels a faint swishing beneath the skin, the timid movements of a new-comer. He rubs his wife's stomach, which is tight as a drum. He taps his fingers on her belly. It's just a hello. *I'm here. I got you.*

Bernie cups his hand in hers. "If you want to do this thing with Kwame."

"I don't."

"If you want to do *any*thing, Jay, that's all you. Don't put it on me. I'm not the one trying to stop you."

"I know," he says.

"Do your thing," she says, her voice slowing down to a sleepy crawl.

Chapter 17

On the first full day of the longshoremen's strike, Jay wakes up to the smell of rain. The ashy black clouds outside his bedroom window threaten to split wide open, to bury the city beneath an angry deluge. He manages to get into the office before the first drops fall. But by midmorning it's coming down so hard that he and Eddie Mae leave their desks and go into the waiting area to watch the summer storm through the front windows. The lights in the office flicker a couple of times, and Eddie Mae goes to look for some batteries for a flashlight. Jay keeps his post by the windows, watching the rain dancing in the wind, like sheets blowing on a line. He used to love storms like this as a kid. He and his sister would make jelly sandwiches and lie on the floor in the den to watch *Howdy Doody* all day or catch a couple of

Roy Rogers westerns back-to-back. Sometimes on stormy days, their mother would make them tomato soup or grits with butter and sugar. She would teach them to play hearts or bid whist. She could be like that some days, sweet and attentive, when their stepfather wasn't around. She could make you feel like you were really something.

Jay pulls himself away from the windows long enough to take a call from Dana Moreland, the hooker. "You're a hard man to get a hold of," she says right away. "What's the deal on this thing anyway? I gotta know, ASAP. I got some personal things going on, and I need to know how much I can expect out of this."

Jay doesn't mention the $7,500. "Let's just be patient for now," he says. "And see how this thing plays out in the next week or so."

Dana makes a *hmph* sound under her breath.

"Remember, if you get nothing, *I* get nothing," he says.

"I'm not taking *nothing*. That's not even in the cards, baby."

Eddie Mae pokes her head into the office. Jay sits up in his chair, thinking it's Rolly Snow on the other line. He told Eddie Mae first thing this morning to put Rolly through immediately, the moment he calls. Jay is still waiting on some word about Elise Linsey. But Eddie Mae is in the doorway to tell him that his father is in the waiting room. Jay leans back in his chair and looks into the other room where Reverend Boykins is standing by the door, shaking rain off his coat.

His father. Right.

The hooker is going on and on about money she owes to some dude who stays down in Corpus, something about him fixing the carburetor on her truck and paying her rent last month, plus she wants to buy shares of a little oil-and-gas outfit down south or maybe get into the real estate game. This is, after all, her big break. "Dana, let's just get through this next week, okay?"

He hangs up the phone.

To Jay's surprise, his father-in-law is not alone. Darren Hayworth and his father shuffle in behind Reverend Boykins. All three men are slick with rain. Reverend Boykins plops into the only open chair. Winded, he pulls a monogrammed handkerchief from his suit-coat pocket and dabs at his face.

The elder Hayworth unzips the top half of his school district uniform, and it occurs to Jay that he took off from work to be here. From inside his uniform, Mr. Hayworth pulls out the front page of today's *Houston Chronicle*. The paper is folded in thirds and dark in spots where rainwater soaked through his clothes.

"We saw it this morning," he says.

Jay looks at the paper, his eyes sweeping across the main headline: "Dockworkers Walk." Underneath there's a picture from yesterday evening's press conference, the dockworkers and representatives from OCAW standing together.

Mr. Hayworth turns to Darren. He nods his head in Jay's direction, nudging his son to say something. Darren, always less spirited in the presence of his father, shuffles his feet a few steps forward. With his good arm, he points to a face on the bottom half of the page. The newspaper photo is smudged with fingerprints, the ink getting pulled in every which direction, sweat and rain blurring the picture. Still, Jay can make out the image of a white man with puffy, pockmarked skin and oversize glasses. His sideburns are long and curling at the ends. The picture is accompanying a substory about the OCAW vote and its history of labor solidarity. The caption identifies the man as Carlisle Minty, Vice President, OCAW, Local 180. "That's him," Darren says.

"Who?"

"The one in the truck the night I got jumped. He was just sitting there watching them beat me, *ordering* them to do it."

Jay reads the caption again. *OCAW. Vice President.*

"Are you sure?"

"If my boy says it's him then that's all I need to know," the elder Hayworth says, folding his arms across his chest.

"That's him," Darren repeats.

"This is what we always said we needed, Jay," the Rev adds. "We just needed a name. Now . . . let the mayor put her money where her mouth is."

Jay skims the article. In essence, it's an OCAW love song to labor struggle and solidarity among working people. Mr. Carlisle Minty is quoted throughout the piece, saying that the Oil, Chemical and Atomic Workers Union "garnered a strong majority vote in favor of a walkout with the ILA. And I, for one, believe in equal pay for equal work, that everybody ought to have equal opportunities to advance." Minty goes on to say that he would not want a similar issue to divide his union, and therefore he and the other OCAW officers made a strong push to get behind the dockworkers.

Everything in the article, every word attributed to Carlisle Minty is in complete contrast to the violent picture Darren painted. Here, it says that Carlisle Minty is 100 percent behind the dockworkers . . . black or white.

Jay looks up from the newspaper article to Darren, looks into his eyes.

"You're *sure*?"

"Yes, sir."

"You tell the mayor to do something about this or we sue," the father says.

Jay walks through their argument in his head, pictures himself telling all of this to the mayor. He runs it down two and three times and comes across the same crack in the logic. "You know, if you make a big deal out of this, make some public pronouncements about this man, an officer in his union no less, beating up a young kid, spreading fear about the strike . . . you may end up sending the message that OCAW ain't really down with this after all, that they might not go the distance in a work-stoppage situation. You're already flying without the Teamsters. In a negotiation, it may weaken your position."

"I don't want to cause no trouble," Darren says in a childlike whisper, not wanting all this on his young head.

The elder Hayworth shakes his head. "I'm not backing down on this. The mayor said she needed a name, and we got a name. Somebody's got to pay for what they did. If the police won't handle it, I will. I know who it is now."

"Wait a minute, now, wait a minute," the Rev says. "We not doing things that way, hear?" The elder Hayworth keeps shaking his head back and forth, arms pressed so tightly into his chest that Jay wonders how he can breathe. The Rev turns back to his son-in-law. "Now, you said the mayor was sympathetic to what these men are trying to do. Give her the man's name then. She said she would take it to the police. That's all we're asking." Then he adds, pointedly, "For now." His voice is firm and crystal clear. "You hear me, son? Let the mayor know we aim to be taken seriously on this." ·

Jay nods. "I hear you."

Cynthia agrees to meet him at an address downtown, surprising him when he calls by saying, "We need to talk," before he has a chance to. He hangs up his desk phone and tucks the front page of the *Chronicle* into his jacket pocket. He steps out of his private office, telling Eddie Mae he'll be out for a while.

The streets downtown are like tiny rivers, the storm turning the city's center into a grid of muddy, shallow creeks, much like the bayous that give Houston its nickname. The rain has not let up, not even a little bit. Jay squints through the wall of water coming down on his windshield, catching a clear snapshot of the road in front of him only once every few seconds as his wipers struggle to keep up. On his car radio, there are reports that some five hundred dockworkers are picketing with rain-soaked signs down at the port.

The address she gave is an alehouse on Travis.

Jay orders a sandwich inside the bar, which is full of dark wood and leather booths and smells like baking bread. He nurses a Coca-Cola while he waits for nearly twenty minutes, burning though two cigarettes, wondering what the mayor meant on the phone, what in the world she wants to talk to *him* about.

When Cynthia finally walks through the door, their eyes lock, and Jay feels a strange, helpless sensation, as if he's been struck dumb in her presence, as if he can't move. He feels a prickly heat on his skin. He doesn't know why she has this power still, to stop him in his tracks. Except that history is a funny thing. Fifty years from now, if they're still walking around on the planet, if they should bump into each other on the street or in a bar somewhere, it'll be just as this moment is now, like a key turning in a lock. They are each other's history, capable, with just a glance, of unlocking hidden truths. She is his witness.

Cynthia slides onto the stool next to Jay.

They're only a few blocks from city hall, but no one in the place seems to recognize her. Among the barflys and afternoon drunks, the mayor has found a little oasis of privacy. She knows the bartender by name. She orders a beer for herself and one for Jay. Some dark German brew that he would never have picked out for himself. But with Cynthia, this kind of shit comes with the territory. She steals a cigarette from Jay's open pack on the bar top. Her nails are bitten past the fingertips, he notices, the pink manicure flaking off at the ends. She inhales, blowing smoke up into the air, the calf of her left leg brushing up against his. She doesn't move it right away. "I didn't think you'd see me again."

From his jacket pocket, Jay pulls out the front page of today's *Houston Chronicle*. He spreads it across the scratched bar top, open to the photo of Carlisle Minty. "The guy in the picture," he says. "He beat up the kid." And then, because she doesn't appear to be following him, he adds, "The kid? The dockworker? I told you about him? Got beat up a couple of weeks ago?"

"Right." She nods, catching up.

"That's the guy," Jay says. "That's the guy who did it."

Cynthia picks up the torn newspaper clipping.

Jay watches her eyes drop to the bottom left, scanning the article just as he'd done earlier this morning. He catches the wrinkle in her brow, can almost guess what she's thinking. When the mayor finally looks up, she has an almost comic look of incredulity on her face. She seems, honestly, on the verge of laughter. "You want to bring charges against the vice president of OCAW?"

"I want you to give this man's name to the police department, tell them what happened, just like you said you would. It's up to the D.A.'s office whether or not they want to bring charges."

"But this doesn't make any sense, Jay. OCAW's all those men have, the only friend they've got. Why would Carlisle Minty go around beating people up, threatening the blacks to drop this walkout idea? Next, you're going to tell me he shot up that house on Market Street too?"

"Kid says this is the guy who jumped him. That's what I know."

Cynthia tosses the newspaper clipping onto the bar top as if she's casting aside this whole ridiculous idea. "I *met* with Carlisle Minty, Jay. Trust me, he's on this strike thing, all the way. He's *supporting* the longshoremen."

"Well, maybe that's his public face. Maybe in private he'd tell you something different," Jay says, sipping his beer for the first time. The taste is bittersweet, the texture thick and warm. It makes him think of a kiss. It makes him hot about the neck and chest. "Isn't that how you politicians do things?"

Cynthia cocks her head to one side, studying his face, a thought just now occurring to her. "You don't particularly like me very much, do you, Jay?"

"I don't trust you. There's a difference."

Cynthia nods, as if she can live with this, as if untrustworthiness were only a matter of perspective, and Jay is certainly entitled to his. But Jay has known her too long not to catch the subtle shift in her expression, like clouds passing over. There is something newly grim and regretful in her eyes. She's quiet a minute, pensive, rubbing out the orange, smoking tip of her cigarette, twirling the butt around in heavy circles inside the black plastic ashtray. "If you don't trust me, Jay," she asks softly, "what are you doing here?"

Jay looks at the mayor, searching for traces of the girl he used to know, beneath the frosted tips and split ends, beneath the heavy makeup, which has, at this hour, begun to settle into the deep creases around her mouth. He can tell how hard she's trying to manage her image, and it makes him kind of sad.

"Hoping I'm wrong," he says.

He taps Carlisle Minty's face in the newspaper. "This is your chance to make it right," he says. "From this point on, you can't say I didn't warn you."

"You should tell those boys to go back to work."

"Why don't you tell them?" He stands, heading for the front door.

"They'll listen to you, Jay."

"Yeah . . . the whole union is going to reverse their vote on my say-so."

"You can stop this thing where it started," she says. "Talk to the Brotherhood, get a new campaign going, get them to see this thing a different way." Then she adds solicitously, "You could help me out a lot, Jay."

"No thank you," he says.

"You know, you're a fool to make this Minty thing public. Somebody could easily use this as evidence that the labor block ain't all that strong."

"So you gon' blackmail me now?" He laughs bitterly. "Well, you got the wrong guy. Do what you want with it, Cynthia. I don't care."

"Oh, I know you better than that, Jay," she says. "Have you forgotten?"

He thinks she's trying to charm him, and it makes him like her even less than he already does. "These men are coming to you for help," he says, standing. "If you betray them, that's on your conscience. Why don't you try to not let yourself down for once?" He starts for the leather-cushioned door to the outside.

"Jay, wait," she says behind him. "There's something else."

"Good-bye, Cynthia."

"I need to know why you were asking about the homicide in Fifth Ward."

Jay stops at the door, feeling a flutter of worry, and the sorry knowledge that Cynthia is incapable of making anything easy for him. "I thought we agreed you weren't going to ask me any questions about that," he says.

"She turned herself in, you know."

"What?" He inches toward Cynthia, not sure he heard her correctly.

"The girl," Cynthia says. "She turned herself in."

"How do you—"

"The grand jury came down with an indictment this morning."

He's aware that he's being watched, studied, that she's following his every move, reading his reaction. "The cops were going to arrest her anyway. This way her lawyer avoided a perp walk. The arraignment's this afternoon."

"I thought you said the evidence was light."

"They turned up something in a search."

"The gun?"

There's something desperate in his tone, a note of panic that makes Cynthia nervous. "Jesus Christ, if you know something, Jay—"

"I don't."

"I know you have people out that way. Bernie's family."

He holds up a hand. *Don't.* It's simply more than he can take: the woman, an arrest, his wife's name out of Cynthia's mouth.

"I know you've done some cases out that way, Jay. I know you've got connections in Fifth Ward. If you know something, you need to talk to the authorities . . . the police or the district attorney's office."

"I can't do that, Cynthia. I can't explain it right now. I just can't."

"Well, I already told them about you," she says.

"What the hell did you do that for?"

"Don't worry, I didn't use your name."

He wishes like hell he had any reason to believe her.

"I told the district attorney that I know someone who might have information about the case. They want to talk to you as soon as possible."

"Jesus, Cynthia."

"I had to say something, Jay. The D.A.'s office is hot as hell on this one," Cynthia says, explaining, apologizing almost. "The girl went and hired herself someone right out of their office, an ex-D.A. by the name of Charlie Luckman."

"Are you shitting me?"

"You know him?"

"Charlie Luckman?"

Jay thinks of all the unreturned phone calls, Mr. Luckman's secretary reporting over and over that her boss was with a new client on urgent business.

"Are you in some kind of trouble, Jay?"

"I'm in a lot of trouble, Cynthia."

He turns and opens the front door, squinting against a blast of white light. The rain has stopped, and the sun has found its place again, its oppressive position on high. The heat is dizzying. On the street, Jay stumbles back to his car, playing the words over and over again in his mind: *she turned herself in.*

Chapter 18

They bring in the defendants in groups of five.

Jay, palms slick with sweat, watches from the back row of the gallery.

He scans the faces in the courtroom, knowing the risk he's taking by being here. There must be a dozen or so spectators in the gallery, mostly men in sports coats and slacks. He wonders if any of them are cops.

If he's asked anything, he'll lie. He decided that on the ride over.

But he needs to know what, if anything, Elise Linsey said to detectives.

For arraignments, the defendants sit in the jury box, to the right of Judge Emily R. Vroland's bench. Two armed bailiffs stand on either side, taking note of any stray movement, any unnecessary shifting or yawning or whispering among those waiting to be formally charged. The men and women in custody are a solemn bunch. Most have spent a night or two in lockup, been forced to trade their clothes and personal effects for a county-issue jumpsuit, and are not exactly in the most cheerful of moods. They stare straight ahead, waiting their turn.

Jay remembers looking out into the gallery at his own arraignment, searching first for his mother's face, then Cynthia's. He knew right away something was wrong. His mother's absence didn't surprise him. It hurt, but it didn't surprise him. But when he looked out into the courtroom and did not see Cynthia, he felt actual alarm. Something was seriously wrong. He felt it before he understood the weight of her absence, how bad things would get for him.

That first court appearance, Bumpy Williams was the only cat who showed up for Jay. After all the organizing Jay had done in support of his brothers in lockup, the arrested or wrongly accused, most of his comrades-in-arms stayed away in those early days. It was the first true indication that the charges against him were more serious than the cops had initially let on. This was bigger than some trespassing charge or a case of unlawful assembly.

He was too ashamed to push Bumpy on the Cynthia issue when it became clear she was pointedly avoiding him, not showing up at the arraignment, never once coming to see him in lockup, and not returning the calls it took great pains to make from jail. He hated to send Bumpy on a romantic errand. But pride aside, he knew the issue of Cynthia's absence was bigger than his personal feelings for her. In order to beat the charges, he needed Cynthia as a witness.

Then, a few days after the arraignment, Bumpy came to see

him in lockup. Jay remembers he held the plastic phone receiver, looked at Jay through the dirty bulletproof glass in the visiting room, and, unsolicited, offered up the information he had, what he'd heard from one too many sources. Cynthia Maddox was gone. Off campus, out of the city, maybe out of the state. Gone.

Elise Linsey is still a no-show.

Nor does Jay see Charlie Luckman in the courtroom.

At the bench, the judge is sipping tea-colored water out of a plastic cup, what could be Jack Daniel's for all Jay can tell at this distance. Emily Vroland is young for a county judge. Ashy blond and prettily made up, she looks like the kind of woman who actually has plans for after work. Maybe jazz at the Warwick Hotel or country and western at a stomphouse down in Victoria. Whatever her social agenda, her afternoon calendar seems to be interfering, running longer than maybe she anticipated. Under the courtroom's fluorescent lights, Judge Vroland listens to her clerk read criminal charges into the record. Solicitation or DWI or felony assault. Misdemeanor theft or city code violation or vehicular manslaughter. She listens as the defendants mumble pleas, defense lawyers waive their pretrial hearings, and prosecuting attorneys argue for a stiff bail penalty. She attends to all of this leaned way back in her chair, saying as little as possible about the sleepy proceedings, seemingly lulled by the constant ticky-tapping of the court reporter's stenograph machine.

Jay checks his watch and glances around the courtroom again, looking for some sign of Mr. Luckman or his client. This time, his eyes land on a familiar face. Across the aisle, second row from the back, the man from the black Ford is staring right at him. The man tips an imaginary hat in Jay's direction, a faint smile on his lips, as if this is all going according to some plan, as if he's tickled by Jay's lawyerly predictability. Of course Jay would show up at the arraignment, and of course the man from the black Ford would be here too, to monitor his $25,000 investment.

Jay will not get up and leave. The decision is made right then. He won't turn tail and run. What he needs is a minute to think, to decide on an approach. He wonders how much the guy knows—Jay's call to the mayor, the trip to the courthouse and to Rolly's bar—and how long he's been watching. Caught, Jay considers whether his best defense is an offense, if he ought to confront the guy right here and now, in a room full of people, to make clear he hasn't technically broken their agreement. He's almost onto his feet when the door behind the clerk's desk opens wide and the last defendant is led in.

Even at this distance, he recognizes her at once.

She's heavily made up for court, wearing a powder-blue pants suit with a pinkish, seashell-colored blouse, primly buttoned all the way up to her chin. There's no county-issued jumpsuit, no handcuffs for her. Mr. Luckman is already earning his fee, and then some. Jay thinks he's maybe underestimated Charlie Luckman's power, his true pull in the courts. Being an ex-D.A. apparently has its perks. Jay would almost bet that Elise Linsey never spent more than a couple of hours in lockup. And here she is now, about to be charged with murder, and the only metal on her wrists is a pair of gold, diamond-encrusted bracelets. Her hair, lighter than Jay remembers, is tucked softly behind her ears.

A bailiff guards Ms. Linsey on one side. On the other, Charlie, in an oyster gray three-piece and matching quill ostrich boots, leads his client by the elbow, gently showing her the way. She's doing a grand job of pretending that this is all new to her, that she hasn't been here a dozen times before, at a defendant's table, in front of a judge. The clothes and the makeup are a cover, the shell that hides the girl from Galena Park, a thief and a prostitute. Jay can't believe the trouble this woman has caused him. He has an impulsive, perilous thought of leaping from his seat and wrapping his fingers around her bony neck.

When the clerk commences the formal reading of the charges, there's a pronounced hush in the room as the words are said out loud:

The state of Texas versus Elise Linsey. Case number HC-760432.

Let it be noted for the record that the defendant is hereby charged with one count of criminal homicide, in violation of Texas Penal Code section 19.02, a felony to wit the defendant, on or about the date of August 1, 1981, did knowingly and intentionally cause the death of one Dwight Sweeney.

Jay makes a mental note of the name.

"Mr. Luckman," the judge begins the proceedings. Gone is the limp and listless late-afternoon handling of the court's business. Her voice has taken on a deep note of sobriety. "How does the defendant plead?"

They all watch and wait.

Charlie Luckman clears his throat, steadies his cowboy boots on the flat brown carpet. He, to Jay's mind, seems nervous. "Not guilty, Your Honor."

Elise Linsey never says a word.

"My client would like to waive the reading of her legal rights under the U.S. Constitution, as counsel has explained all in great detail."

Judge Vroland nods. "Does the state have a problem with that?"

"No, Your Honor," the prosecutor says. The assistant district attorney assigned to the case is a short, squat woman in her forties, with a Peggy Fleming bowl cut and a rather strong resemblance to a bull terrier. "The state would like to request at this time that bail be set in the amount of two hundred and fifty thousand dollars."

"Your Honor," Charlie says, his voice a honeyed drawl. "I don't imagine the court needs reminding that my client turned herself in to authorities. That's about as clear a show of good faith as you're likely to get," he says, putting his best folksy foot forward. Jay imagines Charlie as the type of lawyer who believes that condescension masked as plainspokenness has a winning way with women.

Judge Vroland is not impressed.

"Do you have an actual counterargument to make, Counselor?"

Charlie clears his throat, his voice coming back as flat as a Midwestern plains state. "Defense requests no bail, Your Honor. We ask that the defendant be released on her own recognizance. We believe she has shown her intention to cooperate fully with both the police and the D.A.'s office in this matter."

"The court does not treat that lightly, Counselor."

"Thank you, Your Honor."

The bull terrier at the prosecution's table huffs under her breath several times. "Your Honor, the state asks the court to consider the heinous nature of this crime. The defendant is charged with shooting a man, not once, but twice, in cold blood. She left her victim to die, alone, on a—"

"You'll have plenty of time to lay out your case before a jury."

"We would also like to remind the court that Ms. Linsey has an extensive criminal history."

"Which is of no relevance here, Your Honor," Charlie says firmly.

"Its relevance won't be decided here, that's for sure," the judge says, picking up an ink pen on her desk. "In regard to the issue of bail, the court appreciates Ms. Linsey's show of cooperation with the police detectives and D.A.s involved in this case, but the court appreciates *more* the seriousness of the criminal charges against the defendant. Bail is set in the amount of two hundred and fifty thousand dollars."

"Your Honor," Charlie says quickly. "I'd like to make a motion for a pretrial hearing."

"On what basis, Counselor?"

"Defense counsel would like to make a motion to suppress evidence seized during the search of the defendant's residence."

The slightly panicked look on the D.A.'s face tells Jay that the state's case against Elise Linsey must rely heavily on whatever it is the cops took from her west side town house. He can't imagine what that might be. He would lay money that the gun used to shoot Dwight Sweeney is floating somewhere at the bottom of Buffalo Bayou. It's *his* gun he's not so sure about.

Jay turns his head toward the back of the room, catching a glimpse of the back rows out of the corner of his eye. He sees two men he takes for reporters and an older Mexican man in a plaid shirt. The man from the black Ford is gone.

"Pretrial hearing is set for Thursday, August twentieth," Judge Vroland says, nodding at her court clerk and making a note on the docket papers on her desk. "Bailiffs will escort Ms. Linsey downstairs for processing."

"Your Honor," Charlie says. "I don't think the cuffs are necessary."

"I do." It's her final word on the subject.

The armed bailiffs treat Elise gently. They ask her politely to please turn around, to please place her hands behind her back. "It's okay. I'll meet you downstairs," Charlie says. Finally, Elise relents, pulling her thin arms behind her and turning her backside to the two bailiffs. She looks into the gallery and sees Jay for the first time. Their eyes lock. Jay feels a jolt in his chest. He is her one true witness, the only one here who knows what happened that night. At the sight of him, her posture stiffens. But it's the only outward acknowledgment that he is more than a stranger to her. Her face is impassive, almost stony. She doesn't utter a single word as the bailiffs lead her, handcuffed, out of the room.

Jay is up and out of the courtroom in a matter of seconds. He ducks into the hallway, thinking if he moves quickly enough, he can get to Elise downstairs before her lawyer does. He's half-way to the elevators when he feels a cold grip on the back of his neck. The muscles in Jay's back seize up, his body suddenly taken hostage. Behind him, the man from the black Ford guides Jay roughly down the hall, shoving him behind a nearby door before Jay can adequately defend himself. On the other side of the door, there's a narrow stairwell. Jay falls down several steps, his body rolling onto a landing below. Above him, he hears the door slam and the echo of the man's footsteps in the stairwell. Jay tries to get to his feet. But the man is on him before Jay is even upright. The first blow comes up under his chin. He feels his teeth knock against each other inside his mouth, feels a shot of pain through his skull. He tries to speak. "Wait."

The man lifts him by the collar and tosses him down the next flight of stairs. Jay feels a burn along the right side of his face as he skids across the linoleum. He hears the footsteps again, coming toward him on the stairs.

"I'm not going to have a problem with you, am I, Mr. Porter?"

Jay is on his side, trying to get on his feet.

The man hovers over him, taking his weakened position for obedience.

"Good." He slaps a hand on Jay's shoulder, patting him in a rough, friendly manner, as if Jay were a dog, a thick-headed animal. "Good boy."

It's the word *boy* that does it, launching Jay onto his feet. He charges the guy, butting his head into the man's abdomen. The force of the blow sends them both tumbling down the stairwell. Jay lands on top of him. He pins his knees to the man's chest and punches him twice across the face, knuckles hitting bone. The man from the black Ford pushes himself up at the waist and, using his head as a weapon, bashes Jay across the forehead, knocking him back. Then he socks him good in the stomach. Jay feels his breath leave him. He collapses onto the linoleum floor. When he looks up, the man from the black Ford is standing over him. He lifts his right boot and kicks Jay across the face.

This time, Jay tastes blood.

The man lifts Jay by the throat, slamming the back of his head against the wall. "Stay away from this, Mr. Porter," he says. "Go home to your pretty wife. Don't make this any harder on her than it has to be." He releases Jay, whose head slumps over to one side, his whole bruised body sinking onto the cold, hard floor. Through the slits of his rapidly swelling eyes, he watches the man retreat down the stairwell, the sound of footsteps fading on the stairs.

When he arrives at his apartment, the television is on. Bernie is sitting on the edge of the sofa, the weight of her belly resting between her knees. She's staring at the screen. She doesn't formally acknowledge his presence. She looks up once at Jay, who still has his keys in his hand, bloodstains on his dress shirt. She doesn't mention his appearance, the bruises on his face and neck. She doesn't say a single word. She simply turns back to the television. The news is on, Jay sees, and on the screen, Elise Linsey is standing next to Charlie Luckman on the steps of the Criminal Courts Building. Bernie stares at her face.

"Jay? What is this?"

On the screen, Charlie is doing most of the talking. In fact, as far as Jay can tell, this press conference on the courthouse steps is really Charlie's show.

His first homicide case in years, one reporter says.

What's it like going head to head with his old department?

Does he miss criminal law?

Would he ever think of rejoining the D.A.'s office?

Charlie tells the reporters that he is immensely proud of his private practice, and no, he does not find it odd that he now defends people with money who are accused of the very same crimes he used to prosecute. A bank account has no bearing on the Constitution, he says, adding, "Thank God."

Yes, he would be a fool to say his previous experience at the D.A.'s office didn't give him certain *advantages*, but he knows the men and gals in that office to be tough birds. Still, his prediction for this fight: the case won't even make it to trial. He never says a direct word about Elise Linsey, nor does she speak.

Bernie stares at the girl's face. "We've got to call the police."

Jay takes a deep breath. "We need to talk, B."

He crosses to his wife and kneels before her. She stares at his position on the floor, not understanding. He gently places his hands on her knees. Up close, he hears her quick, shallow breath. She reaches out and touches a bruise on his cheek. Jay winces, the pain cutting to the bone. "What happened to you?"

He tells her everything.

The bit in the paper. The visit to the crime scene. The grounds-keeper. His fears about a setup. The man from the black Ford. The truth about Jimmy's cousin. The break-in. The lies. The mess he made of things. His fears about the feds. The thoughts about his trial, his past. The demons he can't shake. At the end of it, he rests his head in the space between her knees.

"I don't feel right, B," he whispers.

A few minutes pass. He's encouraged by the light stroke of her hand across his hair. He has never felt more that he and B are not equals. Not a man-woman thing. Or even his age. But the simple fact that his wife is whole. And he, at her feet, is not. The reason he needs her so. This family, his child.

Bernie gently raises his chin. "Listen to me. We are going to go to the police. You're going to tell them everything you just told me, just like that."

"I can't do that, B."

"Why?"

He shakes his head. "No police."

"Jay, if this has something to do with my birthday, that night on the boat." She stops suddenly, changing her tone. "You were right, Jay. Is that what you want to hear? You were right, okay? The whole thing was nothing but trouble. But we got to tell the people what we know. We have to tell them what we saw."

Jay looks up at his wife. "There's more."

The money and his missing gun.

He saved the best for last.

"I don't know what I'm dealing with, B. You understand? I don't know who the man is or where he came from. I don't know what he's prepared to do. I don't know anything about him or this girl, if somebody put her up to this."

"Put her up to what, Jay? What are you talking about?"

"I don't know, but the shit ain't adding up. It's just not adding up."

Bernie hugs her arms across her chest, wrapping herself in a tight cocoon, leaving no room for anybody else, especially not him. She gets huffy when she's scared, often angry with him for, if nothing more, bearing witness to her moment of weakness, making it real. She surprises him then, asking, "Where's the money?"

Something in her eyes frightens him. "That money's trouble, B."

"Where is it?"

"In my office."

Bernie is quiet a moment. "Twenty-five thousand dollars?" she says, her voice almost a whisper. "You weren't gon' tell me? About none of it, Jay?"

"I don't want you in it."

"I'm already in it, Jay. I heard her screaming too, remember? I heard *gunshots* too," she says. "Evelyn liked to died when I told her the story. She said from the start we should have gone to the police."

Evelyn. *Shit.*

Jay scrambles to his feet. He forgot that Bernie told her sister about the boat ride. He's got to stop his sister-in-law before she tells anyone else, before the story gets out of his control. "Call her," he says. He tries to help his wife off the couch, but she's resistant, pulling her whole weight away from him, looking up at him like he's plumb lost his mind. "Stop it, Jay."

"You need to call your sister."

"Why?"

"You need to call her and tell her to keep her mouth shut."

"It'll just make her worry more."

"Then tell her *I* already talked to the cops," he says, suddenly thinking of a way to keep this whole thing quiet. "Tell her I already told the police everything."

He starts walking toward the kitchen phone, pleading.

"Call her."

"I'm not going to lie. Not to my family. I won't do it, Jay."

"I just need to buy some time, B. Just 'til I figure out what to do."

"You didn't have anything to do with this, Jay. I don't understand why you can't go to the police," she says, shaking her head at him, the parts she still, after all these years, doesn't understand. "Just tell them the *truth*."

"The man has my gun, B! I have a felony arrest record! What do you want me to say here! What the hell do you want me to do!"

His arms collapse at his sides. He is suddenly very, very tired.

Bernie lets out a soft, featherweight sigh.

It takes her longer to get off the couch than it does to get to the wall phone in the kitchen. Jay stumbles behind her, in a stupor of awe and gratitude for his wife's graciousness, the depths to which she's willing to forgive. She picks up the phone. He puts a gentle hand on her shoulder. "It's just a phone call, B."

Bernie nods, dialing.

Jay walks her through the whole thing, whispering in her ear.

Tell her this is the first you heard of it or you would have said something earlier.

"You know how Jay gets, don't want to worry nobody with nothing."

Tell her I talked to a detective. I told you the man's name, but you can't remember it just now.

"It must have been a few days ago," she says into the phone.

"Tell her you're coming to stay with her," Jay says, suddenly flipping the script. He knew the moment he walked in the door and found her unharmed that he would ask her to leave, demand it even. He saved it until now to avoid an argument about it. "Tell her we had a fight, and you're coming to stay with her."

Bernie shakes her head. She mouths the words, *No, Jay.*

"You can't stay here, B. It's not safe."

"Ev, listen. I'ma be out to your place in about an hour. Is that all right?" Bernie says, looking at her husband. "Yeah, we had a little fight. You know how Jay is, caught up in his head some-where, don't want to let nobody inside." Jay feels the weight of her stare. "Well, frankly," she says, "I'm getting tired of it."

He helps her pack. Toothbrush, change of clothes.

Enough for a couple of days.

They wait until after sundown, Jay checking the back alley and the streets around his apartment complex for any signs of a black Ford. They drive to Evelyn's place in silence. He won't walk her to the door. They've got to keep up the appearance, at least, of marital discord.

Bernie waits a long time before she opens the car door.

"You take care of this. Hear me, Jay? You take care of this so I can come home, so I can have my husband back, Jay. You make me that promise."

He squeezes her hand, nodding his head, biting the corner of his lip.

"You got to get clear in your head about some things." She speaks matter-of-factly, even as her eyes fill with tears. " 'Cause I need you, Jay . . . *we* need you."

He nods, chewing on his lip until he tastes blood.

He knows he's got to let her go.

She twists the straps of her overnight bag. Finally, she opens the car door. Through the car window, Jay watches his wife ring the doorbell at Evelyn's one-story tract home. He waits for the door to open, waits to see that she's safely inside. He waves to Evelyn, in a cotton nightgown down to her ankles, but his sister-in-law slams the door without a nod or a hello.

Chapter 19

Later that night, Rolly finally calls with a lead on where the girl is staying. With Bernie tucked safely away at her sister's, Jay waits 'til after midnight before meeting Rolly out to his place. When he arrives at Lula's, Carla is behind the bar in a grape-colored leotard and her skintight Glorias. She directs Jay down the hallway to Rolly's office, a closet-size room with a desk hidden beneath a mountain of papers and receipts and industrial-size cans of stewed tomatoes. On the other side of the desk is a screen door. Through the wire mesh, Jay can see tiny puffs of smoke blowing in from the alley out back, where Rolly is leaned up against the peeling paint of Lula's back side, smoking a joint. He offers Jay a pull, then nods his head approvingly when Jay refuses, as if the offer were only a test. He pinches off the head before tucking what's left of the joint behind his left ear. He nods toward his car, parked in the alley. The El Camino is waiting.

Jay rides curled up on the floorboard to avoid being seen from the street. His neck is crunched, turned at a severe angle, and the heat from the truck's engine is burning through his clothes. Rolly claims his Louisiana bones can't stand air-conditioning.

"Just drive safe, hear?" Jay says, feeling suddenly apprehensive about putting his life in Rolly's high hands.

They ride for a piece in silence, until Rolly gets down to business. "You might have told me the bitch was wanted for murder," he says.

Jay squirms on the floorboard, reminding Rolly to watch the road.

"Where we headed anyway?" he asks.

"Your girl owns a good deal of property around town. Most of it under a corporation for which she is the sole proprietor. A lot of it she's apparently looking to unload, according to listings in the paper. She lucked up into the real estate game good," Rolly says, reaching across the front seat to the glove compartment, pulling out a pack of Camels. "There's a co-op out to Sugarland, some new development. Pool, workout room, that sort of thing. It's a nice place. The girl owns a unit, and I'm pretty sure she's staying out there."

"She been back to her old place?"

"Not to stay."

"You went out there?"

"Once or twice," Rolly says, lifting the car lighter to his cigarette.

"Cops around?"

"Not that I seen."

"What about a black Ford, LTD model," Jay says. "A white guy driving?"

Rolly cuts his eyes to the floorboard, taking in Jay's bruised and battered face. "You know, I get the distinct feeling there's some shit in this you're not telling me."

Jay ignores the comment. "So what'd you find?"

As they ride, Rolly fills Jay in on the rest of it, what he's learned about Elise Linsey, DOB 5-16-57. She graduated Galena Park High, went all the way to state with their track team in '74. He found that in a little puff piece in the *Pasadena Citizen* under the heading "Local Girls Run Circles Around the Competition." From the front pocket of his leather vest, Rolly pulls out a roll of photocopied papers. "I got a copy of whatever the library would give me. Police blotters, obit notices, any little thing that mentioned her name."

The girl's arrest record speaks for itself, Rolly says, but from a police blotter in the *Chronicle* he did get the name of an after-hours joint where she used to dance and pick up johns on the side. The Peephole, Rolly says it was called. "There's one girl over there who remembers her, or at least was willing to talk to me about it. She says Elise was fired from the strip club. She tried to keep in touch, but Elise never stayed in one place long enough. Last she had heard, your girl was heading to secretarial school or something like that. Which checks out, by the way. I spent part of the day yesterday calling about a half-dozen secretary schools in Harris County until, bingo, I got it. Sloan's School of Business Management had an Elise Linsey graduate just last year. The placement office says her first job out of school was at Cole Oil Industries downtown."

"That's quite a leap," Jay says, still having a hard time believing that Elise Linsey reinvented herself so completely, and of her own volition. "From soliciting in a strip joint to working in a corporate high-rise."

"Well," Rolly says, "the girl mighta had a hand up, just like you said. The counselor in the school's placement office went on and on about one of her girls working at Cole Oil, at their downtown headquarters, no less. I think she would have put the girl in a brochure if she could have, which, of course, is a fucking crack-up. A prostitute on the cover of a school brochure." Rolly chuckles, shaking his head at the thought. "But the thing is, the school didn't get her that job. The counselor was hard pressed to admit that, but once she did, it kind of made sense with something Elise's girlfriend at the Peephole mentioned. One of the barroom regulars at that place was Thomas Cole."

"No shit?"

"Mr. Cole was not only a Peephole regular, he was also one of Ms. Linsey's regulars. You follow me, partner?" Rolly tosses his cigarette butt into an empty pop can on the seat, then tosses the can out the window. "Elise told her girlfriend at the club that Thomas Cole was gon' be her way out."

Jay suddenly has to sit up.

"You got anybody behind you, anyone who's been there awhile."

Rolly checks the rearview mirror. He shakes his head.

Jay pushes himself up with his hands, backing out of the cave underneath the glove compartment. The lights outside the car's windows fishtail and streak before his eyes. It takes a moment before the world settles. He rolls down the passenger-side window as far as it will go, breathing in as much fresh air as his lungs will hold. Rolly turns down the music on the stereo. "The girl didn't make it long with Cole. When I called personnel over there, playing like a prospective employer, you know, they were all too happy to tell me Ms. Linsey was let go after working only six months in Mr. Cole's office."

Jay follows the lines of the freeway through the windshield.

Secretary school. Corporate offices. Thomas Cole.

None of this is what he was expecting.

"And you never came up with anything else?" Jay asks, trying to think of how to put it. "Any other relationships worth nothing? Cops, sheriff's deputies? Federal agents? Anything like that?"

Rolly raises an eyebrow. "What's your deal with this girl again?"

"What about government work?" Jay asks, pushing the issue. "What'd she do after she left Cole?"

"I told you, she got in the real estate game."

Rolly pulls off the 59 freeway somewhere past Beechnut.

"The girl landed on her feet pretty good." He turns off the freeway feeder road into a subdivision called Sugar Oaks Plantation. " 'Cause short of owning your own oil well, real estate is about the best game in town. If you're thinking the girl's got money, it's a good guess that's where she earned it."

Only Jay hadn't thought she *earned* it at all.

In his gut, he had believed the girl was trouble, or at least *in* trouble, and someone had helped her out of a bad situation . . . for a price.

In his head, it was the government, not somebody like Thomas Cole.

In his head, they were using her to get to him.

But he has been known to see things that aren't there, to wake up some nights reaching for his gun, reaching for a world that no longer exists, for friends who are gone. He has been known to jump at sudden noises, to fear a stranger's smile. He is not sure a broken heart, a broken man, can be trusted.

Sugar Land, Texas, the crown jewel of Fort Bend County, was founded more than a hundred years ago as a cotton and sugar plantation. Which, apparently, is license enough for real estate developers to boldly embrace "plantation-style living" as a selling point, with absolutely no hint of irony or restraint. All across the county, savvy developers have sprawled colonial knockoffs and erected white columns over every square inch of newly razed pastureland, wrapping it all up in names like Sweetwater Plantation Estates and Oakville Plantation Homes and Colonial Dreams. At the Sugar Oaks Plantation, there are lawn jockeys at attention on the clipped lawn in front of the clubhouse. They are not black so much as they are tan—not exactly white, but rather some reassuring shade of brown, the universal color of good service. They are meant as a reminder that somebody, somewhere, is working harder than you. The clubhouse, visible from as far back as the 59 freeway, is well lit and alive with good landscaping and fresh white paint. But beyond it, the main road into the subdivision is dotted with stumpish baby pin oaks and clumps of clay and sand where grassy lawns should be. Most of the grand, palatial single-family homes advertised on the painted billboard (FROM THE $120,000s!) on the highway are still in their skeletal phase. They are just skimpy wood frames poking up out of the dirt, casting strange, sickly shadows into the street. Beneath the hazy moonlight, Sugar Oaks looks less like a plantation and more like a cemetery.

At the back of the subdivision is the entrance to the Plantation's "condominium-style living quarters." Rolly's idea is to park the truck inside the apartment complex so as not to draw any attention on the main road. He'll find a spot for the El Camino to hide, and Jay will go in alone. Rolly cuts the engine.

"They pick her up for killing a john?" he asks. "Is that the story?"

Jay shakes his head. "I don't know."

He remembers the groundskeeper's description of the crime scene, the car discovered in a remote, empty field. A couple parked out there alone on a Saturday night, the victim's pants undone. It certainly sounds like it was a date, legit or not. Jay turns to Rolly, thinking out loud, "To hear you tell it, the girl found a new calling. Why would she go back to working backseats?"

"Some habits are hard to break," Rolly says with a shrug. "Maybe if I knew a little more, you know, like what the hell is really going on here . . ."

Jay makes an impulsive decision to trust Rolly with the rest of it: the man from the black Ford, the blackmail money in his office, and his missing gun.

Rolly listens to the whole of it, whistling through his front teeth.

"Damn, man," he says.

"I'm just trying to see what I'm dealing with, you know."

"You don't know who it was? The dead guy?"

"Just his name," Jay says.

Rolly sits up in his seat. "Why don't you let me take a crack at him?"

"What?"

"The dude," Rolly says. "Let me find out who he is."

"You think it's so easy?"

"Shit, man." Rolly shakes his head, as if he's sorely disappointed in Jay's lack of faith. " 'Course, I might need a little extra for it, you know."

Rolly, always hustling.

"You find something," Jay says. "I'll make sure you're taken care of."

"All right, man, cool." He taps another Camel out of his pack.

"What about the phone records from the girl's place?" Jay asks, knowing that Rolly keeps an on-and-off-again girlfriend at Southwestern Bell who has come in handy on more than one occasion. "I'm working on it," Rolly says.

Jay finally starts out of the car.

Rolly leans across the seat. "You carrying?"

Jay thought about going in with a gun. After all, it's more likely than not that this girl shot somebody. But instinct told him to go a different way, that armed he might only cause more trouble for himself. Hell, what if the girl takes one look at him and calls the cops. Empty-handed, he can always say he just came to talk. He shakes his head, waving Rolly off, assuring him that he's fine. But, of course, he doesn't feel fine. His ribs ache and his face is still swollen.

He slams the car door shut, then turns and walks down a pebbled pathway and through a pergola archway that's covered in stiff wisteria branches and thick blooms, which, on a closer look, Jay realizes are made of plastic.

Each unit in the Sugar Oaks Condominiums has its own porch with a white ceiling fan and matching wicker furniture. The pool is kidney shaped and completely empty. Sugar Oaks is not yet operating at full capacity. Jay walks through the desolate courtyard, looking for unit 9B. The condo is tucked in a far corner, on the opposite end of the courtyard from where he entered. The blinds are drawn, but there's light poking through, casting thin streaks of yellow across the painted black slats of the front porch.

He raises his fist and knocks.

There are no footsteps. He hears no padding to the door.

It simply opens without warning.

There, on the other side, is the face he's been chasing.

She takes one look at Jay, takes him all in, head to toe. Then slowly, her mouth curls into a thin half smile. She looks almost reproachful, as if Jay were a tardy dinner guest who's kept her waiting into the night. She does not seem in the least bit surprised to see him at her doorstep after dark. She seems, if anything, to have been expecting him. If not on this night, then some other.

"If it's the same to you," she says, "I'd rather do this inside than out."

He remembers the voice, rusty and sweet around the edges.

"Why don't you come inside?"

He follows her inside the apartment, wincing ever so slightly when she closes the front door, locking them both inside. He doesn't know this woman, only what she's capable of, and he has no reason, as of this moment, to trust her.

The condo smells of fresh paint. It's completely empty except for a pair of tangled sheets and a Louis Vuitton duffel bag in one corner, a bottle of Cutty Sark in another. There's a rotary phone on the floor, near the kitchen.

Elise offers him a drink, making a show of fishing through empty cabinets in the kitchen before simply holding out the bottle of scotch. Jay shakes his head, wanting to stay sharp. Elise raises the bottle to her lips and drinks alone.

Unlike the prim, buttoned-up clothes she wore earlier today at the courthouse, right now she's wearing jeans and what appears to be a man's undershirt. Her nipples and the bones of her rib cage poke through the thin white cotton. She's smaller and a lot younger looking this close up, under the bright white overhead lights in the unfurnished condo. Here, she's open, completely exposed. Beneath the soft putty of her chin, Jay can see thin, ragged rings around her neck, fading bruises that are still visible almost a week after their first meeting on the boat. The colored scars against her white skin startle him. And all at once, he hears her screams again. That night on the boat. The words, *Help me.* He remembers the shrill desperation of it, the I-don't-want-to-die of it. Looking now at the bruises on her neck, he gets the clearest picture yet of just what happened in that parked

Chrysler by the bayou, in those few moments before gunshots tore through the night air.

She stares at Jay, the bottle dangling between her thin fingers.

"Whatever you're thinking about me," she says, "you got it all wrong."

Jay can hear the Galena Park coming out, rounding out her vowels, roughing up the ends of her words. Elise takes another lusty swallow from the liquor bottle, then wipes her mouth with the back of her hand. Jay can imagine her as a girl, growing up in that rough-and-tumble neighborhood. He can see her dusty bare feet, toes dug in the dirt, can picture her begging a quarter from some boy to run up the street for a snow cone or a cherry pop. She has the bony disposition of an alley cat, a wayward thing, hunting for scraps she can use. And like a feral cat, there is the hint of a hulking strength beneath her tiny frame. It's in the way she cuts her eyes at you. If cornered, she will come out fighting.

"He do that to you?" Jay asks, nodding at the marks on her neck. "Dwight Sweeney?"

"I don't know who the hell that is," she says.

Jay stares at her, confused. He thinks she's playing games with him.

"He told me his name was Blake Ellis," she explains.

"He put his hands on you like that?" Jay asks.

"I'm not supposed to be talking about this."

"Your lawyer know he attacked you?"

She shakes her head. "I can't talk about it."

"I don't understand," Jay says, softening toward her in a way he doesn't like or even completely understand. "We dropped you at a police station," he says. "Why didn't you just go in and tell them what he did to you?" He can't help thinking this whole thing might have gone so much differently for all of them. "If this man attacked you, tried to kill you—"

"You never panicked?" Elise asks, her voice rising sharply. "You heard that lawyer in court. I got a record."

The irony is not lost on Jay. He would laugh out loud at the peculiar similarities between their two states of mind if it weren't for the feelings of confusion they engender. He feels a sudden headache coming on, a white-hot point of pressure behind his eyes. He had not been prepared to feel anything but rage toward her. "Who was he?" he asks. "The guy?"

"How the hell should I know?" she says. "We met in a bar. He asked me on a date, took me to some Mexican joint out north. After, he wanted to park a little, which I was all right with." Her words slow to a crawl. "Then he got kind of rough with me and . . ." She looks up at Jay suddenly, the brown color of her eyes going as flat as a puddle of mud. "And that's all I'm gon' say about it."

He can tell by the look on her face that she's decided something just then, decided that he's not entitled to know every god-damned thing about her.

"Look, we don't have a lot of time," she says abruptly, setting the bottle of scotch on the floor next to the telephone. "So why don't you tell me what it is you want, why you're here." She glides across the floor in Jay's direction. "If you wanted to rat me out to the cops, you'da done it by now. So there must be something else you want." She takes another step closer to him, close enough that he can smell a musky sweetness coming off her skin. Remembering her one-time profession, her often enterprising way with men, Jay gets the very strong sensation that she is making him an offer. She has her face tilted up to his suggestively . . . waiting. He might be insulted by the gesture if the whole thing weren't so profoundly sad. "I want you to call him off," he says, pushing her away from him. "I want you to tell him to stay the hell away from my family."

Elise stares at Jay, her eyebrows pinched together. "I'm not sure I know what you're talking about."

"The guy in the Ford . . . the money," he says. "You made your point."

"Is that what this is about? Money?" She actually sounds relieved. "You want money?" She makes a move toward the Louis Vuitton bag.

Jay grabs her by the arm, holding on like a kid who's caught a cat by the tail.

He catches a flash of fire in her eyes, a signal, a warning, even.

"I don't want a goddamned thing from you," he says. "I'll give it back, okay? The money? I'll give it all back. Just call your guy off."

She looks utterly confused. "What are you talking about? What guy?"

Jay doesn't understand where she's going with this, why she would deny it here, now, the two of them alone. He can't follow the game she's playing.

"You telling me you didn't send a guy after me, to pay me off?"

"I don't even know who you are," she says.

"What about the old man on the boat? The captain?"

"What about him?"

"He's dead."

"What are you talking about?" she asks, her voice rising in fear.

"You telling me you don't know anything about it?"

"You're hurting me!"

Jay looks down and realizes he's still holding on to her arm, his fingers digging into her flesh. He feels himself losing control. The pain behind his eyes spikes. The light in the room seems unnecessarily bright. "Where is it?" he asks.

"Where is what?"

"My gun."

Elise shakes her head slowly, as if she's not sure he will understand such a simple gesture. She seems to regard him now as she might a small, highly imaginative child. "I don't know what you think is happening here," she says. "But I'm not trying to get you in any trouble. If anything, I owe you. I know that. You saved my life, and I don't even know your name."

The words have an airy lilt of a question, an invitation maybe. A suggestion that under different circumstances they might have been friends. Her manner seems purposely disarming, almost ingratiating. And it infuriates him as much as it frightens him. The power of it, the pull. Her convincing denial.

It's a trick, he tells himself. *Don't trust it.*

"How do I know you're not going to turn it over to the cops?"

"Turn what over to the cops?"

"My gun," he says, watching her eyes for a flicker, a tell.

"Listen to me, the cops don't know a thing about you. And frankly, I'd like to keep it that way. I was never at the scene. You understand?" she says, wanting to wrestle some cooperation out of him. "The cops don't know a thing."

"Somebody knows," Jay says, raising his voice into a ball of thunder. "He went after the old man on the boat, and now he's coming after me and my wife!"

There's a sudden knock at the front door.

Jay turns and sees the doorknob twisting back and forth,

someone trying to get in from the outside. Jay curses himself for coming in here unarmed. He wishes he'd worked out some kind of signal with Rolly, a backup plan in case shit got rough. Elise starts for the front door. Jay tightens his grip on her arm.

"It's the neighborhood security guard," she explains. "He knows I'm out here alone. He comes by every hour or so to check on me. I asked him to."

Jay is slow to let her go.

"It'll be worse if I don't answer," she says.

When she finally opens the front door, there's a short, stocky man in a red-and-black uniform on the other side. He's wearing riding boots and a pistol on his belt. Elise glances back at Jay. She seems to want him to see that she was telling the truth. The security guard eyes Jay closely, a black man loose on the plantation. "Everything all right?" he asks Elise. "He a reporter or something?"

"He was just leaving," she says, looking at Jay. She seems thankful for the interruption, which, Jay now realizes, she knew was coming. She holds the front door open for him and, in a show of Southern hospitality, steps out onto the tiny front porch, walking him to the little gate, just beyond earshot of the guard. "I'm not trying to hurt you, Jay," she says.

"I thought you said you didn't know my name."

"You just told me," she says, tilting her head to one side. "Inside."

But he didn't . . . *did* he?

He can't remember. His head is starting to ache again.

"I just wish you wouldn't go to the cops about anything, is all. They don't know a thing about you," she says. "I'll give you whatever you want, I swear."

"Why should I trust you?" Jay asks.

He still doesn't understand the man from the black Ford, her insistent denials, or his missing gun. "How do I know you're not trying to set me up?"

"I told you," she says. "I don't even know who you are."

Chapter 20

He told her he believed her. She put a hand on his knee and asked him what he planned to do. They were laid out in the bed of her truck, parked behind an abandoned fairground, next to a faded red barn and a row of sunken bleachers. Underneath a crescent moon, they lay side by side, watching lightning bugs, early for this time of year, dance in the shadows of the pines. Cynthia had walked the grounds earlier, playing on an old swing set while Jay sat smoking cigarettes, watching from the bleachers. She smelled of grass and clay. There were pine needles stuck in her hair. Jay kissed her lips in the back of the truck. She put her hands on the small of his back, inching toward him.

The sex was awkward.

It started too fast and never arrived anywhere. Cynthia kept fidgeting, too much in a hurry and getting in her own way. Eventually, Jay rolled off to one side and pulled up his pants. He lay on his back, listening to Otis Redding crackling on the Ford's tinny radio. *Sitting on the dock of the bay, wasting time . . .*

Cynthia asked again about Roger. What was Jay prepared to do?

The cops had raided Bumpy's girlfriend's place the week before. Cynthia had found Jay coming out of a Spanish lab on the south side of campus and told him he needed to see Bumpy right away. Something big was going down.

Bumpy had been seeing a freshman that spring, a gal studying biology over at TSU. She was living with an auntie in South Park, and against Jay's strident objections, Bumpy had started holding meetings at her place, arguing that they needed to take some of the heat off the Scott Street duplex. They played cards out on the front porch, and sometimes Bumpy's girl would cut hair or let them smoke a little weed if her aunt wasn't home. But they kept no files at the house, no phone sheets or mimeographed flyers. So Jay was more than a little surprised and upset to find that the police had discovered a small arsenal of guns stashed in paper bags under the house. The deputies had made a beeline for the guns within a few minutes of storming the house . . . as if they'd known just where to look. Which could mean only one thing: somebody had snitched.

They had all initially suspected Bumpy's girl. How well did he know her and all that. If she wasn't the rat, it was at least assumed that the girl's aunt, sick of fist-pumping boys coming around her house all time of the day and night, had called the cops. But this assessment didn't hold much weight, especially not after the sheriff's department threatened to arrest the girl *and* her aunt too.

Bumpy went a little crazy over the whole thing. His girl

wouldn't talk to him, and he wanted someone to blame for that, and for his missing weapons, which had been one of the most valuable assets AABL had; the guns were for protection, yes, but they were also a source of income. Bumpy called an emergency meeting at the Scott Street place. Founding members, newcomers, anybody who'd ever made it to even one meeting or showed their face at a rally. He billed it as a rap session, had some of the girls fry up a plate of chicken, made it sound like a party. When the place was filled to capacity, Bumpy shut the door and turned the key, locking everybody inside for almost twenty hours. Lloyd Mackalvy and Roger Holloway were assigned to guard the doors, each armed with a .38.

Bumpy interviewed everybody one-on-one, seeking a second opinion from Jay from time to time, but also grilling Jay when he got the chance, asking if he was talking to anyone outside AABL about the inner workings of their organization. Besides his buddies in AABL, there was only one person Jay talked to, period. And there was no way he would have told Cynthia about the guns.

Jay kept an eye on Roger from across the room. For a soldier on guard, Roger seemed to be having a royally good time. Always a piece of chicken or a beer or a girl in hand, he kept himself far across the room from the heat of inquisition. By the time the sun was coming up the next day, Bumpy had exhausted himself. His eyes were bloodshot, his mouth dry. He had a couple of beers and went to bed before he ever got around to talking to Roger. So Jay took it on himself to ask Roger if he had known about Bumpy's stash in South Park.

"Naw, man," Roger said, picking chicken meat out of his teeth. He wasn't exactly looking Jay in the eye. "I don't even like guns, man. You know that."

"Naw, Roger, that's the thing," Jay said. "I don't know that.

Matter fact, I don't really know a thing about you, man, not really."

"I'm Roger, man," he said, smiling broadly. "Just Roger."

It was an odd, indirect answer. And it kind of sat with Jay funny.

Cynthia was furious about the whole thing and furious with him for not ousting the dude on the spot. She needed no more convincing that Roger Holloway was a snitch. Laid out in the back of her truck, she kept saying over and over that the feds couldn't get away with it. This was *their* government after all, a point he was too tired to argue. He hadn't come out here to talk about Roger, to be lectured by her about whose government it was. Some nights he hated to be reminded of how different they were, how much separated their two views of the world. He wanted to kiss her, to bring her closer. But he felt her slipping away, pulled into some corner in her mind, pouting there like a petulant child. She wanted Roger dealt with. She wanted some show of aggression from him, when all he had was fear and apprehension, and the true knowledge of what *his* government would do to him if he wasn't careful.

Cynthia rolled over flat on her back, pulling her skirt down, covering her knees and every inch of open skin. The silence was there again, popping up between them like mushrooms after a hot spring storm, until there was nothing left except the sound of Otis whistling, and even that faded after a while.

Given the circumstances, the police raid and his growing suspicions about a mole in their midst, Jay had half a mind to cancel the African liberation rally, which was only a couple of weeks away. Stokely, on a swing back from Guinea, was planning to make a speech, and somebody's heard a rumor the *New York*

Times was sending a reporter to cover the event. It was turning into a very big deal. Jay was already worried about drawing any more attention to himself. He knew the feds were watching him closely. The few times he'd traveled out of the state to deliver a speech, he'd been followed on the road, one car clipping the bumper of the borrowed truck he was driving, almost running him into a ditch. Another time, two highway patrolmen pulled him over. They searched his car and made him spend a night in lockup because his right taillight was out. He knew the government was looking for any reason to trap him, and he was afraid of the lengths to which the feds would go to silence him.

Plus, there was no way of knowing if Roger was the *only* government informant on campus. Any fool would guess he wasn't. As Cynthia had taken pains to point out, this was something that affected all of them. Political organizing, free speech, the whole goddamned Constitution. None of it was safe. And if Jay canceled the rally, she said, then they all might as well turn their tails in the air; they deserved every ass-fucking rape of their civil rights the government had in store for them. She said it would be a disgrace if he canceled.

Other than the general principle of the thing, he didn't understand why Cynthia was so worked up, why she cared so much about one rally. He didn't think Cynthia's group, Students for a Democratic Society, nearly blinded as they were by their collective rage over Johnson's bullshit war, gave two shits about Africa. And he didn't want them at his rally no way. The local chapter of SDS was rancorous and full of infighting and prone to gross theatrics. They had once doused the university's provost in pig's blood as he was coming out of a staged production of *My Fair Lady* at the school's performance hall. In an article claiming responsibility for the prank in the next day's edition of the *Daily Cougar,* a senior officer of SDS said they felt they needed to get people's attention any way they could, that marches and rallies weren't making the deaths of American soldiers real enough to folks. Jay didn't understand what the university's provost had to do with Vietnam, or what drowning him in pig's blood was going to do except piss him off and make it harder for everybody else to be heard.

But he did see their point about the fading power of speech.

The sight of kids chanting and marching through the streets with fists raised was getting more and more common. On its face, it was no longer enough to shock, to wake up the masses, and, more important, the powers that be.

Jay was ready to try something new, a different tactic altogether.

Economic boycotts. Or "consumer sanctions," he called them.

He had already leaked the idea to the papers. But at the rally, he would make it official. He planned to call for a nationwide boycott of some of the biggest corporations in America, companies that were continuing to benefit from a history of colonial and economic oppression of brown people, that made money off the continent of Africa and its people. He would name names.

Coca-Cola and Johnson & Johnson.

Shell and Gulf Oil.

The big petroleum companies sucking the Congo dry.

He supposed Cynthia knew what all this meant to him, this push for global uplift, and he liked to think that was the reason she was behind the rally, why she kept pushing for him to protect it, to move forward with his plans.

He had no real proof of Roger's wrongdoings. And he was afraid to get into it with Bumpy for fear of what Bumpy might do to the kid if Jay even floated the idea that Roger was on the wrong side of things. Jay needed everybody to keep a cool head. If the kid was an informant, laying so much as a scratch on his back was a colossally bad idea. And Bumpy was still fuming about his guns.

So Jay kept his fears to himself and vacillated about what to do with the rally. Up until the last thirty-six hours, he was on the fence. He kept running through the evidence against Roger in his head, all of it circumstantial:

1. Roger wasn't even a student on campus.
2. No one was really sure where Roger lived.
3. He had offered to help Jay with the rally, offered to type up copies of Jay's speech, his outline for corporate boycotts, and the call for global unity.
4. He'd also cozied up to Alfreda Watkins, and in the process gotten a good, long look at AABL's fund-raising roster, the names and addresses of people in the community who'd given what little money they had.
5. He'd been hanging around the duplex for months and had occasionally been by Bumpy's girlfriend's place out in South Park. If Roger had been snooping around, he could have easily found the guns there on his own.

Added together, it didn't look good, and Jay had to make a decision about the rally before Stokely got on a very expensive flight from Oakland to Houston.

Because of the bugs crawling all over the Scott Street duplex, Jay made the call from Cynthia's place. She was off campus by then, in a one-room shotgun shack in the Bottoms in Third Ward. He needed a place where he could camp out for a while. It would take hours to track down Stokely, who was back in the country by then, reportedly on the West Coast. Jay needed a secure line where Stokely could call him back if Jay had to leave a message for him. Cynthia made a pot of coffee, rubbed his shoulders while he waited. When the call came, she left him alone. She kissed his forehead and walked out of the house.

Jay lit one cigarette after another and ran it down for Brother Carmichael.

The cops, the guns, the raid.

Maybe, baby, I'm just tripping out on the vibe down here.

Tell me I'm just seeing things.

But if he was looking to Stokely to cool his paranoia, he'd picked the wrong dude. Talking to a Panther about a fed in their midst was like dropping a match in a pool of black oil. The shit was gon' blow. "This is the most elemental expression of fascism in its purest state, my brother," Stokely said, his voice cracking like lightning. "What they cannot silence, they will exterminate. You need to open your eyes to the truth of this thing. They trying to kill us, brother."

The words poured out of the phone like tear gas, filling up every space in the room, burning, stinging, gobbling up Jay's breath. "This ain't no game," Stokely said. "If you got even a hunch about this dude, get rid of him, push him out now. We in a war, brother. You got to get them before they get you."

He was talking fast, moving at a dangerous clip.

Jay shook his head. "But that's exactly what they want, man. We start kicking people out left and right, until there's nothing left. And they sitting back somewhere laughing, watching us tear ourselves apart."

There was a long pause on the other end of the phone.

Stokely came back soft, somewhat reflective. "Fred Hampton, man," he said. "How much more you need to hear to know these cats mean business?"

Now it was Jay's side of the line that went dead silent.

He sat there for a long time on Cynthia's floor, running his fingers through the fringe of a Navajo blanket that was covering the concrete floor. He thought about those boys in Chicago, and he had a clear, sudden image of his mother at his own funeral. She would bring him back to Nigton, he knew. Back to Nig Town. Nigger Town. She would bury him right where he was born, and it would be done and over with, like he'd never even been here, like nothing had even changed. She would bury him right next to his twenty-one-year-old father.

No, he had to fight. But he wanted to do this right.

"I don't know shit about this dude, man," Jay said, meaning Roger. "I don't know nothing for sure. Maybe I ought to talk to him first, you know."

"They not teaching our boys over in Southeast Asia to stop and *talk* to the Vietcong. No, they tell those boys to shoot first, ask questions never. And that's how we need to do things." He said it again. His new catchphrase. A slogan for the new decade. *Shoot first, ask questions never.* "You hear me, brother?" he said.

"Yeah, I hear you," Jay said, though he was not sure he completely understood what Stokely was getting at, what he was really suggesting. Jay couldn't tell how much of this was the rhetoric talking—Stokely sped up by his own language, not able to stop himself—and how much of this was real.

Were they talking about an execution?

In theory or in practice?

"Y'all need to handle that nigger," Stokely said gruffly. "Quick."

"I'll take care of it," Jay said. His last words on the phone.

In the end, Stokely never made it to the rally.

He claimed pressing business on the coast. Brother Huey

was still incarcerated at the time, and there was a growing beef between Carmichael and the Panther Party's leadership. Stokely said he was staying in California to keep the brothers and sisters down there on point, though Jay strongly believed that Stokely's absence was meant as a clear message to him. *Clean your house, brother.*

It was a big blow.

They lost the *Times.* And the *Chronicle* only sent one photographer. Jay put him down front by the stage. He wanted a clean shot of the banner: AFRICAN LIBERATION: GLOBAL UNITY, ECONOMIC PARITY.

Roger Holloway was not supposed to be there.

When Jay finally broke down and told Bumpy and Lloyd and Marcus Dupri about his suspicions and his conversation with Stokely, the founding officers unanimously voted on a course of action: Roger was not to be touched. In fact, they would act as if nothing had changed . . . and use this newfound information about Roger to their advantage. Two could play the spy game.

Lloyd was put on counterintelligence.

His job was to provide Roger with all the pussy and beer and weed he could handle, to make good friends with the boy, and, mainly, to find out where he lived. When the time was right, he was to break into Roger's place and confiscate whatever had been taken from them; he would destroy any incriminating evidence Roger was collecting against the members of AABL.

And Lloyd was supposed to keep Roger away from the rally.

The morning of, Lloyd had Roger drunk and halfway to a cathouse west of Waco when Roger made Lloyd turn the car around. There was no way, he said, he was gon' miss the rally. It was his deal as much as Jay's. He found his way onto the stage in the main cafeteria at the student union, Lloyd right at his side, keeping a close eye on him. Bumpy and Marcus Dupri and

Alfreda Watkins were lined up on the dais, their backs against the north wall, underneath the banner. They were dressed in all black, arms clasped behind their backs. Jay was in an olive-colored dashiki, laced with bits of chocolate and amber and russet. He had an elephant's hair bracelet on his left wrist, a used Timex on the other. It was sometime after three o'clock when he stepped to the podium. He scratched his goatee and looked out across the crowd.

"Brothers and sisters," he said, his voice echoing through the cafeteria. "Despite what our current administration would have the world think of us, we know the young people of this nation to be full of heart and grace, to be appreciators of human struggle and soldiers for justice. *We* are the true patriots."

Jay's voice was strong, sure and focused. He felt at home onstage.

Delores Maxwell, one of Alfreda's sorors, was in the crowd passing out leaflets, glossy foldouts that had cost them fifty dollars at the printers. They listed the main points of the speech, the tenets of this new call for global unity.

"We gather here today out of complete and total necessity, for we know we cannot stand down. For the first time, we intend to hold the American political establishment *and* American corporations to the fire on the issue of global oppression, the continued raping of Africa's natural resources and oppression of its peoples. Injustice abroad is a threat to justice here at home."

Jay watched Delores move through the crowd. Folks were nodding and clapping, flipping through the leaflet. The doors were open and his words were pulling in people from nearby buildings. More students, professors too. They were curious about Jay, this young man with the booming voice and big ideas.

"We have to take this to the next level, people. We have to let these folks know that we are prepared to exercise our power beyond the ballot box or the bullet. We are prepared to exercise our political power as consumers. If big business wants us to buy, they gon' have to show some respect for the issues we got in our hearts and minds. They gon' have to come correct, you hear? From this point on, we take the fight for justice from the political to the economic."

Some of the black cafeteria workers had stepped out from the kitchen. In white smocks and hairnets, they huddled at the back of the room. Jay waved them forward. Today, the floor was theirs. Delores gave them leaflets too.

Jay was just diving into the first of his ten points when he heard the other group come in. It was two dozen of 'em, at least. They came in through the back door, their feet heavy on the linoleum floor, their march exaggerated to get everyone's attention. Cynthia was at the head, her fist in the air.

At the sight of her, Jay lost his place in the speech.

Behind him, he heard Marcus whisper, "What the fuck are they doing here?"

Jay had told Cynthia to stay away. He had told SDS to stay out of it. He was sure this was another one of their stunts.

Cynthia climbed onto the dais.

Jay covered the microphone with his hand. He whispered, "What is this?"

She was wearing a man's vest over a ruffled, coral-colored blouse. She tugged at her shirt, smoothing it out. "This is our fight too, Jay."

Our.

She yanked the microphone right out of his hand.

"Brothers and sisters."

Bumpy grabbed Jay by the arm. "What the fuck?" he said, loud enough for the microphone to pick up the words and lob them across the room. Cynthia turned around to face Bumpy.

"We mean you no disrespect, brother," she said, her voice dulcet, almost cheerful. "But this is something that affects us all."

The spectators on the floor seemed confused. SDS had taken up positions along the walls. Jay, the organizer of the march, had seemingly lost control. The air in the room felt tight, in short supply. The cameraman from the *Chronicle* must have sensed the tension building. His lens cap came off for the first time.

Cynthia was now addressing her comments to the black folks on the floor. "We are here today not as rivals but as compatriots, partners in struggle," she said. "Make no mistake, we appreciate the struggle for our people in Africa."

OUR people.

"But we have some domestic issues that need to be addressed first. Namely, the encroachment of the federal government and their systematic oppression of our right to peaceably assemble. They are infiltrating our groups, people, illegally tape-recording our phone conversations."

Jay reached for the microphone. Cynthia shoved him back.

"We know your group has been hit," she said, looking back at the men onstage, looking a little too long and hard at Roger. "And we stand here in solidarity with you, to say we're not going to take this anymore."

She pointed a pale white finger in Roger's direction. "The rat must go."

Jay grabbed her from behind, and the microphone dropped to the floor, a loud thump echoing across the room. One of the SDS boys yelled, "Let her talk, man. You guys don't own the cafeteria, you know."

Jay had her firmly in his arms. He pressed his cheek against her neck. He whispered in her ear. "Stop this, Cynthia. Stop this shit right now."

She was still glaring at Roger, calling him a rat, over and over.

Roger, a little guy to begin with, was only a few inches taller than Cynthia. He squared his shoulders and stepped to her, hopped up on the balls of his feet, peering down at her as best he could. "What the fuck you just call me?"

"I called you a rat, motherfucker." She took her same white finger and poked him in the chest with it. Not once, but twice. Which was all it took. Roger hit her across the mouth with his fist, knocking her so hard that her head butted back and caught Jay across the chin. When Roger raised his hand to her again, Jay pushed Cynthia aside and clocked the man himself. He got Roger good across his cheekbone, and then once in the stomach.

There were flashbulbs going off every few seconds. The photographer was snapping away. Cynthia had tumbled to the floor of the stage. Jay squatted down and asked her if she was okay. He didn't see Roger behind him. But he felt a swift kick across his ribs and felt himself falling from the stage, dragging Cynthia with him. When he looked up from the cafeteria floor, Lloyd had Roger by the arms. Bumpy had a weapon drawn at his side, ready if need be.

A few months later, Marcus Dupri would testify on the stand that he saw what happened next from the stage. He saw the first chair get thrown. It was a white kid, he said to the judge and jury. It was SDS who started the worst of it.

But in the end, it didn't matter because, after that, all hell broke loose.

First, some of the SDS boys in the back overturned a table.

The rest of them rushed the stage.

The African liberation banner came down in someone's fist.

Marcus Dupri shoved one of the white kids tearing up the stage.

Somebody punched Lloyd across the mouth.

Lloyd let go of Roger and grabbed a member of SDS by the

back of the neck. He whacked the kid across the knees with the microphone stand.

The whole stage exploded into a ball of arms and legs.

Bumpy fired his weapon into the air.

In the back, the cafeteria workers ran.

Jay ducked, covering his head as the first window was broken.

He reached for Cynthia. But she was gone.

In the chaos, they were separated.

He crawled across the floor, staying low.

He was, foolish as it may seem now, looking for her.

It was the university police who showed up first. A huge tactical mistake. Only three officers to deal with two hundred or so riotous college students, some of them armed. They should have waited for the team of HPD officers who were only a few minutes behind them. Instead, the campus cops arrived, ill equipped and unable to stop most of the people from running for the exits.

Bumpy got out. Lloyd and Roger too.

Alfreda and Delores.

Jay was still on the floor when HPD stormed the building a few moments later. The cops lined them up in a paddy wagon, "niggers on one side, whites on the other." The news photographer showed them his press pass, and they let him go, but not before confiscating his camera. Jay, his hands cuffed behind his back, watched as they kicked the photographer out of the van, slamming the door on him while he shouted on the street, going on about his rights.

At the station, the men were booked together, then segregated once again, into separate cells. By the next morning, they were released one by one.

All of them except Jay.

His lawyer tried to prepare him a few minutes before the

arraignment. The charge was inciting a riot. Jay said he wasn't guilty, so that was the plea. It was all cut and dry, he thought. Except the judge refused bail. They wouldn't let him go home. Then, a few days after his arraignment, they moved him from men's central to a holding cell at the federal courthouse downtown. He tried to rap with the officers who made the escort, but nobody would tell him nothing.

He asked to speak to his lawyer.

They sent a new guy. A kid not that much older than Jay.

They met in a dirty room with low light and no windows.

The kid had a folder tucked under his arm.

Jay said, for the dozenth time, that this was all a misunderstanding. He'd given a speech, which the United States Constitution, last he checked, gave him every right to do. He hadn't thrown one chair, hadn't destroyed any property or asked anybody else to do so. And he had the witnesses to prove it. It was a rally, he said, not a riot.

"That," the lawyer said, "is the least of your problems."

From his folder, he pulled out a black-and-white photo.

It was the rally. Jay onstage. A shot of him clocking Roger Holloway.

"The feds want to charge you with conspiracy to commit murder against a federal informant, Mr. Porter."

It was official: Roger Holloway was a snitch.

Jay pushed the photo across the table. "This is bullshit," he said. "I hit the guy 'cause he was being a punk, not 'cause I was trying to kill him."

"They got you on tape, Jay."

"What are you talking about?"

"Something about you, uh, 'handling a nigger.' "

Jay shook his head. *No, man, you got it all wrong.*

Then he remembered.

The phone call to Stokely. The call he'd made from Cynthia's house.

Jay's stomach sank, down past his knees.

It was nearly impossible for him to accept what he was hearing. For yes, it was conceivable that the federal government knew about his relationship with Cynthia, that they had bugged her place as well as his. But he also, in this moment, had to acknowledge the possibility that Cynthia—who had been the first to point out Roger's suspicious behavior, who had chided Jay for not doing something about it, who had shown up at the rally uninvited—had put the bug in the phone herself, had kissed his forehead and walked out the door.

Chapter 21

He wakes up alone, about an hour before dawn, his wife somewhere way across town. He lies curled up on the couch, one hand lifted over his head, balancing a glass of whiskey on the arm of the sofa. His third, if you count the two he downed when he walked in the door tonight, before he collapsed on the couch into a few fitful hours of sleep, his dreams a disjointed parade of faces.

Lyndon "Bumpy" Williams and Marcus Dupri. Lloyd Mackalvy and Alfreda Watkins. Charlie Wade Robinson and Natalia Greenwood. Lionel Jessup and Ronnie Powell and M. J. Frank. Carl Petersen. Cynthia Maddox. He woke up thinking about them all, marveling at the difference a decade makes, between then and now, between their dreams and where they landed. From death to prison to the mayor's office, and the many cramped spaces in between.

Of them all, Cynthia made the greatest leap.

By whatever means . . . Jay may never know.

The true pain of it really, the not knowing.

And the blinding confusion that brings.

Jay rolls over and stares at his water-stained ceiling. He rests the half-empty glass of whiskey on his bare chest, feeling the cool ring of its bottom against his skin. He remembers the promise he made to his wife. The promise to himself. Of a home. A man. One with moving parts. And a working heart.

Because he can't sleep, he pulls the wad of folded-up copier pages out of the pocket of his pants. They are newspaper articles and such, part of Rolly's full report on Elise Linsey. Jay glanced at them once in the dark cab of Rolly's truck. Now, alone in his apartment, he reads through the pages carefully for the first time, absorbing every detail of the life they describe. He reads about Elise Linsey's high school track team, her mother dying, and the arrests that made it into the back pages of the *Pasadena Citizen* and the *Houston Chronicle* and the *Post*.

Slowly, though, as he continues to read, a picture of the new, improved Elise Linsey emerges in the printed pages. Over the last eight months, her name has been mentioned in both of the city's main newspapers as a contact for residential properties newly on the market. One of the real estate listings is for the empty condo at the Sugar Oaks Plantation. The pages give Jay a picture of her current professional life. It *is* entirely possible that Elise Linsey has made a good living selling high-end suburban homes, that she's turned her life around.

The only really curious bit in the stack of newspaper clippings is an article from the *Houston Chronicle* that Jay has to read twice before he understands it, or rather what, at all, it has to do with Elise Linsey. He runs his finger down the columns to find her name in print because he missed it the first time around.

The article is several inches wide, with a large photo in the center—a picture of a craggy-looking man in his early sixties, wearing a baseball cap and overalls, one side of them held up by a large safety pin. From first glance, Jay takes him for a working man, can almost see the dirt under his fingernails and smell the sweat off his back. In the picture, the man is standing on what appears to be his front porch. There's a Texas flag waving behind his head and limp petunias in a box planter hanging from a kitchen window. In his hands, the man is holding an oversize poster board, eight very distinct words printed on it:

JIMMY CARTER, GIVE ME MY DANG JOB BACK!

JIMMY CARTER has been crossed out with two dark lines, replaced by RONALD REAGAN, whose name has been scribbled in an arc over Carter's.

The caption beneath the photo reads:

Erman Joseph Ainsley, of High Point, returns from Washington, D.C.

The piece, from a Sunday *Chronicle* a couple of months back, is printed beneath a boldface heading called "Cityscapes," where readers can find little tidbits of nonessential news, mostly local color and commentary. Stories highlighting a senior citizen beauty pageant or a preschool golf team or a dog somebody trained to barbecue brisket. Cute little stories about local eccentrics or pieces of neighborhood flavor. It's exactly the place you'd expect to find an article about Erman Joseph Ainsley, of High Point, Texas—a man who had, according to the article, just returned from his second one-man march on Washington:

Don't get Erman Joseph Ainsley started about the New Testament's David and Goliath. You're liable to get an hour-long lecture about the pitiful state of humanity, or about the big guns in Washington who, he says, want to take advantage of your fears.

"They think they can get away with any damn thing," Ainsley, a former salt mine worker, says, speaking of the government. "But not on my watch. Not here in High Point."

Ask anyone in High Point, Texas, a small community just outside Baytown, and they'll tell you that Erman Ainsley is not a man easily deterred. For the past four years—since he lost his job a few months short of retirement when the Crystal-Smith Salt Co. closed its seventy-five-year-old factory in High Point—Ainsley has been working tirelessly to save his beloved town. "I've lived here all my life," he says. "I was born in this house."

Ainsley looks young for his sixty-plus years. He talks fast and rarely stops for a breath. "My daddy worked the mine, my granddaddy before him. This is all I've ever known. When they took that, they took everything. What we got left?"

The closing of the mine was a crushing blow to a town with no other industry, save for small coffee shops and a single hotel that served workers who came from as far as Beaumont and Port Arthur to work two- and three-day shifts at the mine. The hotel has since closed. Two small cafés on High Point's Main Street are also considering closing.

"It just ain't enough people here no more," says Wanda Beasley, a woman in her early fifties who favors hot pink jogging suits and Keds sneakers. She's been running her father's restaurant, the Hot Pot, for twenty years now. "I've never seen it this bad."

Most of the houses in Mr. Ainsley's modest neighborhood are boarded up. Ainsley's newest beef is with the real estate developers who are canvassing the town and buying up acres and acres of residential property. "If somebody comes around offering me some money, you can believe I'm gonna take it and get the hell out of here," says one resident in between bites of Wanda's "famous" Frito pie.

It's this lack of town loyalty that gets under Ainsley's skin.

"They sold out," he says.

His crusade started with the local city council, then his state representative, then his congressman—writing letters, calling their offices incessantly, demanding help for his struggling town—but these days Ainsley directs almost as much of his energy toward his own neighbors. Two or three days a week, he stands in front of Wanda's place and passes out flyers, warning people against talking to any real estate folks from Houston.

Some people in the community consider him a menace. He's being blamed for a rash of strange, late-night phone calls in town—lots of heavy breathing and abrupt hangups. A number of townsfolk think that Ainsley is making the calls to scare the residents he feels are contributing to the problem. But when presented with the accusation, Ainsley responded with a single harsh word, "Hogwash." He doesn't seem to care that he's alienating the very people he claims to be trying to help. He just wants the world to know what's going on in High Point. From his personal Rolodex, Ainsley offered this reporter the name and home addresses of the former owners of the Crystal-Smith Salt Co., as well as the name of a real estate agent representing the Stardale Development Company, based in Houston, which has already bought twenty homes in High Point. Pat Crystal and Leslie Smith offered a written statement thanking Mr. Ainsley for his dedication and years of service to their company, adding that the closing of the salt mine was simply an economic decision. Elise Linsey, the real estate agent, could not be reached for comment.

Through the floorboards, Jay hears Mr. Johnson's television set come on.

A few seconds later, he hears the opening theme song to *AM Magazine*, a locally produced morning news show, which his neighbor often listens to at full volume. The song means it's half past six. Jay is still drunk. In a minute, he will get up, make a pot of strong coffee, and call his wife. For now, he remains sunk into the couch, staring at the article.

He doesn't know which is more interesting. The fact that Elise Linsey was, at one point, working for a well-financed real estate development company. Or the byline at the top of the page. The name catches his attention right away. It's familiar to him even before he can exactly place where he's seen it.

When it finally comes to him, the name, it pushes him up out of his seat.

Because the man who wrote the article about Erman Joseph Ainsley and the closed salt mine is the same man who left the note for Elise Linsey at her doorstep—the note that Jay found by chance, days before her arraignment, before her court case had even made the evening news.

By the time he makes it into work, there are two cops waiting for him.

Eddie Mae takes one look at Jay and, unsolicited, brings him a can of tomato juice from the vending machine by the parking lot. She sets the morning-after elixir on her desk. Jay downs it in a single gulp, his hand shaking a bit as he returns the empty can to Eddie Mae. He steals a nervous glance through the open doorway to his private office, where the cops are waiting. Detectives, he can tell by their dress, the starched shirt collars and clean-shaven skin.

"What in the hell happened to you anyway?" Eddie Mae asks, nodding at his bruised face. He knows he looks like hell, and his nerves are only making things worse. He dabs his damp forehead with a corner of his sleeve and straightens his tie. "Lock the door," he says to Eddie Mae. "And don't let anybody in."

"Mr. Porter?"

Jay buttons his suit jacket and walks into his office.

One of the cops, in his late thirties, is seated in front of Jay's desk smoking a cigarette, Jay's ashtray resting on his thigh. The other cop, the older one, is standing next to Jay's filing cabinet, a few inches from the stash of dirty money. Jay wonders how much they know, how much trouble he's already in.

The young one moves first, returning Jay's ashtray to his desk and moving quickly onto his feet. He shakes Jay's hand, the cigarette resting between his middle and ring fingers. "I'm Detective Andy Bradshaw, Mr. Porter. And this is Detective Sam Widman, my partner." Widman is still lingering by the filing cabinet, his eyes scanning the stack of files on top. He appears to be reading the names on the labels. He glances at Jay and gives him a simple nod.

The blinds in Jay's office are open. He takes a measured stride across the room, aware that the cops' investigation began before he even walked into the room; they're marking his movements. He pulls a string to close the blinds, then bends to pick up a stray stack of files on the floor, walking them to his desk as if this is all a part of his morning routine. "What can I help you with, Officers?"

"What happened to your face?" Widman speaks for the first time. He's still standing by the filing cabinet, the heel of his shoe practically touching the drawer where the money is hiding. He's staring at Jay, waiting for an answer.

"I fell down some stairs," Jay says.

Widman cocks his head to one side, eyeing the shape and color of the bruises on Jay's face. "You must have fallen pretty hard, Mr. Porter."

"Can I ask what this is about, Detectives?"

"You know a man named Marshall Hennings?"

"Pardon?" Jay asks, because at first the name doesn't even register.

Widman's partner, Bradshaw, stubs his cigarette into the ashtray. "Mr. Hennings manned a boat you were on, Mr. Porter, the night of August first."

So . . . here we go.

"Yes, that's right," he says.

"Mr. Porter, Mr. Hennings died sometime shortly thereafter," Widman says. "He was found in his automobile in a ditch along Elysian, north of here. It was more likely than not a car accident, but in the course of our investigation, some questions came up. And, you know, we have to look at every angle."

"Sure."

"That's why we're here," Detective Bradshaw says.

"About Marshall?" Jay asks.

"Yes."

Jay looks back and forth between the two detectives. "Marshall?"

"Did Mr. Hennings seem all right to you that night?" Widman asks. "Did he seem well?"

"Well, I'd never met the man before, but . . . sure, he seemed fine."

"And there was nothing unusual about his behavior?"

"No."

"Nothing unusual about that night at all."

Jay pretends to consider this. "No, not that I can recall."

Detective Bradshaw makes a note on a tiny pad he lifts from his shirt pocket. Widman watches him, then glances down at his right shoe, the heel of which he taps lightly against the bottom drawer of the filing cabinet. "Jimmy Rochelle, a relative of Mr. Hennings, said something about you asking if Marshall had talked to any cops," Widman says, looking up. "Why did you imagine Mr. Hennings would have been in touch with law enforcement?"

"Jimmy must have misunderstood me," Jay says, frightened by how easily the words come, the lie leaping from his lips. "When Jimmy said Marshall hadn't been heard from, I believe I asked Jimmy if *he'd* called the police."

"He says you called looking for Marshall."

"Two of his lady friends also said you contacted them," Bradshaw adds.

"Why were you trying so hard to get in touch with him?"

Jay doesn't want them to see him thinking. He goes with the first words out of his mouth. "My wife lost a bracelet. We thought it might be on the boat."

"But you never spoke with Mr. Hennings?" Detective Bradshaw asks.

"No." Then he adds, "And anyway, my wife found it, the bracelet."

Detective Bradshaw smiles. He and Widman exchange a glance. For the first time, Widman steps away from the filing cabinet. Bradshaw tucks his notepad back into his pocket. The two detectives thank Jay for his time.

"That's it?" Jay asks, trying not to sound too relieved.

"Unless there's something else you want to add," Widman says.

"Not that I can think of," Jay says.

"Well," Detective Bradshaw says. "Thank you again, Mr. Porter."

"Sure thing, Detective."

The cops gone, Jay tells Eddie Mae to keep the front door locked.

Then he shuts himself in his office and, alone, reaches under his desk for the phone book. He's got some questions of his own that he wants answered.

The *Chronicle*'s main line is busy. He gets a voice on the fourth try. He asks to speak to a Lon Philips. The line is soon ringing again, twelve times before someone finally picks up. The voice on the other end is thin and high pitched for a man. He sounds young, Jay thinks, green as a new blade of grass.

"Philips." His tone is impatient, distracted. Jay can hear a typewriter clackety-clacking a mile a minute in the background. "What is it?" he barks.

Jay clears his throat. "Sir, I want to ask you about a piece you wrote a couple of months back. Late June, you wrote an article about an Erman Ainsley."

The typewriter comes to an abrupt stop. "I'm sorry, who are you?"

"My name is Jay Porter. I'm an attorney here in Houston."

There's a pause on the line. "The old man got himself a lawyer, huh?"

The question strikes Jay as curious. What in the world does Ainsley need a lawyer for? "No," Jay says. "I'm calling you about someone else, actually."

"Well, I'm in the middle of a story right now." The typewriter starts up again, at full speed. "I'm on a three o'clock deadline."

"I'll be quick."

Jay checks to make sure the door to his office is closed. Then he asks the million-dollar question: "Why have you been trying to contact Elise Linsey?"

The typing stops again. Jay can hear Philips's breathing through the line.

"She was the real estate agent you wrote—"

"I know who she is," Philips says.

"I know you've been by her house," Jay says. "Two months after your article went to print, you're still trying to reach her, and what I want to know is, why?"

"My work is my business, Mr. Por-ter," Philips says. By the way he draws out the name, Jay gets the idea that he's writing it down.

"I guess I just want to know," Jay says, "if this is something to do with the homicide in Fifth Ward."

"You one of Charlie Luckman's boys?" Philips asks. "I'm not doing anything illegal, just so you know. Your client is free to call me back or not."

"I think you've misunderstood me," Jay says. "I don't work for Charlie Luckman. And I certainly don't work for Elise Linsey."

"Well, who are you then?"

"I said my name is Jay Porter. I'm a lawyer here in Houston, which, in this case, is somewhat incidental," he says. "The thing is, I read your piece on Mr. Ainsley, and I was wondering about the connection to Elise Linsey, why you're still following her movements. Is this about her court case?"

"How do I know you're not a reporter?" Philips asks from out of the blue.

To Jay, it's another odd question. "I just told you I'm not."

Philips is quiet a minute, his typewriter completely still.

"Well, that's not good enough," he says.

Jay hears a loud click. It's another second or two before he realizes the line is dead. The phone book is still sitting on his desk, sitting right on top of all the other work he should be doing. He picks it up and opens to the *S*'s.

The Stardale Development Company maintains an office on Fountainview, out west of the Loop, just off the 59 freeway. Jay heads in that direction on his lunch hour, but not before trying the number that's listed in the phone book. He gets a recorded message, five times in a row.

The foolishness of this errand is not lost on him. But he feels reeled in by her, yoked by his own curiosity and his inability to take at face value Elise's promise to leave him out of her troubles. Somewhere deep down, he knows. It's his own fault. He knows what the weight of his past has cost him, then and now. He knows the places where he can't let go. Where his faith falls short.

His wife still out of the house, the dirty money still stashed inside his office, the man in the black Ford still at large, in possession of Jay's .22. . . . He has not slept a solid night in days.

Or is it years?

He gets mixed up sometimes.

Talk radio is hot on the strike.

Almost every number on the Buick's AM dial has callers lined up, one after the other, happy to offer what little information they've picked up. From somebody's brother who works the docks. Or an uncle who's a project manager at one of the refineries. Jay listens to the parade of rampant speculation over a ham sandwich and a Coke as he makes the drive to the west side.

One gal on 740 AM claims to know firsthand that the strike won't make it another week. She's got a girlfriend who answers phones over to the mayor's business development office, and according to this friend, the mayor and the unions and the business heads have already worked out some kind of an agreement. They're just holding out on this thing a little while longer so they can jack up the price of everything from gasoline to coffee. She advises a citywide boycott in protest. To which the next five callers reply that there is no way in hell they intend to live without gasoline *or* coffee. Or any other goddamned thing they want to buy with *their* money. One man calls in to remind the listening audience, "You know, we got it good down here. They're paying near a dollar fifty for gas over to Arkansas and Oklahoma, a dollar sixty out in Arizona and California. We got nothing to complain about."

Jay snaps off the car radio and balls the butt of his ham sandwich inside the waxed paper it came in, stuffing the whole of it into a paper bag. He lights a cigarette as he pulls into a strip-center parking lot across the street from 4400 Fountainview, which is a newly constructed, low-lying office building encased in walls of mirrored glass that painfully catch the afternoon sun. Jay yanks down his car's plastic visor, shielding his eyes. He smokes his Newport and waits.

Twenty minutes pass, then thirty. In the whole time he's watching and waiting, no one, that he can see, has come in or out of the building across the street. When the heat in the Skylark becomes unbearable, he finally gets out of his car. Dodging lunchtime traffic, he crosses the street to the office building.

The doors to 4400 Fountainview are locked. The building, as far as Jay can tell, is completely closed. He walks around to the parking lot in back. There are no cars anywhere, not a stitch of litter, not a paper cup or even a gum wrapper. The building's back doors are locked too. Jay pulls on them a few times. Then, cupping his hands around his eyes and pressing his face against the glass, he peers into the building. Inside, he sees nothing. Not even a desk or a telephone. The Stardale Development Company is, apparently, no more than an empty building.

Chapter 22

He has a dream about dead ends. Streets in his hometown. He's
a boy, five, maybe six years old, dressed in a Roy Rogers vest
and cowboy boots made of cheap plastic and dusty with red clay.
He's got a toy holster on his belt. The matching gun is missing,
has been for some time. He lost it or let his sister take it or some
neighborhood kid ran off with it. In the dream, he can't remember. In the dream, he's looking for something else. He sets out
early in the morning with two ham sandwiches in a knapsack
and a small carton of milk.

He sets out to find his father.

He imagines his daddy tied up on somebody's fort, held cap-
tive by a general's army or maybe taken in by Indians. Jay will
be the one to save him, the one to bring him home. But in the

dream, he's only a little boy, and scared of the dark sometimes. He doesn't have a horse or even a gun. And he can't get out of Nigton. The streets ain't laid out right, not like he remembers. And seems like every road he tries starts out wide with promise, only to stop a few yards later at a point so narrow he can barely pass through. The road suddenly becomes thick with scrub oak and weeds, tall and thin as reeds, with points as sharp as needles. He thinks of snakes and chigger bites and is too scared to venture forth. Each time, he backs up the way he came, starts over again, down another road . . . until he finally accepts that he's going nowhere, only walking in wide circles, always ending up on the same street corner, stuck in the middle of an unworkable grid.

The light behind the trees starts to fade.

His food is almost gone.

He feels himself getting scared.

Jay turns and sees a kid not that much taller than he is. The kid says he's Jay's father, says it more than once. Jay shakes his head over and over, stamps his little foot in the dirt. His daddy is a man, not no boy. The kid kicks a rock with his shoe, tells Jay he can believe him or not. But the truth is waiting for him, if he can just get home. Just look under the house, the kid says. I'll be waiting for you, he says, kicking the rock all the way down the street.

The way home is long and black and full of thorns and mosquito bites.

Jay arrives hungry and tired and without any satisfaction.

His sister is hanging her feet off the porch, telling him he's in big trouble for staying gone so long. He asks her if she's seen a man come by, somebody asking for him. She shakes her head, swinging her matchstick legs in the air.

The kid said his father would be waiting. Just look under the house, he said. In his good clothes, Jay crawls in the dirt, clawing his way under the house. He pretends he's an old-timey soldier, breaking into the enemy's fort after dark. There is no great rescue, though. He never finds his father.

Only a nickel-plated .22 lying in the dirt.

Friday, his other father calls.

The Reverend and his wife invite Jay to dinner. He's told to be at their house by seven o'clock. Yes, sir, he says, sure he'll be asked to explain himself tonight, why he's got the man's youngest daughter staying at a house that is not her home. Jay's plan was to leave the office at six, give himself plenty of time, maybe stop off for some flowers for his wife. But at a quarter 'til, Rolly shows up at the office unannounced. Eddie Mae buzzes him past the waiting room. He strides by her desk with a wink and walks into Jay's office, moving his long legs like a man on stilts, everything slow and deliberate. He's wearing a Rolling Stones concert T-shirt beneath his usual black leather vest. When he smiles, plopping himself in the chair across from Jay's desk, his teeth are tobacco stained. "Guess who rented a gold 1980 Chrysler LeBaron from a Lone Star Rentals out near Hobby Airport on July thirty-first," Rolly asks, somewhat proud of himself. "The day before the shooting that's got you wound up so tight?"

Jay shrugs and states what seems obvious by now. "Dwight Sweeney."

"Nope," Rolly says, smiling, relishing the curious look on Jay's face. "Try a man by the name of Neal McNamara, a man who, I'm made to understand, bears a striking resemblance to Mr. Dwight Sweeney."

"You think it's the same guy?" Jay asks. "The same car?"

"Well, I can tell you this much. That Chrysler was never returned."

"Neal McNamara?" Jay says, repeating the name.

"The guy I talked to at the rental place said two detectives come around wanting to look at the books. They told him the car was being impounded."

Jay shakes his head to himself, wondering why he didn't think to call the rental place himself. "So you think he was using an alias?"

"Something like that."

"Elise said the guy told her his name was Blake Ellis," Jay remembers.

"Three names, one dude. Sounds like trouble to me."

"Maybe he was married," Jay offers. "You know, covering his tracks."

"I can do you one better," Rolly says, leaning forward in his chair, pulling out a couple of pieces of folded-up yellow legal paper, smudged with gray pencil markings on both sides. Rolly slides the pages across Jay's desk. "Dwight Sweeney has quite a colorful background, enough to rival that of the girl's." He pulls a pack of Camels from his vest pocket. "The name thing was a tip-off. It just ain't *normal* to be a Neal on Friday and a Blake on Saturday and come up dead and it turns out your real name is Dwight Somebody. It, frankly, sounds shady. And trust me, I would know. It takes one criminal to spot another."

He lights the cigarette in his hand. "Turns out Mr. Sweeney did a couple of stints at my alma mater in Huntsville."

Jay gets a bad feeling about the guy almost instantly.

He remembers the bruises on Elise's neck, her cries for help.

Rolly turns the pages upside down, trying to read his own handwriting. "Let's see, we got a couple runs for extortion here, a time or two for battery and making criminal threats, blackmail, the works. Plus, my man did seven years for taking money from an undercover officer, all in a scheme to supposedly get rid of the guy's wife." Rolly looks up from his notes, his expression quite serious. "You ask me, the dude sounds like a pro."

"What do you mean?"

"He sounds like a hired gun."

Jay remembers the description of a struggle in the car, a crystal-clear picture forming in his mind. He mumbles it softly to himself. "He came after her." He rented the car the day before, invited her to dinner. It was all a setup, Jay realizes. She walked right into a trap. "He came after her," Jay whispers.

"And he didn't know she was packing," Rolly says, shaking his head to himself. "Fatal mistake, man."

Jay sits at his desk, somewhat dumbfounded.

Here it is, a piece that finally makes sense. A new way of looking at this whole thing. And still he's confused. "I don't understand," he says out loud. "Why not tell the cops he attacked her? Why would she keep that a secret?"

"Scared, probably."

Which, to Jay, would explain why she'd been hiding out in Sugar Land.

"Just 'cause she took out the dude," Rolly says, "don't mean the dude who hired that dude ain't still at large. Maybe she thinks it's best to keep her fucking mouth shut."

"Why the hell would her lawyer go along with that?" Jay asks. "When he's got a good shot at a self-defense angle with this thing?" Of course, as soon as the words are out of his mouth, Jay thinks he has the answer. "Unless her lawyer's planning to get the whole thing thrown out of court," he says, thinking of Charlie's petition to get the contents of the police search tossed.

"The real question," Rolly says, "is why someone wanted to put a hurtin' on her in the first place. 'Course, a girl like that, you know, been around the block once or twice . . . it could be anybody."

"Which Dwight Sweeney or whoever hired him must have known," Jay says. "The guy tried to choke her and leave her in an empty field. The cops were supposed to find an ex-prostitute out there, a throwaway crime that might be traced to anybody."

Rolly scoots forward, to the edge of his seat all the way, sitting himself eye to eye with Jay. "Look, can I offer something here, man, some advice?"

"Yeah."

"If she don't want to tell the police about you, and *you* don't want to tell the police about you . . . what's the problem, man?" Rolly asks. "I was you, I'd leave it alone."

That was of course Jay's entire plan. To stay out of it.

What he has, so far, not been able to do.

"This don't have a goddamned thing to do with you, man."

Jay sits on that a second. "I'm beginning to think you're right."

"And let me tell you what else, whoever put Mr. Sweeney on the girl, I'm guessing he don't want it known," Rolly adds, looking around the office, snooping with his coal-black eyes. "The reason for your sudden windfall, I imagine."

Jay understands the logic now. The real reason for taking his gun. All of it just to scare him away. And he, of all people, fell for it. He, of all people, had made the perfect mark. Rolly looks across Jay's desk. "My feeling . . . I mean, whatever this is really about . . . it's bad, man, real bad. I'd let it alone, Jay."

An hour later, the sight of his wife is breathtaking.

In a bright yellow sundress, tight across her belly, she's barefoot, sitting on the Boykinses' aging porch swing, using the meat of her big toe to push herself back and forth. She's holding a glass of iced tea, watching Jay come up the walk.

"What are you doing out here?"

"Waiting on you," she says, sipping her tea.

He was a fool, he thinks, to ever let her out of his sight.

He can hear voices inside the house, the clinking of silverware and plates. He smells garlic and fried onions, stewed tomatoes and collards brewing on the stove. But he is in no hurry to leave this spot, this moment with his wife.

"You're late," she says.

"I know."

"Everything all right?"

He knows he will not lie to her, not ever again.

"I don't know, B. I don't know."

Bernie rests the glass of iced tea on the swell of her belly. "I'm tired, Jay."

Jay pulls gently on her toe. "I want you home, B, I do."

It's a humble proposal. More so than even his first.

He sits at her feet, not even a bunch of flowers in his hand.

His greatest promise, to keep her safe, an empty one at best.

Bernie scoots herself to the edge of the swing, the wood creaking beneath her. Jay helps her to her feet. She kisses the tip of his chin, the place she can reach. He holds the screen door open for her, letting flies in the house. As she passes the threshold, she whispers in his ear, "Kwame's here."

Time he steps in the house, Evelyn wants to know about the girl.

To her, the whole thing is like something off an old episode of *Barnaby Jones*. She wants to hear about the detectives and what they wanted with Jay. She gets all this out before they're even seated at the dining room table, before grace has been said. Jay looks to his wife for some guidance. But she is no help. She gives him no more than a light shrug, a suggestion that she will neither restrict nor sanction his storytelling. He can talk his way out of this one himself.

Luckily for Jay, no one else at the table is even listening. They're hardly paying attention to Evelyn or Jay. The strike is the real guest of honor this evening. It has been invited to a place at the table along with everybody else, seated somewhere between the Reverend and Kwame Mackalvy to his right.

Soon as grace is complete and the meal officially commenced, Kwame and the Rev start in on the dockworkers' plight and the fate of the strike, outlining, between bites of roast chicken and greens, which strategies have worked for the men and which ones haven't. Kwame is still hot on his idea for a citywide march. He traces the route plan on top of the linen tablecloth, using his silverware and place setting to lay out a mock-up of Main Street downtown. Jay is sitting way on the other side of the table, near his wife, Rolly's refrain running just under his breath: *This don't have a thing to do with you.*

Bernie asks the men about the march, how they think it'll help.

Kwame wipes at his mouth with his napkin, dismantling part of Main Street. "The port commission is holding an open meeting on Tuesday. They're getting all the parties together, see if they can't push a resolution on this thing."

"Unions, stevedores, oil folks," the Rev jumps in. "They're all going to be there. That's the plan, at least," he says. Adding, "The press and the mayor's office, business leaders . . . they're going to have the place full that night."

"And that's the day we walk," Kwame says, sucking down a belch. "We start downtown," he says, placing his napkin back on the table, somewhere between the old Rice Hotel and the back side of Market Square Park, as far as Jay can tell by the crude map. "We start to the south, by Foley's Department Store, at eleven, so that we end up here," he says, pointing to Mrs. Boykins's crystal salt shaker. "At twelve noon, we want to be at city hall. We want as many eyeballs on us as possible. We want the city to stop and take notice."

"This is do or die for these boys," the Rev says, his voice a husky whisper. He peels his black-rimmed glasses off the bridge of his nose, and for the first time, Jay notices the puffy half-moons under his father-in-law's eyes, the strain this is taking. "I'm just worried they won't hold on. A lot of these young ones, they don't remember what it is to fight." The Rev looks up, nodding at Kwame and Jay, as if they are the sons he never had. "I'm talking about even before your time, boys. My time, you understand." His voice cracks under the weight of it, the memory of harder times. "It was a fight, day in, day out. It wasn't no *choice.*"

The whole table has come to a standstill, all eyes on Reverend Boykins.

"You okay, Daddy?" Bernie asks softly.

The Rev manages a smile. "I'm all right, Bernadine."

"The plan is to take this fight all the way," Kwame says, continuing his rant. "From downtown to the port commission meeting."

"You're going to walk from downtown to the port?" Evelyn asks, sounding exhausted by just the thought of walking anywhere in August.

"The Rev and I are working with some local churches, to get busses downtown, something to carry everybody the rest of the way."

"You got a permit for the demonstration?" Jay asks. "They'll nail you on that if you don't. They'll shut you down before you make it a block or two."

How quickly it all comes back.

"I put in the application this morning," Kwame says tersely. "I *have* done this before, you know."

"Yeah," Jay says, nodding.

He folds and refolds the napkin in his lap.

Kwame doesn't want his help anymore.

This, after all, doesn't have a thing to do with Jay.

Mrs. Boykins stands to collect their plates, carrying them into the kitchen. A few minutes later, she returns with a peach cobbler and a fresh pot of coffee. Kwame turns to Reverend Boykins. "You talk to Darren Hayworth about getting together before the port commission meeting?"

Reverend Boykins nods. "We're asking the president of ILA to arrange a sit-down with OCAW, to get this whole Carlisle Minty thing sorted out for good."

"What happened with the kid?" Jay asks.

Kwame and Reverend Boykins, their voices stopping short, lips drawn tight, like heavy drapes, turn to look at Jay. His question, his very presence at the table, is treated with polite suspicion. Neither man answers right away.

"Darren . . . the boy in the sling," Jay says, thinking he needs to clarify.

"What about him?" Kwame asks.

"What's going on with that? You moving forward on something?"

He looks back and forth between the two men, trying to follow what's not being said. But from his chosen place at the table, at such a distance, most of it is lost on him. "Is the kid okay?"

"Darren's fine," Reverend Boykins says, laying his napkin across his dessert plate. "He's handled all this pretty well, if you ask me."

"I think it's terrible what they did to that boy," Mrs. Boykins says, dabbing at crust crumbs gathering at the corners of her mouth.

Jay looks at Kwame. "So what's your next move?"

"Cleanup," Kwame says.

"I don't follow," Jay says, again looking between Kwame and the Rev.

"Well, your mayor came through with the police all right," Kwame says.

"She did?"

"She did."

And because Jay still doesn't believe it, he asks again, "She did?"

"Several officers have been assigned to investigate," the Rev says.

"We got cops coming out the sky now," Kwame says. "Suddenly, they're tripping over themselves to help."

"They came to take a statement from the boy," adds the Rev. "Even drove out to the scene with him. *And* they interviewed Carlisle Minty, went and stopped him on his job at the Cole refinery, out on the channel."

"He denied everything, of course," Kwame says.

"The policemen have said they're going to turn over every stone."

"Cynthia did this?" Jay asks, with an uneasy mix of doubt and hope. His whole adult life, he's wanted nothing more than to be wrong about one woman.

"The problem," his father-in-law says, "is now that the story's out, we're having a hard time controlling these men on the picket line. They feel lied to. They went into this thinking OCAW was backing them through and through."

"What do you mean 'now that the story's out'?" Jay says.

They all turn to him and stare.

"Where you been the last couple days, man?" Kwame asks.

You don't want to know.

"You didn't see it, Jay?" his wife asks.

"Evelyn," Mrs. Boykins says. "Go bring your father today's paper."

"She went on TV, Jay," Bernie says. "I watched it at Ev's."

"The mayor held a press conference announcing an investigation into the beating," the rev says.

"What?"

Evelyn returns from the kitchen with the newspaper tucked under her arm. She hands the paper to her father and plops down into her empty seat, sucking on a slick sliver of baked peach. Reverend Boykins licks his fingertips, flipping through the newspaper. When he finds what he's looking for, he passes the article to Jay. Jay looks down at a photo of Cynthia Maddox at city hall.

The headline: Mayor Pushes for Investigation into Union Beating.

The lines underneath: *A high-ranking member of OCAW is under investigation for the beating of a black member of the ILA on the eve of the strike.*

Jay stares at her face in the paper, the pale eyes, the reassuring smile. It's a brilliant move, he thinks. She goes on television acting like an advocate for labor, a tireless defender of black men unfairly and unnecessarily beaten, when it's clear to him that the press conference's real goal is to undermine the power of the labor coalition and let business leaders in the city know that the boys on the docks won't hold out much longer.

Just wait and see, her smile says.

"She just told the whole city that we got a big, big problem," Kwame says.

"A lot of the men, Jay, white ones too, feel like they were led into the strike under false pretenses. If OCAW isn't really with them, they don't see a way to win this thing," the Rev says. "And, frankly, I don't either."

"Why did this Minty guy do it?" Bernie asks.

The Rev shakes his head, shrugging his thin shoulders.

Jay looks up from the article, the picture of the mayor.

To his father-in-law, who once stood at Jay's side just as he stands by these workers now, Jay says, "I'm sorry." Because he, of all people, should have known Cynthia better.

Chapter 23

It's not until sometime after midnight that he starts to get angry. The mayor, his ex-girl, is only half of it. More immediately, it's the man in the black Ford who's still stalking through Jay's mind; it's the mystery of who was behind the threats on his life. He can't stand the idea of being played with, being treated like a dog thrown a bone. He resents the pull of the money, the power he assigned it, the ways he imagined the hand that dealt it held dominion over him. He's angry with himself for cowering, for not going to the police from the very beginning, as a free man, an innocent man. He is so ashamed of the way he's behaved, so ashamed of his fear, that he feels actual rage toward a face he can't see—the one who sent the man in the black Ford, the one who wanted him scared, who was counting on it. The anger feels good, landing on his tongue, dissolving like a warm, bitter pill. He feels the rush, the high, and remembers anger's power, its ability to clear the head. Unable to sleep, he sits up in bed next to his wife, watching her breath rise and fall, thinking of the one thing that *is* perfectly clear in his mind, the one thing he's absolutely sure of: if he can solve the mystery of who tried to kill Elise, he will know the identity of the person who's after him now.

More than once, the old man in High Point occurs to him as a possible suspect. Though, at least initially, he couldn't tell you why. It's less logic, or a story worked out in his head, and more lawyerly intuition. He was, after all, a onetime criminal defense attorney. He used to deal in motive for a living.

His suspicions about the old man are circumstantial at best. As a game, Jay presents the prosecutorial case in his head, the reasons why Erman Joseph Ainsley could have had a hand in the attack on Elise Linsey's life. He rereads the article in the *Chronicle*, marking the highlights. There's the description of Mr. Ainsley's rage at "real estate folks from Houston." There are the charges of harassment by Mr. Ainsley against members of his community (threatening phone calls and the like), indicating a propensity for violence, or at the very least a shaky mental state. And maybe most important of all, there's the fact, stated openly in the newspaper article, that Mr. Ainsley had obtained Elise Linsey's home address—a sign that he either had contacted her or intended to.

Then, just like the old days, Jay tries to tear down the state's argument, piece by piece, just to see if he can:

Anger doesn't mean murder, else we'd all be in jail, this lawyer included.

He would pause here, waiting for the jurors' smiles.

The harassment mentioned by the prosecution, Jay would add, is no more than one neighbor's word against another's. The state has entered no evidence that law enforcement was called or legal complaints made against Mr. Ainsley.

And as to Mr. Ainsley being in possession of Ms. Linsey's home address, well, I believe some of you might likewise be in possession of that information, or anyone else who has a phone book for the city of Houston in their house.

He would pause again, letting the jurors take in this last bit.

But of course the strongest counterargument Jay can think of is that he doesn't know where a retired mine worker would get $25,000 to blackmail *him*.

The old man sounds more like a kook than a criminal, a man more likely to take his fight to Washington than to an empty field alongside Buffalo Bayou. But then again, Jay knows firsthand what frustration with one's government can do to a person. Many people have taken up arms over far less. Maybe in the end, Ainsley decided Elise Linsey, as a representative of the Stardale Development Company, was an easier target than Ronald Reagan.

It may only be a circumstantial case against the old man, but absent any other workable theories about who wanted Elise Linsey out of the picture, Jay comes back to Erman Ainsley again and again. He can't, for the life of him, get the *Chronicle* article out of his mind. He can't forget the phone call with the reporter, Lon Philips, the mention of Ainsley getting a lawyer, or the empty building on Fountainview where Stardale's offices are supposed to be.

He can't shake the idea that there's more to the story.

So just a few days after Rolly's advice that he back away from a bad situation, Jay loads up the Skylark with ten gallons of unleaded at $1.39 a pop and heads out toward Baytown, his .38 snug in the glove compartment. His only plan is to talk to the man. But if it comes down to it, Jay plans to make his message heard loud and clear: he and his family are not to be touched.

He doesn't tell anyone where he's going—not his wife or Rolly or Eddie Mae—and it's not until he's about twenty miles east on the I-10 that he starts to think that was maybe a bad idea. He is lately coming to the conclusion that secrets, in and of themselves, are dangerous. He makes a vow to call his wife when he gets to High Point.

The town is a few miles southwest of Baytown on the Trinity Bay shoreline, which is north of Galveston Bay and Texas City and the Bolivar Peninsula. Baytown itself is a Gulf city of the classic model, balmy and thick with vegetation. There are rubber plants and banana trees, sandy-colored palms and butter-colored houses, arched high on stilts. They look like rows of startled house cats. The houses have white or blue shutters, all weathered to a soft gray by the constant breath of warm, salt-cured winds, and almost every other house has a motorboat anchored in its front yard. People come to retire here. The ones who can't afford to live in Galveston or just don't want to. Galveston, with its ancient town center full of bead shops and pubs, too closely resembles the tourist trap and liberal cesspool of New Orleans for some. Baytown is where good Christians come to retire, cowboys and refinery workers who made good, saving 15 percent every two weeks their whole working lives. There are American flags waving hello to passersby and more crosses in more front windows than Jay can count. It's not a place he wishes to stay any longer than he has to.

He passes through Baytown, turning south on Farm Road 219.

A green highway sign puts him eight miles outside High Point.

Eight treeless miles of prairie and marsh, the land dotted every half mile or so by shallow ponds and snowy egrets lying in wait. The air is softer out here, more forgiving. It's a good ten degrees cooler than it is in Houston.

The first thing Jay notices coming into High Point is the rise in elevation. It's no more than a few hundred feet. But along this flat Gulf coastland, driving over an anthill can feel like climbing the side of a mountain. Jay feels the pull of gravity on the back end of his car as he drives over the swollen landscape. At the crest, he can see all the way to Trinity Bay, drilling ships and pleasure boats tiny in the distance.

Main Street is easy enough to find. A simple turn off FM 219, and he's in downtown High Point, driving past the elementary school and a hardware store and a United States post office, which looks, inexplicably, closed at three o'clock in the afternoon. A lot of the storefronts are either empty or have their windows covered in cheap plywood. Jay has no trouble finding a parking spot right in front of the Hot Pot, which is sandwiched between a dress shop and a bait-and-tackle store with a handwritten sign in the window: WE SELL GUNS TOO.

Erman Joseph Ainsley is not out in front of the Hot Pot restaurant passing out flyers. That would have been too easy, Jay supposes. He shuts off the car engine and steps out of the car, feeding two nickels into the meter before walking into the Hot Pot café. Inside, he takes an open seat at the counter and orders from the pie case. A slice of lemon meringue and a cup of black coffee. He asks the woman behind the counter where he can get hold of a phone book.

The directory, when it arrives, is thinner than a high school yearbook. Jay opens to the *A*'s, trailing his finger down the inky columns until he comes across an Ainsely, E. J. On Forrester Road. The house number is 39. He leaves a dollar on top of the cost of the pie and coffee and asks the way out to Forrester Road. The woman behind the counter pinches her eyebrows together. "You looking for Mr. Ainsley?"

The question catches Jay off guard. "Why do you ask?"

The woman scoops the bills and loose change from the countertop, crumpling them all together and stuffing the money into
the front pocket of her apron. "He's the only one still left on Forrester, the only one left in that whole neighborhood, in fact. But
I guess you already knew that," she adds, taking particular notice
of Jay's suit and tie all of a sudden. She gives him a cool smile,
letting him know that she's on to him, country girl or not.

"I'm not sure I know what you mean," he says.

"You ain't out here tryin' to get him to sell his place?"

"No, ma'am."

"Hmph," the woman mumbles, studying Jay. He can tell she
hates to be wrong about things. "What do you want with Ainsley
anyway?"

Jay pointedly ignores the question. "Is there a map somewhere
that I can look at?" he asks. "Or maybe you could point me to a
gas station."

"Personally, I wouldn't listen to a thing that man has to say,
but some people are hardheaded, so . . ." She sighs and points
out the front windows of the café, beneath the gingham curtains. "Take Main back to 219 and head south, like you're heading to the water. The next exit you see, get off and go to your
right. There's a line of houses out that way, right off the highway.
That's where Ainsley stays. You can't miss it," she says. "He's out
by the old mine."

The exit sign for the Crystal-Smith Salt Company is still by the
side of the highway. Its lettering is cheerful, red, white, and blue.
And a contrast to the otherwise drab surroundings. There are
tufts of weeds growing around the buildings at the salt factory,
which Jay can see from the highway. The exit Wanda instructed
him to take leads him onto a street called Industry. The factory,

or what's left of it—empty buildings and crabgrass and a couple of shabby-looking trailers—sits to the right. The mine itself, Jay understands, is belowground, beneath the black asphalt he's riding on now, deep below the earth's surface where briny seawater sloshes inside underground caverns and rock salt practically grows on the walls. The salt caverns, or salt domes, as they're sometimes called, are a natural part of the Texas coastline, where the Gulf and land meet.

Just across the street from the old factory is a neighborhood of modest one-story homes. The houses are older white clapboard structures with pitched roofs and wooden porches. Jay imagines this is where the first workers at the Crystal-Smith Salt Company settled nearly a hundred years ago, and where Erman Joseph Ainsely has taken his last stand.

Forrester Road is marked by a small street sign that looks like it was peeled off a tin can, rust creeping around the edges. Jay makes a right, taking note of the house numbers, counting down from 63. He passes empty driveway after empty driveway. Number 39 is the second-to-last house on the right, the only one on the whole street with curtains in the windows and grass clippings in the front yard. Jay recognizes the front porch from Ainsley's picture in the paper. He remembers the American flag and the petunias in the box planter.

Jay takes the .38 from his glove compartment and tucks it into his waistband at the small of his back, pulling down his suit jacket to cover the bulge. The window above the box planter is cracked open. Jay hears a television playing loudly inside the house, tuned to a game show, if he had to guess by the constant stream of canned applause. There are pale yellow curtains in the front window and a few oddly shaped tomatoes or apples resting on the windowsill. A Chevy pickup at least fifteen years old sits in the driveway, next to a station wagon. The homey feel of the place doesn't sit right with Jay. For some reason it makes him uneasy. He wants to get this over with.

Standing on the front porch, Jay wipes his slick palms on his pants legs, then pulls back the screen door, holding it open with his foot. He knocks on the front door, twice. Through a glass window cut in the wood, Jay tries to get a glimpse inside the house, cupping his hands against the glare of the South Texas sun and pressing his face against the glass.

On the other side, he sees a pair of eyeballs staring back at him.

Jay, startled, pulls back from the window. The screen door slips from behind his foot and slams hard against the door frame. Then the door to 39 Forrester opens. From behind the mesh wire of the screen door, Erman Joseph Ainsley pulls a baseball cap low over his weathered forehead, a hood over his cool blue eyes. He stares at Jay a long, long time, one hand on his hip, the other leaned up against the wooden door frame. Jay can hear a television behind him. Wink Martindale is calling for another X on the board. Ainsley keeps his hand on the door, protecting his property, his little piece of something in this world.

"Who are you?" His voice is phlegmy, moist with age.

"My name is Jay Porter." He waits to see if the old man recognizes the name. "I'm an attorney, Mr. Ainsley, from Houston."

The old man moves in for a closer look, coming so close to the screen door that the bill of his baseball cap makes a line of indentation into the netted mesh. He narrows his blue eyes in Jay's direction. "A colored lawyer?" he asks.

Because it's the easiest answer and because he doesn't have time to rehash the entire civil rights movement on this man's front porch, Jay says, "Yes."

The old man nods, as if this is perfectly acceptable to him.

He pushes the screen door open in a wide arc, opening the

house to Jay. "Well, come on then," he says. "I guess you're as good as any other."

He turns then, motioning for Jay to follow, before disappearing into the house.

The darkness inside is disorienting. It takes a frightening amount of time for Jay's eyes to adjust. He can make out Ainsley's shadow moving through the house, but little else. He doesn't know where he is or what the old man has in store for him. Jay, on instinct, reaches for the .38 at his waist. He walks down a long hallway, wandering into the blue light of a television set. It's streaming in from a nearby room where, to Jay's surprise, a woman sits in a seashell-scooped armchair, a pile of yarn in her lap. She glances up from her knitting needles, studying Jay over the half-moons of her reading glasses. He angles the gun in his hand so that it hides in the shadows behind his back. Whatever she makes of Jay, this stranger in her home, her expression is impassive, or uninterested. She nods her head to the left. "He's in the kitchen."

The applause on the television reaches a fevered pitch.

The woman goes back to her knitting.

Jay backs into the hallway, sliding his hand along the wall, feeling his way around to the other side of the house. In the kitchen, he finds Ainsley standing in front of the open door to the refrigerator. "I guess you want some water, a glass of tea or something," the old man says.

The air in the kitchen is thick and un-air-conditioned. The room smells of Mentholatum and vanilla extract. There's a can of Postum resting on top of at least a week's worth of newspapers, spread out across an oval-shaped Formica table.

"I'm fine," Jay says, hanging in the doorway.

The old man shrugs.

From the plastic drainboard, he picks up an empty jelly jar.

He fills it with tap water, then empties the entire glass into his stomach in just a few gulps. He wipes his mouth with his sleeve.

"How'd you find me?" he asks finally.

There's something in the old man's demeanor that Jay doesn't quite comprehend. From the time Ainsley opened his front door, he has seemed to Jay to be, well, relieved, as if he had been waiting for Jay to show up at his doorstep for hours, days, even. "I read about you in the newspaper," Jay says.

It's just enough to set Ainsley off.

"That idiot," he barks. "I told that ding-dang reporter what the deal was, what's really going on here. But, you know, some people got to have every goddamned thing handed to 'em. You see that piece of shit they put in the newspaper, you see how they lied on me? They gone and missed the whole story." He shakes his head in disgust. His neck is the color of a mottled peach, dotted with sun spots and flush with color. "But you wait," he says. "When this all comes out, they gon' be the ones to have their asses handed to them."

Then he notices Jay's gun.

The muscles in the old man's neck stiffen. His jaw rocks back and forth in its joint. He takes a sudden sharp gulp of air.

"Boy, put that up," he says.

He crosses to the window over the sink, yanking on the curtains. "You better believe they got somebody watching."

The old man's eyes are frantic. He is not making a lick of sense. Jay slides the gun into the pocket of his suit coat, tucking it away. "Mr. Ainsley," he says calmly. "Do you have any idea who I am?"

"Thought you said you was a lawyer." He says it quite matter-of-factly, as if he takes this to be the whole reason for Jay's stop at his doorstep. The old man starts for the door. "Come on," he says. "I want to show you something."

=====

He walks Jay along the fence line.

Jay can see the old salt factory from Ainsley's backyard. The old man rests an elbow on top of the metal fence and looks, somewhat wistfully, across Industry Road. "They let us all go in seventy-seven," he says, his voice barely above a whisper, as if he's speaking of a death in the family. "The year after Carter started with that petroleum program. I didn't vote for the man, personally," he adds as an aside. "Ol' Ford woulda been all right with me."

He takes off his cap and rubs the dome of his balding head, which is startling white. He feels around his skull with his fingertips, as if he's looking for something he's lost. "And this one they got up in Washington now," which he pronounces "Warshington." "He ain't a whole hell of a lot better. All business, that's how they do now. That's all these fellas care about. That George Bush got people in oil. So you see how it works? They making hand over foot, crying OPEC this and market forces that, and all the while they got a shitload of black gold running right underneath your feet." He settles his fingers into the rings of the chain-link fence. "I'm short a pension now. I got a wife in there, son. I got to eat." He looks at Jay as if he expects him to do something about it.

Jay, lost in this whole conversation, isn't sure what he's meant to say.

His silence seems to anger Ainsley, or maybe embarrass him.

The old man slides his worn baseball cap back onto his head and looks back at the buildings and run-down trailers on the other side of Industry Road. "I gave my life to the mine," he says. "You have any idea what it's like to work two hundred feet belowground, boy?" He eyes Jay's suit and tie, then shakes his head to himself, answering his own question. "Hours at a stretch, in the dark, the air so tart it burns through your goggles, burns right through your eyes to the back of your skull. And that white salt dust, so fine, like a mist, getting everywhere . . . in your clothes, in your hair, in your lungs, so you can't hardly breathe." He nods his head in a slow, steady rhythm, as if he's counting, one by one, each working day of his life, every hour spent underground.

"I'm not trying to complain. I'm just saying, I don't think it's right, that's all, to kill off a workingman so somebody else can make a dollar."

"Mr. Ainsley . . . what does this have to do with Elise Linsey?"

"Who?"

"The real estate agent from Houston," Jay says, waiting for a flicker of recognition in Ainsley's eyes. "Do you know who I'm talking about?"

There is the faintest smile on Ainsley's lips. He clucks his tongue. "Don't think she ain't in on it too. Buying the land, see, that's just a cover."

Jay thinks of the empty building on Fountainview in Houston, where Stardale's offices are supposed to be. The image comes to him unbidden. And once it's there, he can't easily get rid of it. It lends a sudden weight to this whole conversation, Ainsley's conspirational ranting.

The old man steps back from the fence. He nods his head toward the back side of his house and waves one hand for Jay to come on. "It's over here."

There are three short cement steps leading up to the back door of the house. Ainsley stands with his hands stuffed in his pockets and one foot propped on the bottom stair. He's staring at something on the ground.

"You ever have any contact with Ms. Linsey?" Jay asks him.

"I mean, other than her coming around your place trying to get you to sell?"

Ainsley's eyes are firmly on the ground at his feet. "Take a look."

Jay turns to see what Ainsley is pointing at.

It's coming up around the foundation of the house, black, like raw sewage.

Jay immediately takes a step back, wanting to protect his shoes. "Looks like you got a plumbing problem there," he says, almost gagging at the thought.

"No, sir," Ainsley says calmly. "That's crude."

Jay looks up at the old man. "Pardon?"

Ainsley nods at the ground. "That's oil, boy."

He stands back with his hands in his pockets, as if he's daring Jay to come take a closer look. Jay steps forward, bending at his knees. He touches the stuff with his right hand. It's loose, but thick, like melted gelatin. It slips and slides between his fingertips. "They call it creepage," Ainsley says. "Last year it was just a few spots, mostly places where the grass stopped growing. I had little bald patches coming up everywhere. My neighbors too. See, that oil down there floats on brine water, and when the water level changes for some reason only God can account for, the oil gets pushed up to the top, right up through the ground. It didn't start to get this bad until the last month or so," he says, pointing to the clumpy pool of oil and dirt. "If I had sold my house when everyone else did, I guess no one would have ever known about it, now would they?"

Jay stands, still rolling the oil around on his fingers, rolling this whole thing around in his mind, trying to get a good hold on it. Elise acted as a liaison, getting people to sell their homes. But to whom? The federal government?

"They've had explosions at petroleum reserve sites in Louisiana," Ainsley says. "They don't know if all this is really safe. They don't even care. They just buy up the salt mines, buy off the people. But I'm making a stink, you hear me?"

Jay remembers the old man's relief when he showed up at the front door. And it now dawns on him that Ainsley wasn't waiting for Jay so much as he was waiting for *someone* . . . to come see this mess for themselves. "Did you show this to that reporter from the *Chronicle*?" Jay asks.

"Not that I trust the press any more than a fox in a henhouse, but yeah, I called 'em when this come up," he says, pointing to the oil. "I called everybody I could think of. The Department of Energy, even the goddamned White House."

"Did the reporter come back out?" Jay asks, thinking of the strange phone call with Lon Philips and Philips wondering if Jay was another journalist.

"Yep," Ainsley nods, his voice sour. "And I ain't heard a word back since. The government telling me the whole time they can't do nothing. But I know they trying to get rid of it now. You can hear the tanker trucks coming through in the middle of the night, always at night, just the way they brought it in. Dot used to couldn't sleep through the night for hearing the trucks come through. See, they pump the oil in over at the old factory site, and now they're trying to pump it out, always at night, mind you," he says, lowering his voice. "And your tax money is paying for this, you understand. If this is government business, why ain't it out in the open, huh? Well, I'll tell you why, son, 'cause this is the cleanup part, the shit they don't want nobody to know about. See, they know I'm watching now." The old man nods his head toward the fence line. "It's been real quiet over there, about a week or so now. Suddenly there's no more trucks. Nothing coming in, nothing going out. They know somebody's watching."

Jay still has the stuff all over his fingers.

Ainsley offers him a rag from the front pocket of his overalls. Jay wipes the oil as best he can, but finds that it coats his skin completely, covering his pores, clinging like a parasite that has found an unsuspecting host. He wants to go inside and wash his hands. He wants to sit down somewhere. He wants to know who exactly wanted Elise Linsey killed.

There's a knock on the back door.

Jay and Ainsley look up at the same time.

Dot, Ainsley's wife, is standing inside the house, in front of a window, a somewhat grave expression on her face. She taps the glass, pointing at something over their heads. Ainsley is the first one to turn around.

"Here we go again," he says.

Jay turns and sees it too.

Just over the fence line, on Industry Road, between Ainsley's backyard and the old factory, there's a black Ford LTD parked in the middle of the street. The man in the driver's seat is smoking a cigarette, watching the house.

Jay is over the fence in a matter of seconds. He lands hard in a muddy ditch on the side of Industry Road, his ankle turning underneath him. Still, he runs. He pulls the .38 from his jacket. Behind him, he hears Ainsley hollering but can't make out the words. He thinks the old man is yelling for him to stop.

The man in the black Ford lets Jay get within a few feet of the car. "You're a fool, Porter," is all he says before swinging the car in a wide arc, turning it around in the middle of the street. Jay has to leap off to the far right side of the road to keep from getting run over. He ends up in the ditch on the factory side of Industry Road. The bones in his knees crack and moan. He scrambles up the small incline, slipping in the mud more than once. By the time he's back on his feet, on top of the hot asphalt, the Ford is a good thirty yards down the road. Jay points his gun at the back of the car, his finger on the trigger. Sweat drips into his eyes, stinging and blurring his vision, fucking with his aim. He shoots wildly, shattering the Ford's back window in a crystal rain of glass that scatters across the pavement. The car swerves, its back end swishing left and right like an animal's tail. But the driver never stops. Jay watches the car turn back onto FM 219, heading toward downtown High Point and Baytown.

He hops across Industry Road, back to Ainsley's house. He cuts his right hand on the fence and tears a hole in the seat of his pants. He runs through the old man's backyard and through the back of the house, past Dot and the television room and *Tic Tac Dough*. He runs all the way to his car, Ainsley at his heels. Dot peers out from behind the curtains in the kitchen window. Ainsley hisses at her to get back inside, to shut the windows and lock the back door.

"You know that man?" Jay asks.

"He started coming around a while back, letting me know he's kind of watching things." The old man is breathless from the run, coughing every other syllable. "He's come up on me only once, out back while I was in the yard. He told me to stop talking to newspapers, looked me in my eye and said it."

Jay thinks he can catch the Ford on the highway, maybe find out where the man's going or where he came from. Jay struggles to open his car door. The car keys slip in his bloodied hand. By sheer force of will, he gets the door open.

"You coming back?" the old man asks.

Jay starts the car. Ainsley wisely steps back to the curb.

At sixty miles an hour, Jay tears down Forrester Road.

=====

Down I-45, halfway to Houston, Jay has a sudden panic about his wife, at home alone, remembering that he never called her from the café like he said he would. He never told her where he was going. He pulls off the freeway and into a Shell gas station to call home. He's relieved to hear Bernie's voice. She actually sounds chipper this afternoon, telling Jay she's going to roast a chicken for dinner and wanting to know would he pick up a bag of white rice.

"B, listen," Jay starts. "I want you to hang up the phone now and go make sure the doors are locked, the windows too. And I don't want you to answer the door for anybody but me."

"We went over all this, Jay."

"Just do it, okay?" he says firmly. "I'll be there as soon as I can. If you have any problems, somebody tries to mess with you or get in the apartment, I want you to call Rolly Snow. He can get there faster than I can."

"Why in the world would I call *him*?"

"Then call the police, B."

Bernie's voice comes back soft, frightened. "Jay?"

"Don't argue with me, B. Just do it."

"Jay . . . there's a police officer here right now, sitting in the living room," his wife says. "He said you called the station, wanting somebody to come out and check on me. He just got here. I mean, not two minutes before you called."

Jay feels his knees give. "Bernie, I never called any cop."

"But he's sitting right—"

Her words stop short.

Jay can picture his wife in the apartment, on the kitchen phone, turning her pregnant body to take a second look at the white man in her living room, realizing that something is indeed off about his appearance. The suit that's just a little too nice for city work, the gold on his finger, and the scotch on his breath.

Over the phone, Jay hears his wife whisper, "Oh, God."

"Are you on the kitchen phone?"

"Yes."

"His back to you?"

"Yes."

"Then get out of there, B."

"Should I call—"

"There isn't enough time."

"What is this, Jay? What's happening?"

"Just hang up the phone and walk out the door and don't look back."

He tries hard not to picture his life without her. As he pulls into the alley behind his apartment building, Jay tries to convince himself that there's still a life before him that's worth living, a life with Bernie in it. A few feet from his building, he jumps from the car with his .38, leaving the engine running. He ducks under the carport and races for the stairs. The back door is open. It's the first hint that maybe, just maybe, his wife got out okay. The sun has set by now, and the apartment is dark. Jay steps inside, hardly able to see more than a few inches in front of him. He moves blindly through his apartment, feeling along the walls, calling his wife's name. The silence is unsettling. The stillness in here is all wrong. Jay feels a terrible ache, down to his bones, a painful premonition that behind the cloak of darkness that surrounds him, something awful awaits. It's then that he hears his wife, her voice a soft, gurgling whimper, a sound choked with tears. Jay turns and flips on a switch in the hallway. A path of light falls into the living room, where Bernie is curled up on the floor, her back against the wall. He flies to her side.

"Bernie!"

She is staring blankly across the room.

Jay reaches over her, turning on a lamp by the couch.

The barrel of the .45 catches the light first.

Jay sees the gun, is able to comprehend it, before he sees the man's face. He quickly raises the .38 in his hand. But the man from the black Ford shoots first, taking out a chunk of plaster just a few inches from Bernie's head before aiming the weapon at Jay.

"Drop the gun," he orders.

Jay refuses. The two armed men stand face-to-face.

"Don't be stupid, Porter," the man says. He aims the gun at Bernie again, daring to take a step closer. On the floor, Bernie stuffs her hands over her mouth, stifling a scream, tears streaming down her face. The man from the black Ford looks at Jay. "You really think I'd miss twice? Drop the fucking gun!"

"Let her go," Jay demands.

"You're fucking this up, Porter," the man says, his words clipped, as if he's out of patience, and Jay is out of time. "I like to keep things neat, understand? That's my job. Now you're making two more problems for me to clean up."

"You got me. . . . let her go."

"Drop the gun."

"Let my wife go, and I'll do whatever you want."

The .45 is still aimed at Bernie's head.

The man from the black Ford looks between her and Jay and Jay's .38.

Then, deciding something, he looks at Bernie and barks, "Get up."

Bernie looks at her husband. "Jay?"

Jay steels himself when he thinks of what he's about to do, the script he's already written in his head. He looks into his wife's eyes. He wants her to understand what he's asking of her, that he needs her to trust him completely. He wants her to see the way out. "Go on, B, get up."

The man from the black Ford orders her to stand next to him, on the other side of the room.

"I have to go to the bathroom," Bernie says weakly.

"You're not going anywhere," the man says.

"She's eight months' pregnant, man. Let her go to the fucking bathroom."

Jay lowers his gun finally, placing it at his feet. He kicks it across the matted carpet toward the man from the black Ford.

"Let her go."

The man picks up Jay's .38, a gun in each hand now.

He nods to Bernie, who takes one last look at her husband.

She looks frightened, unsure of herself and what comes next.

"Jay?"

"Go on, B," he says.

He watches his wife shuffle slowly out of the room.

The man from the black Ford calls after her, "And leave the door open so I can hear you." Then he turns to Jay, who raises his arms in a grand show of surrender, counting the seconds in his mind, how many steps to the closet door.

"I'm losing faith in you, Porter," the man from the black Ford says. "You got about five seconds to tell me why I shouldn't shoot you right now."

Out of the corner of his eye, Jay sees her enter the room, leading with the long nose of his shotgun, the rifle he keeps in the hall closet. He tells her to shoot and don't think. The man from the black Ford sees Bernie and the rifle and reacts quickly, pointing his .45 at her. Bernie holds her breath and shoots.

The blow knocks them both to the floor, the kickback pushing Bernie into the wall behind her. The man from the black Ford falls to his knees, blood oozing from the place where his right hand used to be. The stump at the end of his arm is almost unrecognizable as a feature of the human body. Bernie, aiming God knows where, blew the thing clean off. The man, howling in pain, raises Jay's .38, shooting weakly with his left hand. The bullet whizzes past Jay's right ear, but misses him completely. Jay grabs the shotgun from his wife, slides a bullet into the chamber, and points the barrel of the rifle at the intruder. The man sits up at the waist. Jay has a clean shot at the center of his forehead.

"Jay!"

The sound of his wife's voice ricochets inside his skull, lighting up the place where his reason still has a hold. A breath away from pulling the trigger, he moves the gun six inches to the left and shoots a hole through the man's right shoulder. The man's eyes go blank. The .38 falls from his one good hand, and he collapses completely, his body crumpling onto its side. For a moment, the air in the room is perfectly still, nothing moving but gun smoke winding in the air.

"He's still breathing," Bernie whispers.

"He passed out."

Which means they don't have a lot of time.

"Is Mr. Johnson home?" he asks.

Bernie stares at her husband, confused by such a simple question. "Not yet, I don't think," she stutters. "His wife doesn't get off work until nine."

Jay sets the gun against the television.

The sight of this man incapacitated on his living room floor does not relieve his fears about the mess he's in. This guy was only ever a messenger, moving on instructions from someone else. This is not the end of anything, Jay suspects.

He turns and looks at his wife. "You'll have to help me move him."

They drive to Riverside in silence, listening to the whistle of the man's breath in the backseat. Bernie rests her head against the passenger-side window. Jay stares straight ahead through the windshield, following every traffic law of Harris County, Texas, to the letter. When they get within spitting distance of the hospital, Jay turns off his car lights and puts the Buick in neutral, coasting in darkness to the rarely used service entrance around back.

Riverside is a county hospital, its patients mostly black and poor. The hospital staff is used to treating gunshot victims, and they are not known to ask a lot of questions. Jay leaves the man from the black Ford on his knees, a few feet from the service door. As they pull away from the hospital, Bernie starts to cry again. Jay reaches for his wife's hand and trains his eyes on the road ahead.

Chapter 24

Jay lost track of Cynthia sometime after his trial.

She simply vanished from his life, disappearing without explanation or apology, without a word to him or even a kiss good-bye. She was just *gone*.

The rumors on campus were rampant:

Cynthia Maddox was a fed.

No, she had gotten picked up on drug charges in Matamoros, Mexico. LSD, somebody had heard.

No, she was living on a commune in Oregon. Or she had run off with a married sheriff's deputy and was living down in Corpus.

Somebody said she had transferred to George Washington University.

Somebody else said it was UT.

He waited for her to come back. He quietly finished out his final semester, skipping meetings at the Scott Street house and dropping his global equality crusade. He kept his head down, got a job somewhere. He took his old room at Miss Mitchell's boardinghouse, renting by the week. Most nights, he played cards by himself in his room, listening to the radio. And he waited.

One month passed, then another. She never came. She never called.

Every hour he waited was just another brick in the wall he was building at his feet, to shield himself from what he could no longer deny: Cynthia Maddox had betrayed him, plain and simple, one way or another. If she had not sold him to the feds, then she had loved him and left him—if she had loved him at all.

He still longed for her in a way that made him sick to his stomach.

How could he love someone he hated, or hate someone he loved so completely?

So he decided he would do neither. He would neither love her nor hate her. He would simply put her away. It was a beginning for him. He learned that other things could be put away too; whatever hurt could be hidden, if only he willed it so. He set about quietly packing up his life, piece by piece, like heavy luggage, trunks put in storage. Until, slowly, he remade himself.

In July of 1970, the Houston Police Department's Central Intelligence Division shot and killed Carl Hampton, shot him dead from the roof of a Baptist church. When Bumpy Williams, Jay's oldest friend, was killed a month later, Jay walked away from the movement for good. He never looked back.

He went, of all places, to law school. It kept him out of Vietnam (that, and his felony arrest record), and it gave him hope. There could be a life on the other side. He got married, and he pretended to forget all about Cynthia Maddox.

She didn't start showing up again until sometime in the summer of 1976, campaigning for Senator Bentsen. She was running the senator's Houston office, and the *Post* did a big spread about the little gal from Katy who wanted to put Lloyd Bentsen in the White House. Jay had stumbled across the article by accident. Someone had left a newspaper behind in one of the orange vinyl booths in the cafeteria at South Texas College of Law, where he was in his second year. The day Cynthia came back into his life, he'd been in the cafeteria for hours, reading contract law for so long that his eyes were starting to cross. He had picked up the discarded newspaper as a mere distraction during lunch.

Her picture was on page three. A girl he once knew.

He pushed his sandwich across the table, left his coffee to get cold.

The article listed Cynthia Maddox as a graduate of George Washington University and an aide in Bentsen's D.C. office, working closely with him on legislation he was drafting in the Senate's Economic Growth and Transportation Subcommittees. There was no mention of her time in Texas—her years at the University of Houston or her early, more radical political activism—other than to say she was born and raised in Katy, a local girl. She had remade herself as well.

Jay spent that summer on edge. Just knowing she was in the city was a terrible imposition, a burden on his soul. It interfered with his ability to study, to sleep, to even eat some days. Everything in his life had come to a sudden stop.

Somewhere deep down, he was still waiting.

She never came to him, though. She never called.

In the end, Bentsen lost his bid for the Democratic Party's presidential nomination. His campaign office downtown was closed by the fall, and Jay went back to his studies. Cynthia, presumably, went back to D.C. By the time she returned for midterm elections in '78, this time running her own campaign for local office, she was a stranger to him. The hair was blonder, the clothes stiffer, the politics, save for a few perfunctory nods in the general direction of equality and justice, were unintelligible to him. He found he could see her picture daily in the newspaper without a quickening of his pulse. It no longer mattered that she was in his city. He was no longer waiting.

He might have left it at that. If his father-in-law hadn't called on him to get involved with the mayor again, to break their ten years of silence. If he hadn't needed to get his hands on information about the shooting by the bayou. And if he hadn't stayed up 'til two o'clock in the morning last night cleaning blood off his living room floor, trying to make sense of Erman Ainsley's rant against the government. He might have left Cynthia Maddox alone for good. But the mess he's in now is bigger than his past, bigger than his aging feelings for a woman he hardly knows anymore, a woman he may have never known.

He showed up at Cynthia's office this morning, unannounced. There were no smiles from the mayor's secretary this time. She has, in fact, spent most of the forty-five minutes Jay has been waiting with her eyes to the closed double doors that lead into the mayor's private suite, where Kip is standing, likewise waiting, put out of whatever business is going on just on the other side of those doors. The phone has rung exactly twenty-three times, and each time, the secretary looks helplessly at Kip, asking, "How much longer you think?"

It's a quarter after eleven when the doors finally open.

A group of men emerge from the suite first, followed by Cynthia, who is smiling broadly. The men dwarf her, some by as much as a foot. They encircle her like a fresh kill in the bed of a pickup truck, like they're trying to decide which one she belongs to, who landed the final shot. Jay recognizes a few of them from their pictures in the paper: Pat Bodine, president of the longshoremen's union; Wayne Kaylin, president of the oil and petrochemical workers' union; Hugh Bowlin, of the Maritime Association; and Darwood Becker, a commissioner with the Port of Houston Authority. The man to Cynthia's right, the one who's got a hand on her elbow, standing firmly beside her even as the others begin to disperse, is Thomas Cole, whom Jay has seen in person only once before, at the lunch with Luckman and J. T. Cummings. As usual, Cole is the only one in the room who doesn't look particularly frightened.

Cynthia is clearly smitten with him.

As the others say their good-byes, moving on toward the elevators, Cynthia and Thomas stand facing each other, Cole bent over to catch the mayor's every word. It appears the two are whispering to each other. When they pull out of their semi-embrace, Cynthia flashes Mr. Cole a girlish smile. "We'll do fine," Cole says, patting her low on the back. "We'll be just fine."

As he turns toward the elevators, Cole catches a glimpse of Jay, standing just a few feet away. His expression is flat. He is, after all, looking at a stranger. Still, Cole holds Jay's gaze a hair past what is universally considered polite.

"Can I help you with something?" Jay asks.

Cynthia turns, noticing Jay for the first time.

She looks nervous, eyeing the two men, sensing a tightness in the air.

Cole never utters a single word. His eyes soon glide over Jay, like a stone skipping on water. He nods good-bye to the mayor and walks to the elevators alone. Once Cole is gone,

Jay feels the energy in the room shift into a lower gear, as if the others had all been holding their breath in the presence of Texas royalty, no one more so than Cynthia. She quickly waves Jay into her suite without a bit of inquiry, as if she had invited him. Inside, she pulls a Carlton from her purse and lights it. She kicks off her black pumps and tells Kip, twice, to shut the door. She takes a hard pull on the cigarette, inhaling deeply and blowing the smoke through a toothy smile. She receives Jay without ceremony or politesse, treating him as an old friend. "I know what you're thinking," she says, misreading his expression. "But I'm telling you, this is going to work out better for everybody."

She offers Jay a cigarette.

He declines, hands in his pockets, keeping himself at a safe distance.

"There is a way out of this mess," she continues. "A way everybody can win." She pushes herself off the front edge of her desk. "We just need the right person to present it," she says, throwing her voice in a wide, encircling arc, inviting Jay into that *We*. As if they're in this one together, comrades again.

He remembers this Cynthia.

The girl who would get hold of an idea and work it, over and over in her head 'til you could see sparks in those blue-gray eyes. He can tell by the look on her face now, the bright flash in her eyes, that she's sitting on something big.

"Are you going to the port commission meeting tonight?" she asks. "We could really use you on this thing," she says. "*I* could really use you, Jay."

The phone on the mayor's desk rings. From his perch at the back of the room, Kip answers the line. Jay hears him whisper into the receiver, the words lost in the distance.

"I don't see why you and I can't put a lot of shit behind us,

Jay," Cynthia says calmly, almost casually, as if they were talking about something as mundane as an old card game that went sour. "If you came out tonight, if you stood with us, it would send a message to those men, to the Brotherhood camp, in particular, that we're not—*I'm* not—out to hurt them. 'Cause I'm not, Jay. I'm not. And you of all people should know that." She lowers her voice to a sweet drawl. "If you stand with me on this thing, Jay, maybe I can help you out too, you know, maybe get you out of that shithole of an office you call a law practice. I mean, you got a lot of talent, Jay. You just never figured out how to channel it."

"Fuck you, Cynthia."

"People listen to you, Jay." She says it softly, almost wistfully, as if she's never forgotten in all this time what drew her to him in the first place, as if she's carried it with her a long, long way. "You just got to remember to speak up."

"You giving me advice now, Cynthia?"

"I know you, Jay, better than anybody. Don't forget that."

He can smell her perfume from here, woodsy and strong. It makes him think of pine needles and red clay, nights in the back of her pickup truck.

"You haven't forgotten me, have you, Jay?" she asks.

"If only it were that easy."

Behind him, Kip hangs up the phone and they have an audience again. The mayor is dry and businesslike all of a sudden. "I could really use somebody like you in this administration, Jay, as a liaison to some of the more *diverse* communities in the city."

Jay smiles bitterly at the offer, almost charmed by the audacity of it. So that's what this is all about? She wants him to be her blackface.

"If you stand with me—"

"Cynthia, I don't stand with you on anything."

"Oh, come on, Jay," the mayor says, quick to her own defense. "You *know* me. You know where I'm coming from."

"I know you sold out those men with that press conference," he says. "You got management hovering like vultures, just waiting for the whole thing to collapse. That's about all I need to know about where you're coming from."

Cynthia shrinks away from him, her voice suddenly stern and cold, that of a woman refused. "Whether you understand it or not, Jay, I'm doing what's best for those men. Because what's best for this city, and this city's economy, *is* what's best for those men. When business wins, we all win," she says, Reagan smiling over her shoulder. Jay can barely resist laughing out loud.

"A strike," Cynthia says, "is not helping anybody."

She plops down into the wingback chair behind her desk. The phone rings again. Behind him, Jay hears Kip pick up the line. Cynthia rests her elbows on the mahogany desk. "We're losing tens of thousands by the day. Another month, we'll be losing *millions*. You understand? This has got to stop."

"Cynthia," Jay says, trying to slow her down.

"This is one of the most prosperous times in this city's history," she says, shaking her head somewhat incredulously, as if she's only of late discovered that running a city isn't nearly as much fun as she thought it would be. "And I'll tell you what, the shit ain't gon' fall apart on my watch. I won't let it, Jay."

"I didn't come here to argue with you about this," he says.

He pulls his hands from his pockets, runs his fingers along the dark stubble that's come up in patches along his jawline over the last few days. He's shy with his words, which makes him seem more nervous than he intends.

"Is this something to do with the girl?" Cynthia asks.

Jay ignores the question, having decided before he walked

in here that he would not say any more than he had to. "What do you know about the federal government storing oil underground?" he asks. "In salt caverns on the coast?"

Cynthia leans back in her chair. "What in the world are you asking me about that for?"

"You were in Washington in the seventies. You were in Bentsen's office."

It feels odd to say it out loud. The first time they've acknowledged to each other this part of her life, the years after she disappeared, the years after him.

"I figured if anybody would know something about it. . . ."

"Well, it's not some big secret," she says. "Not in the least."

"This was Carter's deal?"

"I'm guessing you're talking about the Strategic Petroleum Reserve?"

Jay nods. *Sure.*

"Well, what do you want to know?" she says with a shrug. "They passed a law in seventy-five, after all that bullshit with the Arabs. The point was to have the stuff on hand so we wouldn't run into another crunch, you know. So, yeah, Carter's administration had to implement it. The Energy Department started buying up oil in rather large amounts. And the question was where to put it. The salt caverns, Texas and Louisiana, they won." She pulls her black pumps from the side of her desk and slides them back onto her feet. "This is all old news, Jay."

The phone on her desk rings again.

"*I* didn't know that much about it," he says.

"Well, you were in law school at the time."

He hates that she knows this, that she knows the facts of his life.

"You know anything about them closing down salt mines?" he asks. "Or buying up real estate?"

The phone lines on her desk start lighting up, one after another.

"Well, if barrel prices keep dropping like they are, I'm sure they're trying to buy up as much as they can and store it wherever they can."

"Right." Jay nods absently, trying to think how this all adds up.

"Why are you asking?"

"You hear about any problems with this? Like structural problems? Underground?"

Cynthia is still waiting for him to answer her question.

Then, realizing his silence is all she's going to get, she sighs. "The technology's not that new, Jay. But the thing is, no one's ever tried to store this much oil in salt caverns before, not in a program this extensive. There were some problems in the beginning. I mean, I heard some things."

"Like what?"

She hesitates for a breath. "There were . . . explosions."

"Leakage?"

"Something like that," she says. Her words slow all of a sudden, as if she's not sure how much further down this road she wants to travel. "But look, if anybody gets hurt, if there's any property loss, the government pays. Somebody always gets a nice big settlement. That's the way I understood it, at least."

Jay thinks of the old man in High Point, the government telling him there was nothing they could do. He thinks of Elise Linsey and the threat on her life, the Stardale Development Company and its empty offices, the man in the black Ford and the hush money—the spirit of secrecy running underneath this whole thing.

"What is all this, Jay?" the mayor asks. "What are you into?"

She stares at him a good while, her blue-gray eyes narrowing slightly. She seems to take him in for the first time since he walked through the door, noticing the bruises on his face and neck. She rises slowly behind her desk and crosses the room to stand before him. "My God, Jay," she says softly, tilting her blond head to one side. Gently, she reaches out and touches the marks on his face. Her fingertips are cool and dry. "You're in something bad, aren't you? Is it the girl?"

"Cynthia—"

"Don't worry," she says quickly. "I said I wouldn't give your name to the D.A., and I won't," she says, adding, "but you got to do something for me too."

"Jesus, Cynthia."

"Help me with this union thing, Jay." She's desperate, beyond any sense of shame. "I need a win, Jay, something that says I can do this goddamned job. Or else they'll make this bigger than it is. They'll make it about my hair or my clothes or what I've got between my legs, as if that's got a fucking thing to do with anything. They'll tear me to pieces, and you know it. I need to win, Jay."

The phone has not stopped ringing.

Kip is now standing at his desk. His expression is grim. "Ms. Mayor."

Cynthia looks past Jay to her assistant. The phone lines are all blinking, calls coming in on top of each other. Just then, the double doors to the suite swing open. The mayor's secretary walks in from the waiting room. She looks at Kip first, then the mayor. "I think you ought to come see this," she says.

Outside the mayor's suite, most of the staffers on the third floor are standing together in front of a wall of windows facing east. As the mayor approaches, Kip and Jay behind her, the staffers part and make way for her. They nudge each other and whisper. They glance at Cynthia, and they wait. She looks out the window at her city and lets out a single, ragged gasp. Jay, behind her, elbows his way through the crowd, edging for a view to the east.

At first, he doesn't get it.

He sees blue sky, the white sun. He sees the larger-than-life C-O-L-E letters on the buildings across the street. He sees the top of the public library, a piece of the federal courthouse, the city skyline that he knows so well.

Then he looks down at the street below.

There must be three hundred people on the street, maybe four. As good a turnout as he ever had, years ago. From a distance, they move as one, like a river, a living, breathing stream pulsing through the heart of the city. They are coming right for city hall. At the sight of Kwame's march, Jay cannot help his smile. It wells up from someplace inside him he didn't know was still there.

He can almost hear them through the glass.

Clap, clap.

The hands in the air.

Clap, clap.

The march of feet on pavement.

Clap, clap.

The rhythm that is in his soul.

Cynthia, the girl he knew, would have been down there too once. But the mayor, the woman standing beside him now, looks absolutely panicked. She turns to Kip and asks how fast they can put something together on the mall in front of city hall. She asks him to call the *Post* and the *Chronicle*. She uses the word *pronto* more than once, barking orders at some of the other staffers. Before long, it seems that everyone on the third floor is on the phone.

Cynthia turns to Jay. "If you had anything to do with this, I swear—"

Kip calls from a nearby desk, informing the mayor that the city news editor from the *Post* is waiting on the line. She shakes her head at Jay, giving him a look of reproach or terror, he can't quite tell. Either way, she's furious with him. Jay, on the other hand, is still smiling, watching as the mayor turns and runs back to her suite, skittering across the beige carpet in her high heels.

Chapter 25

"No one understands discrimination more than I do," the mayor says from behind the podium. Outside in the August heat, she's removed her red jacket and rolled up her sleeves just in time for the camera crews. "As a woman working in politics, I have certainly had to knock down my fair share of doors."

Click. Click.

The news photographers snap away on the mall in front of city hall, where the mayor, to her credit, has managed to pull together a press conference in less than twenty minutes. She stands behind the podium, baking under the August sun, sweating through her makeup and the pits of her white blouse.

Jay stands down below, on the grass with the other marchers.

He stands with Reverend Boykins and the kid Darren.

With Darren's father, Mr. Hayworth.

With Donnie Simpson and his wife and their three kids, the two girls in matching halter tops, the little one asleep on her daddy's shoulder.

Jay stands with the dozens of dockworkers he met along the way.

He stands with his old friend Lloyd.

If Kwame Mackalvy is surprised to see Jay here, he keeps it to himself, offering Jay a brotherly nod and a place down in front if he wants it. Jay, feeling a part of something again, weaves through the crowd, feeling its restless energy. The men are almost punch-drunk with it. The crowd rocks back and forth, shifting its weight every few minutes, relieving aching feet. Someone is passing around an army canteen of cool water. Jay peels off his jacket and tie in the heat.

Traffic has slowed to a standstill on Bagby, rubberneckers leaned out of their front windows, exhaust fumes choking what little oxygen hangs in the humid air. The mayor's coiffed helmet is drooping by the minute, and Jay gets the feeling that she is courting this disheveled image, that she wants to let the long-shoremen and the news cameras see that she is not putting on airs here or concerning herself with her appearance. She is, Jay guesses, betting on the fact that when it comes to women, people often mistake homely for earnest. He is beginning to think she's a better politician than he gave her credit for.

"I want to let you know, first and foremost, that I stand with you," she says. "Since this whole overtime issue came to light down at the port, I have been working tirelessly to see how this conflict can spin us all in a new direction. 'Cause as the city's first woman mayor and a longtime supporter of civil rights, I will accept nothing less. We will move in a new direction or history will move all over us and leave us behind. We stand still at our own peril."

Click. Click. Click.

Early in, the cameras are the mayor's only applause.

The marchers down below listen with their arms firmly crossed.

"I don't know about you," Cynthia says. "But I want more for this city."

Behind her, Kip smiles on the dais. Jay wonders which words are his.

"And I am not alone," the mayor says. "The Maritime Association and the Port of Houston, the unions and the oil companies . . . we all want to see an equitable resolution to this thing, a way that everybody can win. I want us to reach Dr. King's dream, where race doesn't matter, where black men and white men can get equal pay and benefits, overtime and a chance at management."

Jay doesn't remember that part of King's speech.

But it's no matter. The mere mention of Dr. King's name causes a knee-jerk reaction in the mostly black crowd. There's a sudden smattering of hand clapping and head nodding, an amen or two. Here it comes, he thinks. Here comes the seduction.

"And the only way for us to get there," the mayor announces, "is to get rid of preferential treatment once and for all."

The applause in the crowd grows from a smattering to a swelling wave.

"For as long as the stevedores are hiring and promoting on the basis of race, as long as anyone anywhere is picking people on the basis of their skin color, we all lose," the mayor says. "As long as we continue to *see* race, we lose."

The wave of applause spreads through the crowd on the mall, reaching such a fevered pitch that Cynthia actually has to wait for it to die down before she can get out her next words. She plays the moment for all its dramatic effect, waving her hand in the air like a conductor, driving the people where she wants them to go. "If we play into that Southern stereotype, we run the risk of the world seeing Houston as backward and unsophisticated. We run the risk of driving away business. The future of this city depends on putting our best face forward, to let people know that Houston, Texas, is first class all the way."

She pauses to look down at the print reporters scribbling in their notebooks, as if she wants to make sure that no one misses a word of what she's about to say next.

"The answer then, as I see it, is to remove the lens of race altogether," the mayor says. "Now just this morning, Pat Bodine of the ILA, your union president, as well as Wayne Kaylin from OCAW, some members of the port commission and the Maritime Association, and Thomas Cole . . . they were all in my office. We were hammering something out, trying to come up with the right solution. And I'm happy to report that we reached some common ground in there. I proposed a resolution I think we can all be proud of. And it starts here at city hall," Cynthia pronounces. "I am proposing to the city council, as early as next week, that the city of Houston adopt an official policy of race-blind hiring. There will be no more *skipping* over people because of their race, putting one group of people over another. That's where we've gone wrong in the past."

Oh, she has them now, Jay thinks. This is what they've been waiting for. The words they came all this way to hear. He hears whistles in the crowd, sees a few women waving handkerchiefs in the air. The men clap and stomp their feet. Jay, at the head of the crowd, holds up a hand, as high as he can manage. He waves for them to stop, everything in his body telling them to wait.

Just wait.

"And," the mayor says, "there will be no *advancing* people because of their race either. We will judge people by their merits, no more, no less."

It takes a moment for the crowd to get it, for the catch to catch on.

For the dockworkers to understand what the mayor is really saying.

That her plan is to simply wipe the slate clean from this moment forward, to wipe out three hundred years of racial discrimination in a single afternoon.

The mayor's solution: let the problem self-correct.

Out in the crowd, the hand clapping stops short. The faces grow long.

Cynthia is so proud of herself, she is dangerously close to being smug.

"Now, when I proposed this idea to the unions this morning, to the stevedores and representatives from the port," she says, "it took them no time to come to the conclusion that this was the right thing to do, that this was the right solution at the right time for this city." She pauses, waiting for applause that never comes. "So it falls to you men now," she says, putting the onus of this labor problem squarely in their calloused hands. "If the stevedores and the union leaders can come to a consensus on this, then the only question left is, when do you boys want to go back to work?" She looks directly into the TV cameras on the mall and smiles broadly. "The city is waiting, y'all."

When Jay calls home about an hour or so later, Bernie complains that Rolly's got his feet up on her sofa. "Some bodyguard," she mumbles under her breath. Jay asks if she wants him to come home. She says no, "I know they need you there." He asks how she's feeling, if everything's all right. Rolly, she says, "has been watching stories since this morning," but she's glad she's not in the apartment alone. Jay tells her to hang in there, tells her that he loves her.

Outside the ILA union hall, he hangs up the pay phone.

Then he heads back inside, where a labor fight has been raging for at least an hour already, the men more divided than ever. The white ones came here today right from the picket line, their clothes pocked with sweat marks. Everyone in the room is hot and tired on their feet. Jay and the Brotherhood camp came here straight from the mayor's press conference at city hall, Jay driving his father-in-law and Darren Hayworth because the kid had asked him to come along. Reverend Boykins is still hoping for a sit-down with the union president and OCAW, and the kid, looking at Jay, said he wanted a man with him he could trust. It had been impossible for Jay, despite himself, to say no.

This ILA meeting was thrown together hastily, at Pat Bodine's suggestion. There's no microphone set up onstage today, no coffee or refreshments. The union president is up on the stage, alone, in a damp and wrinkled shirt. He waves down the hand of a white man right under the stage, saying, "Naw, I got to you twice already. Let's get some other voices in here."

Another white man in front raises his hand in the air.

He's leaning his weight against the stake of his picket sign, which reads, UNION STANDS FOR BROTHERHOOD. When Pat Bodine calls on him, the man turns to face his union brothers, black and white. "I don't exactly see what there is to talk about," he says. "I thought this is what we was looking for from the get-go."

The applause in the room comes from the picketers, from the white dockworkers who, by their own choice, stayed far away from today's march. The picketers clap their hands and stomp

the posts of their handmade signs onto the meeting hall's linoleum floor. The marchers, the men of the now defunct Brotherhood of Longshoremen, shake their heads vigorously. "This
don't make nothing right," one of the black dockworkers says,
followed by catcalls and claps from his fellow marchers. "This
just puts us right back where we started."

"Look," one of the white picketers says, "if the stevedores say
they'll stop hiring foremen on the basis of race, I don't get it . . .
what more do you people want?"

"We want an equal shot, same as you," Donnie Simpson says.

"I think what the mayor is saying is that a policy like this
would level the playing field for everybody," Bodine says. "There
has never been an official policy like this on the books. It would
be a huge step forward." Then, sensing he's maybe offered too
much of his own opinion, he adds, "In theory."

"But see, that's the problem, jack," Donnie Simpson says from
the floor. "I can't *eat* on theory. You understand me? I can't send
my kids to school on *theory*."

There's an explosive response from the Brotherhood camp,
men calling out, "That's right, brother," and whistling loudly.
Pat Bodine, onstage, tries to call on someone else to speak, but
the marchers are slow to die down. Bodine puts his hands on his
hips, exasperated at having momentarily lost control.

Reverend Boykins raises a hand next. This gets the black
marchers' attention. They *shh* each other and wait politely for
the Rev to speak. "I think what the men are trying to say is that
the policy put forward by the mayor does not redress the wrongs
that have already been perpetrated against them."

"I'm sorry, Pat, but I got to say something here," one of the
white picketers says, a man in a dirty T-shirt, sleeves rolled up to
his shoulder bones. "This is what I don't like about this," he says,
pointing to Reverend Boykins. "Y'all are listening to people who

don't have a damn thing to do with this union. Y'all are getting into all this political crap when the rest of us just want to go back to work."

"We want to work too," one of the black marchers says.

"But we got to get some black men in management right now," Kwame Mackalvy says. The white union men turn to stare at this interloper in a colorful dashiki, a black man who invited himself into the dockworkers' broken family. "Now look," Kwame says, writing policy off the top of his head. "If the stevedores were willing to say that the next, say, twenty or thirty foremen they hire over the next year will be black, or hell, Mexican even, then that's one thing. If there was something in place that said these companies *had* to hire so many blacks—"

"Well, wait a minute now," the man with the rolled-up sleeves says. "Why should y'all get promised something we ain't guaranteed?"

"Putting some of us in management *right now* is the only way to make it equal *right now*," Donnie Simpson says above the buzzing crowd. "Y'all had your time. It's our time now."

"Let me see if I'm getting this straight," the man with no sleeves says. "We stuck our necks out for you, walked out on the docks for you, and now you're saying that this whole time what you really wanted wasn't to be treated equal, but to be treated *better* than everybody else."

"Fuck that," one of the white picketers hollers.

"I got eight years on the job, eight years toward management. I'll be damned if I'm gon' stay on strike so a black man can come take my job," one of the picketers says, letting his white poster board slide to the floor in defiance.

"You'd think people who say they're always getting discriminated against wouldn't want to turn around and do that to somebody else," No Sleeves says. "Well, I don't think it's right. I didn't think it was right when white folks was doing it, and I don't think it's right if blacks are the ones doing it either."

The white men in the room applaud him loudly. Across the union hall, another man boldly drops his sign to the floor. Two more follow. It starts to catch on around the room. One by one, the white men drop their signs.

The black dockworkers seem stunned, hurt even.

Pat Bodine waves his hand over the crowd. "I will say this, men. It will not be easy to go back into that negotiation room and push for more than what's already been offered." He looks out at the black dockworkers, talking as if the debate were already over. "This doesn't have to be a bad thing. Getting the stevedoring companies out of the habit of automatically putting whites first is not a little thing. We can build on that. Now look, we dragged OCAW into this with us. I don't know how much longer those men are going to walk with us if we're turning down what could be a workable solution."

One of the white longshoremen down front climbs onto the stage without invitation, startling Bodine, who immediately looks into the audience for somebody to come physically remove the guy. "We got to go back to work, y'all," the man onstage yells. "For all of us, the whole union. If we hold out for too long, they gon' have them machines down there running everything. And then ain't nobody gon' have a job. They saying they gon' judge us by what we got inside," he says, speaking directly to the black men now. "If y'all can't live with that, I mean, if you don't think you got what it takes to be management, then, hell, don't apply. But don't keep the rest of us from going back to work."

The black men wave him off the stage, booing loudly.

The whites clap and laud the man's plainspoken sense.

At the back of the room, there's an ILA officer dressed in

slacks and a button-down. He motions to Bodine, then points to a wall clock overhead.

The Rev nudges Jay. "It's time," he says.

Onstage, Pat Bodine tells the men they'll have to put this proposal to a vote before the whole union no matter what, something the officers will organize in short order. In the meantime, they'll need to hear more from the Maritime Association on what the stevedores are willing to put in writing. He reminds the men about the port commission meeting at five o'clock. "Those that want to join us might want to think about heading that way in the next few minutes or so. Get y'all selves something to eat, as the thing is likely to run long. Public officials do love to talk," he says, which elicits universal soft chuckles throughout both sides of the room. "Also, you boys remember now . . . they gon' have cameras at this thing. They're talking about getting press from up north. You boys make sure and represent this union well."

As the dockworkers make for the double doors, Bodine walks across the room to where the ILA officer has been waiting for him, next to a door marked PRIVATE. Both men look up as Reverend Boykins, Darren, and Jay approach. Pat Bodine takes one look at Jay and asks, "Who the hell is he?"

"I'm the boy's lawyer," Jay offers, which in this instance means nothing more than the fact that he's not going to let the kid walk into this situation unprotected. Bodine, upon hearing the news of an attorney in their midst, sighs and shakes his head. They follow him down a long and dimly lit hallway.

This part of the building smells like stale coffee, tinged with the metallic edge of cigarette smoke so thick that it's gotten into the curtains and the carpet on the floor. The union officers' private offices are at the end of the long hallway, the vice president, secretary, and treasurer all sharing one large room to the right, and the president housed in a dim, windowless room to the left.

Two men are already waiting inside: Wayne Kaylin, president of OCAW, and Carlisle Minty, vice president of the same union. Jay remembers Minty's picture from the paper. He is thinner in person. He's wearing glasses, and behind them, his eyes are like two white clouds, pale and shape shifting. At first sight, Jay doesn't like the man. The way he's got himself leaned against Bodine's desk, the way he doesn't even bother to stand up straight and off the man's property when Bodine walks into the room. He acts as if this whole meeting is beneath him. Jay immediately looks at Darren to see if there's some recognition there, now that the two men are face-to-face again, to be sure once and for all if this is the same man who orchestrated the attack on Darren from the cab of his pickup truck. Minty isn't wearing a baseball cap today, and he hardly looks twice in Darren's direction, as if the boy were a stranger. Still, Jay can see the kid's back stiffen in Minty's presence. Darren turns and looks at Jay and the Rev.

He nods. *It's him.*

"You're sure?" Jay asks.

The kid nods again. "I'm sure."

Minty is staring long and hard at Jay. The enmity, it appears, is mutual.

There's not room enough in this tiny office for the men to sit down. The only available chair is buried beneath cardboard boxes, phone books, and two poster boards: UNION STANDS FOR BROTHERHOOD and JUSTICE FOR ONE *IS* JUSTICE FOR ALL. The quarters are so close Jay can smell Kaylin's aftershave and from here could probably make an educated guess about what kind of beer Carlisle Minty had with lunch. It's hardly the most decorous place to hold a sit-down of this sort, but maybe, Jay thinks, it's fitting for the sometimes down-and-dirty nature of union politics. Maybe Minty deserves no better courtroom than this.

"Let me just say off the top," Bodine starts. "I don't stand for labor violence. That's not my way of doing things."

He looks at each and every one of them, making sure they get that point clear and out of the way. Then he adds, "But this little incident is causing us a lot of fucking problems. We're on the verge of making some real headway on this equal pay issue, and this shit ain't helping at all. It's goddamned unprofessional, for one. And I can tell you what, this strike wouldn't be worth shit without OCAW's participation," he says, to which Wayne nods assent. "It's the oil that's got people scared shitless. It's the shutdown at the refineries that's got the fucking *Washington Post* coming around. The *New York Times*, reporters from out East. This is all about the oil." He sighs, maybe sensing his own reduced position in this labor fight. The dockworkers might have started the strike, but like almost every other thing in America, it's being fueled by petrol. "The alliance between the two unions is too important to piss it away on some bullshit like this. And I, for one, don't want to see this drag on much further."

"Me neither," Minty says.

"And let me say this to you, Carlisle," Bodine adds, poking a hairy finger in the air. "I've known you a long time, and if you did this, you ought to be goddamned ashamed of yourself."

"Hold on, Pat," Wayne says. "Let's not jump to any conclusions here."

"I never touched that kid," Minty says.

"My understanding," Jay says, not letting him get away on a technicality, "is that the beating took place on your instruction."

"I never seen this kid, okay?" Minty turns and looks Darren in the eye. "You got that?" He takes a step in the kid's direction. "You got it all wrong."

Wayne grabs Minty by the arm, pulling him back. "Why don't you tell us what it is you want here?" he asks the men. "What makes this go away?"

"If Mr. Minty apologized," Bodine starts.

"I'm not apologizing for a goddamned thing."

Wayne tightens his grip on Minty's arm.

Reverend Boykins clears his throat. "An apology is one thing, yes. The other is that we want to make sure our men aren't putting their lives in danger just for standing up for themselves, you understand? And as this thing goes forward, I, for one, need to know that these men are going to be protected."

"It's my understanding that the strike ain't going forward," Wayne says. "My men are ready to go back to work. Let's make that clear right now." He looks at Bodine. "You said we were close, Pat."

Bodine sighs and says to Reverend Boykins and Darren, "If I'm being real with you, there is no way for us to not take seriously the mayor's proposal. If the stevedores adopt a viable program for race-blind hiring, I think there's a very real possibility that the strike will reach a resolution shortly."

"And I'm telling you-all," the Rev says, "pretending people aren't black is not the way to equality. It's not even possible, first of all. Any more than I can pretend you aren't who you are."

"I thought this is what you all wanted," Bodine says sincerely.

"I think the hope has always been that you see what you see, and you take us anyway, for who we are," the Rev says. "Not that we all go around pretending we're the same. I don't see how that helps anybody."

Carlisle Minty lets out an exasperated sigh.

"And let me tell you what else," the Rev adds. "You will never let those men out there know you're serious about setting things right if you let this man get away with what he did. It will hang over this union for a long, long time."

"Why'd you do it?" Darren asks, looking squarely at Carlisle Minty. "Why'd you do this to me? I don't even know you, man."

"Goddamnit, Pat, are you gonna listen to this bullshit?" Minty asks.

"It ain't a bad question, C."

"Aw, hell." Minty waves his hand in the air like he's waving away the smell of horseshit.

"You're the vice president of the damn union," Bodine says. "If you didn't want a walkout, you shoulda talked to Wayne, or me, for that matter. It wasn't necessary to pull a kid into it. He is one of mine, after all."

"I never touched that fucking kid," Minty yells, his face growing red at the jawline. "Jesus, Wayne, you want to jump in here?" he says to his union brother. "I mean, for one," he says, speaking to Bodine again, "we're talking about ten o'clock at night. How in the hell you gon' tell me this kid saw me on a dark street, in a truck somewhere? That don't make a lick of sense."

"How did you know it was ten o'clock at night?" Jay asks. "I mean, if you supposedly don't know anything about it."

"Well, Mr. Smart Fucking Lawyer," Minty says, ignoring a taming hand on his shoulder from Wayne Kaylin. "I got cops coming to my house, to my fucking job. They were real clear on what this kid *thinks* he saw me do. And I'm gon' tell you what I told them, and then I ain't gon' say nothing more about it. It *couldn't* have been me, okay?" he says, looking Darren in the eye. "I was at work. It's on the fucking books. You can check it just like the cops did."

Jay looks to the Rev, who shakes his head. This is news to him too.

"And I can do you one better," Minty says, cooling his tone now that the facts seem to be turning in his favor. "Thomas Cole and a couple of suits from downtown were doing a site visit at the refinery that night. I had a cup of coffee with the man myself. He told the police as much already. Unless he's lying too."

"You were working at Cole Oil when this happened?" Jay asks skeptically. "Ten o'clock at night?"

"I was working the late shift as a matter of fact."

"The story checks out," Wayne says to Bodine. "I mean, legally, the cops don't know what to do with it. They got the kid's statement. But Minty was at work, Pat. It's on the books. He clocked in for the night shift at seven fifty-five PM and didn't clock out 'til morning. And as far as the police are concerned, if a man like Thomas Cole says he saw Minty at work, then it's enough for them."

"Look, kid, I'm sorry about what all happened to you, I am," Minty says, not sounding sorry in the least. "But it wasn't me, okay?" He looks around the room at the others. "And even if it was," he says, suddenly smug, as if he's just dying to admit that it *was* him, as if he's daring them to do anything about it, what with the law and Thomas Cole on his side. "Don't matter much anymore. You got your strike in the end, and now it's done. We can all get back to work."

"Let me get this straight," Jay says, still stuck on one thing in particular, one thing that seems mildly incredible to him, or just plain odd. "You're telling me that Thomas Cole, the CEO of Cole Oil Industries—"

"CFO," Minty corrects him, bragging, kind of, as if it were *his* job.

"You're telling me the *CFO* of Cole Oil . . . is your alibi?"

Minty eyes Jay coldly. He seems to take the question as a personal attack. "I'm not just some peon down there. I put in nearly thirty years at that refinery. I've earned the respect of a lot of people. And yes, Thomas Cole is one of them. I do an important job for him, not that you would know about it."

"He's a production coordinator for Cole," Wayne says, backing him up.

"Senior supervisor," Minty corrects him. "I keep track of the crude."

"Is that right?" Jay asks.

"Yes, that's right. I'm the one seeing to the tankers out there," Minty says, still bragging. "I mark the levels down in the books when the oil comes in off the ships and the tanker trucks. I keep track of how much or how little we got on hand, what sets the prices, you know. So I'd say I'm pretty important down there, somebody Mr. Cole might want to say hello to once in a while."

Jay, all of sudden, feels something hot behind his ears.

He's had this sensation before, like two live wires touching, something in his mind getting ready to ignite. It's something about the mention of Thomas Cole that doesn't sit right. Minty just happened to be working the late shift that night, and Thomas Cole just happened to be by the refinery at the exact time Minty needed corroboration for his whereabouts? There's no doubt that Minty is lying. The real question is, why would Thomas Cole play along? Why would the CFO of Cole Oil lie for a man like Carlisle Minty? Why help him get away with a crime? Unless, of course, Jay is reading it all wrong . . . backward, in fact.

He stares at Carlisle Minty, the callous look in his eyes.

"Who keeps track of the crude during the walkout?" he asks.

"Nobody," Minty says. "The plant's dark."

He says it like he thinks Jay's an idiot.

The strike, of course, has shut down everything.

"Nothing going out," Jay says out loud, rolling the words

around in his mind, then finishing the thought, "and no workers to bring any oil in."

"That's right," Minty says.

Jay gets a sudden image of oil tanker trucks in High Point, the old man's description of them secreting away oil in the middle of the night. The cleanup, he called it, and said it stopped short just about a week ago . . . right about the time the strike got started, when the Cole refinery in Houston went dark.

Pat Bodine looks down at his watch. "So what are we doing here? Are we in a place to put this behind us?" he asks Reverend Boykins and Darren. " 'Cause I'd like to make some statement to that effect as soon as possible."

"So that's it, huh?" Darren says.

"Look, if the police investigation says it wasn't Minty, I just don't know what else I can do here," Bodine says. "The sooner we put this behind us, the sooner I can go out and negotiate the best deal on your behalf. And that's what we should really be focused on. I'm on your side with this thing, I really am."

Jay's got his eyes on Carlisle Minty still, taking in the gold watch on Minty's left wrist and wondering to himself what a production supervisor makes in a year, how he got himself a watch like that. When the meeting breaks up a few minutes later, Jay sees Pat Bodine drive out of the parking lot in a fifteen-year-old Chevy, while Minty climbs into a late-model Cadillac.

Cole Oil has apparently been very good to Carlisle Minty.

Darren tells the Rev he's not going to the port commission meeting. As far as he's concerned, this whole thing is over. "You got to see it to the end," the Rev keeps saying over and over. Darren shakes his head. "It's over, man. They got us in a corner now. There's no way we can win." And anyway, he's tired.

Jay offers to give the kid a ride home.

After he drives to Kashmere Gardens and back, he heads home

to his wife, and Rolly, laid up on his couch. Bernie is reading a paperback at the kitchen table when he comes in. He kisses the part between her two french braids. Rolly, in the other room, is watching a western on television, Jay's .38 resting on his thigh.

"Didn't you tell me Elise Linsey used to work for Cole Oil?" Jay asks him.

Rolly stretches his lengthy arms overhead. "She was a secretary, I said."

"For Thomas Cole. They had a relationship, you said."

"Something like that."

"Well," Jay whispers, "that's some fucking coincidence."

"What are you talking about?"

"I'm going to need those phone records, man," Jay says. "I need you to go back as far as you can, and I need you to do it as soon as you can."

Rolly sits up on the couch, wiping at the corners of his mouth. "I guess you not gon' take my advice then," he says.

"What's that?"

"I guess this means you're not gon' leave it alone."

Chapter 26

By the time Jay makes it to the *Chronicle*'s offices the next day, he's had time to work out a few things in his head, after spending part of his morning in the government records department at the main library of the University of Houston, asking the librarian on duty for anything related to the Strategic Petroleum Reserve. The librarian was an older white lady, in her seventies maybe, with hair dyed black as midnight. She brought him congressional funding records and maps, even newspaper articles, and told him she remembered him from his time on campus, when he used to spend days on end sifting through government records, looking for legislative ammunition. She told him that back then she'd been happy to help him find whatever information he needed, that it was her little way of being a part of things.

"You at it again, son?" she asked, pulling at the thin sleeves of her cardigan. Jay smiled awkwardly, embarrassed that he couldn't place her, that he didn't remember her at all, in fact.

He'd had a kind of blindness back then too, he thought.

In the middle of his political struggles, this woman hadn't even registered to him, no matter her kindness. Of course, it's no secret he didn't trust a lot of white people when he was younger. And the one he did trust—with *everything*—turned out to be a crushing disappointment to him, personally and politically. The mistake of trusting Cynthia Maddox had cost him his sanity and his sense of safety with himself. It's partly why a woman like Elise Linsey had the power to shake him to his core, why he so easily let his fear get the best of him, mislead and confuse him. The whole world around Jay might have changed in the last decade, but his freedom, his true peace of mind, is not yet at hand.

The librarian at U of H left him in a carrel with a hot cup of tea and a stack of papers and offered to bring him anything else he needed. He looked at the maps first, SPR sites going all the way back to the beginning. Bryan Mound in Freeport, Texas, was the first government storage site, and, according to the congressional paperwork in front of him—the records of government contracts and checks cut—the Bryan Mound site was initially managed by ColeCo, an engineering division of Cole Oil. Which meant, to Jay, that Cole Oil either taught the government the technology of storing oil in underground salt caverns or learned it themselves on taxpayer money.

But of course the most interesting thing about the maps of SPR sites located throughout the Gulf Coast was something that, by the time he saw it in print, came as no surprise to Jay. The maps, some dated as far back as 1976, showed no Strategic

Petroleum Reserve facility in High Point, Texas, at all. And in all the pages and pages of Department of Energy records handed to him, there was not one mention of a purchase payment to the Crystal-Smith Salt Company. There was no record, in fact, of the government being involved at all. Which explains, Jay thought while sitting in the library of his alma mater, why the government so insisted they couldn't help old man Ainsley with the closing of the salt mine or the crude coming up in his back-yard. It was never their oil to begin with.

He takes the maps and a stack of papers with him to the *Chronicle*'s offices on Texas Avenue, downtown, where he's in for his first real shock of the day:

Lon Philips is a woman.

Lonette Kay Philips, actually, according to the roster of employees covering a whole wall of the first-floor lobby. Jay calls up to her desk three times from the pay phones by the elevators, and each time, an answering service picks up the line. He would leave a message, but what would be the point? Philips hasn't returned a single one of his calls in the past twenty-four hours. And anyway, he has no way of knowing if she's even in the build-ing. The security guard posted by the elevators is no help. He won't say whether he's seen Lon Philips come through for the day, nor will he let Jay past without an express invitation.

In the end, Jay tries a different approach.

Near the building's front doors, there's a young woman in her twenties sitting behind a wide U-shaped desk made of glass and steel, whose job it is to answer the *Chronicle*'s main phone line and patch calls through to the offices upstairs. She does this while flipping through a thick catalog filled with motorboats and RVs advertised as "Condos on Wheels." The catalog com-

pany offers E-Z financing in bright yellow writing. The receptionist, when Jay approaches, is looking longingly at a Leisure
Mobile V100, which is really just an oversize van with the backseats taken out and a full bar put in instead. I guess we all have
a dream, Jay thinks. For ten dollars, the girl behind the desk is
happy to report that Lon Philips is indeed in the building. "I saw
her myself this morning," she says. For another ten, Jay asks her
to call up to Lon Philips's desk or to get somebody on her floor
to tell Ms. Philips that there's a man downstairs with flowers for
her, and that he's demanding she sign for 'em herself.

"Make it twenty," the girl says.

He has a smoke in the lobby, and he waits.

It's nearly twenty minutes before Ms. Philips comes down.

He spots her by the purposeful gait, the way she impatiently
marches to the receptionist's desk, wanting to get whatever this
is over with, and by the fact that, on her approach, the girl behind
the desk nods her head in Jay's direction.

Sniffing a ruse, Philips puts her hands on her hips. "What the
hell is this supposed to be?"

She is probably ninety-five pounds, wet, and barely five feet
tall. Her hairdo, a Dorothy Hamill sweep puffed up with lots of
teasing and hairspray, looks like it weighs more than she does.
And her voice, which Jay took to be soft and somewhat fey for
a man, actually sounds gruff and salty coming from this slip of
a woman, who for some reason is wearing a man's flannel shirt
in August. Jay thinks she may be only a few years older than the
receptionist.

"I don't have time for a bunch of games," she says, looking
back and forth between Jay and the girl behind the desk, waiting
for one of them to come clean. Jay finally takes a step forward.
"My name is Jay Porter."

Philips looks him up and down, her eyes narrowing slightly.

"The lawyer," she says. Then, "That is, of course, if you're telling the truth."

"You want to see my bar card?" Jay asks, half jokingly.

"Yes."

It takes him a moment to fish it out of his wallet. When he does, Philips grabs the card and the wallet, inspecting them both, making sure to get a good look at his driver's license too. Jay sneaks a look at the receptionist and the security guard. "Do you think we could go somewhere and talk?" he asks.

"No," Philips says. "I'm on a deadline as it is."

Still, she seems unable or unwilling to leave the lobby just yet. She can't help her reporterly curiosity, it seems. It's the very thing Jay was counting on.

"Let me ask you just one thing then," he says. "Are you the reason Elise Linsey got in trouble?"

"Am I the reason she was arrested? What, are you kidding me?"

"That's not what I'm asking," Jay says carefully, inching a little bit closer. "Are you the reason someone came after her? Is it because she talked to you?"

Philips stares at him a long time, saying nothing.

"Did she talk to you about the 'situation' in High Point, Ms. Philips?"

Lonette's hands fall from her hips. She actually looks frightened by the prospect of missing a huge part of her own story. "What do you mean, 'the reason someone came after her'?" she asks. "What are you talking about?"

So Jay knows something she doesn't. *Good.*

He asks a second time, reeling her in. "Can we go somewhere and talk?"

Philips turns and looks over her shoulder at the receptionist, who has long since gone back to her motorboat and RV catalog, now thirty dollars closer to her dream. "Tell Jerry I'm going out for a bit," Philips says. "But only if he asks."

She then turns and walks out of the building without a purse or a wallet, letting Jay pay for lunch at a taco place around the corner, which, for her, consists of two beers and half a pack of cigarettes. She munches on a few nacho strips, but only when she's not smoking or sucking on jalapeño peppers floating in a pool of oily cheese on the plate between them.

"Sweeney was an ex-con," she says to Jay, lighting a Virginia Slim, one with pink curlicues printed around the filter. She waves the lit matchstick in the smoky air before letting it drop on top of the table, which is sticky with lime juice. "He was into drugs or some shit like that, I heard. That gal over to the D.A.'s office is sweating, trying to connect this guy to Elise Linsey. That's the only thing they got for motive. A bad buy or some trick who got rough with her, maybe somebody from her past. Elise Linsey wasn't exactly a Girl Scout. But I'm sure you already knew that," Philips says, pulling on her thin cigarette. She exhales slowly, staring at Jay through a white cloud of smoke. "You think they got it wrong, is that it? You think it was about something else?" she asks. He thinks she's got a pretty good idea as to what this "something else" is, only she wants to hear him say it first.

"Did she talk to you about the old man in High Point?" he asks.

Philips doesn't answer.

He gets the sense she hasn't decided yet how much she's willing to share with a complete stranger. He needs her to know he's not trying to upstage her; this isn't some newspaper story to him. He lays his cards on the table. "I know about the oil," Jay says. "The mess in Ainsley's backyard."

Philips leans back in her chair, her pink-and-white cigarette frozen an inch or two from her lips. She watches Jay closely, silently, giving him the impression that she is, as of yet, unmoved, that she's going to need to hear a lot more. From his lap, Jay unrolls the government maps from the library. He spreads them across the sticky table, pushing the nachos and the beer bottles off to one side. "And I know the old man is barking up the wrong tree," he says, pointing on the map to an inland spot along the Texas coast. "The federal government maintains petroleum reserve sites in Freeport, Texas, and three other places along the Louisiana coast, but they did not buy the salt mine in High Point. I don't believe they had a thing to do with it."

Philips barely glances at the map. She doesn't have to.

None of this is news to her, it seems.

"I know the Stardale Development Company was probably a shell, set up to move those people away from the old salt mine before the walls of that cavern collapsed, before what was hidden came bubbling up to the surface. And I know, in my gut, that Thomas Cole and Cole Oil had a hand in it," he says. Philips cocks her head to one side and smiles. It's a look to suggest she's maybe just the tiniest bit impressed. "All I want to know from you, Ms. Philips," Jay says, "is, did Elise Linsey talk to you about any of this?"

"You can call me Lonnie."

"I just need to know if she went on record with you," he says. "And if this, God forbid, put her life in danger."

And mine.

Lonnie stares at him across the tabletop.

They're early for lunch. It's maybe a quarter after eleven. There's one girl working the bar. She's watching a soap opera on a thirteen-inch black-and-white set on the countertop. The only other customer in the joint is a man in a booth by the front door. There's a newspaper open on his table, and the man, in his sixties maybe, has laid his head on it like a pillow. He's snoring softly, like a baby.

"No," Lonnie says finally. "I never talked to her."

She motions for the girl behind the bar to bring her another beer. "Not for lack of trying, though. I guess by the time I got to her, she was all talked out."

"You think she was talking to another reporter or something?"

"More like the Federal Trade Commission." She pops a jalapeño pepper in her mouth, cooling the sting of it by sucking air through her front teeth. "They've been looking at Cole Oil for about six months now."

"How do you know that?"

She smiles, sly and prideful. "I am a reporter."

"I don't get it," Jay says, shaking his head. "Why are you sitting on this?"

Lonnie rolls her eyes. "It ain't all that simple," she says. She leans across the table, propping her elbows on top of the maps. "What you gotta understand is, this was a joke assignment, that piece you read. It wasn't supposed to be much of nothing. I mean, look, I'm barely two years out of the University of Missouri," she says. "I've had maybe two bylines. I'm a girl, and untested. To send me out to High Point, it was a joke, you understand? Write a little something about the kook by the water, an old man shaking his fist in the air. 'Write it cute,' my editor said. I mean, that is literally what he said. This was never meant to be more than Sunday morning filler."

"So what happened?"

"Well, it started with the fact-checkers downstairs," she says, letting out a soft burp. "I mean, nobody could corroborate any of it. Except for the obvious—the factory closed and the old man was pissed, driving everybody around him crazy. But this shit about the government, none of that added up," she says. "Of course, to my editor, this only added to the 'character' of the piece, you know, 'cause it only made Ainsley sound crazier, which, to him, *was* the story. I mean, one man marching on Washington . . . it's a joke, right?"

"How did you get to the FTC?"

Philips nods her head, as in "hold on," and reaches for another chip. "I kind of knew from the beginning that there was something missing from the story. But we had a slot to fill, so at print time, we went with what we had, what you read. Then about a week later, I get a call returned. A guy from the Energy Department, who's been there since Ford. And lo and behold, just like you said, the U.S. government has only a handful of SPR sites in the country, and High Point, Texas, ain't one of 'em. Therefore, he cannot comment. But then he starts asking *me* a lot of questions on what I know about the whole deal. In the course of my work, had I had any contact with an Alexander Bakker or Elise Linsey? Questions like that, you know. And then he asked if I had spoken with any other current or former employees of Cole Oil."

Three beers, and the heat is starting to catch up to her. She peels the flannel shirt off her shoulders, revealing a rather frilly camisole underneath.

"You get those sometimes," she says. "The ones behind a desk, the type that don't want to make an official statement, but got a lot of shit they wanna say anyway. He was dropping hints left and right. I mean, this whole thing might not have gone anywhere if this dude hadn't called me back."

"Who's Bakker?" he asks.

"A lawyer."

"I thought we were talking about the FTC?"

"We are, we are," Lonnie says. "But it started with the

DOE. They were looking at the big oil companies—your Exxons and Shells and Coles—as early as seventy-four. The Carter administration, what I come to find out on my own, launched a full-fledged investigation round about seventy-seven, looking into charges of hoarding and price gouging while the whole country was in the midst of a major crisis. And it's not just this deal with the salt caverns, of which I would venture to guess there are many, all along the coast, filled to the brim and effectively hidden underground," she says, pointing to the geological maps on the table. "That ain't even half the shit they been pulling." She rests her cigarette in the ashtray, freeing up her hands to punctuate the story, accenting every other word with a two-handed flourish in the air. "But it was a half-assed investigation from the start, never fully funded, so my guy on the inside tells it. I mean, hell, half of the Energy Department's policy was written by oil industry analysts, guys who used to *work* for Cole and Shell and Exxon and Gulf Oil. You understand? The shit went nowhere. And then when Reagan and Bush came in, the investigation was officially closed. Big fucking surprise, right?" she says. "Especially with all the friends the Coles got up in Washington. The whole thing just went away."

A few more customers trickle into the restaurant. The man in the booth lifts his head once, looks right at Jay, then lays it back down. Jay can smell onions and fried corn coming out of the kitchen, chicken mole and cilantro.

"And then here comes Mr. Ainsley, walking on Washington."

Lonnie smiles at the imagery, the sheer lunacy of it.

"And somebody in the Energy Department, and even *I* don't know who, passed some of their information, shit they put together along the way, over to the FTC. All of a sudden, the

word gets passed along . . . those boys down in Texas are setting prices like they ain't got enough to fill a fucking Toyota
when anybody with their eyes wide open can see what's really
going on in this industry." She starts to whisper, as if she fears
just speaking this out loud might cause a panic right here in the
restaurant. "Barrel prices dipping lower than Elizabeth Taylor's
neckline, industry analysts predicting a worldwide oil glut. A
glut, Mr. Porter," she says with a caustic smile. "You understand
what that means, don't you? It means this whole city's economy
is built on a lie."

She picks up her cigarette from the ashtray and takes a long
drag, blowing the smoke through her tiny nostrils, waving it
away from her hair. "And the party's about over. They can't sus-
tain this, and they know it. Hiding the oil, that's just one tactic of
many, to keep the supply-and-demand balance the way they want
it. If the shit hadn't started coming up in Ainsley's backyard,"
Lonnie says, "wouldn't nobody have ever known the difference,
you see?"

Jay thinks about the petrochemical workers, out on strike
alongside the longshoremen, and the shutdown at the Cole refinery. The strike, he realizes, would have made it impossible to
move the oil that was leaking out of the cavern, to tuck it safely
away somewhere else, like back in the oil drums at the plant. The
strike, therefore, made it impossible for the company to hide its
crime, which was, by then, starting to come up in plain sight, like
black water rising in the streets. Jay wonders aloud why, if the
Houston refinery was dark, they wouldn't have just moved the oil
somewhere else—like another cavern, if they were in possession
of one. Lonnie shakes her head at the notion. "Those caverns
only hold so much, and apparently not so well, not long term, at
least."

"Why not move it to another refinery then?" Jay asks. "Don't these big companies have processing plants across the coast, in Louisiana too?"

"The Cole boys closed their refineries out in Iberia and St. Bernard parishes sometime last year, claiming supply shortages and a need to cut back on operating costs. The same year they made something like nine hundred and fifty million in profit, in *profit*," Lonnie says. "You understand the game, right? It's just another way they fuck with supply. It's how they keep the prices up at the pumps."

Stickup artists, Jay thinks. No better than the meanest thugs on the streets of Fifth Ward, dudes who'll jack you for the few dollars in your pocket.

"The truth," Lonnie says, "Cole didn't have anywhere else to put the oil."

Jay's head has started to ache, his palms suddenly moist. Just the mention of a government investigation and he feels unsteady, short on oxygen, as if he's afraid the mere association with any of this shit is enough to get him in deep, deep trouble. He thinks of the hush money in the envelope. He should have cut it loose a long time ago; his own greed makes him look complicit in a crime much bigger than the one he'd first imagined. He remembers the shootout in his apartment, how close he came to losing everything.

"Where does Elise Linsey fit in all this?" he asks Lonnie.

"Why don't *you* tell me?" she says, sitting back in her chair, letting Jay know that it's his turn now. "And start with the dead guy in the Chrysler."

"He attacked her."

"How do you know that?"

"I just do," he says, deciding in that moment that he will leave his wife out of it for now, the boat trip and the screams they heard on the water.

"She told me as much, anyway."

"You talked to her?"

Jay nods. "She said she barely knew the guy. They met in a bar, maybe a night or two before the shooting. He got rough with her in the car. I'm guessing that's why she shot him. She never said word one about a drug buy."

"Would she?"

"I got good reason to believe she's telling the truth."

"I don't buy it," Lonnie says, looking out the front window briefly at the cars passing by on Travis. "I mean, the girl's got a pretrial hearing in a day or so," she says. "If this was all self-defense, why isn't that coming out? Why would Charlie Luckman bother with a hearing? Why not jump to trial? And why the hell didn't he bring all this out in front of the grand jury?"

"You can't mount a defense in a grand jury hearing."

"Right." Lonnie nods, though Jay can kind of tell this is news to her.

"And anyway," Jay says, "I don't know how much she's told him."

"Her *lawyer*?"

Jay nods.

"Come on," Lonnie says.

"Maybe she's afraid no one will believe her, what with her past and everything."

Lonnie stares at him over the beer bottles and maps. "How do you know this girl again? Where are you getting all this from, Mr. Porter?"

"And I'll tell you what else," Jay says, trying to distract her with new information. "Dwight Sweeney, the guy in the Chrysler, also known as Neal McNamara, also known as Blake Ellis, among others . . . he's an ex-con, all right, but it's not drugs. He did a seven-year stretch in the late sixties for taking money from an undercover cop in some kind of murder-for-hire scheme. So you see what type of guy I'm talking about."

Lonnie leans forward. "You think someone hired him to take her out?"

"That depends."

"On what?"

"On whether or not somebody had a reason to."

Jay watches her stab the girly pink-and-white cigarette into the armadillo ashtray. Smoke and the smell of chiles flow in from the kitchen. Somebody, in the last few minutes, has turned up the music. "You tell me, Ms. Philips . . . do you think Elise Linsey talked to the Federal Trade Commission about Cole Oil?"

Lonnie shrugs, twirling the beer bottle in her hand, swirling the last little bit of juice inside. She seems bothered by the pieces of this story she can't put together with any real precision. "I know her name's come up one too many times for it not to mean something. I mean, I know they were looking at her, you know, as somebody from outside the Cole organization who might know something. But I can't get anyone in Washington to say much more than that. I can't get anyone to even *admit* to an official investigation." She presses her mouth into a frown. "I couldn't guess what she would have told them anyway. Far as I can tell, she was just the face on that Stardale thing, the one who went and knocked on doors and smiled and looked pretty for the folks, you know. I don't know what all they would have told her about what was really going on."

"She had a relationship with Thomas Cole, you should know."

"I do."

"Well, I'm just saying, Cole might have said more than he should have or even more than he meant to. Two people get together in the dark, there's no telling what might come out."

"True," Lonnie nods. "But her name's not on any of the paper-work, none of it I've seen. I talked to some of the High Pointers who moved out of Ainsley's neighborhood, and all of the real estate papers these people got came out of a law firm in Dallas, everything signed by an Alexander Bakker."

"What's his deal?"

"He's a former D.C. lobbyist, used to work at a firm that had Cole Oil as one of its biggest clients. But we're talking ten, fifteen years ago. I've been chasing this story on my own for months now, and that's as close as I can put Bakker to Cole Industries."

"That's pretty close."

"Not close enough, not enough for my editor to take on the Cole brothers. They're fucking hometown heroes. I mean, these people got *schools* named after 'em, for God's sake. They built parks and arts centers and all that kind of crap. Not to men-tion they employ, with all their satellites and subsidiaries, some-thing like twenty percent of the workforce in the entire county. Nobody wants to take that shit on unless you're talking about something real serious."

"Price gouging isn't serious?" Jay asks.

"Not unless you can prove it."

"What about the oil coming up in Ainsley's backyard?"

"Prove it's theirs," Lonnie says, setting her bottle down hard on the table. It lands somewhere south of Brownsville on the map. "Trust me, I been round and round on this one."

The music in the restaurant changes. It's something slow and bluesy now, a single woeful guitar and a woman's words in Span-ish that Jay doesn't understand.

"You think Elise Linsey had any idea what she was getting herself into?"

Lonnie shrugs again. "Don't matter no way. She's in it."

Jay looks out the front window of the restaurant. There are

clouds moving in, blackening the sky. It's going to storm again, he thinks. "He used her and then he tried to get rid of her."

"You really think Thomas Cole tried to get this girl killed?" Lonnie asks softly, careful not to let the words drift past their table. They seem to both know that their whole conversation has been leading to this one question.

Jay shrugs.

What the hell does he know, really?

He turns his head toward the window again, watching the changing light in the sky, wondering how long before the clouds break beneath their own weight, how long before the storm hits. "I'll tell you what, though," he says, his eyes still pointed toward the window and the charcoal sky. "If you can put Dwight Sweeney and Thomas Cole together, I mean, find some connection between the two of them." He turns to look at her. "There's your story."

Chapter 27

Rolly's girl at the phone company can give them sixty days, going back to sometime in June, but any records beyond that are stored on the eleventh floor, she says, on a mainframe that she does not in any way have access to. By whatever romantic or pecuniary arrangement he and the girl have worked out between them, Rolly is able to get the phone records in hand by Thursday, the day Judge Vroland had set for the pretrial hearing in Elise Linsey's case. Rolly brings the printed pages by Jay's office around lunchtime. He comes in smelling like a chili dog and drinking a Dr Pepper out of a paper bag. He takes an open seat across from Jay, lights a cigarette, and stretches out his long legs.

Jay flips through page after page of phone calls to and from Elise Linsey's west side town house, marking the numbers that show up repeatedly, careful to note any calls to or from Washington, D.C., of which there are quite a few.

He asks Rolly how many of the phone numbers he was able to identify.

"It's whatever the girl could give me," Rolly says.

Jay starts with the D.C. calls—six to Elise's place through June and early July, and two calls *from* her place to the same 202 number in late July. The most information the girl at the phone company could get, Rolly reports, is that the calls came from a phone line within a telecom network run by the U.S. government. To get more specific about who or what office the 202 number belongs to was a phone call the girl was not willing to make without knowing why Rolly was asking in the first place.

Jay makes a note to turn the number over to Lon Philips.

The Houston calls are easier to identify.

Jay recognizes one of them on his own. He's called Charlie Luckman's downtown office enough to be able to recite the digits in his sleep. According to the phone logs, Elise Linsey made her first call to Mr. Luckman's office on August 3, the day the discovery of Dwight Sweeney's body made the paper.

That she did not call a lawyer right away, on the night of the shooting, even, is not all that surprising to Jay. What *is* interesting, though, is the fact of who she did call at 1:27 in the morning, early Sunday morning, August 2, not two full hours after the gunshots they heard on the boat.

The phone number, 713-247-4475, appears on nearly every page of the computer printout, showing up once, sometimes twice a day, for months. The correlating address, Rolly tells Jay, is a residence located at 1909 Willowick Road, not even a stone's throw from the River Oaks Country Club. According to Rolly's girl at the phone company, 247-4475 is one of two residential phone lines belonging to a Thomas P. Cole.

Jay thinks again of the night of the shooting:

Elise, bruised and nearly beaten, came within an inch of her life, twice. He pictures her in the backseat of that car, how she fought, shooting her way out of a bad situation. He remembers pulling her from the bayou, barely breathing, and dropping her off in front of a police station. Somehow, she had survived it all. And the first person she called was Thomas Cole. The very man Jay suspects of having orchestrated the hit on her life.

"My god," he mumbles to himself. "She has no idea."

From the pocket of his ever present leather vest, Rolly pulls out a bundle of papers, folded over lengthwise and rolled as tightly as a good cigar. He rests the papers on the edge of Jay's desk. "What's this?" Jay asks, opening the pages somewhat tentatively, as if he were opening a present he's already sure he won't like. "Calls from the condo," Rolly says. "Out on the plantation."

Jay spreads the papers across his desk.

Of all the phone numbers printed, calls coming in and going out, one number leaps out at him, over and over, page after page: 713-247-4475.

"He's been talking to her this whole time," Rolly says.

"Jesus," Jay says, whistling at the wonder of it, the devilry it implies. He shakes his head to himself, feeling a pinch in his chest, an unexpected tug in this woman's direction. "Somebody's got to say something to that girl," he says, looking up and pausing at the same time, as if he were waiting, hoping even, for that somebody to walk into the room and volunteer. But Jay and Rolly are the only two people here, and Rolly is keeping his mouth shut.

"She's gon' be on trial for her fucking life, man, and got a snake right up under her," Jay says. "Somebody's got to tell her what's really going on."

"You're all right dude, man. I've always known that about you,

Jay. But might I remind you that it was running to save this girl that got you in all this trouble to begin with?"

"This is bigger than the girl."

"All the telephone activity out at the condo stopped a couple of days ago," Rolly says. "You even know where she is?"

"No," Jay says. "But I know where she'll be."

There are some things in life that can't be avoided:

Death, for sure. Taxes. And court dates.

The pretrial hearing for the matter of the *State of Texas v. Elise Linsey*, case number HC-760432, is already under way by the time Jay makes it to Judge Vroland's courtroom that afternoon. There's a cop on the stand, a detective, Jay can tell by the awkward pairing of a camel-colored sports coat and navy trousers.

Charlie Luckman is standing behind a podium set up between the state's side and the defense table, where Elise Linsey, in a moss green blouse and black trousers, is sitting primly, her back stiff and at almost righteous attention.

Jay takes an open seat on the bench directly behind her.

By Charlie's posture, the way he leans his weight on the heels of his alligator boots, one hand in his pocket, the other relaxed at his side, Jay thinks he sees something familiar in Mr. Luckman's self-assured demeanor. It's the look of a lawyer with all his ducks lined neatly in a row, the cocksure stance of someone who believes the facts are on his side. Any theatrics, at this point at least, are down to a minimum. Charlie speaks in an even, respectful tone, asking the judge if he might approach the bench, as politely as if he were asking her if he might refill her glass of iced tea. He walks two stapled papers to the bench and asks that they be entered in as "defense exhibit A." Judge Vroland peruses the pages briefly, then hands them to the cop at her right. The detective barely glances at them. He seems to know already where this line of questioning will start.

"Detective Stone, do you recognize the papers in front of you?"

"Yes, sir," the detective answers, though the "sir" sounds perfunctory and not at all sincere. Jay wonders if the two men knew each other in Charlie's other life as a prosecutor. "And that's my signature on the second page," the cop says, stepping on Charlie's next question. From behind the podium, Charlie smiles, cool as a snow cone in January. "Very good, Detective Stone. You want to tell us, however, what exactly you're looking at?"

"Your Honor." The prosecutor, the same bull terrier from the arraignment, stands behind the state's table. Her suit is navy and two sizes too big. "The search warrant has already been entered into the record. We've all *read* the thing. Do we have to go through a whole dog and pony show with it too?"

Her tone is so defensive, so pushy and unladylike, that Charlie is right to simply keep his mouth shut. The judge levels a disapproving gaze on the prosecutor. "I can assure you, Counselor, I don't take any of this to be a show. And I will allow the detective to answer Mr. Luckman's question."

"Thank you, Your Honor," Charlie says. "Mr. Stone?"

"It's a search warrant," the cop says. "For 14475 Oakwood Glen, last known residence for the defendant." He nods toward Elise.

"Yes, and as you've already mentioned, it's a search warrant that you yourself signed, along with a Judge Paul Lockhart, is that correct?"

"Yes."

"Judge, may I approach again?"

Judge Vroland nods, waving him forward at the same time.

Charlie approaches the bench with a single typed piece of paper in his hand. He offers it to the judge, calling it "defense exhibit B." Jay leans forward in his seat, waiting, hoping, for Elise to turn around. From his jacket, he pulls a slip of white paper, a receipt from the taco place on Travis. He scribbles the words *we need to talk* on the back, then folds the piece of paper into a tight square, clutching it in the palm of his hand. Then . . . he waits.

"Detective Stone," Charlie says. "This new thing we got here, will you let the court know what it is you're looking at?"

"It's an inventory," the cop says. "What we took from the town house."

"All right, then," Charlie says, tucking both hands in his pockets, looking down briefly at the tips of his alligator boots. "Let's start with the warrant."

When Charlie has the detective read through the warrant, the list of court-approved items that police detectives—one Detective Harold Stone and a Detective Pete Smalls—were legally allowed to remove from 14475 Oakwood Glen, last known residence of the defendant, Elise Linsey, includes:

A .22-caliber pistol.
Bloody or soiled clothing.
Shoes, ladies' size 6½. Possibly soiled. High heeled,
     with a zigzag pattern on the sole.

The detective lays the warrant on the wood veneer ledge in front of him. Charlie has him pick up the inventory next, the list of what the cops *actually* pulled as evidence from Elise Linsey's town house during their search.

"If you would, Detective, why don't you go ahead and read through it."

"The whole thing?"

"The whole thing."

Detective Stone looks at the judge, who nods.

The detective clears his throat. " 'Ladies' shoes, white, size six and a half. Two pairs of shoes, brown, size six and a half. Three pairs of shoes, black, size six and a half. Sandals, brown, size six and a half. Boots, burgundy, size six. Sandals, red, size six and a half. Two pairs of boots, black, size six and a half. Shoes, silver, with some kind of rhinestones on them, size six and a half. Shoes, pink, with rubber soles, size six and a half. Two pairs of tan loafers, ladies' size six and a half. Three pairs of sneakers.' " He looks up from the piece of paper. " 'Size six and a half.' "

"That's a lot of shoes," Charlie says.

"Yes, sir."

"Let me see, did I count . . . ," Charlie says, making a rather exaggerated show of incredulity. "Was that *eighteen* pairs of shoes?"

"That's what I read."

"And those eighteen pairs of shoes are the only things listed on that inventory sheet, the only pieces of 'evidence' that you and Detective Smalls pulled from Ms. Linsey's town house on Oakwood Glen?"

"Yes."

"No gun? No bloody clothes?"

"No, sir," Detective Stone says to Charlie. "It's just the shoes."

"*Eighteen* pairs of shoes."

"All size six and a half," the detective says.

"Well, now, that warrant you signed was asking for shoes with blood on 'em and dirt, and, more important, it was talking about high-heeled shoes with a zigzag pattern on the sole. So, which of the shoes on that piece of paper matches that description?"

"None of them."

"Am I to understand then that you and your colleague did not find any shoes in the defendant's home that had blood on them or dirt from the crime scene, nor any shoes with a zigzag pattern on the sole? Is that right?"

Detective Stone's jaw tightens ever so slightly. "That is correct."

Jay remembers Elise's bare feet on the boat the night of the rescue. He thinks of the black bayou water, the bits and pieces of this story it has swallowed whole, the deeds it washed clean. He thinks of the shoes, the gun, the prosecution's whole case, sunk all the way to the bottom of Buffalo Bayou, hidden in the muddy earth, washed over ten, twenty, a hundred times a day.

But where, then, is *his* gun?

Elise Linsey, seated before him, holds her head remarkably high, following the action in front of her. Jay clutches his handwritten note. He scoots to the edge of the bench he's seated on, not three feet behind the defense table. He coughs lightly, once, then a second time. Elise Linsey never turns around.

Out of the corner of his eye, Jay senses some movement in the gallery. He turns to his right and sees a new face in the courtroom. Among the courthouse lookiloos and beat reporters, there's a man wearing a tailored charcoal gray suit. He's taken a seat to the right of Jay, on the bench behind him, positioning himself closely enough that Jay can see the sea green color of his eyes from where he sits. The man keeps his jacket buttoned, his hands in his pockets. Unlike the others in the gallery, he is not watching the lawyers or the defendant or the witness on the stand. He keeps his eyes on Jay.

"Might you explain to the court then, Detective," Charlie says, "why you saw fit and legally justified to take every shoe in my client's closet?"

"They were in plain sight."

"So was the woman's furniture. Did you pack that up too?"

"The law gives police officers some leeway here. I believed

that the shoes were relevant in terms of putting the defendant at the crime scene. The shoes were in plain sight. So, yes, my partner and I picked them up as evidence."

"And do you still believe the shoes are relevant, Detective?"

"Inasmuch as they establish the defendant as a size six and a half," the cop says, looking at the judge briefly before eking out another piece of information. "The shoe prints we found around the car at the crime scene were a ladies' size six and a half."

"And one more time," Charlie says. "Did any of the shoes you took from the defendant's residence match the zigzag shoe print at the crime scene?"

"Objection, Your Honor, asked and answered," the state's attorney says.

"Nothing further, Your Honor," Charlie says.

Jay steals another glance at the man in the charcoal suit.

He is still, at this moment, staring at Jay, who gets the distinct feeling that the man is no casual court observer. He wonders again if he's being followed. Jay swings back around in his seat. He closes his eyes and tries to recall every detail of the man's face. He wants to know if he's seen this man before.

The prosecutor is soon on her feet for the cross.

Detective Stone sits up in his chair, looking as if someone had just brought something to the dinner table that he might actually be able to stomach. He's careful not to go so far as to smile at the prosecutor. But everything in his posture says that this is the part of the process he's been waiting for.

"Detective, you and your partner, Detective Pete Smalls, interviewed the defendant in the days after Mr. Sweeney's body was found, is that right?"

"Yes, ma'am. We interviewed her twice. The day the body was found, we interviewed her at her home that evening. And then again a couple of days later, the following Tuesday, I believe."

The prosecutor nods. "Can you tell us what led you to the defendant?"

"We found her fingerprints inside the vehicle in which the deceased, uh, Mr. Sweeney, was found. We were operating under the assumption that Ms. Linsey was possibly the last to see Mr. Sweeney alive."

"I see," the prosecutor says. "And what did Ms. Linsey tell you, Detective, in your initial interviews with her?"

Charlie makes no objection to the breadth of the question, no motion to stop this whole line of inquiry on the basis of relevance. Instead, he's set back in his chair, legs crossed comfortably, his demeanor completely unflappable.

"Ms. Linsey said, during both interviews, that she had had dinner with the deceased, at a Mexican restaurant in the Heights. She said they parted company around ten thirty that evening, and she went home."

"How did she explain to you her fingerprints in the victim's car?"

"Ms. Linsey said that she and the deceased had met at a Church's Chicken parking lot and that she rode out to the Heights in his car. She claims Mr. Sweeney dropped her back off at her car when the date was over."

"Did you ask her if she was with Mr. Sweeney on Clinton Road at any time on the night of August 1, 1981?"

"She maintained, repeatedly, to both me and Detective Smalls, that she was never at any time on Clinton Road or anywhere near the field in which Mr. Sweeney's body was found on the night of August First or any other night for that matter. She was real clear on that." He looks across the courtroom at Elise.

Jay turns once more in his seat. The man in the charcoal suit is staring straight ahead now, watching the prosecutor's cross, his elbows resting casually on the seat back behind him. He's chewing a piece of gum, Jay can see, and more than once he glances at the headlines of an abandoned sports page resting beside him on the bench. He seems to have completely lost interest in Jay, and Jay wonders again if his mind is playing tricks on him. A moment ago, he was sure the guy was here because of him, another man with a gun on his tail. But the man in the gray suit hasn't so much as glanced back in Jay's direction.

"Okay, Detective," the prosecutor says, quite courteously. She looks down at her desk, and from a mess of papers pulls a four-by-six-inch photograph. Elise sits up, nervous-like, in her chair. Charlie puts a reassuring hand on her forearm. The prosecutor asks the judge if she can approach the bench.

"What am I supposed to be looking at here?" the judge asks when she has the photo in hand. She squints at it, turning the picture this way and that.

Charlie stands. "You think I might get a look at that too?"

Judge Vroland waves Charlie to the bench, and Jay sees his chance. The judge, the prosecutor, and Elise's attorney are all huddled at the bench. The cop is watching them from the witness stand. Which leaves only the bailiff to worry about. Jay waits for a moment when the bailiff isn't looking toward the gallery. Charlie, at the bench, says something to the prosecutor. It's a mumble at this distance. Then Jay hears, quite clearly, "You can't even tell what this is."

"Well, if we can let the man testify," the prosecutor says.

Jay makes a leap forward, reaching out until his fingers almost touch the silky fabric across Elise's shoulders. He drops the tiny white slip of paper, watching, breathlessly, as it dribbles down her side, landing on her right thigh.

He waits for her to pick up the paper, to notice it even.

Only once does he look back over his shoulder, surprised to find the man in the gray suit watching him again. Jay holds perfectly still, caught in the man's gaze. *He saw me*, Jay thinks. *He had to have seen me.* The man's cool eyes narrow slightly. Then, suddenly, inexplicably, he stands and walks out of the courtroom.

At the bench, the prosecutor asks to enter the photograph as "state's exhibit A," and Charlie returns to his seat.

"Detective Stone," the prosecutor asks. "Did you take that photograph?"

"No, it was a crime scene technician who took this one. But I was present at the time it was taken, yes. It was a few inches from the car at the crime scene. That spot of black right there," he says, pointing to something in the photograph the rest of them can't see. "That's a piece of the tire wheel right there."

"Why don't you tell the court what that is a picture of, in specific?"

"It's a footprint, ma'am, measured as a woman's size six and a half." He points at the picture again. "That mark right here, that's the heel dug in the ground."

Jay's note is still resting on Elise's thigh. At this point, it's likely that Charlie will notice it before Elise does.

"And what relevance did this footprint have for you at the time?"

"Well, we'd already deduced, from the condition of the body, that Mr. Sweeney was with a woman in the minutes or so leading up to his death."

"The 'condition of the body'?" the prosecutor asks.

"The man's pants were undone. He was parked in an out-of-the-way place, you know. Seemed like a lovers' lane type deal."

"Which leads us to Ms. Linsey and the search of her town house on Oakwood Glen," the prosecutor says. "Would you explain to the court why you and your partner believed Ms. Linsey's shoes to be relevant to the case?"

"Well, it was kind of a credibility issue, ma'am," the cop says.

"I mean, here she is saying she wasn't at the crime scene, and we got a ladies' footprint size six and a half, and it turns out Ms. Linsey is a six and a half."

"Did you believe the defendant was lying about being at the crime scene?"

"Well, she'd already admitted to being on a date with the man."

"Yes or no, Detective?"

"Yes, I thought she was lying," he says. "I mean, we found him with his *pants* down, a woman's footprints all around the scene of the crime, same exact shoe size as Elise Linsey . . . ," he says. "It just all added up."

Charlie is on his feet in seconds. "Objection, Your Honor."

"I have nothing further." The prosecutor resumes her seat.

"Fine," Judge Vroland says.

Charlie returns to the podium, jumping right in.

"Detective Stone, do you know if the deceased was a homosexual?"

"Pardon?"

As soon as Charlie's back is turned, Elise picks up the slip of paper in her lap. She glances at the note, but never once turns to look for its sender.

"Do you know if Mr. Sweeney was a homosexual?"

"Uh, no," he says.

"Do you know if Mr. Sweeney had any medical issues with his prostate or his urinary tract? What might make him pull off the road from time to time to relieve himself?"

The cop purses his lips, answering in one terse syllable. "No."

"Then you couldn't know for sure why that man's pants were down, isn't that right, sir?"

"Oh, I think I've got a pretty good idea."

"You can't be *sure*, can you, Detective Stone?"

"No."

"The county coroner put the time of death for Mr. Sweeney at around midnight, is that correct?" Charlie asks.

"Yes."

"And your officers arrived on the scene the next day, was it?"

"August second, Sunday, yes. It was sometime after ten in the morning."

"So between midnight and ten A.M., how many people were at the crime scene?"

"I wouldn't know."

"So, in theory, anybody could have walked all up and down that crime scene, thrown a party out there, between the time Mr. Sweeney was shot and when the police showed up the next day, is that right?"

"Yes."

"So those footprints that you took such care to photograph, they could belong to anyone, is that it?"

Detective Stone answers with a smile. "Any woman wearing a size six and a half."

"Or any person in possession of a woman's size six and a half shoe."

The prosecutor raises her hand. "Is he making a statement or asking a question, Your Honor?"

"That's all right, Judge," Charlie says. "I'm done."

He resumes his seat next to Elise. She turns and whispers something in his ear. Out of the corner of her eye, she glances back at Jay for the first time. There is no outward reaction or acknowledgment of any kind. When the prosecutor returns to the podium, Elise lets her eyes fall away, as if she had been looking at only a stone or a tree, a thing with no meaning for her. It's so convincing that Jay almost believes she never saw him at all.

The only other witness is Detective Pete Smalls, Stone's partner, who essentially repeats the same exact information as the first witness. The whole thing is over in another fifteen minutes, Charlie taking a pass on cross.

It's nearly four o'clock when the judge calls for closing statements.

Charlie's argument is simple: if the cops had wanted every shoe in his client's closet, then they should have asked for it in the warrant, repeating, as many times as he can, what the police officers did *not* find—no gun, no bloody clothing, and no shoes that match the footprints at the crime scene.

The prosecution is left with a shouldn't-we-all-trust-the-instincts-of-law-enforcement argument, citing the detectives' homicide investigation experience, and summing up the reasons why the shoes in Elise's closet were relevant—enough for the cops to take them from the defendant's home "outside the legal protection of a warrant," which is a fancy-pants way of admitting they took the shoes illegally. At a quarter to five, Judge Vroland wraps up the court's business for the day, announcing that she will make a ruling on the evidence shortly.

Jay waits for Elise by the pay phones, the ones by the ladies' washroom.

When she comes out of the courtroom, walking toward him, a leather clutch bag pinched under her arm, Jay sets the phone receiver on its cradle, hanging up on a call he was not actually making. He steps to the side, blocking her path in the hallway. She passes him with two little words, "Not here."

A whisper, and then she's gone, slipping into the ladies' room.

He waits, keeping an eye over his shoulder, wondering how worried he ought to be about the man in the gray suit.

Finally, he smells her perfume behind him.

She presses something into his hand and tells him not to turn around. Then she's gone, walking past him down the hallway, which is quickly emptying at this hour. Jay ignores her instructions and turns around anyway. Just in time to see Charlie Luckman place a guiding hand on Elise's back, leading her toward the elevators. Mr. Luckman looks up briefly. His eyes lock on Jay's. There is a ten-, maybe fifteen-second, delay. Then an odd smile gathers on Charlie's face, as if he can't quite place Jay, but knows that his presence here is remarkable in some way. Charlie wrinkles his brow. But soon the elevator doors open, and the moment is over almost as soon as it happens. Mr. Luckman and his client slip through the sliding doors and are gone without another look in Jay's direction. He is left alone in the hallway with a janitor and the muffled sounds coming from the man's transistor radio. Jay looks down at the thing in his hand. It's the receipt from the taco place. His note to her has been scratched out, and over it, in a sharp, left-leaning print, a new message has been written expressly for him.

Chapter 28

The Blue Bayou is a bar on the north edge of downtown.

Across the water on McKee, it sits on a rough corner out by the railroad tracks, between a uniform-supply house and a boarded-up storefront. The bright lights of downtown fade on this side of the bayou, where industry stops short and developers seem to have lost their imagination, or patience, with this raw urban landscape. The only bright light out here is the neon sign hanging at an angle in front of the bar. A blinking guitar, blue, with yellow strings.

The note said nine o'clock.

Jay was early. He's had a couple of beers and made two phone calls. He called his wife first, over to her mother and father's place. She asked if he'd heard word about the dockworkers' vote on the settlement offer, saying her daddy was asking. He told her no, and to please stay out that way 'til he could come get her. Then he called Lon Philips. He told her about the phone records, the calls to D.C., the fact that Elise has been speaking with Thomas Cole almost daily since the shooting, and Jay's belief in her ignorance of his involvement.

Lonnie said she'd check on the D.C. phone number and offered some new information of her own, telling it with a reporter's finesse, starting the story back nearly thirty years—when Johnson Cole, family founder and oil industry pioneer, made his three sons and heirs, Thomas being the youngest, start work at the very bottom of the family empire. Every last one of the boys spent time working at the company's Deer Park refinery in their teenage years. And they'd all at one point taken part in a rigorous two-week training seminar for aspiring roughnecks, what some men have likened to boot camp for the marines. Some of the friendships formed in these training camps last a lifetime, she said. "The paper did a profile on Thomas Cole a few years back, when he was made CFO. We interviewed his former classmates, men in the same 1954 training class as him. You know, the whole 'How has the big man changed?' kind of story. Well, one of the men interviewed for the story, you'll be interested to know, was a young Carlisle Minty, future vice president of the petrochemical workers' union."

"No shit."

"It's all here on file," Lonnie said. "And you know who else was in that training seminar, way back in 1954, according to a caption under the class photo?"

Jay can hear the delight in her voice, the almost giddy sense of discovery.

"Who?"

"Dwight Sweeney."

Jay is silent for a moment. "Sweeney worked for Cole Oil?"

He had thought of Sweeney only as a career criminal.

"I don't think he was a lifer at the plant or anything. He mighta put in a couple of years or a couple of months. I don't know. They're not too hot on handing out personnel records down at company headquarters," she said. "But hell if the whole thing ain't interesting, you know, that Cole and Sweeney knew each other way back when. I mean, it's some goddamned coincidence."

"Yeah," Jay said.

"Somebody ought to tell that girl's lawyer," Lonnie said. "If this stuff starts coming out in open court, it would be a hell of a lot easier for my editor to give a nod on a story. You know, like, 'Look at what ol' Charlie Luckman said in court today,' as opposed to the newspaper reporting this kind of 'coincidence' on its own, muddying up Thomas Cole's reputation and taking down Cole Oil, one of its biggest advertisers, in the process. You see what I'm getting at?" she said. "This shit gets put out in open court, though, and it's a different story."

"Yeah, well," Jay said offhandedly, thinking of the day's hearing and the weakness of the state's evidence. "She'd have to have a trial first. And Charlie Luckman is doing everything in his power to keep that from happening."

"Well, I'll keep picking at things on my end," Lonnie said.

They hung up saying they would talk sometime tomorrow.

Twenty minutes later, he's ordering his third beer at the bar.

When Elise comes in, Jay stands off his stool at once, more wobbly on his feet than he would like. He can't tell if it's the liquor or the sudden bout of nerves breaking out across his whole body. The words are already in his mind. But to tell her to her face, to tell a woman she's been lied to, that she's been betrayed, her life threatened—he does not relish being the bearer of such news. He knows, personally, what a blow to the knees a betrayal can be, that after this moment she will never be the same.

Elise sees him and smiles, as if she were relieved he actually showed up. She walks at a clipped speed, her size six and a half high-heeled shoes clicking on the concrete floor underfoot. She seems in a hurry to get this over with.

The seat next to Jay is taken. He offers her his bar stool, standing to the left of her once she sits down. She's wearing the same clothes from the courthouse this afternoon, though her hair has fallen now, down around her shoulders. "Can't say that I expected to see you again," she says, pulling a pack of cigarettes from her purse, a shoulder bag, he notices, larger than the one she was carrying earlier. "I was under the impression we had an agreement."

"You're in a lot of trouble, Elise," Jay says, cutting to it.

"You think?" she says, the smile on her face edged with something he may have earlier mistaken for nerves. On closer look, Jay thinks he sees something cagey in her expression, something hard in her brown eyes. When the bartender approaches, Elise orders a shot of tequila and a beer back. "I don't know," she says to Jay. "I thought it went pretty well in there today."

"I'm not talking about your case, Elise."

"Aren't you though?" she says, laying a five-dollar bill on the bar top when the guy returns with her drinks. She downs the tequila shot and lights the cigarette in her hand. "Last we talked, I remember you mentioned something about money, so . . . you want to tell me what this is going to cost me and we can be done with it?"

"This isn't about money."

She laughs then, a girlish trill at the back of her throat. She waves her cigarette in the air, almost wagging it like an extra finger, as if she were scolding a young boy for wasting her time.

"Listen to me, Elise," he says.

"I'm not going down on this," she says, cutting him off, her voice hard and cold as gunmetal. "Not for anything. You understand?"

"Then you ought to know," Jay says, feeling a fire in his belly as the words come up through his throat, "that Thomas Cole *knew* Dwight Sweeney."

The light in Elise's eyes dims dramatically as the words settle around her.

For a moment, Jay actually feels sorry for her, and his pity, it's clear, infuriates her. The skin around her neck, where she was once scratched and bruised, glows bright pink, the color climbing up her throat to the jawline. "I'm not sure I know what it is you're getting at," she says.

"The man who tried to kill you? Thomas Cole *knew* him."

Then, because she says nothing, he asks, "You understand what I'm saying?" Elise looks at him and smiles darkly. "Whatever you think you know about me and Thomas Cole, Mr. Porter," she says, "trust me, you don't."

"I know he had a very good reason to worry about you talking to the FTC."

"Thomas knows I would never tell them anything," she says.

"You so sure?"

"You know, I have to say I find your concern for me to be a bit uncalled for. Frankly, the details of my personal life are none of your fucking business."

"This is not just about you," he says, almost hissing at the girl. "Those men at Cole Oil have committed a crime on a massive scale, and you have helped them. Buying up that land out there, keeping their secrets. You cannot stay quiet about this unless you want to get yourself dug in deeper. You're already looking at serious jail time over some shit that didn't even start with you. You could go to prison. You understand that, don't you?"

"Oh, that's not going to happen," she says, rather confidently. "I told you, it was going good in there for me today."

She has no idea what she's up against, he thinks. "What if you get subpoenaed by the federal government? Huh? What then?"

She shakes her head at the notion. "That investigation is taken care of."

"What is that supposed to mean?"

Elise picks up her empty glass and motions for the bartender to refill it. "And anyway, Thomas and I have come to an understanding. He knows I won't say anything about his business dealings," she says, taking a long drag on her cigarette. "And I know the line he won't cross . . . not ever again."

On the bar in front of her, the bartender pours another shot of tequila. Jay watches Elise throw back the shot, swallowing the heat and the sting of it, a look of bitter resignation in the dim light that's left in her eyes.

"You knew," he says, turning the words over and over, as if he were trying to get a better look at them, to get a better understanding. The one piece in this he had never really considered. "You knew it was him this whole time."

Elise does not deny or confirm this.

She downs her beer without looking at him.

"Why are you protecting him?" he asks softly, as if he were afraid the strength of this sort of basic logic might break her in two.

"Thomas has done a lot for me," she says unapologetically. "He paid for my real estate license, you know that? I wouldn't even have a job if it weren't for him, be back in a shit-hole club somewhere. And I am *not* going back there."

"Elise, the man tried to have you killed."

"And look how that turned out," she says with a sharp, caustic smile. "I got a forty-five and a twelve gauge that says he won't try that shit again."

Here she is. The girl from Galena Park.

The tough little pistol who's not taking shit from nobody.

"You're a fool," he says.

"I told you, he and I have come to an understanding."

"You really think Cole is going to protect *you* over his money? If you're the only thing that stands between him and a federal indictment, you really think you're the one who's gon' come out all right in the end?"

"Mr. Porter, I'm not the one who ought to be scared of Thomas Cole."

If the scene were playing in a movie, in one of Jay's boyhood westerns, the timing wouldn't have been better. Out of the corner of his eye, Jay sees the door to the saloon open. Elise slides off her stool, leaving a few dollars on the bar. "I'm sorry," she says, the very moment Jay makes out the face at the door:

A white male in his forties, with close-cropped hair.

One side of his body looks completely deflated, making his walk an exaggerated swagger. He wears a black glove over what's left of his right hand.

Jay feels his stomach drop, like a stone down a well.

"If you had asked for more money, I had it all here to give you." She pats her oversize purse. "I told Thomas I didn't know a red-blooded American who couldn't be bought. I begged him not to hurt you," she says, shaking her head at Jay, the look on her face one of disappointment. "But you seem bent on doing this the hard way." She turns and looks at the man from the black Ford, who is by now walking directly toward Jay, at the bar. "I'm sorry, Jay," she whispers.

The man from the black Ford never says a word, but the look

in his eyes terrifies. He raises his one good hand, and Jay sees the tiniest flash of light.

The glint off the barrel of a .45.

Jay turns and runs.

Behind the Blue Bayou, he covers the length of an alley, heading in a southerly direction. The gravel beneath his feet cuts through the soles of his cheap dress shoes. He feels every stone, every sharp edge. He never looks back.

The alley spills out on Providence, maybe twenty yards from his car. He's behind the wheel in a matter of seconds. He starts the engine, peeling the car away from the curb. At the intersection of Providence and McKee, he slows, looking to his right. The only two people standing in front of the Blue Bayou are a man and a woman he does not recognize at this distance. They appear to be arguing.

Jay turns left, heading for the bright lights of downtown. He peers into his rearview mirror, taking in the empty street behind him. He feels a sudden stab of relief, hitting him in the chest, thinking, for one grateful moment, that he's lost the man in the black Ford. But as he crosses a narrow bridge over Buffalo Bayou, heading to the south, a pair of headlights suddenly appears across his windshield, momentarily blinding him. Jay slams on his brakes, shielding his eyes. The driver never stops.

The car is coming straight at him.

Caught in the angry blast of white light, Jay thinks of death, the certainty of it, waiting for him on the pavement ahead, a few precious heartbeats away if he doesn't act fast. He slams on his brakes, churning up smoke. There's little room to maneuver on the bridge, so Jay throws his car into reverse. At nearly fifty miles an hour, he drives the Buick backward, weaving all over the street. He drives some two or three hundred yards, forcing other cars to the side of the road, the same bright headlights pursuing him from the front, burning straight through his car. At Providence, Jay swings in a wide arc, switching the car into drive. He heads to the west, thinking he can meet up with Main Street.

In his rearview mirror, he sees a black Ford LTD make the same turn onto Providence, picking up speed on his heels. Jay takes it up to sixty, then nearly seventy miles an hour. He almost clips the bumper of a station wagon as he tries to pass it, pulling onto the wrong side of the road and dodging a city cab. The Ford inches up on the Buick's tail, tapping Jay's bumper.

Jay gets turned around in a tangle of streets by the railroad tracks and somehow ends up on San Jacinto instead of Main. Driving south, cutting across on Allen Street, he's fairly certain he hears police sirens in the distance. As he makes a left onto Main, the sirens sound so close they could be coming from his own car radio. He looks in the rearview mirror and sees not the white headlights of the Ford LTD, but the swirling blue and red of a squad car, fifty or sixty yards back. Jay slows to a decent, law-abiding speed, pulling off to the right, hoping that the squad car will pass, on its way to some other emergency. He wonders to himself where and when the Ford fell off.

He slows the car on the bayou overpass, waiting for the cop car to pass, pulling the Buick all the way to the right, under a streetlamp. It's only then that he sees his gun.

It's been sitting on his front seat this whole time.

A nickel-plated .22.

His missing gun. His illegal, unregistered, missing gun.

It must have been placed in his car sometime while he was in the bar with Elise, laid across the passenger seat as gently as a sleeping baby.

The blue and red police lights fill his rearview mirror.

The squad car pulls in right behind Jay.

So this is the plan, he thinks, the way they intend to shut him up.

He wonders which one made the call to police.

Elise or the man in the Ford.

Behind him, he hears the doors of the squad car open. He quickly pushes the .22 onto the floor, reaching his right foot across the floorboard and kicking the gun under the passenger seat. It disappears into the shadows on the floor.

In his side-view mirror, he sees one of the officers coming up on the driver's side. The other cop, a flashlight in his hand, is walking on the raised curb to the right, which stretches from the street to the edge of the bridge. Jay can hear the water down below, lapping against the bridge posts beneath them. When the first cop arrives at his door, Jay sees the gun at his waist, the metal cuffs. He wonders what would happen if he laid his foot on the gas, if he just drove away, how long before another squad car picked up his license plate on the radio, how far would he get and what would he have to leave behind.

"Can I see your license and registration, sir?" the cop says.

Jay obediently produces a wallet from his back pocket. Through the open driver-side window, he hands his license to the cop. The cop shines his flashlight in Jay's face. Jay is careful not to make any sudden moves. He steals a glance in the right side-view mirror. The second cop, white like his partner, but younger and thinner, is hanging in position at the right rear of the vehicle, one hand on his flashlight, the other at his holster. He's watching Jay closely, as one might eye a cornered animal, a thing whose behavior is dangerous and unpredictable. The cop seems edgy, his hand inching toward his gun. Jay lets his eyes drop, scanning the ripped carpet along the floorboard. He thinks he sees the nose of the .22 peeking out.

My God, he thinks, they cannot search this car.

The first cop, tall, with reddish blond hair and thick jowls, shines the flashlight into the whites of Jay's eyes. "Where you headed to tonight, sir?"

"Home," Jay says, squinting against the light.

"Where you coming from?"

"A restaurant." He tries to remember how many beers he had.

The cop waves over the roof of the car to his partner, signaling him to move in closer to the vehicle. The second cop raises his flashlight. He shines the beam through the back window first, taking even-paced steps along the right side of the Buick, moving closer and closer to the .22 under the front seat.

Jay feels a burn in his stomach.

They cannot search this car.

"You had anything to drink tonight, sir?" the first cop asks Jay. His partner shines his light through the rear window, skimming along the backseat, the trash and empty soda cans piled up on the floor. The beam of light climbs over the front seat, landing in a pale pool in the empty seat next to Jay.

"I asked you a question, sir," the cop at Jay's window says, tapping Jay on the shoulder with the butt of his flashlight. His partner is inches from discovering the illegal weapon. Trapped, Jay makes a sudden, brash decision to go for broke.

He opens the driver-side door, forcing the cop on the other side to stumble back a few paces. "What the hell do you think you're doing!" the cop yells. Jay swings his feet onto the pavement beside the car, puts his head down between his legs. "I feel sick," he says, hanging halfway out of the Buick.

"Get back in the car, sir."

Behind him, Jay hears footsteps along the right side of the car, the cop's partner moving into a new position, as they are suddenly in a situation here.

Jay starts to stand.

"I said get back in the car, sir."

"Please, I feel like I'm going to be sick," he says, wobbling on his feet.

The first cop has his hand firmly on his weapon. The second cop has already dislodged his from his holster. "Sir," the younger cop says. "You need to get to the side of your vehicle and put your hands on the back of your head."

Jay clutches at his stomach, staggering in the street. He looks up at both officers with a pitiful, hangdog expression on his face.

"Jesus," the first cop says, somewhat irritated. "How much have you had to drink anyway?"

"Get your hands on your head, sir," his partner yells.

There's a pickup truck coming down Main from the north. Jay takes a chance, stumbling out in front of the truck, the cops yelling behind him. The young cop raises his weapon, leveling it at Jay. Behind him, Jay hears his partner say, "Don't shoot. Don't shoot."

The truck slams on its brakes, coming within inches of Jay's legs. The driver, a woman, leans out of the cab, screaming.

Jay runs to the other side of the bridge.

He throws himself against the concrete railing, the line of it jabbing against his ribs. What comes out is real. Dark and bitter, flecked with blood, his insides pouring into the bayou below.

Within seconds, he feels his arms yanked behind him, the bones in his shoulders turned at an unnatural angle. He feels the pinch of metal cuffs on his skin. He knows what comes next.

"You're under arrest," the first cop states.

Jay lowers his head to show that he means to cooperate.

They walk him to the squad car, shoving him into the cage in back.

As the squad car pulls away from the curb, going north on Main, Jay turns around in the locked backseat and steals a last look at his car, still parked on the side of the road, the nickel-plated .22 resting peacefully beneath the front seat.

Chapter 29

He said he would never be back here.

Behind bars an inch thick.

His feet aching on a filthy linoleum floor. A pool of urine in one corner, dried vomit in another. Men sleeping on the floor like dogs. No place to relieve himself with dignity. No place even to set himself down so he can think straight.

Ten paces by fifteen.

He's lived his whole life in this tiny cell, it seems.

Lived in fear of it, at least. Which, it turns out, is exactly the same thing.

As being in the sweat and shit of it, the I-can-hardly-breathe of it.

The stench in this place, the way the walls start to pinch at his insides.

It's never left him. He's spent the last ten years right here, on lockdown.

Keep your fucking mouth shut.

Isn't that the law he's lived by?

Keep your mouth shut, speak only when spoken to.

And what good did it do him? The silence?

The freedom he marched for, a lifetime ago.

The speeches he made. The dreams he had.

What good was any of it, really? If he can't get free in his own mind?

So he can eat at a lunch counter.

Drink warm water from a fountain.

And he can vote.

So what now?

Jay is not a praying man, not really. But some moments in a man's life beg for a little magic, a faith beyond what the eyes can see. The morning his verdict came down, he prayed, alone, in a cell smaller than this one. They kept the lights on twenty-four hours a day. The cell was drenched in white light and hot, not a comforting shadow in sight. He got on his knees next to the bed, elbows on a mattress so thin it looked like somebody had laid a cracker across the springs. He closed his eyes and he tried to picture God the way other people did:

As a father.

One who might watch out for him, lay a comforting hand.

He carried that picture in his head and into the courtroom that day. And he made a bargain with God. *You cut me loose, set me free out of this mess I'm in, and I'll lay it down,* he said. It was a promise to walk away from the armed rhetoric, from the political shit storm he was forever stirring, from a way of life that had consumed him. It was a promise to lay his voice down, to silence himself, which turned out to not be freedom at all, not even nowhere close.

And standing now in a urine-stained corner of this jail cell, where he paid a toll of six cigarettes to be left in peace, he strikes a new bargain with himself. There is a way out of here, he knows, out of this prison in his mind. It requires only the courage to speak.

It's nearly two hours before he's allowed to make a phone call. To Bernie, of course. She's still out to her parents' place in Fifth Ward, waiting on word from him, still up at nearly one o'clock in the morning. She answers the phone in a low whisper, then, hearing his voice, curses him repeatedly, softly, so her daddy won't hear. When he tells her where he is, the gist of what has happened, his wife lets out a jagged little gasp that breaks his heart. The pay phone to his ear, Jay can hear Bernie shuffling around her parents' house in the dark, looking for her purse and shoes. He tells her to stay put. He passed a sobriety test at the station, and there are, as of yet, no charges being filed against him.

He's remained remarkably calm, considering.

He's kept to himself, tried to keep his mind clear.

There have been four fights, two of which drew the attention of the guards, but not to the degree that they were willing to open the cage and break up the commotion themselves. Instead, they yelled threats from the safe side of the bars, tapping their clubs against the hard metal and chipping black paint onto the dirty floor. Two of the fights were territorial. Somebody sat in somebody's spot, or maybe it was somebody looked at somebody wrong. The other two fights were about some girl named Thelma who stays over on the north side. Of the nine men locked in the small cell, two of them apparently knew each other on the outside, and both laid a strong claim to this little gal who, it sounded like, is still in high school. Jay has stayed out of all of it. Except for the two minutes the guards let him out to make his phone call, he's done his time in one solitary corner, in a tiny sliver of space down in front, by the bars.

At two thirty, they start calling the first of the men out of the cell. One by one, the news comes down the hallway. Somebody's mama or sister or girlfriend managed to pull together bail money, dipping into next month's rent. Each time the guards call an inmate's name, the man in question stands righteously and gives the rest of them the finger, a final salute before the cage opens, just for him.

By a quarter after three, there are only three men left in the cell: one of Thelma's beaus, Jay, and an older black man, in his late sixties, wearing a soiled undershirt and high-water black pants with white socks. He's having a one-sided argument with himself about how he knows his gal ain't gon' leave him in here, that she'll bail him out, if only so she can get a ride to work the next morning. He goes on and on, complaining about the fact that she don't cook him baked chicken no more, always sending him for McDonald's . . . until finally, Thelma's boyfriend asks the old man, rather politely, to please shut the fuck up.

It's a little after four o'clock when the guards call for Jay. He hasn't seen the two cops who arrested him. He's had almost no communication with anyone, in fact. When Jay asks the guard what, if anything, he's been charged with, he gets a grunt for a reply and is marched to another room down the hall.

Processing, it turns out.

Where his jacket, watch, and wallet are returned to him. His belt and tie.

And he's told that he's free to go.

He's slow to move, and the clerk, a chubby girl in her twenties, ponytail cocked to one side, asks Jay if he's gon' need a goddamned escort out of the building. "You can go, you know," she says. When Jay asks her about his vehicle, she only shrugs.

He walks out of the police station about an hour or so before dawn, hungry and tired, his feet blistered and burning through the soles of his dress shoes. He stands briefly at the foot of the cement steps, the same spot where he left Elise Linsey so many nights ago, and he wishes for the hundredth time that he'd listened to his wife that night, that he'd gotten out of the car and gone at least to the door of the police station, told the truth as he knew it.

This time of night, the sky is somewhere between black and blue, the dying night as tender as a bruise. The air is moist and mercifully mild. Jay starts walking to the east, cutting through his city. He walks along the railroad tracks that run just to the north of downtown, chasing the sun, it seems, and its early morning peek into the sky, the predawn scene of peach and violet, the wispy streaks of white clouds, thin as a whisper, a secret.

He walks east until he hits Main Street and the bridge over Buffalo Bayou.

The Buick is still parked by the side of the road. At the sight of it, Jay breaks into a weary, lopsided trot. He lays his cheek across the dewy roof of the car. He is bone tired, but deeply grateful. The keys are still in the ignition, the doors unlocked.

Overhead, the amber streetlamps shut off one by one.

In the predawn light, Jay looks both ways up and down the

street, watching for any traffic on Main. Then, on his hands and knees by the curb, he reaches into the car and beneath the front passenger seat, feeling along the frayed carpet on the floorboard. When he hits something hard, the metal of his .22, he claws the gun out from under the seat, holding it in the pinkish palm of his hand.

For the life of him, he can't remember where this little thing came from.

If the gun was Bumpy's first or Marcus Dupri's, or if it was the same .22-caliber pistol that Lloyd Mackalvy pressed into Jay's palm on Highway 71, the night they outran the Klan, the night Stokely said they were gon' change the world.

Jay swings his arm in a wide arc, sending the gun sailing through the air and over the bridge's concrete railing, watching as it pierces the skin of the water. Maybe it will find its twin somewhere along the muddy bottom of the bayou, he thinks. Either way, it doesn't matter. He doesn't need it anymore.

At seven thirty sharp, he's standing inside Charlie Luckman's office, on Milam, his dirty shoes sunk into the plush, caramel-colored carpet, the grime and sweat and rank funk of the jail cell still staining his clothes, clinging to his skin. He stands at the front desk looking like some half-dead shit the cat dragged in.

The receptionist, an alarmingly thin woman in her sixties, her neck somewhat shrunken beneath the weight of a blond bouffant, does not appear to understand Jay, even after he gives his name three times. She keeps looking down at the same piece of paper, anything to avoid looking this filthy black man in the eye. "I'm sorry," she says. "But Mr. Luckman has a full, full schedule. He's got clients, you know, and he's due in court for a ruling just this morning."

"Ma'am," Jay says. "I can guarantee you he's going to want to talk to me before he goes into that courtroom. This is about his client Elise Linsey."

It's the name that does it.

The receptionist finally picks up the phone receiver on her desk and dials the extension to Charlie Luckman's office. "There's somebody named Porter here to see Mr. Luckman," she says to a voice on the other end.

He's led down a long hallway then, past the conference room. Charlie's secretary, a pretty brunette in a navy blue wrap dress and flats, smiles through clenched lips when she sees Jay coming down the hall, when she gets a good look at his soiled clothes and knotted hair. She offers him a seat, tells him Mr. Luckman is on a call. Jay nods politely and walks right past her.

He opens the door to Luckman's office.

Charlie is indeed on the phone. He looks up when he sees Jay.

"What the hell is this?"

He's behind his desk, his collar unbuttoned. There's a blue-and-red-striped tie hanging across the back of his leather chair, a glass of milk on his desk. "I'm gon' have to call you back," he mumbles into the phone.

Charlie's secretary steps in from the hallway.

"I told him you were on the phone," she says.

"What the hell is going on here?" Charlie says. He looks at Jay, screwing his face up at the sight before him, or maybe the smell. "I don't know how you run your business, Mr. Porter, but I don't respond to ambush tactics. You got something you want to say on the Cummings thing, you can call a meeting or wait 'til we get in front of a judge. You can't just barge in here, not today," he says, reaching for his tie. "I'm not doing this today."

And then, because he can't resist, "That girl gon' take the five grand or what?" Charlie asks, spontaneously shaving $2,500 off his last offer.

"That's not why I'm here," Jay says.

Charlie lifts up the white collar of his shirt, nods to his secretary. "Get him out of here, would you?"

"I know where the gun is," Jay says quickly.

The office, which is beige and mahogany and smells faintly of butterscotch, is suddenly stilled, the air tight, as if somebody took the whole room in a choke hold, knocked the wind out of them all, especially Charlie. With the loose ends of his red-and-blue tie in his hands, he stares at Jay Porter, maybe just now remembering Jay's face in the courthouse yesterday and what little sense that made to him at the time. He's putting something together in his mind. "The gun that killed Mr. Sweeney," Jay says. "I know where it is."

Charlie clears his throat. "Gail, shut the door," he says.

The secretary pushes the maple-colored door closed with her hand. Charlie sighs. "Might you kindly put your behind on the other side of it?"

Behind him, Jay hears the door open and close again with a carpet-padded whoosh of air, soft as a baby's breath. The room is starkly, almost painfully quiet. Charlie steps from around the corner of his desk, moving toward Jay slowly, tentatively, as if he were actually physically afraid of Jay, of what he has to say, but feels forced to close the gap between them anyway, if only to keep their voices at a minimum, down to a whisper. "How do you know my client?"

"Why don't you ask her?"

"Don't you dare play games with me," Charlie says. "Don't come in here and say something like you just did and play games with me."

"Why don't you ask her how she got those marks on her

neck?" Jay says. "Why don't you ask her why she *really* shot that man?"

"How do you know . . . ?" Charlie asks, almost stopping himself before he gets the words all the way out. "How do you know she shot him?"

"Because I was there."

There, he said it.

The words, once out, are like a locomotive on the tracks, with too much physical strength behind them to stop on a dime. He cannot, will not stop the truth. He tells the whole thing: the ride on the boat, the gunshots, the screams, the water rescue, the late-night drop in front of the police station, the black Ford and the money, Elise's cagey behavior, the news from High Point, the old man and the oil, the cover-up, the real estate buys, the government's sudden curiosity in Ms. Linsey, the calls from D.C. He runs the story all the way to its breathless end, plopping the meat of it at Thomas Cole's doorstep. He ends grandly on the link between Thomas Cole and the deceased, the man who tried to kill Mr. Luckman's client. This is his mess, Jay says, speaking of Cole. "And somebody ought to do something about it."

Charlie walks to the office's one window, which covers an entire wall. There's a small bar parked in the thick carpet in front of the window. It's got a mirrored tray on top, a pitcher of water and a coffee carafe and three different types of scotch. Charlie pours himself a glass of water, downs it, then pours a scotch. He looks up at the view in front of him, the green spread of Allen Parkway, cut in half by the serpentine bayou, the city's main vein.

"What do you want?" he asks.

"I want to testify."

Jay has never been on a witness stand in his life. He didn't even speak at his own trial. His court-appointed attorney said they would tear him to pieces, getting into his reputation as a rabble-rouser, a troublemaker, a man with no love for his country. Jay was silent through the whole thing. But not anymore.

"They set her up. Let me get on the stand. Let a jury hear what really happened that night, who wanted to harm this girl, and, more important, why."

"Mr. Porter, this case is not going to trial. They don't have the evidence. Emily knows that," Charlie says, calling the judge by her first name. "And I wouldn't put you on the stand no way. My client says she was not at the scene, and the state has yet to provide any substantial evidence to say that she was. So why the hell would I ever put up a witness who says she was *right* there? Especially if you're telling me that gun's buried and gone, somewhere at the bottom of Buffalo Bayou. As far as I'm concerned, they got nothing."

"I could go to the other side," Jay says.

"You coulda done that this morning. But since I'm looking at you right now, I'm going to guess that's not the way you wanted to handle things." He cocks his head to one side, regarding Jay from a distance. "I don't think you want to see that girl hurt. The state, though, they got other plans for her."

"Thomas Cole is the one who belongs behind bars," Jay says.

"I don't have nothing to do with that, I don't want to know nothing more about it," Charlie says. "My job is to keep that girl out of jail, that's it."

" 'That's it?' You're just going to ignore the rest?" Jay asks, mildly incredulous. "You're sitting up in this big firm, got all the resources in the world, and you're just going to let this guy get away with what he did?"

Charlie tucks his hands in his pockets, studying the tips of his boots. He's trying to find the right way to put this. "I don't think you understand what's really going on here. You really think a girl like Elise Linsey . . . forget the clothes, the diamonds and all that . . . you really think a girl like that can afford me?"

The words hang in the air for a minute before they finally settle in. "Thomas Cole hired you," Jay says, finally getting it.

"Look . . . I'm gon' do us both a favor, Mr. Porter," Charlie says, his boots already gliding to the door. "I'm gon' pretend like we never had this conversation." He opens the door to his office, pausing at the threshold, where the two men pass each other, only inches apart. Here, Jay gets the closest look yet at the downward turn of Charlie's green eyes.

"You're afraid of him," Jay says. Then, "You're a coward."

The insult washes right over Charlie, as if Jay had been stating something as matter-of-fact as the color of the drapes or describing the carpet on the floor. He pats Jay on the back and actually manages a smile. "Mr. Porter, I wouldn't spend another minute worrying over any of this," he says, holding the door open. "This whole thing'll be over by lunchtime anyway. You'll see."

Lonette Philips sits on the bench directly behind Jay.

Just before the judge comes in, she puts a hand on Jay's shoulder, leans forward, and whispers, "The calls from D.C. to Elise Linsey? That number you gave me? It was a Martin Burrows, an employee with—surprise, surprise—the Federal Trade Commission. He was in their consumer protection division."

Jay has not been home or changed his clothes or showered since his arrest. Lonnie is mercifully silent about his haggard appearance in Judge Vroland's courtroom this morning. She's in another flannel shirt, rolled up to her elbows.

"*Was?*" Jay says.

"Mr. Burrows is no longer employed by the FTC," Lonnie says flatly, repeating the information she received. "He was terminated three weeks ago."

Jay stares straight ahead.

Elise and Charlie are side by side, at the same table they occupied yesterday afternoon, he in the same suit he was wearing in his office only an hour ago, and she in a white pantsuit, a thin gold belt at the waist. They're facing straight ahead, passing the time in silence, not speaking to each other.

"I guess Cole really did it, huh," Lonnie says to Jay. "The son of a bitch made a whole federal investigation go away."

When the judge comes in, they all stand.

Lonnie whispers over his shoulder. "What happened to you anyway?"

Because there is no quick answer, Jay doesn't even try.

Judge Vroland takes her place at the bench. Jay looks back and forth between the prosecutor, nervously fidgeting at the state's table, and Charlie Luckman, whose legs are comfortably crossed, his hands resting in his lap.

The whole thing plays out exactly as Charlie said it would.

First, the judge offers her ruling on the search: the shoes are out. They were *out* of the bounds of the search warrant, and therefore *out* of any trial in her courtroom. Second, she asks the prosecutor if the state can proceed with their case without the shoes. "I mean, tell me you weren't hanging this whole deal on every shoe is this young lady's closet. Tell me you got something else to work with," she says, to which the prosecutor, standing at her desk, responds, "We've got her fingerprints in the car, Your Honor, the very car they found the victim in."

"If I'm remembering it correctly, the defendant has admitted to being in the man's car, out to dinner or something like that." Charlie, following the action from his seat, nods his head. The judge leans forward in her chair, her eyes focused on the state's attorney. "Do you have anything that puts the defendant at the scene of the crime? An eyewitness, a murder weapon?"

"No, Your Honor," the prosecutor says.

Charlie, on cue, stands and asks for a dismissal of the case, based on a supreme lack of evidence. Judge Vroland announces to the room that she's inclined to agree with Mr. Luckman. She doesn't seem particularly pleased by this fact. She looks at the prosecutor as if her hands are tied, advising the attorney to pull together some more evidence and take it back to a grand jury. "I just can't see you mounting a case with what you got now."

Behind him, Jay hears Lonnie whisper, "Oh, boy."

A moment later, Judge Vroland makes her second ruling of the day, granting defense counsel's motion for a dismissal of the case.

In less than twelve minutes, it's all over.

Elise is free to go. The gun, and the truth, still buried beneath the surface.

She kisses her lawyer on the cheek, looking, only once, over his shoulder. She spots Jay in the gallery. Across her thin, pinkish lips, he sees something he takes for a smile as the clerk calls the next case on the docket. Lonnie puts a hand on Jay's shoulder. "What now?" she asks.

Jay says the only thing he can think of. "I have to go pick up my wife."

He stops in the washroom on his way out of the building. For five whole minutes, he stands alone over an empty sink, watching water run. When he feels he has the strength, he splashes cool water on his face, wiping at his eyes with his sleeve. Behind him, one of the stall doors opens. A man, taller than Jay, glides to the row of washbasins. Jay catches a glimpse of him in the bathroom mirror. The man is lean, his features seemingly cut from stone. The face is instantly familiar.

Thomas Cole is standing at the sink right next to him.

Jay stands perfectly still, watching Cole admire his own reflection, smoothing a few wayward hairs on his dark blond head. When Cole finally looks up, catching Jay's reflection in the mirror, he smiles, an odd twinkle in his steely gray eyes. "Don't make me regret I didn't kill you when I had the chance," he says, his tone mannered and cool, the smile belying his true menace.

Just then, two lawyers enter the men's room. They stand at the urinals rehashing a prosecutor's performance in Judge Kupperman's courtroom; they are both convinced the prosecutor passed gas at some point during her opening statement. In the mirror, Cole gives Jay a wink. He tucks his hands into the pockets of his linen trousers and saunters out of the men's room. Jay stays behind at the washbasin, feeling a heat radiate through his whole body. He is almost faint with it, a rage that has the power to break him if he doesn't hold himself together. Everything, he knows, depends on him keeping a cool head.

Bernadine is waiting for him on the front steps of the church, one hand on her swollen belly, the other tangled in the straps of her purse. She's biting her bottom lip when he comes up the walk, and one of her french braids has started to come loose in the back. She looks to have slept as little as he did last night. When he's within loving distance of her arms, she grabs hold of his neck. In his ear, she exhales. One breath, one syllable. She whispers his name, his father's first initial. On the stairs, she's two steps taller than he is, and it is something, he feels, to look up to this woman, to feel held up by his wife.

She's the first to tell him about the strike, the vote that ended it.

They're going to take a chance on this race-blind thing, she says.

"Daddy's up in the office, on the phone right now. I know he wanted to say something to you about it."

"Not now," Jay says, feeling her belly close to his. "Let's go home."

He steals her away then, carrying her purse for her to the car. They leave without a word to anybody, ride the whole way to Third Ward in silence.

When they get to the apartment, Bernie takes a pair of chicken breasts out of the freezer for a late lunch. She lays the raw meat in a shallow pool of water in the kitchen sink. Jay takes off his jacket and tie. He lines up two beers on the dinette table, downing the first in a matter of seconds. Bernie, never one in favor of daytime drinking, watches him without saying much of anything. She keeps an eye on the chicken thawing in the sink, and when she gets bored with that, she shuffles across the kitchen floor, taking a seat across from her husband at the table.

Finally, Jay tells her what he's thinking about doing next.

"Leave it alone," she says, speaking softly to him, as if the baby were already here, already sleeping in the other room. "It's over, Jay."

"They brought this to my doorstep. They did this, not me." He raises his voice in a way that makes her wince. He realizes she has never seen this side of him, that she came into his life long after he thought his anger had run out. He stares into the living room, his gaze falling on the bleached-out spot on the floor, where he scrubbed blood with his bare hands. "They came into my house, Bernie."

"*I* was here, Jay, alone," she says. "This has to do with me too."

"They came into *our* house," he says. "I didn't ask for any of this."

"Then walk away."

He shakes his head slowly. "They're stealing from people, B.

People like me and you. People like your daddy, your sister, the ladies at your church, working people. We're paying more at the pump, paying more for our clothes, the shoes on our feet, the food the grocers pick up from their suppliers in those big, gassy eighteen-wheelers. This oil thing touches everything. You're paying an extra fifty cents on that chicken breast for the cost of the plastic it's wrapped in. That's made from petroleum too," he says, looking at his wife under the dim white light of the overhead bulb. "They're cheatin' people every which way. And I'm not gon' be pushed into keeping my mouth shut about it."

Bernie, listening to all this, bites her bottom lip.

Jay sets his beer can down, pushing it away.

There was a man, he says, a man who used to come around his granddaddy's place, a little restaurant the family had up in Nigton. The man was a soldier, a vet, and a drunk. He used to come in every day in his old uniform, which was coming apart at the seams. He never had any money. And sometimes Jay's mama would pay him a quarter to sweep up out front and get himself a little lunch. Mostly the man would just sit for hours at a stretch at one of the tables. He would stare out the window kind of mumbling to himself. And sometimes he would cry for no reason. He wasn't all right in his head. Shell-shocked, the old folks called it. The man used to grab hold of Jay sometimes, used to grab him by the shoulders real hard and look the boy in the eye. He spoke in short, broken-off sentences, barking, kind of, like he had something caught in his throat. *Same thing make you laugh make you cry. The quinine rooster was a purly-curly, you hear me, boy?* Then he would shake Jay by his shoulders until the boy's head hurt. *You hear me now . . . they coming to get you too.*

Jay looks up at his wife.

"I don't want to be that man, B. An old soldier, a man who can't hardly talk. I can't walk through this life like that." He says this last part as an apology, for revealing to his wife, this late in the game, the man he truly is. "I just can't."

Bernie studies his face for a long time, the shadows beneath his eyes.

Finally, she gets up and walks to the sink. With a wooden spoon from the drain board, she pokes the chicken breasts encased in plastic wrap in the sink.

"I need you to be safe, Jay. I need that, understand?"

"I know."

"I mean, they came after you once, Jay, what makes you think they won't do it again?"

"I'm taking it right to the courts, B," he says. "I'm taking it right to court."

That night, sometime between *The Dukes of Hazzard* and *Dallas*, the dishes put up and his wife asleep in front of the television, Jay stands over the kitchen counter. He picks up the phone and calls the old man in High Point.

"You still looking for a lawyer?" he asks, after introductions are remade.

The old man is silent for a long stretch on the phone. Jay can hear his phlegmy breathing, a rattle and a rasp. There's a television playing somewhere in the background. Jay thinks it's tuned to the same station. He hears the same beer commercial that's playing in his living room coming through the phone line as well. He pictures Mr. Ainsley's wife sitting in the blue light of their television screen, a pile of knitting yarn in her lap. He thinks of their white A-frame house. The yellow curtains in the windows, the American flag hanging limply out front.

"I understand you got some encroachment onto your property," Jay says, using the same tone of voice he uses with all his prospective clients, one that's gentle and encouraging. "Seems to me somebody ought not get away with it. Somebody ought to be made to answer for that, Mr. Ainsley."

The old man is quiet still.

The laughter on their televisions raises to a high pitch.

Ainsley clears his throat. "You that black fellow that come by the house?"

"Yes, sir."

The old man makes a humming sound, like he's pausing to catch his breath . . . or think. "I don't have a lot of money to pay you," he says.

"You let me worry about that," Jay says, already counting, in his mind, the $23,200 he's got stuffed in the lockbox in his office. He thinks it may be enough for at least one expert witness . . . and enough to pay Eddie Mae overtime.

Chapter 30

The day he files the papers, Bernie goes into labor, some two weeks early.

Jay races home to find his wife bent over the kitchen table, her face screwed up in pain, the packed suitcase at her feet. They make it to Ben Taub Hospital in a record eleven minutes. He holds her hand for the first hour in the waiting room. Once they've been assured the doctor is on his way, Jay does everything he can to make his wife comfortable, fluffing up the pillow she brought from home and offering her a can of soda from one of the machines. Then he has a smoke outside and starts making the calls on her list: her mother and father, her sister, some of the ladies from the church.

Jay doesn't have a list, not a soul he can call.

It kind of eats at him a little, not for the first time, and not the last.

Back at his wife's side in the waiting room, he chews his nails to the bone, picks up one magazine after another, even starts flipping through one of Bernie's romance novels, one with a field of corn and a nearly naked lady on the cover. By the time Bernie's family starts to trickle in, the doctor has already come and gone. False labor, he called it. Not at all uncommon, but a sign they're getting close. The doctor said he couldn't check them into the hospital this early, nor did he believe they'd want the extra expense. His best advice was to send them home and tell them to be alert for the real signs: contractions that grow longer and stronger, any mucus or discharge, and certainly if Bernie's water breaks, they should come back in. It could be anytime now.

Jay and Bernie wait around to make sure her whole family gets the news. Then they all make a caravan back to Jay and Bernie's apartment. Evelyn and Mrs. Boykins get into the kitchen right away, doctoring up a couple of cans of chicken soup, throwing in fresh onion, garlic, and salt, and toasting up half a loaf of white bread. Reverend Boykins sits on the couch with his baby girl. Jay brings his wife a cool glass of water. He tells her he's got to run by the office for a bit, that he won't be gone more than an hour. "I'll be all right here," she says, patting a hand on her daddy's knee.

Reverend Boykins looks up at his son-in-law. They haven't spoken about the court case, but Lonnie's article about Jay's civil suit against Cole Oil Industries made the front page of the *Chronicle* this morning. The story is officially out.

Reverend Boykins gives Jay a nod of approval. "Go on, son."

It's not until he's out of the house that Jay realizes how hard it was for him to breathe in there, how much being around Bernie's family makes him pine for something he thought he'd long ago given up on, the someone he thought he'd lost.

When he arrives at the office, Eddie Mae has a stack of pink message slips for him, more than triple the amount of calls he usually gets in a single week. There are calls from newspaper reporters and at least one magazine, and three calls from the same law firm claiming to represent Cole Oil and Thomas Cole personally. Jay takes the message slips into his office and shuts the door.

He picks up the phone and calls, of all people, Rolly Snow.

He pictures Rolly behind the counter at Lula's, bare-chested beneath his black vest, as, even in the first week of September, the thermostat hit ninety in Houston today. Jay pictures Rolly plucking a stubby pencil from behind his ear, jotting notes on any little slip of paper he can find, a bar tab or a parking ticket.

Jay gives him all the information he has. His sister's maiden name, different from his own. The neighborhood in Dallas she called home more than a decade ago. And a loose description. Hair, rust-colored. Her skin, fair, with a mess of freckles across the bridge of her nose. "Tell her I'm having a kid."

There's a pause on the line.

Then Rolly's voice, coated in nicotine. "Man, I'll do everything I can."

Jay spends the rest of the time at his office tying up loose ends, calling several prospective clients to let them know that he won't be able to take their cases after all, that his dance card is full. For the open files on his desk, he draws up paperwork for some of the smaller civil suits, requesting extensions.

The last call he makes is to the hooker, Dana Moreland.

He tells her he can get her $5,000 from J. T. Cummings, can have a check drawn up as early as this afternoon, in fact.

But if she wants to take Cummings and Charlie Luckman to court for more, she's going to have to do it with someone else. He, unfortunately, cannot represent her in this matter any further.

As Mr. Cummings had originally (and accurately) guessed, the girl jumps at the money and wants it in her hot hands as soon as possible. She has, since they last spoke, broken up with the mechanic from Corpus and is no longer interested in real estate or oil. She's thinking about getting into the cosmetics game now, selling door-to-door, for which she will need a new car. She's got her eye on a two-toned Pontiac Grand Am at a dealership out by AstroWorld.

One phone call and it's over and done with.

He's got at least one satisfied customer.

Sometime after four o'clock, he's clearing up the scattered paperwork on his desk when Eddie Mae pokes her head in the office, her eyes as wide as milk saucers. It's a moment or two before she can get any words out, and Jay sighs, thinking this is Eddie Mae working up her nerve, readying herself to ask him if she can cut out a little early today. He tells her he needs her to stick around until at least five o'clock from now on. He reminds her that's the deal they made.

"Somebody's here to see you, Mr. Porter," she says.

When his office door opens all the way, Jay sees Cynthia Maddox standing on the other side. She's come alone, in a dark blue suit. She smiles at Jay, then briefly, shyly, looks down at the tips of her black shoes. She's waiting to be invited past the threshold, into his private space. He, admittedly, feels a flutter in his chest at the sight of her, but whether it's a longing that may haunt him the rest of his life, or just a lingering rage that flares up from time to time, he can't tell. And anyway, like almost anything, it starts to fade after a while.

"Can I get you something, Miss Mayor?" Eddie Mae asks.

"No," Jay says, answering for Cynthia. "Just leave us alone."

"Oh, surely, Mr. Porter," Eddie Mae says.

She raises a single eyebrow before shutting the office door.

There's nowhere for Cynthia to sit. Jay's papers and files and two phone books cover the only available chairs. He makes no effort to clear a space for her to sit, and she is maybe too prideful to ask. "This is a surprise," he says.

"There've been a lot of surprises today, Jay."

She looks around the tiny office. For the first time, he sees the place through Cynthia's blue-gray eyes: a cheap strip-center rental with bad flat carpet, stained in too many places, and yellowing blinds on all the windows. A long, long way from the mayor's office. "What do you want, Cynthia?"

"I read the paper this morning," she says.

"And you came all the way down here to tell me that?"

"I came here to see if you really know what you're doing, Jay."

"Cynthia, this doesn't have a thing to do with you."

"It's happening in my city, it has everything to do with me." Then, taking a step toward him, she asks, "What are you trying to prove here, Jay? I mean, think about who you're taking on. This thing is much bigger than you."

He shrugs. "It's just a little property dispute, that's all."

"You won't win."

"It doesn't matter, not really. It only matters that I remember to speak up." He looks at Cynthia, looks her right in the eye. "Isn't that what you said?"

"Oh, Jay," she says, her voice a near whisper. She seems disappointed in him, or else exasperated, as if he grossly misunderstood her. "I'm asking you to reconsider," she says. "Think about your practice, your family, and reconsider."

He resents the mention of his family. He thinks he knows why she's really here. "How much did you get from Cole for your campaign last year?"

"Listen to me, Jay," she says. "These people do not fuck around."

"How much?"

"Oh, please, Jay," she says, waving away the thought with her hand.

"No, really, I'm asking," he says. "How much?"

"My god, Jay," she says faintly, kind of shrunk down in her clothes, looking as if he had struck her with his hands, as if he'd deliberately set out to hurt her. "Did it ever occur to you that I might be here 'cause I care about you?"

"No."

The light in her eyes changes them from blue to gray, then back again. "You don't think much of me anymore, do you?"

It's a ridiculous question, one they're long past.

Jay stares at Cynthia, across the room, thinking this is what it must feel like to sit with a loved one in their final hour, the body sometimes twisted and bloated to an unrecognizable degree, when there is an often childish wish to turn back time, to remember the person the way they once were, at their very best.

"Come on," she says. "Let's take a walk."

"Cynthia," Jay says, shaking his head.

"Come on . . . one last time."

Outside, they make the block around his building in silence, ending up at a small park to the left of a barbecue restaurant and an office-supply store. Somewhere near a rusted swing set, Cynthia stops, kicking the toe of her high-heeled shoe into the trunk of a nearby tree. She looks softer in the shade.

"I didn't do what you think I did," Cynthia says to him finally, what she dragged him all this way to say. "I just want to get that straight right now." Her voice is shallow, not quite shaking, but damn near. "I didn't set you up, Jay."

He's standing a few feet from her, his back against one of the metal posts of the swing set. He nods in her direction. But it doesn't mean anything. What she said doesn't change a thing. "What if you did, Cynthia?" he says. "What if you *were* working both sides? What if *you* put the bug in your phone that day? Then used your government connections to get a post in Lloyd Bentsen's office up in Washington, used my arrest to jump-start your political career? I mean, what if, Cynthia? Would you really tell me the truth now?" He stares at her. "Be honest."

She thinks about it for a long time. Then, softly, she says, "Probably not."

"Well then," he says. "You see my dilemma."

"I was a kid, Jay. I was a scared kid."

"So was I," he says. "The difference is . . . I was in a jail cell."

When she looks up again, their eyes meet only briefly. She turns and looks over her shoulder toward a black Lincoln Town Car parked across the street. A driver, in uniform, tips his hat to the mayor. The walk was choreographed, Jay realizes, for them to end up here, for her to have a safe out. She lingers for a few moments by the tree trunk, crunching pine needles underfoot. "You really going to do this thing?" she asks, meaning the lawsuit.

"Yes."

Cynthia nods.

Before she turns toward the waiting Town Car, before she says her final good-bye, she regards him for a good long while, a faint smile on her lips. She is remembering him too, maybe, remembering Jay Porter at his very best.

======

When he gets home, Evelyn is the last of the family left at the apartment. She's looking at the news on channel 2, eating a slice of buttered bread and drinking one of his beers. She nods at Jay and tells him his wife is lying down in the bedroom. He peels off his jacket and tie on his way to her.

Bernie is lying on top of the covers when he walks in.

The air-conditioning unit is shaking in the window.

His wife, somewhere between asleep and awake, lifts her head off a mass of pillows under her neck and calls out a "Hey," light as a feather blowing across a warm wind. Jay kicks off his shoes and shuts the bedroom door. He crosses the room and lays himself next to her on the bed, still in his work clothes. He buries his nose inside a favorite nook, the space between his wife's neck and shoulder, which smells milky and sweet. Her breath falls into a soft, whistling key. A few minutes pass in silence.

Jay lies in bed thinking about his father.

As he feels himself start to drift off to sleep, he puts one hand on Bernie's belly and gets a sudden image of his father's hand on his mother's womb, a lifetime ago. His only true contact, their only hello. He tries hard to remember. He tries with all he's got to recall the sensation from the inside, to remember what he can, in reality, have no way of ever knowing . . . what were his daddy's hands like? His body jerks across the sheets, fighting the inevitable slip into darkness. Here, on the edge of sleep, just before the final descent, Jay feels, for the first time in his life, a reassuring weight across his chest, a caress, a man's touch, a sudden faith in things unseen . . . *I got you, son. I'm not gon' let you fall.*

Acknowledgments

My thanks go first to my editor, Dawn Davis. Thank you for believing in this book and especially in me as a writer. A very big thank-you to my agent, Richard Abate. This book grew by leaps and bounds because of your candor and insight. Thanks also to Brian Lipson for reading an early draft and pointing me in so many right directions, and to Bob Myman for your friendship and advocacy. Special thanks go to Michelle Satter, Lynn Auerbach, Ken Brecher, and Bob Redford for my summer on the mountain, the lessons of which are with me still. To my father, Gene, thank you for accepting phone calls at all hours to answer my many questions about Houston and the civil rights movement. Thanks also to Argentina James for arranging my tour of the Port of Houston, and to Captain John T. Scardasis for explaining the culture of the longshoremen's union. To my mother, Sherra, who always gets the first read, thank you for dreaming with me. And a heartfelt thank-you to Mrs. Odell C. Johnson, my earliest inspiration. I also wish to thank my sister, Tembi, for her sharp suggestions and her deep and abiding faith in me, and also my brother-in-law, Rosario, for finding the gentlest way to ask me some very tough questions. And I will always owe a debt of gratitude to Julie Ariola for teaching me to hold everything lightly. Likewise, this book would not have been possible without the unyielding support of Cheryl Arutt. Thank you for reminding me to trust myself. Special thanks also go to my daughter, Clara, for waiting until Mommy had at least a first draft before showing your beautiful face. And finally, to my husband, Karl, who has more patience than any man ought to, there simply aren't enough ways to say thank you. Your love has been a light in my life, helping me find my way.

About the Author

ATTICA LOCKE is a screenwriter who has worked in both film and television. A former fellow at the Sundance Institute, she is currently at work on an HBO miniseries about the civil rights movement. A native of Houston, Texas, she lives in Los Angeles with her husband and daughter.